ECHO IN ONYX

Books by Sharon Shinn

Uncommon Echoes:
Echo in Onyx
Echo in Emerald
Echo in Amethyst

Samaria series:
Archangel
Jovah's Angel
The Alleluia Files
Angelica
Angel-Seeker

Twelve Houses series:
Mystic and Rider
The Thirteenth House
Dark Moon Defender
Reader and Raelynx
Fortune and Fate

Elemental Blessings series:
Troubled Waters
Royal Airs
Jeweled Fire
Unquiet Land

The Shifting Circle series
The Shape of Desire
Still-Life with Shape-Shifter
The Turning Season

Young adult novels:
The Safe-Keeper's Secret
The Truth-Teller's Tale
The Dream-Maker's Magic
General Winston's Daughter
Gateway

Standalones, Collections, and Graphic Novels:
The Shape-Changer's Wife
Wrapt in Crystal
Heart of Gold
Summers at Castle Auburn
Jenna Starborn
Quatrain
Shattered Warrior

Echo in Onyx

Sharon Shinn

Echo in Onyx

Copyright © 2019 Sharon Shinn
All rights reserved.
This edition published 2019

Cover image by Dave Seeley; cover design by Andy Holbrook

ISBN: 978-1-68068-162-8

This book is published on behalf of the author by the Ethan Ellenberg Literary Agency.

This book was initially an Audible Original production.
    Performed by Emily Bauer
    Executive Producers: David Blum and Mike Charzuk
    Editorial Producer: Steve Feldberg
    Sound recording copyright 2019 by Audible Originals, LLC

Where to find Sharon Shinn:
Website: www.sharonshinn.net
Facebook: https://www.facebook.com/sharonshinnbooks/
Amazon: https://www.amazon.com/s?k=Sharon+Shinn&ref=dp_byline_sr_all_1

THE KINGDOM OF THE
SEVEN JEWELS

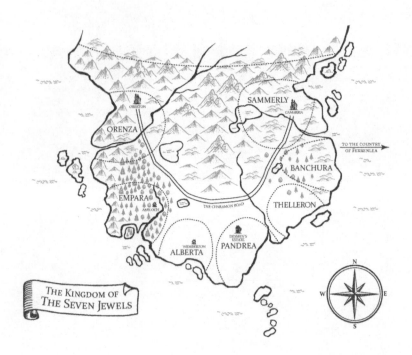

Cast of Characters

ROYALS
Harold: the king
Tabitha Devenetta: the queen, Harold's second wife, the mother of
    his daughter
Cormac: the king's oldest legitimate son and heir
Jordan: the king's second legitimate son
Annery: Harold and Tabitha's daughter
Jamison: Harold's bastard son

Edwin of Thelleron: the first king of the Seven Jewels (long dead)
Amanda: the first queen

NOBLES
Garvin Andolin: governor of the province of Orenza
Lady Dorothea: his wife
Marguerite: his daughter
Patience, Purpose, and Prudence: Marguerite's echoes

Elyssa: from the province of Alberta
Cali: from Alberta
Leonora, Letitia, and Lavinia: triplets from Banchura
Deryk: from the province of Banchura
Dezmen: from the province of Pandrea; a close friend to the princes
Darrily: Dezmen's sister
Vivienne: from Thelleron; Cormac's former fiancée

PROFESSIONALS & WORKING CLASS FOLKS

Brianna: An innkeeper's daughter, maid to Lady Marguerite

Jean: Brianna's aunt

Nico Burken: an apprentice inquisitor

Taeline: a priestess in the temple of the triple goddess

Constance: housekeeper to governor Andolin

Rory: a footman in the Andolin house

Del Morson: the head inquisitor in Orenza

Lourdes: the head housekeeper at the palace in the royal city

Malachi Burken: the king's inquisitor and Nico's uncle

Chessie: an acquaintance of Nico's

CHAPTER ONE

B ecause I was born the same year as the daughter of the governor of Orenza, I was always fascinated by the life of Lady Marguerite Andolin. Whenever travelers arrived at my mother's posting house, fresh from Orenza's capital city of Oberton, I quizzed them for information about Marguerite. By the time I was ten, I knew every detail there was to know: Her eyes were blue, her hair was blond, her favorite color was purple. She had a brood of brothers almost too numerous to count. And she was one of the few people in the whole province of Orenza with three echoes. They showed up overnight three days after she was born.

I knew the story so well I might as well have been the nursemaid who entered the room that sunny morning to find the four small bodies wailing in the crib. One was still in her frilly nightshirt, while the other three were naked, pale, and shivering. The maid shrieked and ran from the room to call for the governor's wife, the nanny, the housekeeper, anyone who could help her bathe and dress the new arrivals. She was so excited that she couldn't even form the words to describe what she had found. When the nanny finally grabbed her and shook her and demanded, "Are there echoes?" the girl was only able to reply by nodding and holding up three fingers. Whereupon the nanny fainted.

It was what everybody had hoped for, of course. The governor and his wife had two echoes each, but their sons hadn't been particularly blessed in that regard, since none of them had more than two and one didn't have any. Three echoes had always been a rare phenomenon, rarer still in recent decades. Some said there were

1

fewer than fifty people in the whole kingdom who could boast of such a thing.

By the time I was twenty-three, I had seen only a handful of echoes, and I still found them both magical and a little unnerving. They looked just like their originals—absolutely exact copies, down to the placement of freckles and quirks of expression—yet just a shade or two paler, a few pounds less substantial. They ate and drank like ordinary men and women—and they slept and performed other human functions, or so I understood—but they never spoke. They had no independent thoughts. And they all replicated their masters' movements without variation, turning their heads to the same precise angle, blinking in concert, smiling and frowning and laughing like reflections in a mirror.

What would it be like to have such a constant shadow? What would it be like to have *three*? Glorious and gratifying, I thought— and perhaps irksome and awkward at the same time. My mother had gotten married when I was ten, and I now had almost as many siblings as Marguerite. I could hardly find an hour when there wasn't some sister or brother underfoot. Privacy probably wasn't as hard to come by in the governor's mansion as it was at an inn, but for a woman with three echoes, solitude was never a real option. I would probably hate such an existence, I admitted to myself, but that didn't mean I didn't envy it.

Perhaps I envied it all the more because, the summer I was twenty-three, I had become disenchanted with my own life. My mother was expecting her sixth child, which meant my two younger sisters were now sharing my room, and I never had a moment alone. It was time to move on, I knew. I had acquired a good number of skills during the years I had acted as my mother's assistant—I could cook, sew, garden, groom a horse, rock a baby, and calm the angriest customer—but I was itching to move on to something a little grander. A job that I had chosen, a life that was *mine*.

For the past couple of years, I'd thought my future would include a boy named Robbie, and we would run his family's farm together once his father passed on. But then Robbie decided he was in love with the miller's daughter, and they ran off together one cold night last winter. . She was already pregnant when they came back three months later. Never in my life had I seen a girl so smug.

It was hardly a wonder that, this summer, I was about as unhappy as a girl could be.

It was the hottest day we'd had so far when my mother drew me aside after we'd fed the last of the travelers who'd taken rooms for the night. My stepfather and my brothers were making a last visit to the stables to check on the horses, and my sisters were cleaning the kitchen. My mother picked up a folded envelope to fan her face with and motioned for me to follow her outside. The day's heat had finally started to fade once the sun went down, though the air was hardly any cooler in the back garden. But it had that dense, hopeful smell of rich earth and green, growing things, and I felt my mood lift a little.

My mother made her way to a stone bench situated next to the tomato plants and carefully lowered herself down. She was eight months along and had grown big and ungainly. More than once I'd seen her refuse the opportunity to sit because she didn't think she'd have the strength to push herself back to her feet.

"You'll have to help me up in a few minutes," she said. The light from the kitchen window cast just enough illumination that I could see her faint smile. "A woman my age has no business being pregnant."

"You're not that old," I said, taking a seat beside her. She wasn't even forty. She'd been only sixteen when she had me after a summer romance with a boy from the next town. He'd had the misfortune to die before he could marry her, though I'd often thought my mother was relieved, not disappointed. "Anyway, you like being pregnant. Or at least you like having babies in the house."

"I do," she admitted. "I might not stop with this one."

I groaned and then I laughed. "Pretty soon we won't have room for any paying guests."

"Well," she said, "I know you think there's not much room for *you*."

I shrugged. "It's time for me to start my own life, I think," I said. "As soon as I can figure out what it should be."

"No one figures out what her life should be," she said. "It just happens. You can plan and plan, you can save all your money, you can open a shop in the heart of the city—and then a fire burns down the building and all your hard work comes to nothing." She turned her head to look at me. "Or you can think your life is over and one day a handsome stranger shows up at your door, and suddenly the world is made new again."

I spread my hands. "Well, I'm ready. Where's the shop? Where's the handsome stranger?"

She fanned her face again with the envelope, then she held it out to me. "Maybe you'll find one of them in Oberton."

I took the envelope from her hand, but didn't open it. It was too dark to read—and anyway, I was too busy staring at her. "What's this?"

"A letter from your aunt Jean. I wrote her a while back asking if she could help you get established in the city. If she'd let you stay with her while you look for work."

Jean was my father's sister, an intelligent and formidable woman who always made me feel as if I had forgotten to comb my hair or honor the triple goddess. She lived in a small house on a busy street and worked as a bookkeeper for an attorney. She'd never been married and didn't seem to have much of a maternal streak, but she'd always been kind to me in an offhand, matter-of-fact way.

But maybe she was about to become the best aunt ever. "And she said I could?" I breathed. *"Gorsey!"*

That made her laugh. It was a word much beloved by country folk, a corruption of the common prayer *Goddess have mercy on my soul.* My mother and I only used it with each other when we were being silly or melodramatic.

"Better than that," she replied. "She's already set up an interview for you for a job you'd love to have."

How could Aunt Jean know what job I would love when I didn't even know that myself? "What is it?"

"Lady's maid to Marguerite."

I could only stare at her in the darkness.

"Jean is second cousin to the head housekeeper at the governor's mansion," my mother said. "She asked about getting you a position there, and it turns out Marguerite is in need of a maid, as her current one is leaving to be married. You have an interview with the housekeeper next week. You'll leave for the city the day after tomorrow."

I nearly shrieked with excitement and then threw my arms around her, feeling the hard mound of her belly pushing against my waist. "I can't believe it!" I exclaimed as I drew back. Then suddenly I was flooded with horror. "But what will I *wear*? Every single dress I own looks like I've been scrubbing the floor in it, which I have. I'll hardly appear suitable to be a lady's maid if I can't even dress myself right."

My mother smoothed back my hair and dropped a kiss on my forehead. "I've got a little money saved to send you on your way, and Jean will take you to the right shop to get a proper dress made. You'll look just fine. And if you don't get a position with Marguerite, well, there are plenty of other jobs in Oberton. You're such a hard worker, and you're good at so many things. You'll find something."

"You're the most wonderful mother," I said.

She laughed. "That's right, I am. And to remind you of that fact every day, I want you to take this with you and wear it from now on."

She took my hand and dropped a ring in my palm. Even in the dark, I immediately knew what it was—a thin silver band that twisted into a triskele to honor the triple goddess. Each spiral of the triskele was set with a smooth chunk of onyx: one black, one white, and one red. It was the piece of jewelry my mother wore most often, except for her wedding band.

"That's to remind you of where you come from, no matter how far you might go from here," she said. "And to remind you that, wherever you are in the world, someone loves you."

I slipped the ring onto the fourth finger of my right hand and found it a perfect fit. I held my hand up to the light seeping out from the kitchen, trying to get a better look. "I've always wanted this ring," I told her. "But I can't take it from you! It's yours! Your mother gave it to you!"

"And your mother is giving it to *you*," she said. "Anyway, my hands are so swollen I can't get it on."

"But once the baby is born—"

"Once the baby is born, I'll be so busy changing diapers and cleaning up messes that I won't be thinking about folderols like this!" She took my hand again and folded my fingers into a fist. "You keep it, Brianna. Take a part of me with you when you go out into the world."

Of course I started crying. I threw my arms around her neck, and said I couldn't possibly leave behind all the people and the only place I knew. But already my mind was turning. Already I was planning what I would pack to take with me, what I might need to buy once I was in the city. Already I was looking forward to my new life.

CHAPTER TWO

It was a day's journey by the slow public coach from our posting house to Oberton. The city's dramatic backdrop was the dark, serrated mountain range that contained dozens of onyx mines, which was the reason Orenza took onyx as its traditional symbol. Empara province, to the southwest, was surrounded by lush forests, so its symbol was emerald; Alberta, even farther south, took its cue from its extensive lavender fields and claimed amethyst for its badge. Altogether, the seven provinces of the kingdom were known as the Seven Jewels—though I myself had never seen any jewel but Orenza, or any city but Oberton.

And what a sight it was. I couldn't stop myself from staring out the windows at the tall buildings and the rows of shops and the throngs of people. The whole place thrummed with an energy that seemed to radiate up from the streets themselves, animating the people riding or striding by; everyone moved with purpose, bent on extraordinary tasks. From the coach windows as we drove along, I saw a bookstore, a butcher's shop, a milliner, a horse trader's barn, a temple, beggars on foot, fine ladies in carriages, and local soldiers in strict formation. I hugged myself with excitement.

Aunt Jean was waiting for me at the bustling inn where all the passengers gratefully disembarked. "I see you didn't bring much. Good," was her brisk greeting as I grabbed my shabby bag. "We don't have far to go. We won't need to hire anyone to haul it for us."

"Thank you so much for inviting me here," I said, hurrying to keep up as she set off down the street. She was twenty-five years older than I was, but age hadn't slowed her down any, and my bag was heavier than it looked. "If I could get a job with Lady Marguerite—!"

"No reason you shouldn't, but we'll see," she said. She glanced at me appraisingly. "You're a smart girl and you're used to hard work. You'd make a fine lady's maid—a fine worker no matter where you end up. It won't be difficult to get you situated."

Within a few blocks, we arrived at Aunt Jean's house, a tiny two-story building crammed between two much taller structures on a lot so small it might once have been a common garden. In fact, the only windows were on the front and back of the building because the side walls were built right up against the neighbors' bricks. The house was sparsely furnished and scrupulously clean and exactly the sort of place you would expect Aunt Jean to live if you'd known her for even five minutes.

Over a light dinner, she filled me in on local gossip, which mostly revolved around the fact that within the next six weeks, Prince Cormac and some of his friends would be traveling to Oberton from the royal city of Camarria. They were expected to stop in Alberta and Empara before their journey was over. This was big news, since there had been hostility for years between the three westernmost provinces and those in the east—including Sammerly, where Camarria was situated. I couldn't remember the last time a royal delegation had come our way; and I most certainly would have seen one, since it would have had to pass my mother's inn on the Charamon Road, even if the company was too grand to stop at a small posting house like ours.

"Everyone thinks King Harold is pushing for greater peace among the provinces," Jean said.

"Why now?" I asked.

"He's getting old, I suppose, and he wants to make sure his sons inherit a stable kingdom once one of them ascends to the throne."

"Or his *daughter*," I insisted.

Jean made a face. "Queen Tabitha would like to see that girl wearing a crown, no doubt, but the two boys are older and have been groomed for the position much longer. Anyway, Harold loved his first wife and he hates Tabitha. He would pick Cormac or Jordan for that reason alone."

I took another slice of bread and covered it with jam. "How do you know all that?" I demanded.

She laughed. "Well, it's what everyone says. I have no idea what actually goes on in the palace. But you'd be surprised how often gossip turns out to be true."

"So what else does everyone say about the prince's visit?"

Jean poured herself another cup of tea. "That Cormac is looking for a wife."

"He's already betrothed, isn't he? To Vivienne of Thelleron?"

Jean nodded. "A love match, or at least that's the rumor. But the engagement's been called off. The speculation is that Harold wants him to take a bride from one of the three western provinces as a way to improve relations."

I carefully set down my half-eaten piece of bread. "You think he might want to marry Marguerite?"

Jean shrugged. "You know the governor has been urging Alberta and Empara to join with Orenza and secede from the Seven Jewels."

I nodded. *That* news had been the talk at more than one dinner when travelers gathered around the table at the inn. Orenza had a history of being the most fractious of the provinces, and more than once in the distant past had declared its independence, only to be brought back into the fold by force or negotiation. It was well positioned to be self-sufficient, since the mountains created two very defensible borders, and there was enough land and enough water to sustain everyone who lived there. From what I'd been able to determine by listening to the talk, though, there was only half-hearted enthusiasm for the idea of seccession—except when taxes were raised on crops or onyx. Then everyone thought it was a good idea.

"So if Cormac marries Marguerite, Orenza stays in the kingdom," Jean said. "It makes a lot of sense from Harold's point of view."

I picked up my bread again. "I wonder what Marguerite thinks about the idea of marrying a prince."

Jean snorted. "I suppose it depends on the prince."

I nodded. It sounded very romantic to be married off to the heir to the throne, but I knew that reality often wasn't romantic. I'd met my share of unsavory men as they paused at our posting house or spent the night under our roof. Plenty of them were nobles who thought their wealth and status entitled them to behave any way they chose. A prince might be gracious and charming—or he might be selfish and insufferable. It was hard to know.

"Well, maybe someday I'll be able to ask her myself," I said.

"That's right. When you're working as her maid."

I smiled and then I sighed. "I can only hope."

The next week passed in a whirlwind of shopping and sightseeing and dressmaking. It turned out that—between the money my mother had given me and the sum I had saved for myself and the amount Jean bestowed on me, with a gruff observation that her brother would have wanted her to do right by me—I had enough to buy three dresses. I also could afford a pair of good shoes and a cloak that I wouldn't have a chance to use for at least two months. But it was not only warm and fashionable, it was on sale—and I could not resist.

On the morning of my interview, I arrayed myself in one of the gowns (a bright blue that splashed a little color into my gray eyes), buttoned on my new shoes, and slid my mother's triskele ring onto my finger. I was ready to face my future.

Aunt Jean accompanied me, which was a good thing because I would have been lost without her. She knew which of the manor's half dozen entrances we should use, she knew exactly what to say to the servants who asked us our business, and she exchanged a few friendly words with the housekeeper before introducing me. Constance was an imposing woman—at least six feet tall and solidly built—and she looked me over for a full minute before she began asking questions. I was polite but not obsequious, and I thought she liked my forthright manner.

However, I could see her growing a little cooler after we had been talking for about ten minutes. "Am I to understand that you've never been a lady's maid before?" she asked.

"Not formally, no," I said. "Though I've cleaned and pressed clothing for hundreds of women who stayed in our rooms overnight. And I've sewed buttons on their jackets and helped them into their dresses."

"She hasn't been raised to know all the latest fashions, but she has a good eye for style and color," Jean volunteered.

Constance nodded. "Do you have much experience styling hair? Are you familiar with curling tongs and the various pomades?"

I was starting to feel a little anxious. "I've used tongs often enough myself, and I was usually the one braiding my sisters' hair—with ribbons and lace, even, on fair days."

Her expression said that I could not have supplied a more provincial answer. "But feathers and headpieces—the newest cuts and styles—you don't have knowledge of how to incorporate those into a lady's toilette," she said.

"I can learn," I said.

"She's very clever," Aunt Jean put in.

"No doubt," the housekeeper said. "Well, I'll be frank, I'm not sure you're what Marguerite is looking for, but she expressed an interest in meeting the most promising candidates." She flicked a look at Aunt Jean that clearly said, *Although this girl is not one of them.* "And as I know this is important to my cousin, I will introduce you to the lady. But I would not get my hopes up, if I were you."

"Thank you. No. I won't," I said, my voice subdued.

Constance got to her feet, and Jean and I hastily rose as well. "I will see if she is available now," she said. "I'll return shortly."

"Plenty of other jobs," Jean said the minute Constance was out of earshot.

I forced myself to nod and smile. "That's true. At least I'll get to meet her." But it was hard not to feel both glum and a little embarrassed. Why had I ever thought I would be suitable for this position?

Twenty minutes later, Constance reappeared and said, "Come with me."

I followed her through miles of narrow servants' corridors and down one long, airy public hallway before she led me through a wide door. "This is Brianna," she announced, then departed without another word.

I was suddenly face-to-face with Lady Marguerite.

I tried not to stare as I made a deep curtsey and shakily rose, but there was so much to take in at once. In person, Marguerite looked very much as she had always appeared in paintings and pamphlets. She had fine blond hair simply styled, smoky blue eyes, and a heart-shaped face with a sweet expression. But she had a quiet presence that didn't come across in the portraits; she had a look of intensity that would have drawn my attention even if she wasn't someone I had been curious about my entire life.

Then there were the echoes.

I had been shown to a large, sunny room that seemed to exist merely as a meeting spot. There were chairs and small tables and a coatrack near the door, and a sideboard in the corner holding a pitcher of water, some glasses, even a bowl of fruit. But there wasn't a book or an embroidery frame or a sheet of writing paper to be found. People didn't come here to do anything useful. They just came here to sit and talk.

Or merely to sit.

The three echoes had taken chairs across the room from Marguerite, and there they remained, eyes cast down and hands folded primly in their laps. They didn't even glance up when I walked in. Like Marguerite, they were dressed in gowns of pretty seafoam blue, though perhaps two shades lighter in color. Their fair hair was pulled back from their faces in styles identical to hers. I couldn't see their eyes, but I guessed they were the same color as Marguerite's. Their expressions were different, though—more vacant, more placid. I never would have mistaken one of them for the real woman.

"Have you never seen an echo before?" Marguerite asked in a lovely voice, light and musical.

I quickly gave her all of my attention. "I have! A few. But never three at once."

"I understand that it is quite rare for someone to have three," she agreed.

"And I've never seen them sitting separately like that, away from their originals," I added. "They're not copying your every movement."

"Sometimes they do. But I can release them if I like. In fact, I often do." She surveyed me a moment. "Where have you encountered echoes in the past?"

"My mother runs a posting house on the Charamon Road, and all sorts of travelers pass through. Now and then someone comes with one of the shadow creatures." I couldn't help smiling. "The first time it happened, we didn't know what to do! We charge by the bed, and a traveler with an echo needs two beds. But that first lord insisted that the echo was not a separate person, and so he shouldn't have to pay a separate fee. My mother said, 'Fine then, he can share your bed,' and they argued for five minutes. In the end, she gave him blankets and let him make up a pallet on the floor for free."

"Poor echo," said Marguerite.

I glanced at the three sitting across the room, then back at Marguerite. "So they can feel discomfort and pain and fear the way ordinary people do?" I asked, wondering if it was an impertinent question but curious to know. "I have never been sure."

All this time, I had been standing politely in front of her, but now she waved me to a straight-backed chair placed a few feet away from her. I sat down, too nervous to do more than perch on the very edge of the seat.

"Some people think they don't feel anything," Marguerite replied. "Some people think the echoes are no more than—" She lifted a delicate hand and made a short, graceful gesture. "Images in a mirror. Reflections flickering through a filtered life. Completely devoid of thought or feeling or emotion."

I was fascinated. "You don't agree?"

She turned her head to survey her companions as if she had never seen them before. "They eat. They sleep. If one stumbles against a door, a bruise forms on her skin. When I am sad, they come and sit by me and put their arms around me." She shrugged.

"I don't believe they think and reason and grow and understand the way an ordinary human would, but they are more than reflections."

There were so many questions I wanted to ask to follow up on those observations, but the one that rose to my lips first was, "What sorts of things have made you sad?"

I saw surprise come to her face, but she quickly banished it with a laugh. "Oh, isn't everyone sad from time to time? And for no particular reason."

I studied her a little more closely now. I was used to gauging a traveler's mood by the expression on his face or the way she held her shoulders—an essential skill when so many clients were likely to be tired and irate—and I would have bet that something was making Marguerite very unhappy. I could hardly ask her about it, however. "Yes, no doubt," I said. "Though I don't like to think of anyone being miserable!"

She shifted in her seat and tried a smile, answering me as if I had actually posed the question. "I just have a slight headache," she said. "It's been with me all day."

"I'm so sorry," I said quickly. "I can come back some other time. It's just that the housekeeper said you wanted to meet all the candidates—"

"I do," she said. "I suppose I should now ask you questions about your credentials as a lady's maid."

All my wonder at being in the presence of Marguerite and her echoes faded away as I recalled that I really had *no* credentials. But I tried to cover up my discouragement with an air of confidence. "I can sew and iron and help you dress. I don't have much experience with fashionable hairstyles, but I'm sure I can learn the ones you like. I'd be happy to run errands and I'm *very* discreet and— What exactly do you want to know?"

Her smile became more genuine. "Those very things," she assured me.

I glanced at the echoes again. It was odd to see three people sitting there so quietly, not talking amongst themselves, not playing

14

games, not embroidering, not doing *anything*. Just existing. "Does your maid help them dress, too?"

Marguerite shook her head. "They dress themselves—or, if something needs to be buttoned or laced up the back, they help each other."

I maintained my silence, but I couldn't help wondering why, if they were that adroit, they couldn't help Marguerite with her clothes as well. She must have read my expression. "Yes, I know," she said. "If the echoes are near me at all times, why do I need a lady's maid at all? Everyone would be quite shocked if I didn't have one. They would think me—defective or inferior. Or perhaps radical."

I ventured a smile. "You don't look to be any of those things."

"No. And that is why I must have a maid of my own."

I wished with all my heart that I was suitable for the job. I said, in deeply respectful tones, "I hope you will consider me as you make your decision."

Marguerite shifted in her chair and something flickered across her face. I thought it might be uneasiness. "I will. I suppose I should ask you a few more questions—" She paused as her uneasiness increased.

"Yes?" I said in an encouraging voice. "Another question?"

She stirred in her chair again, then laid a hand across her stomach. "I'm sorry, I think I'm going to be—"

And she leaned forward and vomited at my feet.

I jumped up, and the three echoes did the same. They were at Marguerite's side when she threw up a second time, but they did no more than hover there, agitated, their hands outstretched to touch her shoulders and the top of her head.

I was more used to handling a crisis. "Quickly—one of you bring her some water. Someone else empty that fruit bowl and bring it to me in case she retches again." They didn't move, except to look at Marguerite and at each other, their agitation increasing. I bent over Marguerite, putting one arm around her shoulder and one hand against her forehead. Her skin was hot and her body was shaking.

"Are you strong enough to stand? Would you like to lie down on one of the sofas, or would moving make it worse?"

"Worse, I think," she panted.

"All right, then, just stay put for a moment," I said. I put my hands on the back of her chair and shifted it just enough so she no longer had to look down at the puddle of vomit.

I quickly circled the room, picking up the items the echoes had declined to fetch, then returned to Marguerite's side. After settling the bowl on her lap, I pulled a handkerchief from my pocket and dampened it with water from the pitcher so I could wipe her face. Over my shoulder I said, "Can one of you go get help?"

I wasn't surprised when the echoes all stared at me uncomprehendingly. None of them made a move for the door.

"They—don't leave me," Marguerite gasped. She doubled over the bowl and her body heaved, but nothing else came up. "And even if they could find a servant, they wouldn't be able to explain what was wrong."

Well, they could jump up and down and wave their arms and point back toward the room, couldn't they? I wanted to demand. But apparently not. They might be more mirror reflections than Marguerite liked to think.

"Then I'll go find someone just as soon as it's safe to leave you," I said. "Would you like a sip of water, or would that make it worse?"

"Worse," she whispered, and then threw up again.

It was probably another twenty minutes before Marguerite's stomach settled a bit and she let me guide her to a sofa, where she lay down with my handkerchief draped over her eyes. The room was taking on a decidedly sour smell and the echoes were still hovering, distressed but silent. I wondered if *they* would start vomiting soon, sparing a moment to think how unpleasant the situation could become. I hustled out into the hallway and stopped the first servant I could find.

"Lady Marguerite is sick and someone needs to go to her," I announced.

Within five minutes, there were a half dozen attendants in the room, some cleaning up the mess and some helping Marguerite to her feet. Nobody asked me who I was or what business I had at the mansion, and no one offered to see me out. I stood there a few moments after Marguerite was gone, watching the undermaids soaping the carpet, and then I shrugged and headed for the door. Soon enough, I had made my way down the hallways and found the kitchen, where the housekeeper had her office.

Constance wasn't there, but Jean was, taking advantage of a bit of quiet time to check entries in a ledger she had brought with her. She came quickly to her feet when I knocked on the door.

"How did it go?" she demanded.

I shrugged. "Well, Constance made it clear I had no hope of landing the job, but Lady Marguerite was very kind. She seemed tired and said she had a headache, then all of a sudden she started throwing up. I had to call for some servants, but—" I spread my hands. "I'm not sure she'll even remember I was there."

"That's most unfortunate," Jean said. "I'll send a note to Constance in the morning, inquiring after Marguerite's health and asking if you should come back another time."

I shrugged again. "I'm sure she'll say no. I could tell I'm not what she is looking for."

"There are other jobs in the city," Jean said, looking around with a slight frown of irritation. "I suppose no one will bother to see us out. Let's go, then. If you can't be Lady Marguerite's maid, what would you like to do?"

I spent the next two days meeting roughly a dozen of Jean's city friends, inquiring into possible employment. To me it seemed she must know everyone in Oberton, though in reality everyone she introduced me to fell squarely into the same social class. In the Seven Jewels, society was strictly divided into five categories, and people rarely strayed above or below their station. There were the high nobles, such as the governor and his family; the low nobles, who had some money and status but came from inferior bloodlines; the merchants and professionals, who owned property and made good livings, but weren't from landed families; the working class, like my mother and the tradesmen who kept the city running; and the poor, who existed at the margins.

Jean's friends were all merchants and professionals, and she appeared to know dozens who were looking for a trustworthy employee. The baker would have hired me on the spot, and the milliner said if I could set a straight seam she would take me on part-time, but the job I found most intriguing was the one working in a bookseller's shop. There had never been much time to read— or very many books to choose from—back at the posting house, but I had always enjoyed the activity when I had a spare moment. I thought if I was surrounded by words all day, some of them might seep into my skull just by association. I would gain knowledge, learn stories, and discover the mysteries of the world every time I brushed past a shelf heavy with leather-bound volumes. The job paid next to nothing, however, and Jean insisted I talk to at least two more business proprietors before I made a decision.

"Don't be shortsighted," she said on the evening of the second day as we were returning from a visit to an attorney's office. I had hated the place the minute we stepped inside: It was small and cramped and poorly lit and smelled like sweaty despair. The attorney liked me and named a salary that made Jean smile, but I told him I had more people to talk to before I made a decision. Once we were out on the street, I informed her that I would never work in such a place, but she urged me to reconsider. "People will always need legal help, and lawyers will always need assistants. You're a bright girl and you deserve a job with a future."

"What I want is a job that's interesting."

She snorted. "The better it pays, the more interesting a job is."

"I just don't think that can be true."

It was almost the dinner hour by the time we arrived back at her narrow house, and Jean wondered aloud whether she should stop to pick up another loaf of bread. "There's plenty for tonight, but perhaps not for the morning," she was saying when I touched her arm and pointed at a tall, slim figure waiting outside her door.

"Who's that?"

"Courier, it looks like," she said.

Within a few steps we could tell that he was not only a courier, but that he was wearing the governor's livery. "I'm looking for a woman named Brianna," he said, and handed over a sealed envelope when I identified myself.

It was from Constance. The note read bluntly:

Marguerite wishes to employ you. Present yourself in the morning.

I stared at the message, stared at Jean, and read the letter again. Then I threw my hands in the air, let loose a cry of sheer delight, and started laughing uncontrollably. My *real* life was about to begin.

CHAPTER THREE

I spent almost a full day at the manor before I saw Marguerite again. First, Constance spent at least an hour reviewing etiquette with me, telling me where I fit in the hierarchy of the servants and what I would be expected to do and who might order me about. From what I could tell, I answered first to Marguerite, then to the housekeeper, then to the butler, then to the cook, but anyone else had to *ask* me to do something and I could say no. I didn't need Jean's voice in my head, admonishing me to *make friends*, to resolve to be a cheerful and willing coworker.

Next, a footman named Rory took me on a long, bewildering tour of the mansion, which consisted of four wings built around a central, enclosed atrium. On the top four levels of the five-story house, there were balconies that ran around the entire perimeter of the atrium; on each level, in each wing, there was single door that led to that balcony. Rory and I were on the third floor when he showed me the trick to identifying those doors—they had special, decorative moldings around their frames—then we stepped out onto the gallery to look around.

The two times I had come to the mansion, I had entered through a servants' door in the back wing, so I hadn't had a chance to see the magnificent public space.

The floor was veined white marble polished to such a high shine that it reflected back the sunlight pouring in through the glass panes of the ceiling. Tall potted plants, some bursting with blossoms, stood under the various archways that led from the atrium into the four wings. There were glowing copper statues and cheerful small fountains and banners and baskets and flags. Too many details to take in.

There were also people moving across the space in a constant stream. Some were clearly servants hurrying off on urgent tasks; others appeared to be merchants and nobles come to seek an audience with Lord Garvin, the governor. We could catch snatches of their conversations and hear the bright tapping of their feet across the hard stone floor. The whole place seemed to swirl with sound and color.

Suddenly Rory pointed. "See there? That's Lord Garvin himself."

I craned my head to look, but the governor was impossible to miss. He was a tall man with brushy gray hair; he was dressed in blue and silver and striding so fast that his navy cloak billowed behind him. Behind him, on either side, were his two echoes. They were dressed in the same blue clothing, held their shoulders just as he did, and put their feet down at the precise moment his touched the floor. Someone called out a greeting and Lord Garvin's head whipped around in response. In unison, both echoes also snapped their attention in that direction.

"Do they always move exactly the way he does?" I whispered, even though the governor couldn't possibly hear me from this far away.

Rory nodded. "It's spooky to watch."

"But they never speak?"

"Not a word."

We stood at the balcony a few more minutes, resting our elbows on the rail, and he pointed out other noteworthy figures as they passed through. I didn't make much effort to commit names to memory, since I wouldn't be mingling with the nobles who visited the mansion. Suddenly I felt Rory grow tense and watchful as he stood beside me, and he elbowed me in the arm.

"See him? The tall man wearing all black?" he asked in a quiet voice.

I nodded, peering down at the figure making his way across the atrium. He was exceptionally thin and moved with a sort of sinister grace, sliding across the floor so smoothly that his outer garments didn't flare or billow the way everyone else's did. No one accompanied him, no one approached him; indeed, it seemed from my vantage point that he was surrounded by a small bubble of space that everyone else was being very careful not to disturb. He was walking in our direction, so I could get a fairly good look at his face, which was narrow and bony and pale. I couldn't see the color of his eyes from this far up, but I could tell how they darted around incessantly, taking in every detail of his surroundings. I would have sworn he even glanced up once to take note of Rory and me at the railing.

"Who's that?" I breathed.

"Del Morson. The governor's inquisitor."

When I just looked at Rory and shrugged, he amplified, "He's the one who keeps order in the city. He can have anyone arrested, anyone questioned. They say sometimes Del Morson keeps people locked up so long they don't remember what crime they've been accused of." Rory shook his head. "Don't do anything that grabs his attention. Never catch his eye. If you're in a room, even a public plaza, and Del Morson walks by, you just freeze in place until he's out of sight."

The advice would have sounded melodramatic if I hadn't actually been staring at Del Morson at that very moment, but given that fact, it seemed like a perfectly reasonable recommendation. "I'll do that," I said.

We waited until Del Morson disappeared through one of the archways and the other visitors resumed their normal patterns of walking across the polished floor. "Well, then," Rory said, turning away from the railing, "let's see the rest of the house."

As we continued the tour, Rory explained how the rooms were laid out, how the servants' routes mirrored the more public corridors, and how to travel most quickly between the different wings. "It'll get easier," he said, after I got turned around for the third time. "Anytime you're lost, just find a door to the balcony, and you'll be able to orient yourself."

Finally, he showed me to my room, which was situated on the fifth floor. It was a small, spare cell with a narrow bed, a high window, and a lock on the door to which Constance and I would have the only keys. "Not very fancy," he said, "but you don't have to share. Last place I worked, a lord's house, there were four of us in every room. I like this better."

"So do I," I assured him.

He then made me find the way from my room to Lady Marguerite's suite, though he followed me and dropped hints when I was about to make a wrong turn. I made mental notes about statuary and wall hangings that would serve as landmarks on my return journey, and thanked him gravely for his help.

"It was fun," he said, flashing me an easy smile. "I'll see you at dinner."

Neither Marguerite nor the echoes were in her rooms, so I cautiously explored. In the village where I'd grown up, there were whole families living in houses that weren't as spacious as these chambers. There was a large sitting room with a picture window overlooking the back gardens; by the sewing baskets and lap harp and piles of books lying around, I guessed that this was the place Marguerite spent most of her time. One door led off to the left, one to the right. I tiptoed first through the door to my right.

It led to a long, narrow room with three beds lined up in a row, all neatly made and piled with the same number of pillows. Across from each bed stood an armoire. I peeked inside to find each one filled with identical dresses hung in exactly the same order, matching shoes arranged precisely beneath them. On one wall hung three oval mirrors; beneath them were three small vanities set with hairbrushes, powders, and jewelry boxes. I didn't sort through the jewels, but I was pretty sure the contents would all be the same.

I slipped back into the sitting room and through the door on the left, which led to three more chambers—a dressing room, a closet almost as big as the dressing room, and a bedroom. Not unexpectedly, Marguerite's amenities were far more lavish than those of her echoes. The bed was mounded high with what looked like down mattresses, and covered with lace-edged duvets; I couldn't count the number of pillows in satin cases. The rugs were thick and featured intricate patterns of roses and violets. Vases of flowers stood on almost every flat surface.

The one thing that surprised me was a small statuary grouping I found in her bedroom. Not that the pieces were shocking. Not at all. They represented the triple goddess, the deity who watched over all the people in the Seven Jewels. This sculpture set was particularly lovely, containing figures that were approximately a foot tall. The one showing justice was rendered in black onyx with her hands stretched out to the sides; the one representing joy was carved in red with her arms lifted up toward the heavens; the one for mercy was made of white stone with her hands extended before her, palms up, supplicating.

What surprised me was that the statues had been placed in a shadowy corner that was as far as it could be from the main door; someone would have to make a pretty thorough inspection of the suite to discover them. This led me to think that either Marguerite felt a deep, personal connection to the sculptures—or she didn't want anyone else to know she kept them in her room. Not only that, it was clear that Marguerite worshipped before the statues on a regular basis. There were half-burned candles set before each goddess, and stone dishes blackened with the residue of incense. Flower petals, both fresh and faded, littered the floor all around the grouping, as if Marguerite tossed a few down every day and rarely bothered to sweep them up.

It made no sense. Who would care if Marguerite regularly paid homage to the goddess? I had never heard any rumblings suggesting the governor was a nonbeliever. As far as I knew, Lord Garvin supported the temples and attended services on holy days. And I'd seen a few paintings of the triple goddess on the mansion walls during the long trek up and down its hallways that afternoon. Marguerite's parents couldn't possibly mind that she was a dedicated follower of the faith.

I stroked a finger across the smooth white head of the sister who stood for mercy. What might prompt the governor and his wife to look on Marguerite's devotions with suspicion? The goddess was served by a select group of attendants, mostly women, who lived in quarters near the temples and carried out sacred duties. Priestesses in black robes always attended executions and were present in the legal courts to ensure that justice was done; women in white robes usually could be found in the slums and infirmaries, ministering to the poor and the sick. Of course everyone was always happy to see a priestess in flowing red vestments at a wedding or any other celebration. Even in my village, we had a small temple and two women who served it. One of the girls my age had almost decided to forgo the idea of marriage and apprentice with them, though I'd always thought she was just nursing a broken heart and would change her mind as soon as she met a kinder young man.

Most of the women who joined the temple were older, having participated in the rough-and-tumble of ordinary life long enough to understand the sorts of passions that make regular people go mad sometimes. But a few girls felt the call very early and donned the robes while they were still young. I didn't know how strictly the rules were enforced, but I knew that, generally speaking, the women in the temples were expected to be celibate. They watched over the world, but they were not a part of it. And while I knew enough about human nature to suspect that more than a few of the priestesses took lovers, I was pretty sure that none of them ever married.

I touched a fingertip in turn to the heads of the red and black statues. Maybe Marguerite felt that call. Maybe her heart was drawn to the temple, to the serving of justice, the offering of mercy, the celebration of joy. For a powerful man hoping to marry his daughter off for political advantage, there could hardly be a more disastrous development. That could explain why Marguerite hid her statues of the triple goddess in a back corner of her room.

Making my way out of the bedchamber, I paused in the dressing room. I decided I might as well make myself useful while I was there. It didn't take much searching through Marguerite's closet

25

to find a small section devoted to gowns and cloaks and undergarments that needed repair. I gathered up a half dozen items and returned to the sitting room, choosing a chair in front of the big picture window to take advantage of the late afternoon sunlight. I snagged a basket of sewing materials from a nearby table and began mending a long, jagged tear in a green silk gown. The work was intricate but not very difficult, and I rather enjoyed myself. I wasn't sure what my new life at the manor would entail, but *this* part of it, at least, I understood how to do.

I had been stitching for about an hour when there was a clatter at the door and Marguerite and the echoes stepped inside. They were all wearing sunny yellow dresses and carrying armloads of summer blossoms, which made me suspect they had been shopping at the city's famous flower markets. When I'd noticed all the vases in the room, I'd just assumed the housekeeper or a maid kept them filled with fresh blooms, but now I wondered if Marguerite made her own selections.

I put aside the green dress and came hastily to my feet, curtseying as they swept in. "Brianna! You're here!" Marguerite exclaimed. She handed her bundles to one of the echoes and came across the room to greet me. "And look at you—working already. Just what I would have expected of you."

I glanced up from my curtsey, honestly surprised. "Would you? You don't even know me."

She was smiling. "You don't seem like the type to sit around idle."

I smiled back. "No, I suppose not. I like to keep busy." I clasped my hands in front of me. Jean had told me I must express my gratitude for my new position, and in truth I wanted to. "My lady, thank you so much for giving me this opportunity. I want to be the best maid you ever had. I don't even know why you decided to take a chance on me, but I'm so thankful you did."

Her smile lingered. "Why did I take a chance on you? Because you took care of me when I was sick. No one else has ever done that."

I was bewildered. "No one—none of your other maids?"

She shook her head. "Winifred—the last one—she was very fashionable. She couldn't abide anything inferior. Her favorite thing to say was, 'It's not *quality*.' If I had vomited at her feet she would have scurried out the door. And Daniella, the one before her. She was almost too timid to speak. She never did anything without a direct order. If I'd been sick while she was in the room, she would have just stood there and watched me."

"Well, maybe they would have fetched someone else to come take care of you."

Marguerite shook her head and turned toward the bedroom, motioning to me. I followed her, and the echoes trailed behind us. "The housemaids would have brought me tea and cleaned up my mess, but I can't think of anyone who would have sat by my bed and wiped my face." She paused by one of the tables holding a vase of flowers, pulled out the wilted bunch inside it, and shook water off the stems. Laying them on the table, she selected new flowers from one of the echoes and began arranging them in the vase.

"Your mother, maybe—?" I suggested.

That just made her laugh. "No."

"But then what happens when you're ill?"

She examined her new arrangement critically, swapped a red rose for a pink one, and moved on to the next vase. "A nurse is hired to stay with me."

I wasn't sure what to say to that, since *How very sad* didn't seem like an appropriate response. I finally managed, "Well, I've sat up with my sisters and brothers dozens of times when they had every kind of cough and fever and horrible, disgusting symptom you can imagine. It never bothered me. I certainly wouldn't ever *want* you to get sick, but if you do, I'll be right there."

"That's what I thought," she said. "That's why I told Constance I picked you."

In a few more minutes, she'd replaced all the flowers in the suite. Without being told, I gathered up the discarded ones and placed them in a pile by the door. I could take them downstairs on my way to dinner and toss them into one of the scrap barrels in the kitchen that—I had learned during my earlier tour—were filled and disposed of every day.

Marguerite was yawning. "I think I'll rest for an hour," she said. "Then you must help me dress for dinner tonight. It is just family and a few local businessmen, so I don't need anything fancy."

"Do you pick your own clothes or am I supposed to advise you?"

"Winifred never let me pick and Daniella never expressed an opinion so— I don't suppose I care." She tilted her head to one side. "You could choose three possibilities," she suggested. "Then we will see how well your tastes align with mine."

"What if you hate all the ones I pick?" I asked nervously. I didn't want to fail during my very first day on the job.

"Then I will select something else! But we must learn how well we work together, and tonight is as good a time to start as any."

I nodded and watched her slip away into her bedroom, shutting the door behind her. The echoes filed into their own room—also to sleep, I supposed, though I couldn't be sure, since they closed their door as well. I was left with the run of the other three rooms and a puzzle to solve.

A quiet family dinner with no one to impress but my new employer. What kind of outfit did that call for? I had already browsed through some of the contents of Marguerite's closet, but now I sorted through the dozens of dresses with a greater sense of purpose. It was clear they'd been arranged to some extent by category—ball gowns in one section, warm morning dresses in a second section, lightweight summer evening wear hanging on another rod. I thought there were probably certain rules that I didn't know—for instance, were particular colors and fabrics appropriate for some hours and seasons, and not for others?—but I would learn those as time went along. For now, I weighed what I knew of Marguerite's preferences and chose three gowns and three different sets of accessories.

Sunset was falling and I was lighting lamps in the sitting room when Marguerite and the echoes emerged simultaneously from their chambers. I glanced at the three echoes before turning my attention to Marguerite. How had they known she was awake? I hadn't even heard her stirring as she moved through her suite.

"Did you have a nice nap?" I asked her.

"Indeed. I feel quite refreshed and ready to take on my family over dinner."

"That makes it sound like it will be a battle."

"Sometimes," she said. "My brothers vie with each other for my father's attention, so the conversation can be quite—clamorous. They are generally better behaved when there are others present at the table and they know they must show some decorum."

"My little brothers were always very loud," I agreed. "I had to shout if I wanted to be heard."

"I rarely bother shouting," she said.

"Do you and your mother sit together and talk while the men are all showing off for each other?"

Her smile was ironic and brief. "No."

It was early days yet, but I was not forming a very favorable opinion of Marguerite's family—or the place that Marguerite held in it.

"Then I hope there is someone at the table tonight you will enjoy talking to," was all I said.

"I hope so, too. Let's see what you've picked for me to wear."

Somewhat nervously, I indicated the three dresses I had laid over the back of a sofa. They were all simple, with relatively high necklines so she didn't have to be watchful about bending over and with loose sleeves so she was comfortable in the summer heat.

"I thought the pale purple one was such a lovely color. It's very plain, but you could wear that lace shawl over your shoulders to dress it up. The dark blue might be too heavy for summer wear, but it's the kind of color that brightens up your face if you're feeling tired after a long day. And the pink dress—if you liked that one, I could braid a few of those tiny roses into your hair just for something light and pretty. You wouldn't do braids or flowers for a formal dinner, but if it's just a casual meal—" I shrugged. "It might be fun. You seem to like flowers so much."

Marguerite was smiling, rubbing the fabric of the lavender dress between her fingertips. "You have chosen my three favorite outfits from my whole closet," she said. "I would hardly have been able to pick from among them, except that you mentioned the roses! Now I *must* have roses braided into my hair! Can you really do that?"

I nodded, relieved and pleased. "I did it all the time for my little sisters. I had to teach my mother how to do it before they would let me leave for the city."

"Then let's get started."

We moved into the large dressing room, Marguerite sitting in a plush chair before the vanity, the echoes clustered behind me, watching intently as I began to fix Marguerite's hair. It was a very simple style, two long locks pulled back from the sides of her face and woven together down the back of her head, with a scattering of small blossoms tucked between the plaits.

"Will the echoes be able to braid each other's hair?" I asked Marguerite. "Or shall I do it for them?"

"They learn quickly, as a rule," she said. "Let's see what they're able to manage."

Indeed, they had already moved a few steps away and started the job of replicating Marguerite's look. One echo stood quietly while another worked on her hair and the third one waited nearby, handing over sprigs of roses. I could tell that the plaits were not as tight as the ones I'd put into Marguerite's hair, but otherwise the echo had done a competent job of copying me.

"I'm impressed," I said. "It took my mother a couple of hours to get it right."

"Patience is usually the first one to pick up any new skill," Marguerite answered.

I had turned to reach for her dress, but at that I turned back. "'Patience'?" I repeated. "They have names?" Then, even more surprised, "You can tell them apart?"

Marguerite looked slightly flustered, as if she hadn't intended to let slip that piece of information. "Most people say that echoes have no distinctive traits—no personalities at all—but I've always been able to see very slight differences among them," she said. "Patience is the one who's most focused, the one who stays calm even if I'm upset. Prudence is the one who holds back. If I'm getting in a boat, for instance, she's always the last one on board." She smiled. "And Purpose is always the *first* one on board. The one who always seems most in tune with my moods."

I glanced doubtfully between Marguerite and her shadows, who were now engaged in making sure the second one had her hair correctly braided. "I don't think I'm ever going to be able to make those distinctions."

"No, well, most people can't," she answered. "I asked my mother once what she'd named her echoes and she called the nurse because she thought I was feverish. I was pretty young at the time," she added. "I would never ask anyone that kind of question today."

"Maybe your brothers would tell you," I suggested. Having watched her father and his lookalikes striding across the atrium this afternoon, I didn't even have to wonder if she would ask him about differences among his attendants. It had been clear even from that brief glimpse that there was no variation among them at all.

"I don't really have conversations with my brothers," she said.

"No. Well, brothers can be difficult," I replied. From what I could tell, Marguerite didn't have conversations with anybody in this household. Which seemed like a lonely way to live, but naturally I couldn't say so. I made a little motion that indicated she should stand up. "Let's get your dress on."

By the time I had slipped the pink silk over her head and laced it up the back, the echoes had finished with their coiffures and filed out of the room, presumably to gather their own clothes.

"I thought the echoes dressed just like you, but their closets aren't nearly as big."

Marguerite shook her head. "No. All of *their* clothes are identical, but they have a much more limited range. I have seven blue dresses—they each have two. I have three white dresses, they each have one. The styles are similar enough to suggest that we are dressed alike. Although for certain very important functions, we do dress the same and their clothes are identical to mine in every detail except for being a shade or two lighter."

"What sorts of very important functions?"

She smiled, but I thought the expression was sad. "When I marry, for instance, they will wear dresses that are exact replicas of mine."

Privately I thought that would be the *last* time I would want to run the risk of anyone mistaking me for someone else. The last time I would want someone to dress like me, too. But I spoke in a cheerful voice. "Well! That will be something to see on that day, won't it?"

"Yes," Marguerite answered without much enthusiasm. "It will be something, indeed."

CHAPTER FOUR

By the end of my first three weeks as a lady's maid, I felt I had found the position I had always been destined to hold. Marguerite had received enough compliments on her new braids-and-blossoms hairstyle that she started to adopt flowers as her signature look. I began to accompany her on visits to the flower markets where we debated which blooms would look best with her gowns, which would stay freshest the longest and not wilt before the end of a long dinner. She could not wear such a simple hairstyle to fancy events, but it was surprising how many elegant coiffures could be enhanced by one or two carefully placed blossoms.

I was delighted that my offhand suggestion had inspired Marguerite's favorite new fashion accessory, but that wasn't all that made me so happy in my position. Truth be told, I simply loved the life. I loved the constant bustle of the mansion, which seemed to be the beating heart powering the entire city. I loved that there was always work to be done, and that I had to constantly think about the next event, the next outfit, the next impression that Marguerite would make. I had never been thrilled with the endless *busyness* of the posting house, but so much of the work there had been sheer drudgery: cooking, cleaning, laundering, gardening. Here, the work was sometimes hard and the demands were unceasing, but the urgency was exciting, and the need for creativity kept me constantly at a high level of alertness.

And Marguerite could not have been an easier mistress. She was never short-tempered, always appreciative, and unfailingly generous. I guessed this made her fairly uncommon among highborn women. It even made her unusual within her own household where, naturally, the residents were a constant topic of conversation among the servants.

Marguerite's mother, Lady Dorothea, was the family member who was most disliked by the other servants. She was rumored to be cold to her husband, despite having presented him with so many children; and she never showed much interest in her offspring, either. Her interactions with servants only had two modes: ignoring them as if they were invisible, or berating them for making mistakes. Naturally, everyone attempted to be invisible around her. The household staff greatly preferred Lord Garvin, considering him a fair man who could be counted on to thank someone for extraordinary service. Marguerite's many brothers roused neither hatred nor devotion in the servants' hall. And as I had no dealings with them, I formed no opinions about them at all.

I did have the chance to observe Lady Dorothea for myself not long after I took my position as Marguerite's maid. We had begun assembling Marguerite's wardrobe for Prince Cormac's upcoming visit, and Lady Dorothea accompanied us one day as we visited various modistes' shops. "You know I must come along," she said as she settled herself into carriage, "because otherwise who knows what kind of unsuitable dresses you might be bamboozled into ordering."

The carriage was the biggest one I'd ever seen, large enough to hold Marguerite, Lady Dorothea, their echoes, and me. It was an oddly built vehicle, with two backward-facing benches, one behind the other, and one forward-facing bench. Lady Dorothea and her echoes had the prime seat, while Marguerite and two of her echoes sat across from her. I shared the final seat with the one I assumed was Prudence. At any rate, she had been the last one to climb into the carriage, and Marguerite had said Prudence was always the laggard of the lot.

From my vantage point, I had an excellent opportunity to study Lady Dorothea, whom I had never seen up close before. She looked a great deal like her daughter, with the same fair hair and heart-shaped face, though her eyes were a faded brown instead of

Marguerite's misty blue. And her expression was far different, bitter and dissatisfied; her mouth was twisted in a perpetual frown. She passed the first half of the trip in absolute silence—except to complain about the heat or criticize Marguerite's posture.

What fascinated me about her was that every slight gesture she made, every brief change in her expression, was perfectly imitated by her echoes. When she glanced out the window, they did, too; when the carriage jounced over a rut in the road and she audibly sighed, both of them sighed in unison. What made this even more impressive was that she never even glanced at them. It was as if they were not even in the carriage with us.

Though apparently she was highly aware of echoes. Just not her own.

This became obvious as the carriage jolted to an abrupt halt and all of us were nearly pitched out of our seats. In fact, both Patience and Purpose, on the bench in front of me, grabbed wildly at the hanging straps to keep their balance, while Marguerite clutched at both of *them*, and managed not to fall on her face.

"And that's another thing," Dorothea said, as if she hadn't sat utterly mute for the past mile. "You exercise no control over your echoes."

"Of course I do," Marguerite replied.

Dorothea sniffed. "You treat them as if they were playthings—even friends. Independent creatures. It's unbecoming. People have remarked on it. I can't imagine what Prince Cormac might have to say."

At first, Marguerite didn't reply, but by the rigidity in her shoulders, I could tell she was seriously annoyed. After a moment, she straightened on the bench—while beside me and in front of me, her echoes did the same. Then, with slow, delicate movements, Marguerite crossed one leg over the other, lifted her right hand to her cheek and pressed her left hand to her heart. The echoes matched her, gesture for gesture.

"Don't be afraid I will embarrass you in front of the prince," Marguerite said in a quiet voice. "I know exactly how to behave."

"Oh, you *know* how," Dorothea replied. "You just don't bother to do it. I can only suppose you want to spite me."

"I'm sorry that I'm a disappointment to you," Marguerite said, folding her hands in her lap. The echoes did the same.

"A mother's life is nothing *but* disappointments," Dorothea replied. "As you will find out for yourself someday when you marry."

"You certainly make it sound like an attractive prospect."

Dorothea loosed an unexpected crack of laughter. "Attractive enough if you marry the prince, as you very well might!" she exclaimed. "So don't argue with me when we arrive at the dressmaker's. I know exactly what colors and cuts look best on you. The prince's visit is too important for us to leave anything to chance."

The day was long and exhausting and I wasn't even the one patiently enduring all the measuring and poking and prodding. Marguerite turned to me occasionally for advice, but Dorothea had little interest in the opinions of maids, so mostly I waited in the background, always ready with a smile or a nod if Marguerite looked in my direction. But my main responsibility was to stay out of the way.

Despite the tedium, I rather enjoyed the outing. I had never been to a really fashionable dressmaker's shop before, and I practically gaped at the piles of exquisite fabric, as well as the spools of lace, the feathers and buckles and jewels on display. Beside every bolt of vibrant emerald green or luscious pink silk was a second pile of the same color, one or two shades lighter in hue. These modistes catered to the very highest echelons of society and knew they would be making dresses for echoes as well as highborn ladies; they stocked up accordingly.

I was also interested to see that, while each dressmaker carefully took Marguerite's measurements, no one bothered to do the same for the echoes. At one shop, after Marguerite had called me into the dressing room and we were alone for a few minutes, I pointed this out.

"Their measurements are always the same as mine," she answered.

"Really? If you gain five pounds, they do, too?"

"Yes."

"Then you didn't even need to bring them with you today, did you? They could just have waited for you at home."

For a second, incomprehension made her face so blank that she almost looked like one of her imitation creatures. "But they always accompany me," she said.

"Yes, but they didn't *have* to."

She just spread her hands. For the first time I realized, really understood, that Marguerite didn't see the echoes as separate from her—a delight or an inconvenience or a symbol of status, as the mood struck her—but as parts of herself. I had viewed them as being roughly equal to shoes or hats—something she wouldn't choose to leave at home, but something she could dispense with if she wanted. She saw them more as arms and feet. Parts of her body. Essential. Inseparable. I wondered if Dorothea felt the same about her echoes. Probably so, or they would not have accompanied us today. Dorothea didn't seem to have sentimental attachments to people or things; she was accompanied by the echoes because there was nowhere else she could imagine they would be.

"I guess someone who doesn't have an echo can't understand it," I said at last.

"I guess not."

"And something *else* I don't understand. Your mother's echoes do exactly what she does. So do your father's. Ever since I've met you, you've always let your echoes move of their own volition—except suddenly today in the coach, when all at once they started mimicking you perfectly. How do you decide when to control them and when to let them go? And how do you *do* it? You didn't even say a word."

Again she looked bewildered, as if someone had asked her to explain why she had teeth or hair. "I just—how can I— You know what it's like when you're breathing? Sometimes you decide to take in a really deep breath—" She inhaled noisily and held the air for a moment before slowly letting it out. "And you can do that for as long as you like. Other times, you just forget about it, you think about other things, but you keep breathing all the same. That's what it's like in terms of controlling the echoes. Sometimes I do it on purpose and sometimes I don't. But they keep existing right alongside me anyway."

I squinched my face up, trying to make sense of that. "It seems like it has to be more complicated than that."

"I suppose it is. I find that when I'm most relaxed, it's easier to let the echoes go. When I'm very focused on a task, or when I'm upset about something, they're most likely to copy my every move."

She thought for a moment and then went on, "I was still a little girl when I realized I *could* let the echoes go. Up until that point, they had always mimicked me, every movement. Then one day I found myself just staring at one of them and wondering what it would be like if she didn't always copy me. And I—I just *released* her. I don't know how else to explain it. And she picked up her hand and looked at it a moment, and then put it back in her lap." Marguerite smiled. "I'm guessing that was Purpose. I couldn't tell them apart then, but now I know she is always the first one to try anything. Over the next fifteen years I learned how to release all of them at once for as long as I want—and to gather them up again when I want, as well."

"But then do they—have their own thoughts? Make their own decisions?"

She shook her head. "Not that I can tell. I don't believe they could exist apart from me. To this day, they breathe when I breathe. Their hearts beat at precisely the same rate as mine. They sleep when I sleep and wake when I wake. It's just that I can let them go if I want to. I don't know how else to say it."

I wanted to ask more questions, but just then, the modiste hurried back in, several lengths of fabric thrown over her left arm. "I had an idea about this deep lavender satin, and I wanted to ask you before I said anything to your mother," she said to Marguerite. "I have a lighter color in stock, but I thought perhaps this time, something slightly different—a purple with a brighter strain of pink in it—that might be a lovely contrast for your echoes."

"Let's take a look," Marguerite said.

The dressmaker draped the darker fabric around Marguerite's shoulders and then motioned me over. "Your maid is your same height. Have her stand next to you so I can show you what the fabrics look like side by side—yes—that *is* very nice."

For a moment, Marguerite and I stood shoulder to shoulder, studying our joint reflection in a tall mirror. We *were* the same height, which I'd never noticed before, and close enough in weight that I could probably wear her dresses if I did a few minimum alterations. Of course, my hair was much darker and my eyes were gray, not blue, and the bones of my face were stronger and wider than her elegant ones.

"I like that," Marguerite said. "Brianna, what do you think?"

"It's pretty," I decided. "It will make you distinctive, especially if there are lots of other ladies there with their own echoes."

"Oh, I imagine every girl with an echo will make her way to Oberton when Prince Cormac is around," the dressmaker said. "Waving her handkerchief and trying to get his attention."

"Yes," said Marguerite dryly, "we will all have to work very hard to make ourselves distinctive enough to stand out from the crowd."

"As to that," the modiste said, "I had an idea the other day when I got a very large shipment of netting. Wouldn't it be pretty to make colorful veils to go with every outfit? You could enter the room with a veil across your face, then slowly draw it back to reveal your features. It would be very dramatic. Everyone would notice you."

Marguerite and I exchanged glances of amusement. Marguerite wasn't much for engaging in drama. "Well, I suppose that might be an interesting accessory," Marguerite said politely.

The modiste produced a long, spiderweb-fine length of tulle and draped it over my face. It was exactly the same shade as the satin still wrapped around my shoulders, but so light and transparent that it was like the memory of color, not color itself. In spite of myself, I liked the way it softened my features and brushed a hint of shadow onto my cheekbones. "And what about the days when you're tired, or ill, and you simply don't look your best?" the dressmaker said. "Wouldn't it be nice to hide your face so no one sees the circles under your eyes?"

"Or the days when I don't feel like smiling," Marguerite murmured, sounding more intrigued. My guess was that she had a lot of those days.

"I rather like it," I said, still watching myself in the mirror. "It might be worth buying the tulle in a few colors and seeing what we can do with it."

Marguerite reached up and slowly began unwinding the satin from around her shoulders. "Why not? It might be pretty after all." She smiled at the modiste. "Thank you for the suggestion."

The tradeswoman smiled back. "You're my favorite customer," she said. "I save all my best ideas for you."

Naturally, whether or not she started incorporating veils into her wardrobe, Marguerite intended to continue wearing blossoms in her hair. I was learning how to dry flowers and sew them onto hair clips so they could be used more than once, though the dried petals were fragile and had to be handled very carefully. We headed to the flower markets every two or three days to buy fresh supplies; I had come to love the rich, mixed smells of soil, water, and greenery.

One day we spent more time than usual searching through the flower stalls and making our selections. The sun was particularly hot and we were all as wilted as summer violets by the time we made it back to the carriage. Marguerite slumped in her seat, resting her head on one echo's shoulder; the other two sat beside me on the facing bench, similarly collapsed against each other. I tried to remain alert and upright, but I fought off yawns for the first ten minutes of the return trip.

Some disaster on the roads had snarled traffic while we were still deep in the heart of the commercial district. The sun beat down heavily on the roof of the stalled carriage. Marguerite sighed and straightened.

"Patience, you have the boniest shoulder," she said, rubbing the side of her face. "It's so *hot*."

"We'll get you a nice, cool bath as soon as we're home," I promised.

She was looking out the window. "Maybe we could get out and wait somewhere more comfortable until the roads clear up."

"Maybe," I said doubtfully. "I don't know where."

She pointed. "There's a temple."

I glanced out. Indeed, yes, there was one of the temples to the triple goddess. In fact, it was the largest temple I had come across so far during my time in Oberton. I guessed it was the main one serving the city, despite the fact that it was nothing more than an unpretentious gray stone building surrounded by a simple green hedge. The only remarkable thing about it was the arrangement of the windows I could see on this side. Each one consisted of three panes designed in some distinctive fashion—three interlocking circles, three diamond shapes, three triskeles. At the entrance to the building stood a small, pretty fountain consisting of a trio of women standing in a circle, facing outward, their hands stretched above them, before them, to either side. Just like the statuary in Marguerite's room. Water dripped from their fingertips in a never-ending bounty.

"Do you want to go inside?" I asked.

She had already tapped on the roof of the carriage to signal the driver to stop. "Yes, let's. It's bound to be cooler in there," she said.

A few minutes later, I trailed Marguerite and her echoes as we entered the building. Aunt Jean had taken me to a much smaller temple during my first week in the city. We had done no more than light candles before a carved representation of the goddess and say the standard prayers. But that place had been the size of a child's bedroom, a sort of outpost on a busy street where harried trades-men could stop to make a five-minute obeisance.

This one was much larger, maybe as big as a merchant's house. The dim light admitted by those tripled-paned windows showed perhaps twenty wooden pews lined up, facing a central dais where another grouping of statues held their arms out in arbitration, sup-plication, and celebration. A heavy wooden door just to the left of the dais stood half open, and through it I could see a narrow hall-way stretching back. Apparently the sanctuary was connected to another building—living quarters for the priestesses, I supposed, if this really was the main temple for the city.

About a half dozen people were already inside, widely scattered across the wooden benches. Some sat with their hands folded and their heads bent, praying silently; others seemed to be merely lost in thought. Two white-robed priestesses moved slowly between them, sitting beside each visitor and carrying on quiet conversations before going on to speak to the next one.

I felt the sweat chill on my body and realized that Marguerite had been right: It was definitely cooler inside. "How long do you want to stay?" I whispered.

She moved forward, pulling the four of us in her wake. "I don't know," she whispered back, "awhile."

She took a seat about midway down the last pew. The echoes settled beside her, and I sat closest to the left-hand aisle. I folded my hands like I was supposed to, but I didn't have any prayers ready and I wasn't feeling contemplative, so I glanced around. The walls were painted with murals depicting the three goddesses among the people, meting out justice, offering mercy, or reflecting joy, as the occasion dictated. The paint was pale and faded, and the gray stones themselves looked softened with age. *This place must be very old,* I thought. Perhaps it was Oberton's original temple.

We had been inside maybe five minutes when one of the priestesses slipped into our row from the right-hand aisle and sat beside Marguerite. "Blessings upon your head," she said softly. "What brings you to the temple today?"

"Heat and chance and flowers," Marguerite replied, her voice so low it was hard for me to make out the words.

"Three reasons for three goddesses, though I would wish for weightier motivations," the priestess answered. I thought I could hear a smile in her voice, but I couldn't be sure without seeing her face. And I could hardly lean past the echoes and stare at her, making it clear I was eavesdropping on the conversation.

"Would you?" Marguerite asked. "I find I prefer the weightless days."

I frowned. An odd thing to say.

"Whether the days are heavy or light," the priestess said, "I hope you remember to say your prayers daily."

"I do. Sometimes I pray with great specificity. Other times I just ask for general guidance."

"The goddesses are not in the habit of granting wishes, though I admit life would be easier sometimes if they were," the priestess answered. "But they can give you the strength and willpower to achieve even the most difficult goals."

"Or the endurance to make it through the realities that shape your life."

"There are some who would say a fine lady with three echoes has no cause to complain about her realities," the priestess said softly, "when so many others suffer illness, poverty, and abuse."

"I would agree with them," Marguerite said.

"Yet, I am sure your own sufferings are real," the priestess added. "Tell me your woes, and I will petition the goddess on your behalf."

I was staring straight ahead, still pretending I was not listening, so I could not be sure if Marguerite glanced in my direction, but I thought she did. At any rate, she bowed her head and dropped her voice to a whisper, and I could not hear anything she said to the priestess after that. Or anything the priestess said in reply. But it was clear to me that she did not want to be overheard—that she had deliberately positioned all of us in the pew so that the echoes would be between the two of us—and that something indeed was weighing heavily on her heart.

It made me sad to think she had no one to confide in except an anonymous temple priestess. No sister or friend, no loving mother or aunt. I supposed she could pour her heart out to the echoes because they'd never repeat a word, but they could hardly draw her into their arms and comfort her and promise they would love her no matter what. I twisted the triskele ring on my finger and felt, for a moment, intensely homesick.

Out of the corner of my eye, I saw Marguerite straighten in her seat, and the priestess lifted her head as well. "Very good," the woman said, shifting somewhat so she was facing Marguerite. "I will share your prayers with the goddess. Until then, may you know she is with you as you go through your days seeking justice"—she touched a fingertip to Marguerite's forehead—"mercy"—to the general region of Marguerite's heart—"and joy"—her lips.

"Thank you," Marguerite said. "I feel better for the prayer."

The priestess rose to her feet, so the rest of us scrambled up as well, and we followed her out of the pew. One by one, as they stepped into the aisle, the echoes paused, and the priestess bestowed the triple benediction upon them as well.

I was the last to emerge and, as the priestess appeared to be waiting for me, I also came to a halt. Now that we stood face-to-face, I realized she was an inch or two taller than I was, and slender even inside the shapeless robes. Her thick brown hair was pulled back in a severe and not particularly flattering bun; in the temple's low light, her eyes appeared to be an even darker shade. I guessed her to be in her mid to late twenties, though her tranquil face and guarded expression didn't give much to go by. I was used to sizing people up at a glance, but I had the thought that it would take a great deal of time and effort to understand this woman and what had brought her to this place.

"A benediction?" she asked quietly. When I nodded, she repeated the ritual she had performed on the others. I nodded again in thanks and followed the other four out the door and back into the coach.

Truth to tell, the outside air seemed as hot as ever, and the traffic was just as bad as it was when we had alighted at the temple. But as we inched along the clogged roadway, I covertly watched Marguerite. She seemed calmer, or happier, or maybe lighter in spirit; perhaps the priestess had managed to ease her burdens with those whispered prayers. I knew it was not my place to speak, but once the pace of traffic started to pick up and we were only a few blocks from the mansion, I found I couldn't keep silent.

"I hope you know," I said abruptly, "that I would never betray you."

She had been leaning her head against the echo again, but at that she drew herself up and stared back at me. "What? I never said you would."

"I don't gossip with the servants and I have never exchanged a word with your mother and even if someone offered me five times my yearly salary I would never repeat anything you did or said," I went on, determined to say the whole thing. "If you need something, I'll help you get it. If you have a secret, I'll help you keep it. I just thought you should know that."

She didn't shrink back like I was a lunatic; she smiled instead. "Thank you, Brianna, that's very sweet. But I don't need anything. I'm not looking for any help."

I was a little embarrassed. "That's all right, then," I said with a nod, turning my head to look out the window. But I thought I could still feel Marguerite smiling for the duration of that short trip.

CHAPTER FIVE

Two days later I headed out to the flower market on my own, since Marguerite had obligations the entire day. I took advantage of the rare free time to have lunch with Aunt Jean, catching up on news from home and sharing my observations of life in the governor's manor.

"What do you think of Lady Marguerite?" Jean asked when I was done.

Mindful of my promise, I didn't go into great detail. "She's the kindest woman there could be," I said. "But I don't think she leads a happy life. Her mother is...well... *not* the kindest woman. Her brothers are boisterous. Her father is busy. She doesn't seem to have close friends. I know it's presumptuous of me, but sometimes I feel sorry for her."

"Not presumptuous—wasted," Jean said dryly. "Folks like us never need to lavish sympathy on folks like her, who have so much in their lives they don't need happiness, too."

"I think I'd want happiness even if I was the highest noble in the Seven Jewels."

"Good health and a good job are all you need to be happy," Jean replied.

I didn't agree, but it was pointless to argue with Jean. We turned the conversation to other topics, and then I was on my way to the flower markets.

I enjoyed myself as I picked through the wares on display: gladiolas and roses with their long stems tucked into metal pails of water, clusters of hydrangeas and lilacs floating in shallow pans. A good number of the flowers for sale were out of season, so I assumed they had been forced in some hothouse on the outskirts of the city and gathered before dawn that morning. I chose blossoms of every hue, thinking to make Marguerite a colorful headband that she could wear with almost any dress.

I hadn't requisitioned the carriage, so I had a rather awkward armload to carry as I walked back, but I didn't mind. I dawdled a bit on the return trip, taking my favorite route through the city, even though it was somewhat out of my way. It was a narrow road that wound through a wealthy part of town, where grand houses were perched on a hill overlooking both the busy commercial district and the residential neighborhoods that crowded close to the governor's mansion. I liked seeing the whole city laid out before me, the grays and tans of the buildings brightened by roofs of green and terra-cotta and red. I liked watching the patterns of traffic, the ceaseless movement of people and horses too far away to see clearly, realizing that each one was on a journey I would never know anything about. I liked picking out the roads that led south, to my mother's posting house, and west, toward the mountains. I liked the idea that, as big as this city seemed to me, there was even more outside its borders. I liked wondering where I might go next.

I had taken a few steps off the main road and set my bouquets at my feet so I could stand and stare at the vista below. I had been distantly aware of intermittent noises behind me, as carts and carriages and horses carried travelers up and down the hill. But I didn't pay much attention until I heard someone call out a quiet "Whoa there," then I caught the sound of boot heels hitting the hard pavement. I turned to find that a man had climbed out of a peddler's wagon pulled by a pair of horses, and he was heading my way. He looked to be in his middle thirties, solidly built, wearing the coarse-weave clothing of a workingman instead of the finer cloth of a merchant. He was smiling.

"Hello, pretty lady," he said as he came to a halt a little closer to me than I liked. "Looks like you're on your way somewhere. Would you like a ride? How far do you need to go? I could take you any-where in the city—for a little fee."

"Not far," I replied, taking one discreet step back. "Thank you, but I enjoy walking."

He continued smiling and came a pace closer. "But it's such a warm day! You'll be faint with heat before you go another quarter mile."

"Not me," I said. "I'm not the kind of girl who melts in the sun."

His smile faded. "Rich girl, though, aren't you? All those buds and blossoms cost you something, I bet."

He was right about that. I could see his eyes wandering over my silhouette, but he didn't appear to be interested in my body so much as the quality of my clothes. At a guess, he'd hoped to cajole me into his wagon and then rob me when he got me to some isolated spot. Now his plan might be simply to rob me on the side of the road.

I bent down to scoop up the flowers and managed to withdraw another couple of steps when I straightened. "Cost my employer something," I corrected. "I have hardly a cent to my name."

"I don't believe you," he said, grabbing my arm.

The flowers spilled from my fingers as he jerked me toward him and I flung up my other arm to try to keep him at bay. With his free hand, he raked at the side of my dress, trying to rip open my pockets and spill out the contents. When that yielded him nothing, he clawed at my neckline to see if I had tucked a purse down the front of my dress.

I stomped on one of his feet, and when he staggered back I shoved my knee, hard, between his legs. That made him howl and back off even more. The minute I had enough room to swing, I punched his nose with all the power I could muster. At that, he cried out and backed away, one hand over his genitals and the other over his bloody face.

"You bitch!" he exclaimed. For a moment I thought he was so angry that he would attack me, knock me to the ground, and beat me senseless. Then I heard the sound of laughter and light applause coming from the direction of the road.

We both spun to look that way and saw an elegant man sitting astride a gorgeous satin-black horse. I didn't have time to study him, but both his animal and his attire indicated a comfortable level of income.

"Well done!" the stranger called. "I was prepared to be gallant and intervene, but I see the young woman can take care of herself."

My erstwhile assailant spat out a mouthful of blood and growled at the newcomer. "Get along with you. This is none of your business."

The well-dressed man slipped easily from the saddle and strolled over. It was not the fashion in Oberton for men to be armed, but I saw a sheathed dagger hanging from his belt, its hilt positioned in such a way that he could grab it with one quick swipe of his hand. "I'd wager that this woman is none of *your* business, either," he said in a steely voice. "Best for you to be moving on."

For a moment, the rough peddler stared back at the elegant stranger, but he apparently realized that it was going to be difficult to steal from me when I was so combative and this onlooker was prepared to meddle. He made another growling sound, then backed up toward his wagon, cursing under his breath the whole way. The stranger and I stood in silence until he had goaded his team into motion and clattered down the road out of sight.

Then the stranger turned to give me a critical inspection. "You don't look much worse for the mauling," he said. "I'm impressed by your fighting skills."

All my senses remained on high alert. Just because a man had come to my aid didn't mean he wished me well. "I've had some experience dealing with men who think they can take whatever they want," I said. "I've learned some things."

He smiled. Despite my wariness, I found his expression attractive. Well, I found the man attractive. He was of medium height and medium build, though I suspected muscles under the tailored clothing. He had curly dark hair, which gave him a friendly aspect, and the confidence that I usually associated with money. But I couldn't quite place him in one of the five levels of the social hierarchy. He didn't have the arrogance of a high noble, the belligerence of a low noble, the calculation of a merchant, the purposefulness of a workingman, or the desperation of the poor.

"*Many* men try to take whatever they want," he observed. "No doubt your experience is broad and varied."

"Thank you for your help," I said.

His smile widened. "Now you're wondering if I offer even more of a threat."

"Well," I said candidly, "you seem smarter than he did—which instantly makes you more dangerous."

He laughed. "Not a bad assessment," he agreed, "but I swear I mean you no harm." He glanced back to where his horse waited with more patience than I would have expected. A very well-trained horse, then, possibly even military. More intrigue. "Unfortunately, I don't think I can provide you much assistance, either, since I don't have a carriage and something tells me—" He brought his attention back to me. "You would not agree to ride pillion with me even if I offered to take you wherever you're going."

"I wouldn't," I said. I bent over to pick up my scattered flowers and was surprised and pleased when he crouched down to help.

"I'm afraid some of these blossoms are beyond rescue," he said, showing me a few stalks that had been hopelessly trampled in the struggle. "Do you still want them or shall we leave them behind?"

"Leave them," I said. "I can buy more another day."

In a few moments we had gathered all the flowers that were still intact and had taken the few steps back to the road. As he reached for his horse's reins, I said, "Thank you again for your assistance."

"You can thank me once we arrive at your destination," he said. "I'll walk you there."

I should have politely refused, but in truth, I was pleased. Opportunities for flirting had been few and far between in Oberton, since Constance discouraged relations between the servants and I scarcely knew anyone else in the city. I still meant to be cautious, since I didn't know a single thing about the man, but I could enjoy myself anyway.

"That's kind of you," I said, setting out at a gentle pace. He fell in step beside me, leading his horse. "But if we're going to walk so far together, I probably ought to know your name."

"Nico. And yours?"

"Brianna."

"What do you do here in the city, Brianna?"

I glanced over at him. "If you ask me questions and I answer them, I get to ask you questions and have you answer them."

He looked amused. "A very good bargain. I wonder what prompted you to want to make it?"

"There's something about you that seems mysterious," I said honestly.

His amusement intensified. "It is true I am a man who knows how to keep secrets," he said, "but I can't think you'll be asking me about any of them today."

"Then what do *you* do in the city?" I asked, wondering if he would notice that I hadn't actually answered the question that he had posed first.

"I'm visiting," he said. When my silence indicated that I felt that was an incomplete response, he burst out laughing. "I'm visiting in advance of Prince Cormac," he elaborated. "He will be arriving in a few days and I'm here just to—" He waved his free hand. "Get a sense of the place. Make sure all is secure."

"So you're in service to the king!" I exclaimed. That explained both his expensive clothing and his confident attitude, though he hadn't said exactly what role he played in the royal household. "That must be exciting."

"Ah, my own position is insignificant," he said, though I had the sense he didn't actually believe that. "I work for my uncle, who works for the king. But I do like the excitement and the pace of the royal city."

"So you haven't always lived there?"

He shook his head. "I grew up in Empara, but I moved to Camarria to apprentice with my uncle."

"I've only been in Oberton for about a month," I confessed. "But I love it, too. All the people. All the motion. Even when nothing is happening, it seems like something *could* at any minute."

"Where were you before?"

I gestured in a generally southern direction. We had been traveling steadily downhill as we talked, so we could no longer see the city's layout and I couldn't point out a specific road. "In a village some miles south of here. My family owns a posting house on the Charamon Road."

"I may have stopped there on the way into Oberton," he said. "Was it called the Barking Dog? I thought it was very well run."

"Yes! That's it!"

He turned his head to give me another close inspection. "I would have said the woman who ran the place was too young to be your mother," he said. "She had a baby in her arms that she managed to keep quiet the whole time she was registering me and showing me to my room."

I laughed. "That's her! And if you tripped over any other children during your stay, those were my brothers and sisters."

"So you worked at a posting house," he said. "That must be where you learned to deal with rude men."

"Learned to deal with all kinds of people," I said. "As a rule, travelers are irritable and hungry and tired and in a hurry. A lot of them are expecting trouble at the end of the journey, so it's common to find them in dour moods. My mother would sometimes make a game of it—try to take the angriest, crabbiest, most unpleasant traveler and see if she could make that person smile. More often than not, she could."

"Now there's a skill," Nico said. "Do you have it, too?"

I wrinkled my nose. "I usually don't bother to try," I confessed. "But I did learn how to size people up quickly. To figure out if they were honest, if they were truly mean or just exhausted, if they could afford to pay or if I had to watch to make sure they didn't sneak off in the morning. And I learned how to get along with almost anybody."

"More useful skills," Nico said. We heard the sound of wagon wheels behind us, so we moved over to the side of the road. The action brought him close enough to me that I could feel the silk of his shirt against my bare arm. His horse snorted and tossed his head, and Nico's shoulder pressed briefly against mine. I had been right about the muscles.

The carriage passed and Nico pulled back to a more polite distance, picking up the conversation where we had left off. "So how do you employ those skills here in the city?"

"I'm maid to the governor's daughter. Lady Marguerite."

His eyebrows rose as if he was surprised or impressed. "Do you like the job?" he asked.

"I love it," I confessed. "I love all the activity. I love the feeling that I'm doing something important—that everything that happens in the mansion matters to the people of the city, and I'm somehow a part of that."

"Do you like the lady herself? I don't know much about her."

"She's wonderful."

"Oh, now, surely you can be more specific than that."

I laughed at him. "Maybe I'm not as mysterious as you are, but I know enough not to gossip about my mistress! *With* a complete stranger!"

He grinned in response. "But I'm the king's man! Anything you share with me could be valuable information for the kingdom itself."

"I suppose you would tell me all about Prince Cormac," I scoffed.

"Ah, he's a handsome young man—and wealthy, too," Nico said. "Isn't that all a young lady really cares about?"

"I assure you, we're not all so shallow. There are plenty of rich, handsome men who are quite despicable."

He glanced over with a grin. It was the first time I noticed the color of his eyes. Not brown, as you'd expect from someone with hair so dark, but a complicated blue-green that probably changed color depending on what he was wearing. "I've met my share of those," he agreed, "but I wouldn't put Cormac in that category. At any rate, all the ladies I've ever seen in his company have appeared to find him entirely satisfactory."

"Is the same true of his brother?"

"Which one?"

I had to think a minute to realize what he meant. The king and his first queen had had two sons, Cormac and Jordan—but before he was ever married, the king had sired a bastard child named Jamison. Jamison was never going to be in line for the throne, especially not since the king had three legitimate heirs, so people didn't tend to talk about him much, though I'd heard he was very wild.

"I meant Prince Jordan."

"If possible, Jordan is even better liked than his brother. He seems to feel the weight of the world a bit less than Cormac, who is generally quite serious."

"And Jamison?"

Nico grinned again. "What's the phrase people use? 'The less said about him, the better.' You'll have a chance to judge for yourself, however, since Jamison will be accompanying Cormac to Oberton."

I tried to think of a tactful way to phrase it. "So Jamison is freely included in court life."

Nico laughed. "Well, Queen Tabitha is none too fond of him, and I think Cormac and Jordan are embarrassed by some of his behavior—but yes, he's an accepted part of the family. He has his foes and his detractors, but he has his champions as well."

"I look forward to getting a glimpse of him," I said. "I know Prince Cormac has three echoes. What about his brothers and his sister?"

"Jordan has three and the princess two, but Jamison has none, I'm afraid."

"I confess I'm still getting used to the echoes," I said. "It seems like an odd way to live—trailed all the time by these living, breathing creatures that are so much a part of you and yet—separate." I cut a quick glance at him. "Not that I mean to give offense if you have echoes of your own," I added hastily.

He laughed at that. "None," he assured me. "The story goes that my great-grandfather was a noble of some standing, but a creature of extreme secrecy. He was born with two echoes, though some of the family tales say he had three. He took on a commission for the queen that was so delicate he put all his echoes to death so that there would be no witnesses to his deeds. Buried all their corpses in the family plot. Since that day, there has never been an echo born to any of his descendants."

I couldn't hide my shock. "That's awful!"

Nico shrugged. "Maybe. Or maybe it's just like amputating your own toe. It's yours. You can do with it what you want."

I had a feeling that Nico's great-grandfather hadn't given his shadows names like Prudence and Patience, or he would have been less inclined to murder. Or, who knows? Maybe more inclined. "I still don't really know how the echoes came to be," I admitted. "They're lovely and strange, but what good are they? I haven't had the nerve to ask Lady Marguerite."

Nico didn't answer until two horsemen riding up from town passed us at a loud gallop and the sound of their hoofbeats faded behind us. "From what I understand, the echoes first came about more than five hundred years ago, long before the Seven Jewels were united as one country. All the provinces were constantly at war with each other. There were skirmishes on the roads and assassinations in the cities. Every time a new prince or lordling would be raised up, someone would kill him."

"I wouldn't think people would be so interested in being the next prince, then," I said.

"People are always interested in taking up the mantle of power," Nico answered. "But it's true they were not eager to die. The high nobles began praying to the triple goddess to protect them from this ever-present threat of death. And because she herself is one being split into multiple parts, she gave the same gift to the lords and princes. That is, she caused the next generation of heirs to be blessed with echoes. These echoes looked and acted just like the originals, so that, from a distance, you couldn't tell them apart.

Eventually, when a noble needed to travel from one city to another, he would bring all his echoes along, and no hired killer would be able to guess which one was the lord and which was the imposter. It greatly cut down on the murder attempts."

"I can see why it would," I said.

"Then Edwin of Thelleron rose to power and began his campaign to unify the provinces," Nico went on. "According to legend, he had been born with seven echoes, and all of them rode beside him when he launched the Great War. So there were eight of them leading the charge at what turned out to be the final battle. Lady Meredith of Empara led the opposition—and as she had two echoes of her own, she was better than most at discerning the original from the copy. So with her own hands, she shot the arrow that went right through Edwin's heart."

"That can't be right," I objected. "Everyone knows he was the first king."

Nico nodded. "Exactly. She killed the real Edwin—but his spirit somehow flowed into the body of one of his echoes, and he continued to lead his armies forward. So Meredith shot and killed him in his new body. But again, his spirit moved on to inhabit a third one. He was so in tune with his echoes—they were so much a part of him—that it made no difference to him which body he inhabited. He could change it the way he changed a suit of armor."

I looked up at him suspiciously. "Is that true?"

He laughed. "Well, it was five hundred years ago," he said. "And who ever knows if any story is true? But I like the notion."

"So what happened to Lady Meredith?"

"She managed to knock off five of the eight versions of Edwin, but before she could destroy them all, the armies clashed together. Meredith and her forces were defeated—she and her echoes were captured. He told her he would spare her life if she would let him marry her daughter, Amanda. So she did, and that's how the Seven Jewels were united under the first king."

"I can't imagine that was a very loving household," I observed. "If I were Edwin, I would always expect to be murdered in my bed.

And by that time he only had, what, two echoes left? Not very many spares!"

"Well, that's the interesting thing. They say that, shortly after the wedding, another echo spontaneously appeared in Edwin's room one night. So he had three again, just as Amanda had three. And they ruled the kingdom as equals, in harmony."

I was skeptical. "Another echo just showed up? That seems even less believable than the notion that his spirit could move from body to body."

"I know," Nico replied. "But maybe you've heard tales about Queen Toriana. The early histories say she had four echoes—but the later ones say five. One theory is that she, too, benefited from the arrival of a spontaneous new echo one strange night."

"Why would she need another one?"

"The explanation I've read is that she was negotiating with foreign visitors and more echoes gave her more consequence."

I privately doubted either story could be true, but both were certainly interesting. I didn't ask more questions, though, because by that time we had reached the base of the hill and started walking down the main city streets. Traffic was heavier and conversation more difficult, so we fell back on desultory topics. I pointed out a few prominent buildings, and he asked what local foods he should try. I noticed as we passed a temple that he casually touched his fingertips to his forehead, heart, and mouth. A religious man, then. Although I was not particularly devout myself, for some reason it pleased me that he was.

"Here we are at the manor," I said as we finally strolled up to our destination. We came to a halt at the front entrance, the one that led to the great central atrium, though once Nico departed I planned to circle around and go inside through the back door. There was the usual commotion of people leaving and arriving; this entrance was never quiet. I waved at Rory when he hurried by, and I saw him give Nico a quick appraisal before he slipped around back. "I expect you'll be here a great deal once Prince Cormac arrives."

"I expect I will," he said. He reached out to flick the pink petals of one of the roses that had escaped destruction. "And I might browse through the flower markets from time to time, to see what the vendors have brought in for sale."

"The flower markets," I repeated, trying to hide my smile. "Somehow I hadn't pegged you as a man who would be interested in anything so frivolous. Perhaps I am not as good at assessing people as I always thought."

He grinned. "I'm adaptable," he said. "I like to learn new things."

"Well, I myself go to the markets every few days," I said. "Perhaps I'll see you there."

He smiled, gathered the reins more tightly, and swung himself onto the glistening black horse. "I'm counting on it," he said. "I'm sure it will be the most interesting venue in the city."

I was still smiling as I executed a brief curtsey and turned away from him, making my way around the side of the building to the entrance in the back. I was a little surprised to see Rory loitering there, clearly waiting for me. His expression was strained and I felt a flicker of apprehension tremble down my spine. Had something happened to Marguerite?

"What's wrong?" I asked, when he started forward to meet me a few steps away from the door.

"How do you know him? Why were you talking to him?" he demanded without any preface.

"Know who? What are you talking about?"

"That man—the one you were with by the front door! Don't you know who he is?" When I shook my head, he looked even more uneasy. "Nico Burken. The king's inquisitor."

CHAPTER SIX

It was three days before Marguerite needed me to return to the flower markets. I couldn't decide if I was glad or sorry. I told myself that Nico Burken wouldn't be there, anyway—surely the *king's inquisitor* must have more important things to do than loiter among the flower stalls, admiring the roses. Such as interrogating criminals and gathering information for the crown.

So it was with mixed emotions that I learned, on that third day, that Marguerite had a commission for me.

"The prince arrives tomorrow and my mother says she needs me all day to finalize plans," Marguerite told me as I brushed her hair into the simple style she wore when no guests were expected. "Would you be willing to run some errands?"

"Of course. What do you need?"

"First, flowers to accent the dresses we've picked for the next few days." We had spent several enjoyable hours going over wardrobe options and deciding which accessories should go with each dress, so I knew very well the colors I needed to match. "And then—" She paused and pressed her lips together as if trying to hold back words.

I met her gaze in the mirror. "Anything else? I won't mind."

Her pretty face showed indecision and something else I couldn't quite identify. Something darker. "It's just that—you told me once— There's a message that I'd like delivered, but I don't want my mother to know—" She folded her lips together again.

I put aside the hairbrush, set my hands on her shoulders, and continued to regard her in the mirror. "I'll take the message," I said quietly. "I won't tell anyone."

She stared back at me, her expression earnest. No—pleading. No. Desperate. "It's just that it's so important."

"Then I'll make sure it's delivered."

She dropped her eyes and began playing with her rings. "You remember the temple where we went a few days ago? There was a priestess who gave us all blessings? Taeline. If you deliver the message to her, she'll make sure it gets sent on."

I tried not to be hurt. "You don't trust me to take it to whoever is supposed to receive it?" I asked, lifting my hands.

She spun around in her chair and raised her gaze to mine again. "I *do* trust you, Brianna, but you don't know—you don't understand. Anybody could see you leaving the mansion and follow you. Del Morson—he watches everyone in the household, though my brothers don't believe it! My mother's maid—*she* could see you leaving, get curious, and go after you. One of the footmen. Anyone. I just have to be so careful."

I nodded, mollified. I couldn't imagine who she was so determined to get in touch with, but if the note was that clandestine, she was right to take this tortuous path. "The temple is safe. I see that," I answered. "I'll be happy to take a note."

She tried a smile. "And not read it."

Now I allowed myself to look insulted, but in an exaggerated way so she knew I was only playing. "My *lady*. I don't know what kind of inferior servants you have engaged in the past—"

"Well, Daniella couldn't read, but Winifred could, and I didn't dare trust a private letter to her hands," Marguerite answered. "And you can read, too, because I've seen you with a book."

"I *can*," I said. "But I *won't*."

"Will you be offended if I seal it?"

"No. But even if I would be, it's not my place to say so!"

Her smile grew a little more genuine. "Well, you're the one person I can't afford to alienate," she said. "So I want to be sure."

I dropped a low curtsey, as deep as I'd give to the queen. "You can always be sure of me."

About a half hour later, I slipped out of the mansion and headed toward the temple, the sealed letter in my pocket. The slim, folded packet felt like a live coal that might catch my dress on fire. Not because I was burning to read it, but because Marguerite was so on edge that I caught some of her agitation. It seemed as if everyone who glanced my way would be able to tell I was carrying combustible goods—I felt more at risk than if I had filled my pockets with gold and was running through the poorest neighborhoods of Oberton, dribbling coins behind me. If I happened to encounter Del Morson and he so much as glanced my way, I was sure my face would flame with guilt and I would freeze to the spot.

Fortunately, I did not meet him on my way to the temple. Not him or any other inquisitor who might be temporarily residing in the city.

I went on foot, since there was no reason to have a royal coachman know my destination, and I made it to the temple with no trouble. Just as well, since my mind was occupied with trying to figure out who Marguerite was trying to contact.

It seemed most likely that she had fallen in love with some unsuitable man—maybe a noble, maybe not, but certainly not Prince Cormac—and she was either bidding him farewell or telling him to keep his distance until the prince and his party had left the city. Her level of despair had seemed so great that I guessed she believed she would never be allowed to marry him, even if it turned out that King Harold didn't want her for Cormac's bride. This led me to think he was probably a low noble, or maybe even a merchant. Or already married to someone else.

I supposed there could be other reasons she needed to carry on a secret correspondence. Maybe she had committed an indiscretion and someone was blackmailing her. Maybe she had incurred great debt and was trying to structure a plan of repayment. I thought it less likely that she was addicted to one of the powerful narcotics that had brought both higher- and lower-class citizens to ruin, since I'd never seen any evidence of such a vice. But in truth, most people are very good at hiding things they don't want anyone else to know. And Marguerite was clearly hiding something.

When I arrived at the temple, I paused briefly outside to say a prayer in front of the fountain, then I stepped through the door into the cool, dimly lit interior. As before, there were a few other people sitting on the benches, praying or meditating. As before, two priestesses moved among them, offering advice or benedictions. Neither of them was the one I had come to find. I took a seat in the very last pew, folded my hands in my lap, and stared at the goddess statues lined up on the front dais. Justice, joy, mercy. Which goddess would oversee this particular errand? I was putting my money on mercy.

I had been there maybe ten minutes when one of the priestesses slipped into the pew and sat beside me. "Have you come here today to seek guidance or merely to settle your soul in silence?" she asked in a pleasant voice. I liked the idea of *settling my soul*. I wasn't sure I'd be able to manage it during this outing, however.

"I need guidance, but I need to speak to Taeline," I said. "She understands my troubles." I found the words awkward to say, but Marguerite had assured me many people found it easier to pour their hearts out to one priestess over another, and no one would find the request strange.

"I will fetch her."

Another five minutes and then Taeline was the one dropping gracefully to the bench at my side. I couldn't tell from her quick glance if she recognized me from my one previous visit. "What can I help you with today?" she asked.

"I brought you a message."

At that, she stiffened very slightly and then relaxed. "I see."

"I was told you could deliver it to the right person."

"I will happily do so. Just put it on the bench while we talk."

I casually reached into my pocket and casually laid the folded paper between our bodies. She did not immediately reach for it. "I don't really have much else to talk about," I said.

She smiled slightly. "Perhaps not. But since you have requested my attention, it will look very odd if you do not at least ask me for a prayer or two."

"You might pray for the governor's daughter," I said. For some reason, I did not think I should use Marguerite's name. "I think she is not very happy." "We all pray for her every day," Taeline replied. "And for the governor and his wife and their sons, and for the king and queen and their children, and for all the people of the Seven Jewels. All of them. Every day."

I think Marguerite deserves extra attention, I thought. I had no idea what else I should say, so to pass the time, I started asking questions. "How long have you been a priestess?"

"Three years. And an acolyte for three years before that."

I gave her a quick sideways look. As before, I found it hard to read much in her serene face, but I thought it unlikely that anyone could attain the rank of priestess before the age of twenty-one. So she was probably at least twenty-four. Most likely a little older. "Do you like the life?"

"I do. I love the goddess, but what I was not expecting was how much I would love the people of Oberton. They come to the temple with all their sorrows and all their joys, and I am reminded every day of the richness and complexity of human existence."

"But you stay apart from it," I pointed out. "You don't participate in it."

Now she turned to gaze at me, her brown eyes appraising. "I can see why you might think that," she said. "But it feels to me as if I am in the middle of all of it every day. It does not feel at all vicarious."

I savored the word, which I had not come across often. "Even so, I think I would find such a life too narrow."

"What would you describe as your ideal life?"

I smiled. "The one I'm living now."

"Ah, but to *me,* a life in service to a human master would seem to be the narrow one," Taeline replied. "Confined to one person's desires, limited to that person's experiences."

"Maybe, but my mistress's experiences are likely to be pretty broad." I gestured toward the temple door. "And I am not always at her side. There is much of the world I can see on my own."

"Then you sound like you are indeed happily situated," she agreed. "A lucky thing for both of you."

As she spoke, she let her hand rest on the letter lying on the bench, and as she stood up, she absentmindedly tucked the envelope into her pocket. "I must attend to other matters," she said as I hastily came to my feet. "I hope you will return in the days ahead."

Which was when I realized that Marguerite might be expecting an answer from her correspondent. The chances were good that I might soon seem to be the most devout person in the governor's mansion. "I'm sure I will," I said, following her into the aisle.

She stopped and faced me. "Tomorrow, even."

"I will see what activities are on my lady's schedule."

She nodded and lifted her hand, and I leaned slightly forward into her benediction. Head, heart, mouth. Justice, mercy, joy. "Then I will see you whenever there is time."

My only answer was a nod in return. She made her way down the aisle, heading for an older man who had just settled on a bench, and I turned toward the door. I stopped for a moment as soon as I stepped outside because the sunny day was almost painfully bright after the dimness of the temple. I was still squinting into the distance when I was startled by a man's voice directly behind me.

"A benediction upon your head," he said. I whirled around to find myself staring at Nico Burken.

"And upon yours," I replied, but my tone was more accusatory than benevolent. My expression wasn't very friendly, either.

He didn't seem to notice or, at any rate, didn't seem to mind. He looked quite cheerful as he smiled at me—and his expression and the curly hair as well as the bright sunlight were all conspiring to make me want to smile back. "You haven't been to the flower market in three days," he said.

"And you have? I hope you didn't make the vendors nervous with your loitering."

"Oh, I made enough purchases to keep them happy. With the result that my rented rooms are now overflowing with blossoms. So it's the maids at the inn who are wondering what I might be up to."

That made me laugh, to my great annoyance. "Well, that's where I'm headed now, but if you've already been there this morning—"

"I'm happy to return," he said, falling in step beside me as I began to walk in that direction. He seemed to be on foot; at any rate, I didn't spot his horse nearby. "I can advise you on which sellers are running bargains today."

"So how did you find me here at the temple?" I asked abruptly, wondering if he would tell me the truth. Oberton wasn't *that* big, but I couldn't believe random chance led him to the very spot I happened to be.

"I followed you," he said promptly. "Speaking of loitering. I was at the mansion quite early this morning, waiting to see if you would emerge."

Oh, Marguerite had been right to send her letter through an intermediary! How many eyes must be upon her—and because of her, on me? "Why didn't you just approach me and ask if you could escort me?"

He glanced down at me, his expression pained. "What if you were headed off to meet a fine young man and while away the afternoon? I would have been an awkward encumbrance then."

"As opposed to what you are now," I said.

He came to a halt right there on the street. Once we had stepped away from the temple, the walkways had grown crowded with other pedestrians, and a couple of people glared at him as they had to abruptly veer around him. Around *us*, as I had stumbled to a stop as well.

"If you don't want my company, just say so," he said. "I'll be on my way."

"What I don't understand," I replied, "is why you want *my* company."

He shrugged. "I enjoyed our conversation the other day. You impressed me. You made me laugh. I liked the way you looked at the world."

"You liked the fact that I serve Lady Marguerite," I countered. "You want to learn more about her any way you can."

He eyed me for a moment, the smile gone from his face. "You have a low opinion of yourself," he finally said, "if you think a man would only like you for the job you hold."

I felt my face heat, but I refused to be distracted. "Plenty of people like me," I said. "But none of them are paid to act as informants."

"Oh, someone warned you away from me, is that it?" he asked. He started moving again, gesturing to me to keep up, so I fell in step beside him. I supposed we might as well argue while we were in motion, since I still had errands to run.

"Someone told me you're the king's inquisitor, if that's what you mean."

"Not me. My uncle. I am merely his apprentice."

"That's just as bad. That's probably *worse*," I said. "You probably do all the nastier things that your uncle doesn't want to sully his hands with."

He made a slight back-and-forth motion with his head, as if considering and not entirely rejecting my accusation. "I'm still learning the trade," he said. "But I view it as a nobler one than you seem to."

"Intimidating people?"

"Protecting the kingdom," he said softly. "Keeping the king and his family safe. I have seen assassins with their confiscated bags of weapons and traitors with their stolen documents—thwarted through my uncle's vigilance. How is that dishonorable?"

Put that way, it wasn't so terrible. But if his uncle was anything like Del Morson, there would be something remorseless and implacable about him, and it would be hard to picture him as heroic rather than sinister. "I suppose it depends on your methods," I said somewhat stiffly. "It depends on what you do to get your information."

"You'd be surprised at how willing ordinary citizens are to gossip about their neighbors," he said, regaining his good cheer. "I've never yet had to resort to torture and threats because people are always eager to tattle on their friends."

I was surprised into a laugh. "Well, I'm sure *that's* true," I admitted.

"You, for instance," he went on. "You're a great favorite in the village where you grew up, so everyone is happy to say how little it matters that your mother wasn't married to your father and how sorry they were when that young man—Bobby? Robbie, that's it—when he ran off with another girl. They think your stepfather could be a little friendlier, but your mother's a hardworking, honest woman who always has a kind word for everyone."

Now he was the one who was forced to stop as I came to a complete standstill on the crowded walk. "You're investigating *me*?" I demanded. "For what possible reason? And how have you had *time*?"

His face was surprisingly serious. "*I'm* not," he said. "I got every one of those details from Del Morson. Though I do admit to asking *him* about you."

Now I was even more astonished. "Del Morson? But why would he— What would I—"

"You've taken a job inside the governor's house. His daughter's life could conceivably be in your hands," Nico replied quietly. "Of course you had to be investigated. Nobody knew a thing about you."

"Constance did!" Then, in case his espionage hadn't yielded all the names of the governor's servants, I added, "The housekeeper. She's second cousin to my aunt. She's the one who brought me in for an interview."

"Distant relatives of the household staff are as unreliable as they come!" he exclaimed.

It was so absurd that I couldn't help laughing, but I was still seriously ruffled. He motioned me forward, so I starting walking at his side again; but I wouldn't look at him. I was going to need some time to think this over. "Well. I never expected to be considered important enough—or dangerous enough—to have someone looking into my life. Which has been very ordinary and dull up till now!"

"Oh, I don't know. The failed romance sounds pretty spectacular."

I shot him a quick look of exasperation, then refocused my eyes on the path in front of me. "Who doesn't have one or two broken romances in the past? That's the most ordinary thing about me."

"Nevertheless, I was sorry to hear about it. Though not *really* sorry," he added. "Unless it broke your heart."

"It felt like it at the time. But then I realize that if I had married Robbie, I never would have come to the city. I never would have met Marguerite. And then I'm glad."

"I'm glad, too," Nico said. "Robbie did me a favor."

"You don't even *know* me," I said.

"No," he said, "but now I have the chance. Seems like it might be fun."

I glanced up at him again, tart words on my tongue. But he was smiling, and I found myself smiling back.

He was right. It did seem like it might be fun.

Some of my previous trips to the flower market had been a little tedious, but this one was delightful. True to his word, Nico guided me to the various vendors who were offering sales, keeping up a whispered commentary about who would give me the best prices and who might be trying to palm off yesterday's roses as today's fresh-cut flowers. He was shockingly frugal, insisting that an expensive bunch of lilacs wasn't worth the price even though the mulberry color was not only rare, but a perfect match with the dress Marguerite planned to wear tonight.

"I pity your poor wife," I informed him as I paid for the lilacs despite his disapproval. "You'll only buy her daisies in season, just to save a few coins."

"Buy them? I'll pick them from a roadside ditch!" he exclaimed.

"I don't know why you're so cheap," I said. "I have to think the king pays you a handsome salary."

"He does. I could buy every flower in the market if I wanted to. It's just hard to overcome early training."

I gave him an inquiring look as we moved on to the next stall. Even I wouldn't pay the prices for the goods on sale there, tall stems of thornless white roses, each petal veined with a complex tracery of pink. I loved them, though, and I bent closer to inhale the delicate scent. Faint but exquisite. "'Early training'?" I repeated.

"Those are pretty," he said. "Are you going to buy any?"

I shook my head and moved on. "Not right for anything Marguerite will be wearing. And they're even more expensive than the lilacs. I don't need another scold from you. So? Your life?"

"My father died when I was young, and my mother was too proud to ask for money from his family. They were low nobles and she was a merchant's daughter, and they'd never thought she was good enough for him," he explained. "We were never to the point of starvation, but I always knew how to get the best value for any coin I ever spent. To this day, it hurts my soul to see waste and overspending."

"Your soul must be in agony, then, living at the king's palace."

"Some truth to that," he acknowledged. "But I can stand to watch *other* people spend their money more than I can stand to spend my own."

"I repeat my observation about your wife," I said.

"Careful," he warned. "I might start finding reasons to pity whatever chap you take it in your head to marry."

I selected a cheerful bunch of fiery red begonias and paid the vendor. Red was not a color that looked good on Marguerite, but it could serve as a fine accent in many arrangements. "I would say you don't know me well enough to list my faults—but then I remember. Del Morson has told you all about me."

"I'm sure he overlooked some of the more interesting bits," Nico answered. "For instance, he never found out why that Robbie fellow decided to marry someone else."

"I never found out, either," I said. I considered a spray of yellow forsythia but I didn't think the blooms looked very sturdy. They would wilt too soon for Marguerite to wear them fresh and crumble too soon for me to try to dry them. "Maybe he didn't like my taste in flowers."

"Maybe he just fell in love with another girl."

I glanced up at him, feeling unwontedly serious. "Does that happen? If you truly love one person, can someone else just appear in your life and suddenly abduct your heart? Against your will, against your wishes? Don't you have to be open to such a thing?"

He looked down at me, his expression as solemn as mine. "I don't know much about it," he said. "I don't know if a heart is ever safe. But I've never thought one could be stolen. Just given."

I shrugged. "And then taken back if you change your mind."

"Well," he said, "you wouldn't want to think it was in a prison somewhere. Fearing the jailor and hoping to break free."

For some reason, that made me smile. It was an odd conversation to be having with a stranger. Especially with a stranger who probably spent most of his waking hours breaking people's hearts, one way or another. I handed him a few of my purchases so I could do a better job of arranging the bundles in my straw bag. He stood there stoically, his arms full of flowers, while I shook off droplets of water and carefully sorted the stems.

"But I do know most of my flaws," I offered. "Things that might make a man think twice before marrying me."

"Such as?"

"I don't like to sit around, fretting over what might happen. I prefer to *do* something to fix the situation, even if what I do might turn out to be wrong. I would be sympathetic if my husband lost his job, for instance, but it wouldn't be long before I'd be saying, 'Well, what else can you do? Let's try that.'"

He handed me the begonias when I reached for them. "I'm not sure that's a flaw, exactly."

"It is if you're the kind of person who wants a lot of coddling."

"What else?"

I put the last bundle in place and decided I'd purchased enough for the day. Besides, I might be back tomorrow, if Marguerite sent me to the temple in the morning to look for a reply. No need to overbuy. "I don't always share everything I'm thinking," I said, turning in the direction of the mansion and strolling that way. Nico fell in step beside me. "Some people appreciate that. Some people don't."

"Do you want me to carry that for you?" he asked.

"Thank you, but no. It's not heavy."

"I can keep my own counsel, too," he said. "Though I don't know that I like the idea of my wife keeping secrets from me."

"Everybody has secrets."

He grinned down at me. "Not once Del Morson's been after them for a while."

I lifted my brows, meeting his eyes with a steady gaze. "Even then," I said softly. "There will always be something that surprises you."

"Well, then," he said. "I look forward to being surprised."

We stepped around an untidy group of nursemaids and small children. "What about you?" I asked. "Besides your excessive frugality, what are your flaws?"

He seemed to think that over. "Sometimes I insist on my own way. I tend to keep arguing even when I've already won—or lost. And I ask a lot of questions." He glanced down at me. "Some people don't like that."

"I don't mind," I said. "Some men can't be bothered to ask a question. They don't care what anyone else is thinking."

"Good. Then I have one for you."

"All right."

"That pretty ring you're wearing. Did Robbie give it to you?"

I couldn't help laughing. "Well, now," I said. "You're getting to know me a little. What do *you* think?"

"I think the minute he came back with his new bride, you marched to his house and *flung* down the ring he gave you, right at his feet."

"I would have," I agreed, "except he never gave me a ring. He couldn't afford it. It was something we were going to save up for together after we were married."

"So where'd you get this one?"

I transferred the straw basket to my left arm so I could hold up my ring and admire the triskele. "My mother gave it to me before I left. Her mother had given it to her."

"Does it make you homesick when you look at it?"

"Sometimes. Or when I get a letter from home with all the news. But mostly I'm too happy with my new life. What about you? Do you miss the people you left behind?"

"I didn't expect to," he admitted. "But once in a while—" He shrugged.

"How long have you lived in Camarria?"

"Two years."

"Tell me more about it."

"It's three times as big as Oberton, and easier to navigate. Wider streets, laid out in a much more orderly fashion. But the best part is the bridges that are all over the city. Some of them don't seem to have any real purpose, they just connect one back alley to another. Some are major thoroughfares that people are crossing at all hours of the day. A few are high over the busiest streets in the city, built to let pedestrians get from one place to another without being trampled by horses or carriages. I'll find a place on a bridge and stand there half the day, watching the city from above. I learn a lot just by watching."

It seemed like exactly the sort of activity that would appeal to an inquisitor, but I didn't voice the thought. "Do you live at the palace?"

"Yes."

"Tell me what it's like."

He spent the next ten minutes describing the building and its history. It sounded impossibly grand.

"Maybe I'll get to see it someday," I said a little wistfully when he was done. By this time we had arrived at the main door of the governor's mansion, with its usual chaos and cacophony. I was eager to get to Marguerite's room and put the flowers in water—but truly sorry my conversation with Nico was at an end.

"I hope so," he answered. "I think you'd like it."

"So the prince arrives tomorrow," I said, though surely Nico was more aware of that fact than I was. "Will you come with him when he visits the governor?"

"He will have a fair number of people in his train, but yes, I expect I will be one of them."

"Then perhaps I'll see you again from time to time while he's here."

He smiled down at me. "Oh, yes," he said, "I think you might be seeing quite a bit of me in the days to come."

CHAPTER SEVEN

Prince Cormac was a tall, serious man who seemed so perfectly suited for the part of royal heir that he might have been an actor playing a role. His handsome face had pronounced cheekbones and a rather pointed chin, and it was set off by sleek black hair. On some men, such a sharp look might have been off-putting, but his earnest smile softened his hard colors and angles.

He was dressed all in black, with touches of dazzling color. His cloak was lined with red silk; his hat sported a blue feather. Over his pleated black jacket, he wore a chain of linked gold disks, each one holding clusters of gems representing one of the Seven Jewels. It was both an homage to the provinces, I thought, and a reminder that his family ruled them all. Even the ones like Orenza, which might be testing out the idea of independence.

"What a beautiful man," breathed the undercook, who happened to be standing beside me when the prince arrived with his impressive retinue. We were among about a dozen servants who had squeezed together in the frames of the doors that overlooked the atrium, trying not to push each other out onto the balconies where Lord Garvin or Lady Dorothea might spot us spying on them. We had been joined by Rory and two of the upstairs maids at one of the fourth-floor doors, and we had an excellent line of sight for the main entrance, though we had to peer through the slats in the railing to get a clear view.

Rory sniffed. "Men aren't beautiful."

"*He* is."

"All of them are," added one of the housemaids.

She gestured at the three echoes who strode in right behind Cormac. They doffed their hats when he did, smiled when he did, stepped forward when he did to accept the governor's outstretched hand. For a moment my vision blurred as I tried to keep straight which were the real men and which were the two sets of echoes, all clasping hands at the same time. Of course, Cormac had one more echo than the governor, so that creature mimicked the rest of them, appearing to interact with a ghost invisible to the rest of us.

"That is *so strange*," I murmured.

"Oh, you get used to it," Rory said.

"Wonder how you get used to it in bed," the undercook asked. One of the maids hissed at her, but she went on, defiant, "Well, if they do everything he does, does that mean all four of them have a go at you? Or are there other girls lying in other beds, providing a service to the shadow men?"

"If Constance heard you talk like that, you'd be sacked in a second!" Rory said.

"Maybe. But I'd like to know."

It hadn't even occurred to me to wonder before. But now I wanted to know, too.

Cormac and his attendants were now turning to greet Lady Dorothea, and the strange ritual repeated. Then it was Marguerite's turn to step forward as Patience and Purpose and Prudence stood in a row beside her. All four of them offered their hands. Cormac bestowed a warm smile on Marguerite as he made some favorable remark, and she responded with a pretty smile of her own. He lifted her hand to his lips. His echoes copied the gesture. Marguerite and her echoes sank in curtseys halfway to the floor and then slowly rose again. I thought Cormac gave her hand a squeeze before he released it.

Next, each of Marguerite's brothers took their turns meeting the prince, their own echoes ranged alongside them; then they all exchanged light conversation for a few moments. Again, my vision blurred slightly at the almost impossibly choreographed scene below—Cormac and Marguerite shadowed by three exact replicas, the others by one or two, each set moving and nodding and laughing and motioning in concert. They looked like ripples undulating across a cornfield or starlings darting across the sky, perfectly synchronized, utterly in tune. It was dizzying to watch.

When I was able to separate out individual actions again, I realized that Cormac was waving his hand toward a group of men who had followed him into the house. Only then did I think to look for Nico within the prince's entourage, but I didn't see him. And no wonder. Even I could tell that Cormac's fellow travelers were high nobles, whereas an inquisitor would no doubt be part of the professional class; they would hardly be socializing together. At first, I thought Cormac had brought eleven companions, but then I realized that several had echoes of their own, and I had to concentrate to get a more accurate count. I finally decided he had brought five friends; two had two echoes, two had one, and one had none. The one with no echo—a burly fellow with red-gold hair as bright as a coin—looked to be loud and a little rude on top of it. None of his friends were as striking as their prince.

Dorothea sailed up to Cormac again, gesturing to different areas of the house. By the direction her hands were pointing, I assumed she was explaining that they would all withdraw to one of the inner salons before continuing on to the dining room. Rory and the undercook had already slipped away, since their services would be called upon during the meal; but unless some disaster befell Marguerite's wardrobe, there would be nothing for me to do until she returned to her room at the end of the evening. So I stood there a few moments longer, watching the crowd in the atrium slowly thin out as people filed through the archway that led toward the salon. Soon the big room was empty except for a few self-effacing figures that I took to be guards, valets, or other attendants brought by Cormac and his friends. They would wait there or in the servants' hall by the kitchen until their masters were on their way home again.

One of those unobtrusive fellows was on the move, prowling along the perimeter of the atrium like a cat sniffing through an unfamiliar space. He stayed under the overhang of the balcony and wove between pillars and tall planters as if trying to stay hidden, so it was hard to see him clearly, but after a moment, I recognized him. Nico. He was there, after all, gathering information on behalf of his prince.

I didn't sniff or scowl or make any sudden movement, so I don't know how I caught his attention. But just as I decided it was time for me to quietly withdraw, Nico came to a halt and looked up at me. Not as if he'd just that moment discovered my presence—as if he'd spotted me the minute he walked in and had been glancing my way every so often for the past ten minutes, just to see if I might do something interesting. Despite the fact that I was so far away and almost entirely obscured by the railing, he seemed to realize that I had seen him. He smiled and raised a hand in greeting. I couldn't help smiling in return as I slipped away.

I headed one flight up so I could enjoy a couple hours of solitude in my room before Marguerite needed me again. I was still smiling as I unlocked the door, but my expression turned to surprise when I stepped inside. There was a long, narrow box lying on my bed, sealed with a wide silk ribbon tied in a bow, and beside it lay a note in Constance's plain handwriting: *This was delivered this afternoon for you.* I wondered if she'd opened the box to look inside, but I thought she probably hadn't. Constance was all about observing rules and boundaries.

The only people I could think of who might send me packages were Jean or my mother—but Jean wouldn't bother with a bow and my mother would assume, correctly, that the stress of travel would shred a ribbon before it could arrive, so she wouldn't bother, either. Then who was sending me presents?

I stood beside the bed a moment, savoring the mystery, then slowly pulled at the end of the ribbon and lifted the lid of the box. Inside, nestled in a length of red velvet, were a dozen tall-stemmed white roses, their petals veined with faintest pink.

I bent down to inhale the sweet, faint scent. Nico Burken had sent me flowers, a time-honored gesture of courtship. Not only that, he had selected the most expensive of the blossoms that we had seen at the market yesterday, remembering that they were the ones I liked best. I sniffed again at the blossoms and felt a brief inclination to fall into a romantic swoon.

I reminded myself that this was nothing more than a flirtation. Within a few days, Nico would be back in Camarria and I would remain in Oberton, and I might never see him again in my life. But for this single moment I could allow myself to be giddy with pleasure and silly with delight. I liked a man and he fancied me; coming to that realization is always one of life's most beguiling moments.

I would have to fetch a vase from the kitchen—or, even better, appropriate an empty one from Marguerite's room, since she was less likely than Constance to ask why I wanted one. Leaving the box on the bed, I turned toward the door—which was when I saw the small, folded piece of paper on the floor. Someone had slipped it under the door earlier in the day, perhaps when I had been out running errands.

It was brief, and it was in Marguerite's handwriting. *Come to my room tomorrow at dawn. Tell no one.*

The big picture windows in Marguerite's room showed nothing but blank, dark skies when I arrived before sunrise. Nonetheless, she was awake and perched on one of the sofas in the sitting room. The echoes were huddled around her, looking oddly unhappy. It took me a moment to realize why they seemed so strange, but then I saw it: They were still in their nightclothes while Marguerite was fully dressed.

Or, well, *sort of* dressed.

"My lady," I whispered, because the hour was so early it didn't seem right to speak out loud. "What are you *wearing?*"

She glanced down at her rough-spun brown dress with the workaday pinafore. "Winifred used to put it on when she snuck out to meet her lover. I confiscated it one day and told her she didn't have to indulge in such pretexts—I didn't care that she was involved with a young man as long as she still did her job. She gave her notice three weeks later."

"That explains why you *have* it but not why you have it *on*."

"I need to leave the house in secret. No one will look at me twice if I'm dressed like this."

That was probably true. Lady Dorothea wasn't the only person in the mansion who thought servants were invisible. On the other hand, all the household staff knew each other, so even servants who didn't expect Marguerite to be masquerading as one of them would realize this woman did not belong in the mansion. Except Constance had hired extra help to manage the workload while we were entertaining the prince. Marguerite just might be able to pull this off.

"What's so important that I can't handle it for you?" I asked.

Marguerite shook her head. "I can't explain it. I have to go. But I want you to come with me."

I nodded and pointed at the echoes. "And them?"

"No. They'll stay behind."

That explained both why the echoes were still in their night-clothes and why they were so distraught. "I didn't know they *could*," I said.

Marguerite sat straighter, a look of determination on her face. "They must," she said.

I was curious. "Have they ever? Been separated from you before?"

Marguerite hesitated, then shook her head.

"What if they follow you?"

She held up the key to her door. "I'll lock them in."

This was getting more and more strange, but we didn't have time to argue. The blackness outside the window was starting to haze to gray, and the sun would be up before long. "Then let's get going." *And see how far we get.*

The echoes were *really* uneasy as we stepped through the door and refused to let them follow. They didn't speak, but their mouths were open and they made small, distressed sounds, like kittens or mice. One of them reached through the door, trying to catch Marguerite's arm, and she had to shove it back with a firm, "Purpose, *no*. Stay here. All of you. Just wait for me." She resolutely locked the door, then took a deep breath and said, "Let's go."

I figured some of the staff would already be up, so it was safer to take the public hallways than the back corridors, and we boldly made our way down the main stairs and across the atrium. A startled footman opened the door to the front entrance for us, too bemused to ask why servants had picked that exit, and we were out of the house with no trouble.

"One hurdle down," I said under my breath. "Where are we going?"

"The temple."

I nodded. I should have guessed that. "Follow me, then. If we're walking, there's an easier way to go than the road you take in a carriage."

We moved quickly and mostly without speaking through the nearly empty streets. The brighter the skies grew, the more people we found on the road with us—bakers opening their shops, dairymen delivering their goods, day workers hurrying toward their jobs. Marguerite seemed edgy and ill at ease, pulling an old shawl closely over her shoulders, sticking as close to me as she could, and constantly glancing over her shoulders.

"I don't think anyone followed us from the house," I said at last.

"What? Oh. No. I keep thinking—I'm so used to having the others with me. I keep looking for them. It's so strange."

"I imagine it is. But if you were trailed by three echoes, anyone who saw you would instantly know who you were. You had to leave them behind."

Her voice was so soft I almost didn't catch the words. "That's not why I did it."

The sun was up, but still very low on the horizon, by the time we arrived at the temple. As usual, I paused at the fountain to dribble my fingers in the water and make a silent prayer. I didn't know why these representatives of the goddess seemed friendlier to me than the ones inside.

"You stay here," Marguerite said.

I looked up, my hand still in the spray of water. "But—"

"I'll come out when I'm done," she said firmly, turning away from me. I watched her push open the heavy door and disappear inside.

A moment longer I just stood there, staring after her, then I shook my hand dry and looked around for a place to wait. There was a rigid metal bench situated under one of the triple-paned windows, so I made my way over to it and sat down. It was just as uncomfortable as it looked. I squirmed for a minute, trying to find a better position, then just gave up and slumped against the hard back. My body was as relaxed as I could manage, but my brain was working feverishly.

What in the world had brought us here in such a clandestine fashion? Although nothing untoward had happened so far, I couldn't help but feel we were running terrible risks and that to be discovered would be disastrous. But why? A respectable lady had come to visit a temple, very properly escorted by her maid. What fault could anyone find with that?

And yet the air of ruination lingered. I could imagine only two reasons Marguerite might want to come to the temple in such secrecy that no one, not even her echoes, could bear witness.

The first, and most likely, explanation was that she was meeting with her lover, the one she had been corresponding with in secret. That made it even more ironic that she was wearing Winifred's clothing, since she had urged the maid not to hide her own romance. I had to assume that the message I had brought to the temple a few days ago had set up the time and place for this assignation. My supposition was that she would exit through a back door where her lover's carriage was waiting. I was tempted to creep around the side of the building to try to get a glimpse of him, but I did not want Marguerite to catch me spying on her.

Besides, I could be wrong. She might not be carrying on a forbidden romance after all; she might be here to meet with the abbess in charge of this temple. I had not forgotten the small, pretty triple goddess statue that Marguerite kept in the far corner of her room. Every day when I arrived, I found that she had scattered fresh flower petals at the feet of the women offering justice, mercy, and joy. My first day in the mansion I had wondered if Marguerite was a passionate follower of the goddess. The only times I had seen her truly at ease were when we were inside the temple.

Did she want to become a priestess, then? Was she desperate to throw off all the trappings of a noble life, to escape the attentions of the prince, to refuse to play the pawn in the king's attempt to reconcile the warring provinces? My guess was that—if Marguerite did not end up married to the prince—her parents would rather have her become a priestess than take a lover, as that course of action would bring significantly less disgrace to the household. But maybe not. Nobles survived scandals all the time. A woman caught with a lover might be repudiated by royalty, but she could still catch the eye of a man who would overlook such irregularities in favor of her family connections. Whereas a woman who dedicated her life to the goddess might as well be dead if her only value came from her potential as a bride.

I supposed there might be a third reason Marguerite had indulged in such a charade, but I couldn't come up with it.

I sat there perhaps an hour, trying to still my chaotic thoughts, trying to look like someone who was perfectly happy to sit on an unyielding metal bench and watch the world walk by. There was slow but constant traffic in and out of the building, as some visitors concluded their devotions and others arrived to begin theirs. A few people cast curious glances my way, but no one seemed very interested in me. I maintained my abstracted expression.

Just as I had begun to wonder if Marguerite would ever rejoin me, she emerged through the temple door, pausing a moment to let her eyes adjust to the light. I was on my feet and at her side before she had time to look around for me.

"Ready to go?" I asked quietly.

She simply nodded, and we headed back toward the mansion at a brisk walk. As we strode along, I stole a few quick glances at her face and thought she looked decidedly more peaceful than she had at any time since I'd known her. That still didn't provide a clue about what she'd been doing while she'd been out of my sight.

"What's the plan for today?" I finally asked.

"My father will take the prince on a tour of the city. My brothers will accompany them, but I won't. There's to be a light luncheon, and then tonight is the ball."

I knew about the ball, of course. Aunt Jean had told me that every woman in the city had prayed to be invited. Marguerite and I had spent days debating what she should wear, while Lady Dorothea had offered her own decided opinions about Marguerite's wardrobe choices.

"So—two different outfits. Two different hairstyles?"

Marguerite nodded. "Simple for the luncheon, ornate for the evening."

"You'll look beautiful."

She glanced over at me. Behind her calm exterior, deep in her blue eyes, I saw sadness and resignation. "It doesn't even matter."

I could hardly contain myself. "Lady Marguerite—"

She lifted a hand. "Don't ask."

"But if there is something I can do—"

"You're doing it."

I spread my hands. "I haven't done anything!"

"You've been my friend."

I didn't even know how to answer that. Finally I just said, "Always."

When we arrived at the mansion, people were already coming and going through the front doors. There was no way to avoid being seen. "I think the back entrance is our best bet, but we'll surely run into servants who recognize you," I said, frowning.

Marguerite shrugged. "I don't mind if people realize I left. I just didn't want anyone to stop me from leaving."

"Some of them might carry tales to your mother."

A faint smile touched her lips. "Then that will be interesting."

Indeed, as we went in through the kitchen door, we encountered no less than nine staff members, from Constance to the undercook. Each one first stared, then dropped into a hasty bow or curtsey, then gave me a sideways look of astonishment. But everyone knew by now that I wouldn't spread stories about Marguerite. They might ask me later what she meant by the servants' garb and the secretive arrival, but they wouldn't expect me to tell them.

We made it to her room without encountering any family members—not entirely a surprise, since it was still early in the day for nobility to be about. The echoes were clustered at the door when we walked in, as if they had stood there the whole time we were gone, and they fell on Marguerite with inarticulate gladness, patting her arms and shoulders and shoving their faces close to hers, as if inhaling her scent. Or—I don't know. Inhaling her very breath as it escaped her body. As if they had almost asphyxiated in her absence because she wasn't there to breathe for them.

She seemed just as glad to be back among them, wrapping her arms around all of them at once and drawing them in for a communal embrace. I saw her close her eyes—saw all of them close their eyes—and for a moment a different kind of peace smoothed Marguerite's features. She was home. She was whole. She was in balance. I marched past them toward the dressing room to start sorting through Marguerite's closet. I didn't belong at that reunion.

CHAPTER EIGHT

Marguerite wore a pink-and-white dress to the luncheon and a crown of pink asters in her hair. I considered presenting her with one of the white roses even now gracing my room, which would have added a touch of elegance to her ensemble—but I didn't. I was being greedy, but I wanted to keep all of them for myself.

She was somewhat flustered when she returned to her room after the meal so she could nap for a couple of hours before the ball. "What's wrong?" I asked as I helped her undress. The echoes followed us into the dressing room and proceeded to unbutton each other's gowns.

"That man. He's so rude." When my face showed inquiry, she explained, "Jamison. Cormac's bastard half brother. Apparently he is a fixture at court and the king expects him to be welcomed everywhere, but he is familiar and offensive and very unpleasant! At least two of the other women at the luncheon made some excuse to leave the table rather than be near him—but, of course, they can't complain about him for fear of offending Cormac! It is most infuriating."

I was mentally reviewing the companions I'd seen arriving with Prince Cormac yesterday. "Is he the one with the red-gold hair and the full beard? He was handsome, I thought."

She slipped her arms into the silken robe I was holding for her, then she tied the sash. "Yes, that's him. Within five minutes I thought he was so ugly inside that he was no longer handsome on the outside. When did you see him?"

I wrinkled my nose, embarrassed to be caught out, but couldn't manufacture a quick lie. "I was watching from one of the balcony doors when they arrived," I admitted.

She laughed. "I suppose you weren't the only one!"

"No. We were all so curious!"

"Well, pick a good place tonight," she advised. "The ball will be held in the atrium, you know, and it'll be an impressive sight. When I was a little girl, I used to sneak onto the balcony and watch whenever my mother and father hosted an event. There's nothing like seeing echoes at a ball."

I had never given it any thought before. "Do they dance when you do?"

Marguerite nodded. "In exactly the same motions at exactly the same time."

"What if one person has more echoes than another? Does one of the echoes sit on the sidelines?"

"No! They dance alongside you like demented children, dipping and twirling in time with the music. But my mother and most of the other nobles always hire dance instructors who can fill in whenever there is a mismatch in the number of echoes. Some of the instructors are men, some are women. So *anyone* with echoes can be sure there will be enough partners available so that they actually enjoy the ball. Otherwise, it's just too distracting."

"One of the maids said—well, I probably shouldn't even ask—"

Marguerite flicked her hands at her echoes and they headed out the door, toward their own room. She climbed onto her bed and I pulled the covers up to her chin. She was the same age I was, but when she lay there on the big bed, surrounded by pillows, she looked so young and small. "Ask me what?"

"Well—once you're married, and you and your husband—oh, never mind."

But her face showed a certain cynical comprehension. "Oh, yes, the marriage bed for a woman with echoes," she said. "I want you to imagine me having *that* conversation with my mother when I was about twelve years old."

I did, and I had to swallow a giggle.

Marguerite nodded. "But, yes. That's one of the reasons it's preferable for people with echoes to marry people with the same number of echoes. Because they all perform the same act at the same time."

"And if the numbers don't match up? Do you find—dancing partners?"

She made an inelegant sound. "I don't know! I suppose some people do and some people don't, depending on how much they care about the well-being of their echoes."

"And do they—I mean, if they're having sex—do the echoes ever get pregnant? Or *make* someone pregnant?"

Marguerite shook her head, tangling her blond hair on the pillow. "They're sterile. They just mimic the motions."

I tried not to shudder. "The whole thing is a little unnerving to think about."

"I think it wouldn't bother me at all if I liked the man I was married to," Marguerite said. "But if I *don't* like him, I think it will be horrid. Not only will *I* have to endure something unpleasant, but I will be forcing Patience and Prudence and Purpose to endure it as well."

"Well, you never know," I said. "The man you end up with may be courteous and kind, loving and generous. *All* of you might enjoy your time in the marriage bed."

She hesitated a moment, then asked in a small voice, "*Is* it something women generally enjoy? My mother didn't make it sound as if that was very likely."

I obviously hadn't been married to Robbie, but we hadn't held off on that account. For one of the first times since he'd broken my heart, I allowed myself to remember how much pleasure we'd had in each other's bodies. Really, there had been times I had found Robbie's lack of ambition frustrating and his sense of humor annoying, but I'd loved every minute of intimacy we'd spent together. It had always been the best part of our relationship. "Well, *I* enjoyed it a great deal," I said firmly, hoping she wasn't shocked to learn I wasn't a virgin. "But it's probably a whole different story if you don't like the man in your bed."

She closed her eyes. "Which is highly likely, I'm afraid. My mother hates my father, after all. I don't think I know a single noble-woman who loves her husband."

"Some people think you might end up married to the prince," I said casually, wondering how much she might tell me.

She opened her eyes again. "Is that the gossip in the servants' hall?"

"I heard it said before I even met you. The king thinks if you marry Cormac, it might repair relations between Sammerly and Orenza. And the other western provinces."

"And make my father a very rich man into the bargain, because my father already has a list of concessions he's drawn up for the king to consider," Marguerite responded. "You can guess how much pressure I am under to make a good impression on the prince during this visit!"

"Would you *want* to marry him?" I asked. "If he asked you?"

"You mean, if our fathers worked out the arrangements."

"I suppose."

"I don't know. I never thought about it until recently." She closed her eyes and turned on her side to snuggle into the pillow. "I don't want to think about it." When she added something, her words were muffled by the pillow and spoken almost inaudibly. But I thought what she said was, "I don't think I want to marry anybody."

It took more than an hour for Marguerite to dress for the ball. First she bathed in scented water and rubbed perfumed oils into her skin; then she sat quietly while I arranged her hair in complex coils, pinning blossoms into each tight curl. A few discreet cosmetics for her cheeks and eyes and lips, then it was time for her to step into her dress. It was a lovely layered confection of starchy taffeta and smooth silk, white with delicate accents of red ribbon and black lace. The whole ensemble had been created to accentuate the spectacular necklace I fastened around her throat, a collar of burnished onyx stones in white and black. The collar was six stones deep around her neck and fed into a wide V that narrowed to a point above her décolletage. A single bloodred stone hung at the very tip as if about to drip between her breasts.

When she lifted her left hand to touch the lowest gem, I noticed her bracelet. Though it, too, was constructed of onyx in red, white, and black, it was done in a much simpler style, as it featured small, flat disks of stone connected by plain silver links.

"That's new," I said.

"You just haven't seen it before," she replied.

I didn't contradict her, but I knew she was lying. I was familiar with every piece of jewelry and clothing she possessed. "It's pretty," I said. "Maybe not as ornate as it should be for tonight, though."

She twisted her hand back and forth to watch the disks sway slightly as they hung from her wrist. "I've decided I should wear it every day," she said. "As a perpetual statement that I am a daughter of the province of Orenza. Like you wear your ring every day."

We had talked about my ring before. "That's not why I wear it. My mother gave it to me so that I would always remember that someone loves me."

Marguerite met my gaze in the mirror. "Well," she said.

After a moment's silence, I said, "And now your shoes."

Finally she was completely ready, a delicate, perfect creation of beauty and artifice. I thought Prince Cormac would find her hard to resist.

The echoes filed into the room and arranged themselves behind her. Their gowns were very similar, but sewn from blush-colored fabrics; their necklaces were simple strands of multicolored onyx beads, and their coiffures didn't incorporate quite so many flowers. Still, as they stood silently behind her, they looked like reflections of Marguerite captured on a tarnished silver surface—fainter, more ethereal, much more likely to melt away.

"I hope you have a wonderful time at the ball," I said.

She stifled a sigh as she lifted her chin and headed for the door, the echoes trailing in her wake. "I hope so, too," she said.

I headed to the kitchen to see if I could grab a quick meal but found the place so chaotic that I just started helping any way I could, carrying plates and washing out pans. Once the meal was served in the grand dining hall and cleared away again, the pace dramatically slowed down. I was able to swallow a few bites and then sneak out, lured by the muffled strains of music. I realized the dancing must already be under way.

I made my way to the east wing of the third floor—where Lord Garvin and Lady Dorothea had their studies, and where no one was likely to be present at this time of night. I slipped through the doorway that led onto the balcony. I had carefully dressed in neutral colors that would blend with the wallpaper and the wood, and I stretched out full length on the floor, my head propped on my fists and my face a few inches from the railing. Someone in the atrium would have to look very carefully to spot me staring down at the scene below.

And what a sight it was. The musicians were set up under the overhang of the balconies, as were the chairs and the tables of food brought in for the comfort of the guests. So there was nothing to be seen in the atrium except the dancers themselves. For a moment, my eyes could hardly take in the riot of colors. All the women wore ball gowns of lime and strawberry and tangerine and wine; all the men sported dark trousers and bright jackets. Everywhere were flashes of gold and sparks of silver, and the whole gorgeous mix was in endless motion, driven by the lively music. But eventually I began making sense of the patterns and was able to pick out the individual dancers. And then I was even more impressed.

Marguerite had been right—there was nothing to compare to the sight of echoes dancing together on the ballroom floor. Marguerite and the black-haired prince turned and spun in the very center of a stately pattern of color, and around them, in perfect orbit, wheeled three identical pairs of dancers. Smaller clusters of paired dancers spilled out around them in a bright, twirling constellation. Each set moved with flawless precision; it was as if the partners glided between invisible mirrors, danced with their own reflections. A woman pivoted so quickly her lavender skirt flared behind her, and two more skirts billowed in exactly the same way. A man threw back his head and laughed. Two other men laughed in concert. It was dizzying. It was extraordinary. It was magical.

The spell was briefly broken when the music stopped and it was less obvious that certain groups were acting in concord. The dancers fanned themselves, murmured a few words to each other, or took the opportunity to change partners. I noticed that the prince still kept a light hold on Marguerite, and his echoes remained similarly close to Prudence, Patience, and Purpose. But the governor bowed to his wife and sought out a large, dour-faced matron wearing a violent shade of fuchsia. I could only see one other figure who might have been her echo—and then I noticed a slim, simply dressed woman step out from under the balcony and sidle up to one of the governor's echoes. When the music started again, she did her best to emulate the large woman's steps and gestures. No doubt she was mostly following the lead of her shadow partner. If I squinted through the slats in the railing, I could hardly tell that she was not exactly synchronized. On the dance floor, her mistakes would probably go completely unnoticed.

It was the most surreal and most mesmerizing scene I had ever witnessed.

I had probably been lying there for a half hour, staring at the dance floor, when I heard the door behind me quietly open. Assuming it was one of the other servants, I didn't even turn around to see who had arrived. So I was caught completely off guard when a solid shape dropped to the floor on my right side and I glanced over to find Nico Burken sitting there. My *"Oh!"* of surprise was so loud it would have been heard below except that the musicians were playing a particularly rousing passage.

"I thought that was you," he said. "Do you often find vantage points like this where you can come ogle your betters?"

"No!" I said, breaking into a laugh and motioning for him to lie flat. "You're not dressed right! Your clothes are too dark and someone is likely to see you."

He stretched out beside me, just a few inches away, but he didn't look too worried. "None of them will bother to look up," he said. "They're too full of their own consequence to think anything of importance could be happening somewhere else in the house."

This tallied with my experience, but I still didn't want to attract attention. "And keep your voice down."

"If you're always this bossy, I don't wonder that none of the other servants wants to join you to watch the entertainment."

I choked back a laugh. "Most of the ones who would like to see the ball are still cleaning up the kitchen," I retorted. "But they'll be at one balcony door or another before the night is through."

"So are you enjoying the evening?"

I nodded. "I can't take my eyes off the dancers. I've never seen anything like them."

"And this is a small gathering, compared to some of the events the king has hosted," Nico answered. "Imagine, if you will, a room in which everyone has at least one echo, and all the sets of dancers spin around each other like stars in some kind of celestial pattern. From above, it is an absolutely amazing sight to behold."

For a moment I felt an intense desire to witness such an impossible sight. Then I said, "So you're in the habit of spying on people even when you're not touring the kingdom?"

He grinned. "I make it a habit to watch everyone every chance I get."

"Thank you for the roses," I said. "They're so beautiful."

"I wanted to buy something less expensive, you understand," he said, "but by the time I made it back to the market, there was nothing else left."

"I was astonished that you bothered buying me anything at all."

"Were you? Then you must not be paying attention."

I wasn't sure how to reply to that. Fortunately a clatter below caused both of us to quickly look down. On the edge of the dance floor, right under an archway, there was a small disruption in the ripple of color and movement. It looked as if someone had stumbled, then bumped into another couple, then tried to get out of the way. Most of the dancers hadn't even noticed, and they continued spinning around the floor as if nothing had occurred.

Nico was frowning, so I peered harder through the slats. A young woman was hastily exiting the dance floor, clutching folds of her dress in her fists so she didn't trip over the fabric. A man stared after her, his back to us. "What happened?" I asked.

"Looks like Lord Jamison is up to his old tricks," Nico replied.

I looked again. Yes, that was the man with the red-gold hair that I had spied yesterday afternoon. His navy jacket hugged broad shoulders that indicated a certain physical power. I wondered if he had been holding his erstwhile partner a little too tightly. "Such as?"

"Somewhat forcefully displaying his interest in winning a young woman's attention."

I raised my eyebrows. "Is this how he always behaves at social events?"

"Let's just say, it's not unusual. You can find women across the Seven Jewels who despise him."

"Why does Cormac tolerate him, then? Why does the king?"

"You've got it backward," Nico said. "Jamison feels free to behave as he does *because* his father and his half brother put no checks on him. Harold, I suppose, feels some guilt about the fact that Jamison is illegitimate. He can't give his son the crown, but he allows him every other indulgence. Cormac—who knows? Perhaps he chafes at the restrictions put on him by virtue of being the heir, and he likes to see how Jamison flouts such restrictions in his own life. At any rate, Jamison is free to do his worst—and he frequently does."

I gave an exaggerated sigh. "I would like to think nobles and royals were *better* than the rest of us, not worse."

Nico laughed and gestured toward the scene below. "They're certainly not better, but they're more interesting to watch."

I trained my gaze back on the dance floor, and a companionable silence fell between us. Nico seemed content to watch everything that was happening below—not just the patterns of the dancers, but the conversations going on along the sidelines, the discreet entrances of the servants carrying in more platters of food. I had the feeling that, if I asked him, he would be able to tell me how many people were in the room, who had danced most often with whom, and how many glasses of wine each one had tossed back. I thought it must be an exhausting way to live.

"So do you dance?" he asked presently.

"I do," I said. "I like it, too."

"Reels and line dances, or fancy ones?"

"You *do* think I'm provincial."

He grinned over at me. "You're a country girl. It seems like a reasonable assumption."

"Until I was fifteen, I only knew the simple dances," I confessed. "But that summer, we had a visitor who stayed at the inn for a month. She had to be fifty years old and not at all fashionable, but she'd spent half her life running a dance academy for young ladies. She had run low on funds and couldn't pay for the rest of her trip, so she started dance classes in the village for any girl who was willing to pay. I got to attend for free, since she couldn't afford rent on the room, either. Once she'd earned enough to finish her journey, she was gone, but we'd learned all the steps. At local weddings, we still play waltzes."

Nico was still grinning. "But who do you partner up with, if she only taught the women?"

I laughed. "With each other! We all tried to teach our brothers and beaus, but they weren't nearly as interested in learning."

"No," Nico said. "As a rule, a man would rather fight."

"What about you?" I challenged. "Can you dance?"

He nodded. "My father was a low noble, as I think I told you, and my mother was determined that I should know every skill that fell to my station, so she insisted that I learn. I resisted as much as possible, and I'm not very good at it, but generally I don't disgrace myself if a dance becomes inescapable."

I rolled to my side and propped my head up on my left hand. "And how often does it happen that you are forced to dance?"

He laughed. "As infrequently as possible! But from time to time I attend royal balls in the role of extra dancer—filling in for a man who only has two echoes and who has solicited the hand of a woman with three."

"How many of your dance partners are aware that they are waltzing with the king's inquisitor?"

He turned his head to inspect me. "You mention my profession in almost every other sentence," he said. "Do you find my occupation that horrifying?"

I rolled back onto my stomach and rested my head on my left fist, so that my chin was almost on the floor. I curled my right hand around one of the slats on the railing and stared down at the dancers again. It hardly mattered what *I* thought about his line of work. "I think it could be ugly," I said. "For all that you justify the ugly parts."

"I suppose any profession has less savory elements."

"All jobs probably have elements that aren't very *pleasant*," I allowed, thinking about cleaning up a room at the posting house where the occupants had celebrated a little too enthusiastically. Nothing like day-old vomit to make you never want to eat again. "But many of them are still honorable."

"Well! Now we've gotten down to the truth of it!" he exclaimed. His tone indicated outrage, but I was pretty sure he was amused. "I think you're provincial, and you think I'm dishonorable."

"Good thing you'll be heading back to the royal city soon."

"Not quite *that* soon," he said. "I think the plan is to stay here three more days. And once we leave, we head to Alberta, not Camarria."

I gave him a quick look. "But you'll still be leaving Oberton."

"We'll still be leaving here," he echoed. "Yes."

I shrugged. "So."

"Not for three more days. A lot can happen in that amount of time."

I shrugged again and didn't answer. But I didn't pull away when he reached up and gently pried my right hand from the railing, then laced his fingers between mine. We lay like that for the longest time, side by side on the balcony floor, not speaking, not touching except for where our fingers intertwined. Every note of music that played for the duration of the ball seared itself into my brain as if to make certain I would never be able to forget a minute of that night.

CHAPTER NINE

In the morning, Marguerite wanted to visit the flower markets. Both of us had gotten to bed late and risen late, so there was no chance of sneaking out before anyone else was awake. But it was soon clear that sneaking was exactly what she wanted to do. We took a carriage to the markets, telling the coachman to park somewhere for a couple of hours because we planned to take our time picking out purchases. We had not spent five minutes winding between the flower stalls when Marguerite and her echoes all pulled out plain silk shawls and draped them over their heads as if to shield their faces from the sun.

"Come on," Marguerite said, turning in the direction of the temple.

I muffled a sigh and followed. At least she'd had the forethought to give each echo a wrap of a different color and she'd released them enough from her control that they didn't walk behind her in perfectly timed steps. But it wouldn't be too hard to pick them out from the throngs of people on the street if anyone had been paying attention.

Once we arrived at the temple, we took our usual seats in back. Well, the echoes and I did—Marguerite stood in the aisle, staring at the echoes with eyes so fierce they seemed to burn.

"You must sit here, do you understand?" she whispered in a low, intense voice. "You cannot follow me. I will only be in the next building, not far at all. I will return as quickly as I can. Do you understand? You must stay."

They rustled uneasily on the bench, one of them half-rising until Marguerite pushed her firmly back in place. "Stay here," she whispered again, then turned and strode away without once looking back. A moment later, she disappeared through the door near the front of the sanctuary.

The echoes stirred and whispered, wringing their hands and bobbing their heads. The same one came halfway to her feet again, and this time I hauled her back. *This must be Purpose,* I thought. Always the first one to act, the first one to understand. She didn't look at me as she settled back on the seat and I could feel the tension emanating from her coiled body. I didn't know how to soothe her and I didn't know how long Marguerite would be gone and I didn't know what dangerous adventure she might be pursuing. I wanted to sigh and chitter and shake my head, just like the echoes, but I didn't; I sat there, hands folded, head bowed, every muscle corded with readiness. It felt like the longest hour of my life.

This time, when Marguerite reappeared, she didn't look particularly peaceful. She looked sad. *Maybe she's told him she has to stop this nonsense,* I thought, following her and the others out of the temple, into the light, into the crowded and cheerful streets. *Maybe this is the last clandestine visit we'll have to make.* I hoped so—but I was pretty sure I was wrong.

That evening, the governor and his wife hosted a dinner to which it seemed half of the city had been invited. As the event was held in the grand dining hall, there was no convenient balcony perch from which I could look down on the visitors. But since I had no specific function to fulfill during the meal, I could step outside to enjoy the cooler air of evening. I was not entirely surprised to find that Nico Burken was loitering behind the mansion, near the servants' entrance, and that he, too, fancied a casual stroll through the nearby streets. Later, Marguerite said that the dinner had seemed endless, but I thought our slow promenade was much too short.

The next two days were, like Marguerite's echoes, almost exact copies. A trip to the temple in the morning. An event at the mansion in the evening. A few hours of dalliance with Nico.

Clearly, Marguerite did not want to relinquish her lover after all. I had to say, knowing how quickly Nico would be riding away, I could sympathize.

On the fourth day after the ball, which was the last day the royal visitors would be in town, there was no chance to visit the flower markets—or the temple—as Lady Dorothea had scheduled activities that would keep Marguerite at her side for the entire day. I had plenty to keep me busy putting Marguerite's wardrobe back in order because there had been very little time to clean or mend anything during the hectic pace of the past week. I chose a sofa in the sitting room and spread a half dozen garments around me so I could sew by the light of the picture window. I was only about halfway through my task when Marguerite and the echoes returned and plopped down in nearby chairs.

"Back for a nap?" I asked, glancing up. Then added, with more concern, "What's wrong? You look like you've been slapped across the face."

Marguerite put a hand to her cheek, and all the echoes did the same. She must really be disturbed, then. She had told me it took her some concentration to let the echoes go free, so when they mimicked her this closely, I assumed it was because her thoughts were elsewhere. "Do I? That's sort of what I feel like."

I laid aside my sewing. "What happened?"

"The prince said—the prince wants me to go to Camarria—so we can get to know each other better."

"Oh, my lady! Does that mean—"

She shook her head. "He's not asking for my hand. Not yet. But if all goes well, he *will* ask for it."

"But then—"

"I'm not the only one being invited to Camarria because he does not want to appear too particular in his attentions. There will be a dozen eligible women from across the Seven Jewels. We are expected to assemble in the royal city in about three weeks and stay for a month."

"And at the end of that month?"

"If we find we get along—if his parents find me suitable—and, I suppose, if our fathers can work out their bargain—then he—then he—"

"Then he asks you to be his bride."

She nodded dumbly.

I took a deep breath and let it out again. It was hard to know how to respond, whether to offer comfort or congratulations; every reaction seemed wrong. She could leave for Camarria the governor's daughter, and return as the woman next in line to be queen. A deliriously exciting prospect for someone who desired such a life; a horrifying notion for someone who craved a different existence altogether.

"And if you *don't* get engaged? What happens then?"

She made a fatalistic gesture. "Then I come home, to find my mother disappointed and my father furious. No! Worse! My father would be more convinced than ever that the western provinces must secede, and determined to whip up a rebellion with the support of Empara and Alberta. So there would be war and bloodshed and death, and all of it my fault."

"Hardly your fault, not if your fathers are the ones who can't come to terms," I said in a dampening tone, since her voice had risen to the edge of hysteria. "Anyway, the provinces have been quarreling for years, and there hasn't been a war yet. I don't think the consequences will be so dire."

"Maybe not," she said a little more quietly. "Maybe I just come home and try to resume my old life until my father picks out someone else he thinks I should marry to give him political advantage."

I tried to infuse a little hope into my voice. "Maybe you come home and your parents let you pick your *own* husband," I said. "Wouldn't that be nice? Can you think of someone you might *want* to marry?"

I said it in a playful tone, but it was clear she took the question with utmost seriousness. She lifted her head and stared at me, her blue eyes huge with longing and grief. Then she glanced away, down at her hands, and began plucking at the design embroidered into her skirt. "Oh, yes," she whispered, "but I'll never get the chance."

"Are you sure?" I said in a gentle way. "Times change. People's circumstances change. Someone who is unsuitable or unavailable might become acceptable and free."

She looked up again, attempting to force her mouth into a smile. "It's a nice thought. But I don't expect it to happen. I need to push this person out of my heart."

"Camarria might be just the place to do it," I said, in what I hoped was an encouraging voice. "Maybe, if you don't marry the prince, you'll meet someone else in the royal city. Someone who's young and handsome and rich—and has a large estate."

"I don't care about money and a big house," she said. "A kind heart and a gentle temper are all I want."

"You'll care about a big house when you're trying to find beds for your echoes!" I told her. "Unless you think they can curl up in front of the kitchen fireplace, like puppies on a blanket."

Her smile was more genuine now, though still streaked with wistfulness. "If I lived in a small cottage with barely enough room to turn around, would you still come take care of me?" she asked.

"I would," I said firmly. "Though I'm *not* sleeping on a blanket in front of the hearth. I at least need a cot of my own."

"Well, we'll do better than that for you in Camarria."

"'In Camarria'?" I repeated, puzzled.

"You're coming with me, of course."

I had been so focused on Marguerite's predicament that I hadn't even thought about what her news might mean for me. Suddenly I was overcome with so much excitement that I was speechless. Of course I would be traveling with Marguerite! Of course she would need her maid with her! I would be going to the royal city! I would get to see the king and queen, the spectacular palace, the famous bridges!

Nico would be there.

Goddess have mercy on my soul, *Nico would be there.* He must have been well aware that Cormac was considering Marguerite as a bride—and he had probably known that the prince would be inviting her back to the royal city. He must have realized that our light

101

summer romance would be extended—by a month, it seemed, and possibly for a lifetime. For a moment I was tempted to advocate for Marguerite's marriage to the prince. *I've reconsidered. It's your duty to marry to please your father. It's your responsibility to save the kingdom from civil war. The prince is handsome, and you will be a beautiful queen. Marry him! Marry him now!* But that was silly and selfish and even a little cruel. Besides, maybe I wouldn't be so keen on Nico once I knew him better. But it looked like I would get the chance to find out...

"Well?" Marguerite demanded. "You *are* coming, right? If I have to go, you have to."

I hopped up from the sofa just so I could sink down into a curtsey that practically brought my nose to my shoes. "My lady, I would be honored and delighted to accompany you to Camarria," I said. "Thank you so much for bringing me! I know you don't want to go—but I can hardly wait."

I could hardly wait for the dinner hour, either, so I could discuss this turn of events with Nico. But there were several long hours in between. I continued mending her wardrobe while Marguerite napped, then we began the lengthy process of dressing her for dinner. She had saved her most spectacular ensemble for last: a sleek lavender gown accented along the deep neckline and cap sleeves with rows of dangling pearls. Most of her jewelry this night consisted of amethysts and pearls, though she insisted on wearing the new onyx bracelet despite my protest that it did not match. But her headband, covered with carefully preserved violets and snowdrops, was perfection.

The echoes wore a darker shade of purple—and headpieces fitted with net veils that drifted prettily over their faces. It was the first time Marguerite was trying out the new fashion accessory in public. Prudence didn't like the veil; she kept tugging at the hem as if to pull it more tightly under her chin. Purpose found it annoying, I thought, as she repeatedly swiped her hand across her eyes as if to clear her vision. But Patience fooled with the placement of the headpiece until she had it exactly right, and then she stepped over to help Prudence adjust hers. I smiled as I watched.

Then I gaped at them. *I could tell them apart!* At this particular moment, as they were learning something new, I could see their distinct personalities. As soon as the stress passed, I was sure, they would all subside into anonymity again, since there was nothing except their behavior to differentiate one from the other. Still, I found it both amazing and a little unsettling that I had seen even this much separation between them.

"Oh, I do like the veils," Marguerite said, surveying them critically. "They'll cause a stir, don't you think? But a lovely one."

"I hope the echoes can manage to eat without getting food all over the netting."

Marguerite laughed. "I hadn't thought about that. Well, we'll see how it goes."

I made a few minor tweaks to her dress, patted her hair one last time, and then saw her out the door as the echoes trailed behind

Five minutes later, I was slipping through the kitchen, deaf to the undercook's muttered curse as she tried to scrape the leavings out of a pan of potatoes and scallions. I could have stayed to help, but I wanted to be outside. In the cool evening air—away from the chaos of the dinner party—on the street where some passing visitor might chance to be walking by...

Nico was waiting for me just around the corner of the mansion, standing in shadows thrown by the setting sun. At first I couldn't see him because his clothes were so dark and the shade was so deep, but I knew he would be there. He was always there whenever I went looking for him. He was always watching from some hidden spot—

I shook my head and summoned a saucy smile. "I thought you might be here," I said in a cheerful voice.

He took my hand and placed it in the crook of his bent elbow. "You *knew* I would be here," he corrected. "My last night in Oberton."

Without discussing any kind of plan, we started strolling down the street, skirting the main entrance of the mansion where carriages were even now rolling up and disgorging passengers.

"I have to give you credit, though," I said, my voice warm with approval. "You do know how to keep a secret."

"Uh-oh," he said. "I have a feeling this is a secret I should have shared."

I shot him a quick, accusing glance. "You knew, didn't you? That Marguerite would be invited to Camarria—and I would be going, too. You knew that this wouldn't be the last time I'd ever see you. You could have *told* me."

"Would it have changed anything?" he demanded. "Would you have spent more time with me—or less?"

"I don't know, but at least I wouldn't have felt so *bleak* about everything."

He grinned. "Maybe I liked you feeling bleak. Maybe I thought that would make you realize how much you were going to miss me. How much you like me."

"I won't like you very much if you insist on keeping things from me."

He laid his free hand over mine where it rested on his arm, and gave it a tight squeeze. "But how could I tell you? What if Cormac had determined there was no chance he and Marguerite would suit, so he decided not to invite her to Camarria after all? What if she had decided to take someone else with her—a different maid, more experienced than you? Why would I get your hopes up just to see them dashed? I *hoped* you would be coming to the city, but I didn't know for certain."

That was the problem with Nico, as I was starting to learn. Anytime you accused him of something, he had very reasonable answers to explain away his bad behavior. "You could at least pretend to apologize, even if you don't mean it," I informed him.

"Then I am sorry. *Very* sorry, especially if it ruins our last evening together here in Oberton! Because it will be three weeks before we are all in Camarria again, and that seems like a very long time for you to be angry with me."

"Well, I won't be angry if you find me something to eat," I decided. "I just walked out of the kitchen without looking anyone in the eyes, and I'm starving."

"I can find you food," he said, guiding me down a narrow side street.

I glanced back over my shoulder. The governor's mansion was the largest building in this section of town, and its big, rectangular bulk was coming to life as candlelight flared from half the rooms on every level. "I can't go far," I said. "She might need me."

"We'll buy food and bring it back," Nico promised.

We visited three nearby specialty shops that probably did a brisk business catering to the wealthy folks who frequented the mansion. One sold cheeses and fine breads, another wines and the raw fruits that made them, and a third sold pastries and exotic sweets. We loaded up with what was bidding fair to be the most decadent meal *I* had ever had, though I wouldn't have placed any bets on Nico, and headed back toward the mansion. There was a small square of parkland just a stone's throw from the back entrance—not much more than a carpet of grass, three trees, and a doleful fountain, but it served as greenery on the days any of the servants missed their rural roots. If, by some chance, Marguerite needed me during the course of the meal, any of the servants would know to step out the back door and look for me there.

Nico and I made our way to the park and settled right on the ground, our feet pointing toward the mansion and our backs against the stone of the fountain. Both the grass and the rock were pleasantly warm from the heat of the day, but the whole place was overhung with shadow—and, even better, deserted except for us.

We didn't have glasses or utensils, so we ate with our fingers and drank from the bottle. "To Camarria, and the old friends we might meet there!" Nico toasted me before handing me the wine.

I smiled and toasted back, "To Oberton, where those friendships began."

"How soon can you leave?" he asked. "How quickly can you arrive in Camarria?"

"You just said it would be three weeks before we were all in Camarria!" I exclaimed. "Doesn't the prince have other stops to make upon the road?"

"He does," Nico said, squirming a little to situate his back more comfortably against the fountain. "We're going to Alberta next, but I don't think we'll linger. He hates the young woman we'll be visiting next. Lady Elyssa."

"If he hates her, why visit her at all?"

He toasted me with the wine bottle again. "Because the king is trying to mend relations with all the western provinces, of course. There is much talk that there will be a marriage arranged between Elyssa and Prince Jordan, so I'm certain she, too, will be invited to the royal city."

"It sounds like it will be a very pleasant gathering," I said dryly.

Nico laughed. "Well, I do think it will be, for *some* of the invited guests. Cormac is also bringing in a handful of wealthy and eligible young men from the seven provinces, so there will be many opportunities for flirtation and romance. Cormac said he expects half the visitors will be betrothed before the year's end. Jamison said, 'No, there will be a crop of bastards by next spring.'"

"The more I hear about Lord Jamison, the less I like him."

"That puts you with the majority. But the king loves him, so don't be surprised to see him often when you're at the royal court."

"All right, but we don't have to talk about him any more tonight! Tell me who else might be in Camarria when we arrive."

So he offered names I didn't recognize, and I imagined them all dressed in lace-edged silk and trailed by echoes. He told me more about Camarria, its shops and markets and high bridges, and promised he would take me to visit its famous gardens. He said that the royal palace was so large that all of the visitors, and their echoes, would be given rooms within it, so that we would never be more than a few steps away from the next dinner, the next dance.

"Do you have rooms at the palace as well?" I asked in a low voice. We were by this time sitting very close, and various points of our bodies were touching—our shoulders, our hips, our knees, and our ankles. As soon as we finished our meal, he took my hands in his, and we alternately laced our fingers together and pulled our hands free. When I flattened my palm against his, I could see our hands were about the same size from heel to fingertip, but I was fascinated by how very differently they were shaped. I had long, quick fingers, thin and nimble; his were thick and broad, powerful, built for heavy work. I wondered how they would feel on my body, and then I blushed in the dark.

"I do have rooms at the palace," he answered, his voice as soft as mine. "So you will never be more than a few steps away from me, either."

"Well, I imagine you are often busy," I demurred. "Investigating situations for the king. You're probably gone a lot."

"True, but I always return. I don't think you'll have trouble finding me."

"If I'm ever looking for you."

"If you ever are," he said and leaned in and kissed me.

I kissed him back, straining up to meet his mouth and feeling my whole body flush with heat. He dropped my hands so he could wrap his arms around me, drawing me closer. Pulling my hips against his, he tightened his grip and rolled us so that I was lying with my back on the ground and he was above me, his mouth still on mine. I lifted my hands to the back of his neck, slipped my fingers beneath the collar of his shirt, felt the bunched muscles along the tops of his shoulders. His skin was warm and a little rough, and I splayed my fingers wide so I could feel as much of it as possible.

He made a grunt of satisfaction and freed one hand so he could run it the length of my body, from my thigh, up the curve of my hip bone, along my ribs. I caught his hand before he could do more than cup my left breast through the fabric of my dress. "Not yet and not here," I said breathlessly. "I'm not quite so wanton as all that."

"I suppose you need four walls and a bed," he said, sounding more amused than disappointed. I doubted he had expected me to allow more than a passionate embrace or two, though he wouldn't have minded more. "Women are just too civilized."

I kissed him quickly then pulled myself out of his arms, sitting up again so I could pat my hair and clothes into place. "I certainly need more privacy than I'd find outdoors in a park, not a hundred yards from where I work!" I exclaimed. "If you really hope to see me in Camarria, you'd better not do anything to get me sacked in Oberton."

"Excellent point," he said, flicking my nose with his finger, then bending down to kiss the spot his finger had touched. "Do you suppose you'll be fired if we just sit here, chastely embraced?"

He slipped one arm around me and I snuggled against him. "Well, Constance would probably want to send me packing, but I think Marguerite would give me another chance." Marguerite knew all about the allure of an illicit romance.

He rested his cheek on top of my head and reached for my hand with his free one. "So is she looking forward to the visit as much as you are?"

I didn't plan to gossip about Marguerite with the inquisitor's apprentice, so I answered cautiously, "She is quite pleased to be invited, but she realizes there is a great deal at stake, so she doesn't see it simply as the adventure I do."

Nico interpreted this with no trouble. "She realizes the king wants to improve relations with Orenza, so she could very well end up married to the prince."

"Which, of course, would be a great honor," I said, still speaking carefully, "but also a great responsibility."

"And a great sacrifice—if she doesn't fancy Cormac."

"I have no reason to think she doesn't like him."

"But does she like him enough to marry him?"

"Well," I said, perhaps more candidly than I should have, "I'm sure Marguerite expects her father to marry off to *someone* who will bring some advantage to Orenza. It might as well be Cormac."

"Even if she has another preference?" he asked. "Even if she'd rather marry whoever she's been meeting in secret at the temple?"

It was a moment before I registered what he'd just said. Then my whole body turned to ice and stone. Slowly, stiffly, I sat up, shook off his arm, and withdrew my hand from his. There was just enough light coming from nearby buildings that he could see the cold rage on my face.

"Brianna," he said, reaching for my hand again.

I hit him once, hard, in the chest. He caught my wrist before I could hit him again. "Brianna," he said a little louder.

"You've been *spying* on her," I said.

"It's what I do."

I broke free of his hold and scrambled to my feet. He jumped up and grabbed my arm before I could take a step. "You don't have to answer me," he began.

I wrenched away and shoved him in the stomach. I knew I couldn't win a physical fight with him, and that I probably shouldn't provoke him, but I was too angry to think clearly. But part of me was certain—even now—that he would never strike me back. At any rate, he didn't.

"I'm not *going* to answer you," I said furiously. "I'm not going to tell you *anything*. I'm not going to speak to you ever again!"

I whirled to leave, but he grabbed my arm again and this time he held on. "You don't have to tell me anything," he said, "but you should know—"

"I should know better than to fall for the king's sneaky inquisitor!" I cried. "You used me to find out about Marguerite! You tricked me and lied to me and pretended to like me—"

His fingers tightened on my arm. "I wasn't pretending."

"It wasn't even an accident that we met, was it?" I demanded. "You must have *followed* me that day. You were looking for a way to ingratiate yourself—"

"I did follow you, but I had no plans to introduce myself," he said, his voice rising a little as he started getting angry as well. "If you hadn't found yourself in trouble—"

"*Which* I got out of, not needing any help from you!"

"—I wouldn't have stopped. You never would have known that I was watching you. If you hadn't had that encounter on the road, I never would have bothered to speak to you."

"I wish you hadn't!"

There was a moment of silence between us. "Don't say that," he said quietly. "I know you don't think you can trust me. I know you think I'm being insincere—but I've enjoyed these hours with you so much. More than anything I can remember, really."

I jerked at my arm and this time he let me go. Once again I smoothed down my hair and my skirts, once again I gave him a look of pure venom, and then I began striding rapidly back toward the mansion. He quickly caught up and loped along beside me.

"You don't want to hear anything I have to say, but you better hear this," he said. "I don't know who Marguerite is meeting. I don't know what she's doing. But whatever it is, she needs to be careful."

I frowned in his direction but didn't slow my pace. "I didn't tell anyone what I saw," he went on. "And I won't. But I'm not the only inquisitor in the Seven Jewels. I never saw any of Del Morson's men nearby when I was following Marguerite, but that doesn't mean they weren't there. And if Prince Cormac decides he wants her for his bride, the scrutiny will be that much more intense. Once she's in Camarria—"

I stopped so hard he slammed into me, and it took us a moment of clutching at each other before we could regain our balance. Once we had, he immediately released me. "Nothing will happen in Camarria," I said. "Whoever he is, he won't be there."

Nico watched me in the dark. "How can you be so sure?"

I stared back at him. I couldn't be, of course. Even if her lover was married, even if he was an impoverished but handsome young street performer without a coin to his name, that didn't mean he couldn't show up in the royal city to trouble Marguerite's days. "Because it's too risky," I answered at last, then turned away and continued on toward the mansion. By now I was half-running, but Nico maintained an easy jog to keep up.

"It's risky for you, too," he said stubbornly.

I rolled my eyes. "What do you mean?"

"If you're aiding her. If she's doing something dangerous. If she gets caught, she won't be the only one swept up in the net. You might say you don't know anything, but who will believe you? I bet Del Morson could ask a lot of uncomfortable questions, and he'd keep asking until he broke you."

I'm not afraid of Del Morson, I wanted to say, but it wasn't true and Nico would know it. I had never been so furious in my life—no, not even when Robbie returned to the village with his pregnant wife on his arm—but I was also sick with fear. Nico was right; he wasn't the only inquisitor in town. Del Morson was more likely to be focused on the governor's enemies than his family members, but a man who'd gotten in the habit of curiosity could decide to wonder about any-body. Who knew what he might suspect? One thing seemed certain, though. If he was aware of Marguerite's questionable activities, he hadn't told Lady Dorothea. I couldn't even imagine the fit of rage she would have thrown if she thought Marguerite was jeopardizing her chance to marry the prince.

We were almost at the servants' entrance when Nico spoke again. "One more thing."

I didn't answer and I didn't stop, so he caught my arm again and pulled me to a halt. "I'm done talking to you," I snapped, but he didn't let go.

"One more thing," he repeated. "I'm not the only inquisitor in Camarria, either. My uncle must have a dozen men who report to him. You might look around and think no one's following you because you don't see *me*, but that doesn't mean you're safe."

"I've already told you, nothing's going to happen in Camarria."

He watched me a moment in the patchy light. "I want to see you when you're there," he said after a moment.

I yanked my arm free and loosed an exclamation of disbelief. "I don't think so!"

Now his face was starting to look stormy. "I didn't have to tell you," he pointed out. "I didn't have to let you know I was watching you. I chose to do it. I chose to warn you."

I was even angrier now. "You didn't tell me to *warn* me! You thought I would betray her! You thought I would tell you who she's seeing!"

"That's not why I said it!"

I came a step closer, though I managed to resist my urge to punch him again. "You thought all you had to do was kiss me and

I would whisper secrets about Marguerite," I hissed. "You thought I would pick you over her."

"I picked you over Cormac," he shot back. "I told *you* what I haven't told *him*."

I stuck my face right up in his and said in an evil whisper, "You haven't told him *yet*."

Now he grabbed both of my shoulders with a grip so tight I figured he was calling on all his willpower to resist shaking me until my eyes fell out of my head. "I won't," he ground out. "And I won't pressure you by pretending I *might* tell him. But you have to listen to me, Brianna. The minute Marguerite is engaged to Cormac, she will be watched from every corner. She cannot play games in Camarria."

"We'll be fine in Camarria," I said. "You can stop worrying about us."

"I think that won't be possible," he said. He bent his head and kissed me again, hard and fast. I was so surprised that, for a moment, I didn't even fight to get free. But the minute I shoved at his chest, now as angry with myself as I was with him, he let me go.

"I'll see you in a few weeks," he said in a somber voice.

The only retorts I could think of were childish and untrue, so I merely glared at him a moment and then ran away, pushing through the back door into the light and heat and clamor of the kitchen. I wanted nothing so much as to flee up to my room and huddle on my bed and think over all the emotional ups and downs of the evening. But the minute I stepped inside, the cook spotted me.

"Brianna! Gorsey, girl, can you lend us a hand? The pans need cleaning and the sweets need serving and that silly girl's gone into a fit of hysterics. If you could help—"

Work was always the best remedy for turmoil of the heart. "I certainly can," I said, grabbing an apron from a hook and heading for the sink. "Just tell me what you need me to do."

CHAPTER TEN

Marguerite and I set out for Camarria two weeks later, spending the first night of our journey at the Barking Dog. It had been Marguerite's suggestion, but I had been delighted by the notion, and I had instantly written to my mother to secure our rooms at the posting house. We were traveling in a large carriage with one coachman, two guards, and three echoes, so we were rather a numerous party for my mother's inn, and I wanted to make sure she could accommodate us.

"But this is utterly charming!" Marguerite said, peering out the window when the coach pulled to a halt.

Indeed, I felt my throat swell shut as I followed her gaze and looked out at the familiar scene. The main house was built of pale gray stone softened by climbing ivy and warmed by a terra-cotta roof. In these hot days of late summer, the flowerbed was a vibrant tangle of roses and dahlias, which my mother cultivated, and enthusiastic wildflowers, which she did not. Behind the main house were the other buildings so necessary to the running of the business— the stables, the smokehouse, the storage cellar. There were living creatures in motion everywhere: my stepfather leading horses into the barn, my brothers chasing down a pig, my sisters feeding the hens that strutted and squawked out back. If someone wanted to paint a mural of a bucolic paradise, this was the place he would come with his brushes and easels.

"How could you ever leave behind such a picturesque spot?" Marguerite demanded as she waited for the coachman to secure the horses and open the door.

I managed a laugh. "Well, this is the entire collection of delights," I told her. "A pretty scene at sunset on a warm day. But the rest of it is hard work and demanding customers and nosy neighbors, and nothing else to do with your time but dream about a better life."

"*I* think I could be quite happy here," Marguerite said

I could only laugh at her as the door swung wide and I took the coachman's hand. From the front door of the posting house, I saw my mother hurry out, the baby in her arms. Not until I clambered down from the coach did any of my siblings notice who had arrived—and even then, they didn't seem to realize who the really important visitor was.

"Brianna's here! Brianna's here!" my sisters cried, running toward me so fast that their braids streamed out like flags behind their backs.

A minute later, I was the center of a circle of laughing, shouting, jumping bodies. Even the dogs had joined us and, true to their namesake, they were barking their heads off. I was trying to answer my sisters' questions, return their kisses, and make sure Marguerite was safely out of the coach, all at the same time. But my mother had made her curtsey to the governor's daughter and drawn her out of the chaos, so I figured she would be just fine.

Suddenly everyone fell silent. I knew without looking that the echoes had climbed out of the carriage and arranged themselves behind Marguerite.

What will impress your family more? Marguerite had asked about an hour before we arrived. *If my echoes mimic my every move, or if they seem a little independent?* That was easy to answer because I think it was true for everyone in the Seven Jewels who didn't have echoes of their own: That flawless synchronization was absolutely spellbinding. That was what everyone wanted to see.

Marguerite lifted a hand to indicate the main building; Patience and Purpose and Prudence repeated the gesture. "Thank you so much for making room for us," she said. "I have been wanting to see this place ever since Brianna described it."

By this time my stepfather had joined us, and he made a stiff little bow. "We think it's special," he said. "We're glad you brought our girl back for at least a night."

"Let me show you to your room," my mother said, turning toward the house.

"You could at least give me the baby!" I exclaimed. That made everyone laugh, and the formality melted away as she handed me my newest little sister and everyone cooed over her blue eyes and goofy grin. Then my stepfather and my brothers took charge of the coach and the horses, as well as the coachman and the guards, while all the women paraded through the house.

"I've given you the biggest room, with two double beds," my mother said as she showed Marguerite into the prize room of the house. It was all blue chintz and white lace and handmade rag rugs—*so* unsophisticated, now that I knew what a truly fancy suite looked like—but Marguerite seemed delighted by its airy, welcoming feel. "But if you don't like to share a bed with one of your echoes, I can bring in a cot."

"I don't mind at all," Marguerite said. "No more than you mind sleeping with your own foot."

My mother's face went blank for a moment as she considered that. "I never thought of it that way," she said.

Marguerite perched on the edge of the bed and bounced a little, as if to test the springs; the echoes did the same. "But where will Brianna sleep?" Marguerite asked. "You might bring *her* a cot."

"She'll stay in her old room with us!" one of my sisters cried, tugging at my arm.

"Careful, don't make me the drop the baby," I said, smiling down at her, though inwardly I sighed. Three to a bed, and the youngest one kicking and muttering all night; not exactly conducive to sound sleeping, as I knew from experience. "We'll be leaving early in the morning," I warned her.

She stuck her tongue out. "*We* have to get up early to start the bread," she said. "We'll be awake before you are."

My oldest brother showed up just then, carrying some of the luggage. "Is this all you need for tonight, or should we bring all of it?" he asked. Glancing at my mother, he added, "There's a *lot*."

"And a separate coach coming behind us with more," I told him. "You have no idea how many trunks you need to clothe four women for a month's worth of balls and dinners."

"This will be fine," Marguerite answered him. "Thank you so much for bringing it up."

"We'll just let you get settled," my mother said, taking the baby from me and shooing all the children toward the door. "Dinner's in half an hour, unless you need more time."

"I'm starving," Marguerite said. "That's perfect."

Dinner was much plainer than the fare Marguerite was used to, but she seemed to genuinely appreciate it. When she learned we were the only guests for the night, she insisted the whole family join us at the table, and it was a merry meal indeed. Marguerite went out of her way to be gracious to everyone, and I could see that her warmth and sweetness were making my mother glow. Not because she treasured the kind words on her own behalf, but because she was thinking, *My lucky Brianna, to have fallen in with such a good mistress!* The girls vied for her attention and my brothers alternated between staring at her and giggling, for all the world like schoolboys nursing a crush on the teacher. Even my stepfather, who could be taciturn to the point of rudeness, exerted himself to join the conversation and appeared to be dazzled by her charm.

Within a remarkably short time, they'd all gotten past the strangeness of the echoes, though every once in a while I caught my stepfather or one of my sisters shooting a quick glance their way. We had placed Patience and Prudence and Purpose at the foot of the table, and they sat there with their usual placidity, eating when Marguerite ate and smiling when she smiled. They were odd but not obtrusive, and everyone managed to ignore them for the bulk of the evening.

"I hold to my original opinion," Marguerite said that night as I undressed her for bed. "I cannot imagine how you ever managed to tear yourself away from this place."

"You'd be begging for city life if you lived here more than a week," I told her. "No balls, no parties, no company to speak of, nothing but hard work and family meals and more hard work."

"And hours spent in the garden and sunshine on your face and no Del Morson creeping around behind you, trying to pry out your secrets," she countered.

I laughed and glanced around the room. "Del Morson would die of boredom here," I agreed. "Anything else you need?"

"I don't think so. I'll see you in the morning."

I made my way to my old room and got ready for bed in the few minutes of privacy I had before my sisters came tumbling through the door. As I braided my hair, I thought over that last exchange with Marguerite.

I had told her about my conversation with Nico, even though I didn't want to. I thought she might dismiss me on the spot, and I cried to myself to think I was losing the first job I had truly loved. But I couldn't bear for my silence to put her at risk; I couldn't bear for her to think she was safe when she was under such close observation. She had grown very still and withdrawn for a moment, then she had nodded once.

"Very well. Thank you for telling me. I know I've gotten careless."

"My lady, I am so, so sorry if I've put you in danger in any way—"

She shook her head. "It sounds like he would have followed you whether or not you flirted with him," she said. "The only difference now is that we know. If you had never spoken to him, he would still be watching you—watching *me*—but we would be entirely unaware."

"I didn't tell him anything. I would never tell him anything— well, I'll never speak to *him* again, but I won't tell anyone else, either! Please believe me! You can trust me with your life."

She'd impulsively reached out to lay her hand on my shoulder. "Brianna. You're the first person I ever *have* trusted. I'm lucky to have found you."

She felt lucky that I had come into her life and I felt lucky that I'd secured this spot in hers. I knew there was no such thing as friendship between two people at such different stations in life, but nonetheless, I thought that was what we had.

We were on the road shortly after dawn, stuffed full of a breakfast of eggs, bacon, bread, and cream. My mother and sisters cried to see me go, and I had to fight back tears, too, though I wasn't nearly as sad to leave as they were to see me go. Marguerite and the echoes blew kisses out the windows, and that cheered everyone up so much that they laughed as they waved goodbye.

Marguerite settled back against the seat cushions with a sigh. "Now, a long, dull four or five days of travel," she said.

I had brought a workbag with me and was already arranging some of the contents in my lap. "*I* will make good use of the time," I said.

"I can't believe you can sew with the carriage bouncing along the road."

"I'll probably stab my finger with the needle more than once," I admitted. "You'll have drops of my blood all over your headpieces."

She laughed. "If this was a magic tale, your blood would protect me from evil."

"If it would do that," I answered, "I'd gladly bleed on every piece of clothing you own."

She smiled and closed her eyes, preparing to nap. "I think the hairbands will be enough."

She had created quite a sensation, at that final dinner during Cormac's visit, when her echoes appeared behind her wearing their gauzy veils. That very night, we had decided that we should alter all the echoes' headpieces to include veils that could be pulled down anytime Marguerite wanted.

"Because my mother assures me I must do something in Camarria to seem unusual," she had said, her voice full of mockery. "I must have an *affectation*. Everyone must realize that I am special enough to deserve Prince Cormac's attention."

We passed much of that day and the next two in silence, with me sewing, Marguerite and the echoes sleeping or staring out the windows. Now and then I lifted my eyes from the project in my hands to watch the changing countryside. Orenza was in the northwest tip of the Seven Jewels, cradled by mountains and marked by brisk sunshine. Camarria was in the province of Sammerly at the northeastern edge of the realm, but to get there, we first had to travel fairly far south. The kingdom was roughly the shape of a very large, very fat V, with a deep cleft on the northern border created by an impassable rocky range. Orenza, Alberta, and Empara lay to the west of the cleft; Sammerly, Banchura, and Thelleron to the east. Pandrea was situated almost exactly halfway between the two halves of the kingdom, and had always managed to maintain good relations with the western provinces, even while staying loyal to the crown.

Our path lay along the Charamon Road for almost the entire journey. The farther south we traveled, the flatter the land became and the smoother the road. I spotted fewer sheep, more wheat fields, the occasional fruit orchard, and acres of farmland given over to all kinds of flowers. I didn't think the landscape was as spectacular as the countryside where I'd been born, but I suspected the life was easier.

On the third day after we left my mother's, we started heading northward again as we made it past the cleft. The terrain on the east side of the divide was neither as flat as the farmlands nor as rocky as the mountainous regions, but full of rolling hills and leafy valleys. I suspected it was at its most appealing in the autumn months, but it was pretty enough now. Though I still missed my mountains.

The following day, maybe a couple of hours past noon, the coachman made an unscheduled stop at a posting house that offered a haven between two widely separated towns. "Front horse has thrown a shoe," he told Marguerite as he came around to open the door. "Might need to be here an hour or two to get it replaced."

"Then let's go inside and see if there's a room where we might wait," Marguerite said. So we gathered up our things and followed her inside.

The proprietor, a large woman with an air of authority, was used to dealing with high nobles, and she whisked us off to a private parlor with a large picture window overlooking the back of the property. When she returned a few minutes later with a tray of refreshments, Marguerite pointed toward the glass.

"It looks like there's a path leading to a little gazebo," she said. "Could my companions and I go for a stroll?"

"Yes, it's a lovely walk, and you'll find a little lake if you continue just another quarter mile," the proprietor said.

Marguerite turned to me. "Oh, let's do that! I'm so tired of being cooped up in a carriage."

"Certainly, but you'll need to put on sturdier shoes," I said. "This is a country path, and likely to be rougher than you're used to."

The owner nodded. "It is that. I'll have one of the boys fetch your suitcase."

A half hour later, the five of us were fed, refreshed, and wearing our walking shoes. Purpose was right behind Marguerite as she headed for the door, but Prudence hung back, glancing around the parlor as if reluctant to leave. I couldn't help grinning as I followed them into the hall, down the stairs, and out the back door that led to the path.

The day was perfect—not too warm, cheerily sunny but not so bright you had to shield your eyes with your hand. Marguerite was feeling relaxed enough to completely release the echoes, so they dawdled behind her, each one looking at different aspects of the scenery and stepping at a slightly different pace. Patience even paused at the side of the road to watch a bee make its erratic route from one flowering bush to another.

We arrived at the gazebo and sat for a few moments, admiring the view, but Marguerite was restless. "I want to see the lake," she said.

"I don't mind, but it makes the walk back that much farther," I answered.

"Oh, pooh. I'll sleep in the carriage if a little exercise fatigues me that much."

I thought Prudence looked disapproving as we set out again, but Purpose was once again right on Marguerite's heels. We had to wind through a grove of elms and climb over a low hill, but then we saw the lake below us, curled sleepily between grassy green banks. A dirt path meandered around the whole perimeter, disappearing now and then behind small stands of trees. About fifty yards from where we stood, there was a tiny island off the left-hand shore and an arched wooden bridge connecting it to the mainland. Wooden benches were located at various points along the path so people could sit and enjoy the landscape.

"Isn't that pretty!" Marguerite exclaimed. "Let's go walk over the bridge." When Patience drooped with dismay, Marguerite patted her on the wrist. "And then we'll go back. I promise."

Before I could say *Let's go*, we all caught the sound of hoofbeats coming our way. Marguerite's features settled into a pout that reminded me of my sisters.

"How annoying. Now we have to share our adventure with strangers."

"Maybe they'll just keep riding," I said.

A single horse crested the hill and continued down toward us. What I noticed first was the sleek beauty of the animal, the fine clothing of the rider. A low noble, at the very least. Not until Marguerite muttered, *"Oh, no,"* did I squint at the rider to try and identify him. But his red-gold hair and beard, bright in the afternoon sunlight, were too distinctive to miss. The king's illegitimate son.

He trotted right up to us and, uninvited, swung down from the saddle. His handsome face was creased in a smile. "The landlady mentioned that exalted visitors had gone walking along this path, but she didn't tell me just how exalted they were!" was his greeting. He swept a deep bow that managed to seem insolent even though he performed it quite properly. "Lady Marguerite. How pleased I am to see you."

"Lord Jamison," she replied in much cooler tones. "What brings you here?"

He jerked his head toward the lake and the six of us began a slow stroll toward the walking path. "I had—ah—business in

Alberta, so I'm a few days behind my brother and his other companions," he said. "I stopped for lunch at the posting house and saw the fancy carriage and wondered who it might belong to." He ogled Marguerite with no attempt at subtlety. "I never dreamed it would be the onyx lady of the rocky north."

"One of our horses needs a shoe," she said, her manner barely civil.

"It's always one inconvenience after another on the road," he said. "But I'm glad I fell in with you. We never had much chance to talk in Oberton."

"Surely there will be plenty of chances in Camarria."

He appraised her again. "I like to take the opportunities as they arise."

Marguerite came to a standstill and we all skidded to a stop behind her. "I'm tired. My companions and I were just about to head back to the inn. Enjoy your walk."

"Hold a moment," Jamison said. Something about his silky tone made me jerk up my head and narrow my eyes. Marguerite must have had the same sense of misgiving. At any rate, she stayed in place. "I have something I want to ask you."

"What?" she said in a flat voice.

Now his eyes flicked over the echoes, lingered a little too long on me. He smiled. "Something I'd like to ask you in private, where no other interested parties can overhear."

Marguerite made no attempt to hide her irritation. "These are my echoes, and my maid. Anything you say to me can safely be said in front of them."

His gaze returned to her. "Can it?" he said softly. "Are you sure there's a name you're ready to have anyone hear when it's said aloud?"

I saw Marguerite flinch before she gave me one quick, wild look. I knew we were thinking much the same thing. *What does he know? Did Nico lie when he said he told Prince Cormac nothing? Did he keep silence with Cormac—but share his information with Jamison?* Given how contemptuously Nico had spoken of Jamison, I found that difficult to believe. But then, I obviously had no idea what Nico was capable of.

"Very well," she said in a glacial voice. "I will walk on a few paces with you. My companions will wait for us here."

Here was one of the benches set up to overlook the water. "Excellent," said Jamison, looping his horse's reins around the top slat. "We will only need to go a short distance."

Marguerite took a moment to sweep the echoes with one compelling glance. "Stay here," she said, gesturing at the bench. With great reluctance, the three of them perched on the very edge of the seat, all their bodies coiled in readiness to spring up if she changed her mind. Now she looked at me. "Keep them here," she said. "We'll be back in a moment."

As reluctant as the echoes, I sank to the bench as well. "My lady," I began, but she shook her head.

"Let's go," she said shortly to the royal bastard and took off at a quick walk. He caught up in two paces and attempted to take her arm, but she snatched it away. I saw him laugh.

The echoes and I stared after them, our eyes fixed on their diminishing forms. It was bad enough when they moved so far away we could no longer catch fragments of their conversation, but within five minutes, they'd disappeared into one of those inconvenient stands of trees. All of us strained forward, waiting for them to reappear farther down the walking path. Another five minutes passed, and they were still out of sight. Ten minutes.

The echoes moved restlessly on the bench, and I felt my own tension ratchet up. I imagined that they had stopped to argue and that the conversation had grown heated. Jamison had probably taunted Marguerite with the name of her lover—threatened to expose her—perhaps offered to stay silent if she paid him excessive sums of money. How would Marguerite respond? She was already convinced that the kingdom would descend to war if her marriage to Cormac did not go through. What might she promise to this disgraceful young man to keep him from sharing any revelations with the king?

The echoes grew more agitated, making those strange mewling sounds that proved they were deeply distressed. Purpose even came to her feet and stood there a moment, trembling. "Sit *down*," I said, tugging at her wrist. She allowed me to pull her back, though I could feel her yearning toward Marguerite with every ounce of energy in her body.

I was still holding on to Purpose when Patience shot up from the bench, uttering a wordless cry. I was so astonished that I released Purpose, and then suddenly all three of them were on their feet and running down the path. I pelted after them, trying to catch at their arms and shoulders, calling, *"No, no, no, turn back!"* But they raced on even faster, skimming weightlessly over the ground like the shadows they were.

They were blocking my vision just enough that I couldn't see clearly into the stand of trees, but all at once I heard a cry of fear or anger. *Marguerite!* I redoubled my speed and pushed through the line of echoes—and came upon a scene that flooded me with icy terror.

Marguerite was on the ground, struggling in Jamison's grip as he tried to force himself between her legs. Her skirts were bunched up over her bosom, and he clutched both of her wrists in one hand, high over her head. His own trousers were unlaced and he was thrusting at her with ugly eagerness. She was fighting hard but it was clear he would overcome her in a moment.

"My lady!" I shouted and flung myself forward, the echoes at my heels.

Jamison snarled and rolled to his knees, releasing Marguerite and lashing out at the four of us as we surged closer. Purpose was the first to reach him and start punching at his face, but he caught her around the waist and flung her from him so forcefully she crashed full length to the ground. Then Patience and Prudence and I fell on him, striking at his head and shoulders with our bare hands. Prudence clawed at his cheek hard enough to draw blood. He swiped at us, grunting and groaning like an animal, beating us back with his elbows and his fists. Not until Patience howled in pain did I realize he'd pulled a knife and was slashing at our flailing limbs.

Out of the corner of my eye, I saw Marguerite scrabble away, desperately trying to pull her clothing back in place. Patience was nursing a bleeding arm, but Prudence snuck up behind Jamison and kicked him ferociously in the back. Still on his knees, he howled and spun around, grabbed her around the thighs, and slammed her savagely to the ground, once, twice, a third time. I saw her mouth fall open, and her whole body grew ominously still.

"Prudence!" Marguerite shrieked, and Jamison swung her way. She, too, was on her knees, crawling toward the echo, when Jamison backhanded her across the face.

"Call them off!" he raged. "Call them off or I swear I'll break the neck of every last one!"

Unseen behind him, Purpose came running up, clutching a large rock she had found on the ground, and brought it crashing down on his head. He cried out and tried to spin around to swing at her, but he couldn't keep his balance. As he teetered there, one hand upraised to block her attack, she hit him with the rock again and again and again. Even when he crumpled to the ground, twitching in pain and shock, she continued to rain blows on his head.

"Stop! Purpose—*stop*! Great goddess, all of you *stop*!" Marguerite panted. "Brianna, help me! I'm not sure—I think—she isn't breathing—"

I hesitated a moment, standing over Jamison's still form with my fists at the ready, but he looked too battered to offer us much harm in the immediate future. Taking a few steps over, I sank to the ground next to Marguerite, who was cradling Prudence in her arms. Purpose and Patience dropped down beside us, making thin, keening sounds as they reached out to pat Marguerite and Prudence with their thin, nervous hands.

"Let me see her," I said, gently taking the echo's body from Marguerite's hands. I checked for a pulse, but it was hardly necessary. She wasn't breathing and her neck was twisted at an unnatural angle. It was clear that she was dead. "Marguerite—my lady. I'm so sorry. He killed her."

Marguerite loosed a heartbroken sob and doubled over so her face touched her legs, wrapping her arms around her head. Purpose and Patience wailed alongside her, crowding closer, their arms around her and each other in one tight knot of mourning. I smoothed back Prudence's blond hair and wiped some of the dirt from her cheeks and laid her gently on the ground.

Then I turned back to Marguerite and the remaining echoes and tucked my hands under their interwoven arms and urged them all to sit up. "Come on. It's terrible, I know, but we have more terrible work ahead of us. We have to figure out what we're going to do next."

Marguerite forced herself upright, showing me a face blotched with grief and marked by rage. "He *killed* her!" she repeated. "Prudence! The shyest, most harmless creature in the kingdom! How could he *do* that?"

"He's an awful man," I said. "But what do you do now? Do you tell Prince Cormac what happened? Do you tell the king? Will they believe you?"

Marguerite wiped her sleeve across her runny nose, so I hastily found a handkerchief she could use instead. "Of course I'll tell them! I'm sure my father wouldn't want me to do anything that might set the king against me, but everyone needs to know what an awful man he is."

I watched her steadily. "But Jamison knows something, doesn't he? Will he reveal it if you expose him?"

"He doesn't know as much as he thinks," she said grimly. "He can't harm me. Any more than he's already harmed me." She started crying again.

I pushed Purpose aside so I could scoot closer and put my arms around Marguerite. "I'm so, so sorry," I whispered into her hair. "I shouldn't have let him take you away from us. I should have followed no matter what he said. But it's all right now. We got here in time. Didn't we? Didn't we? Are you all right?"

"I'm fine," she answered in a shaky voice. "He was going to—but then you all showed up—"

"Purpose leading the charge," I said. "As you would expect. It was the echoes who knew that something was wrong. I just followed them."

Marguerite took a deep breath, smoothed back her hair, and visibly willed herself to calm. "I didn't know they could do that," she said quietly. "I didn't know they could fight for me."

"And fight so hard," I added. I looked over my shoulder to make sure, but Jamison was still unconscious. "But what are we going to do with Prudence? I'm not sure we can bring her with us to Camarria."

"Perhaps there's a cemetery nearby where they will let me lay her to rest."

"What happens to a person like you when one of her echoes dies?" I asked.

She looked so sad that I was sorry I had asked, but she answered anyway. "It doesn't happen very often. Echoes don't get sick unless their originals get sick, so they only die if there's an accident. I don't know what it will be like. I suspect I'll feel as if I've come down with a lung disease and I can't breathe normally. Or as if I'm dreaming and I can't make myself wake up."

I glanced at Purpose and Patience, who were kneeling beside us, almost motionless, like marionettes that had been set aside and weren't going to move again until someone came along and pulled their strings. At the moment, they were neither mimicking Marguerite nor acting independently—unless this show of stunned grief was their expression of independent thought. At the moment, I could only tell them apart because Patience was the one whose arm was still bleeding. "What happens to them if you die?"

She spread her fingers in a quick gesture of dispersal, like someone flinging water from her hands. "So do they. Instantly. Falling at my feet."

"I suppose that makes sense. Though it seems sad, somehow."

Marguerite nodded and lifted a hand to brush it lightly across first one echo's head, then the other. "I know. On my darkest days, when I thought it might be easier to die, I couldn't bear the thought that I would take them with me from this world."

Marguerite had been so unhappy she had thought about killing herself? When was this? "My lady," I began.

She shook her head and came to her feet, lifting her shoulders and giving the appearance of someone determined to pull herself together. Purpose and Patience rose beside her, and I more slowly stood up as well. "Now," said Marguerite, "we have to decide what to do with *him*. Do we just leave him here and let him wake up to his own blood and broken bones? Or do we revive him so we can let him know what stories we will carry to his father the king?"

"Revive him," I said. "Maybe we can fetch water from the lake and throw it in his face."

Marguerite stepped closer to Jamison and stooped over to give him a close inspection. "I think he's more badly hurt than I realized," she said uncertainly. "He's not moving at all."

Without consciously summoning the words, I began silently chanting a childhood prayer. *Great goddess, lady of mercy. Lay your hand upon us; oh never say you will abandon us now...*

"Let me see," I said, dropping back to my knees beside him. I put my hand to his cheek, to his neck just above his collarbone. His skin was warm and supple, but there was an odd quality to it, a stiffness. I couldn't find a heartbeat, though I pressed my fingers to his jugular, slipped my hand down the front of his shirt to flatten it over his chest. When I leaned closer, my cheek against his mouth, I couldn't feel a single exhalation of breath.

"My lady," I whispered, "he's dead."

CHAPTER ELEVEN

Marguerite clapped her hand over her mouth to muffle a cry, and spun away as if she couldn't bear to look at his body. The echoes copied her exactly. By the time I was on my feet, Marguerite had started shaking. She bent over, bracing her hands on her knees, and started choking as if she would vomit on her shoes. The echoes shivered and coughed beside her.

I rushed over to grab her and haul her upright. "Not now," I said grimly. "Not now! You cannot break down. We have to think."

She stared at me, her eyes so wide and unfocused that I wasn't sure she was even seeing my face. "Dead!" she cried. "I killed a man!"

I couldn't help glancing at Purpose. "Not you, exactly."

"The echoes are mine! They're *me*! They couldn't have killed him if I didn't want him dead! I killed him, and I'll be executed for murder!"

"If we explain what happened—"

She covered her cheeks with her hands and shook her head. "Maybe, if he were any other man!" she said wildly. "But he is the *king's son*!"

"My lady—"

She pressed her hands harder against her cheekbones. "I can't think. I don't know what to do."

"We'll go back to Oberton," I began, but she shook her head even more violently.

"I can't go home! Sweet goddess, my father sent me off to marry the prince and instead I murdered Cormac's *brother*! Oh, if the provinces weren't at war before, they will surely be fighting now! The king will *destroy* Orenza! And it's all my fault— I have to flee," she said suddenly. "I have to run, but where? Where can I possibly hide?"

Her desperation was swamping me with a reckless combination of fear and determination. "If no one knows he's dead, no one can accuse you of murder," I said. "We'll hide the body."

"How? Where?"

I pointed. "We'll weigh him down and throw him in the lake. By the time they find him, if they ever do, his body will be so rotted no one will recognize him." I knew this because a young man had died in such a manner not far from the Barking Dog when I was a little girl. We never learned who he was.

"His clothes—"

"We'll strip him and donate all his belongings to one of the temples in Camarria."

"His horse—"

"We'll strip it, too, and set it free. Trust me, some small freeholder in the area will come across it in a day or two and take it for his own, asking no questions."

"Maybe. It might work. Maybe," Marguerite said, looking slightly less dazed.

"It will work. It has to. Let's find some logs and rocks to tie to his body," I said, turning away.

"Oh, but Prudence!" Marguerite exclaimed.

"We can think about her later."

She caught my arm. "I can't ride into Camarria with only two echoes," she said in an intense voice. "It will be odd. And when Jamison fails to arrive, *that* will be odd. Someone will start putting those two odd things together. If not the prince, then your friend Nico. They will figure out that Jamison passed through here at much the same time I did—it will not be hard to reconstruct our journeys."

She was right. The landlady herself could tell any inquisitor that Jamison had gone looking for Marguerite just minutes after she stepped out of the inn. *You'd be surprised at how willing ordinary citizens are to gossip about their neighbors,* Nico had told me weeks ago. *People are always eager to tattle on their friends.*

Even more eager, no doubt, to tattle on strangers.

"Then you'll just have to have three echoes when you arrive in Camarria," I said calmly.

Her expression was hopeless. "How will I manage that?"

I laid a hand across my heart. "I will have to masquerade as Prudence."

She stared at me a moment in silence. They all did, their identical faces wearing identical looks of disbelief.

"You can't possibly be serious," she said at last.

"I am. We're the same height, almost the same build, so with a few alternations I can wear all of her clothes—"

"Your hair is five shades darker and your eyes are a different color, and your face looks nothing like my face—"

"Some lemon juice and vinegar and I can lighten my hair—maybe even buy a wig once we're in Camarria."

"But your face!"

"The veils," I said. "The three of us will wear veils all the time. It will be your affectation. No one will look too closely."

Now she pressed the heel of her hand to her forehead. "I can't think," she said again.

I pulled her hand away. "It will work. It has to. People will expect to see you with three echoes, so they'll see you with three echoes."

"But—but—eating! And dancing! And just walking into a room—"

I shrugged. "I'll mimic you as best I can. We can make sure I'm always between the other two so that I can watch them *and* you."

Once again, she stared at me for a long moment in silence. "It's so dangerous," she said at last. "One mistake—one person realizing you're not who you're pretending to be—"

"It's already dangerous," I interrupted.

"Dangerous for *me*! Not for you! But if you play this game alongside me and we get caught—your life could be forfeit, too."

I motioned with both hands, and Patience and Purpose came a few steps closer. I put my arms around their shoulders, and they put their arms around Marguerite, and we all drew so close that our foreheads touched. "I'm not leaving you," I said in a low voice. "I'm not betraying you. We will go to Camarria, and we will play this game, and no one will ever know."

Marguerite and the echoes all closed their eyes. I knew she didn't believe me—I wasn't sure I believed me, either—but I absolutely could not see another way. After a moment, she nodded.

I pulled back and pressed my hands together, nerving myself for a hard job. "All right. Let's get rid of the bodies."

I don't want to describe the next hour, which was as gruesome and sad and unsettling as any I've ever spent. I'll just say that we carried out my plan, horrific as it was. We took from Jamison's body every piece of jewelry, every bit of clothing that might identify him. Then we stuffed rocks and branches down his underthings to add weight, and dragged him over the path and up the bridge. It took all four of us, each holding one of his limbs, to heave him over the railing and into the water. We stood there watching for ten fearful minutes, but he did not bob back to the surface. It seemed we had bought ourselves at least a little time.

We treated Prudence much the same way, though we were gentler with her broken body than we had been with Jamison's. And we did not throw her half-naked into the lake. Once I had swapped my clothes for hers, we put mine on her. Nothing in the details of my dress would give away my identity or link her to Marguerite, and we could not bear to send her to that unfriendly grave without giving her the smallest scrap of honor.

Then we stood there on the bridge, arms linked, staring down, waiting to see if our efforts were thorough enough. Apparently they were. Prudence did not rise to the surface, either.

After a long, silent, dreadful spell of waiting, I tugged on Marguerite's arm. "Come on. We have to get back to the inn. The coachman's probably been waiting half an hour already."

We crossed back to land and did what we could to erase all traces of the skirmish. Jamison's clothes we folded into a square bundle covered tightly with his velvet jacket. My hope was that it might look like a pillow Marguerite had brought along on our walk.

Then we put a little more attention into my appearance. As I had suspected, I was easily able to fit into Prudence's dress, though it was a little tight in the bosom and waist, since I was heavier than Marguerite. The biggest problem at this point was my hair, so much darker than Marguerite's blond. But, as luck would have it, today the four of them had been wearing blue summer dresses ornamented with exaggerated lace collars almost as sizable as shawls. We carefully ripped each collar from its neckline to fashion impromptu scarves to wear over our heads and shade our faces. The disguise was imperfect—but I hoped it would be good enough for any casual observers.

"If anyone asks, say the sun was hot and you wanted to shield your complexion," I told Marguerite. She nodded. She had hardly spoken at all during these grim activities and showed almost no volition of her own. If I had not been there to direct them, I thought she and the echoes might have simply sat on the ground between the two corpses, crumpled against each other, and waited until someone came along and found them.

Disastrous on so many counts. Though I could not be certain our present course of action would be any less ruinous.

Our last chore was to strip and free the horse. Marguerite had no idea how to remove a saddle or bridle; fortunately, I had plenty of experience with those tasks. Within a few minutes, I had tossed the final items into the forgiving lake. *We better hope there's not a drought in the next few months,* I thought as I watched the last ripples fade away. By the time I returned to the others, the horse had already drifted off a few yards, nibbling at the wilted green grass. I figured it would only be a matter of hours before he had wandered a couple of miles away.

I gestured at the path. "Nothing else to do here. Let's go back. Marguerite, I'll walk behind you and try to copy your movements. Purpose, Patience, you walk on either side of me. I think people are less likely to notice me if I'm in the middle of the group. Nudge me if I do something wrong."

Without a word, Marguerite set off, the three of us right behind her. I studied her posture, the set of her head, the way she held her hands very carefully at her sides as if she had been told that swinging her arms while she walked was unladylike behavior. The sun beat down on my makeshift veil and threw a spiderweb of shadows across my face. I tried not to sweat, but between the heat and the tension, it was hard to stay cool.

I had hoped we could slip unseen into the posting house and up to our private parlor, but the proprietor appeared to be on the lookout for us, for she greeted us the minute we arrived at the back door.

"Your coachman says he's ready to leave when you are," she said. "We've already had your things put back in the carriage."

"Thank you," Marguerite said in a faint voice. "Might we have a few moments in the parlor to tidy up? It was so much hotter than I expected."

"Certainly! I'll have tea brought up, shall I?"

"I would appreciate that."

The four of us had just filed past her into the kitchen when the landlady spoke again. "What happened to your maid, then?"

I froze, and not just because Marguerite did. Even if I could have thought of a response, I couldn't have uttered it; echoes never said a word. But it scarcely mattered—my mind was a blank.

Marguerite hesitated only a moment, so briefly perhaps the other woman didn't notice. "She encountered a friend and stayed behind to visit. She'll catch up in a day or two."

I was watching the proprietor, praying she would accept this flimsy excuse, so I saw sharp comprehension come to her face. "Oh! That fancy man who came through here, wanting to know who owned your carriage."

My stomach clenched, but Marguerite nodded. "You're exactly right. I was—ah—surprised to see how well they were acquainted."

"I know it's not my place to say so, but anytime one of my servant girls starts carrying on with a noble, high or low, I just let her go on the spot. Nothing but trouble comes from such things, I'm sorry to say."

Marguerite turned away from her. "I'm afraid you're right. If she ever does show up in Camarria, I'll be astonished."

Marguerite and I were out of the kitchen, Patience and Purpose at our heels, when the innkeeper called after us, "If you need a maid, now, my sister's girl is just a ten-minute ride away."

"Thank you, I shall make do until Camarria!" Marguerite called back, and we all kept walking.

The minute we arrived in the room, we threw the door shut and all four of us sagged against it, trembling and trying not to break down. Only for a moment—there was too much still to do. I was the one to pull myself upright and square my shoulders.

"Now. We must clean ourselves up. Bind that wound on Patience's arm. Make sure none of us have blood on our clothing. And put on better disguises! Here's my workbag—excellent. I have three headpieces ready to go."

Within twenty minutes, we were refreshed and fed, and we had exchanged our erstwhile lace collars for actual veils. Standing between Purpose and Patience, I studied myself in the mirror. With the headpiece in place, the netting pulled down to my chin, I looked enough like them that it would take a hard second look for someone to notice that my hair was darker and my body softer. It was possible we would pull this off, after all.

"The netting hides my face and eyes well enough," I said. "My hair is the real problem. I just have to design headpieces with a lot of fabric, I think."

Marguerite came close enough to make a fourth nearly identical shape in the mirror. "Brianna, are you *sure*—"

I turned away and began gathering up my things. "I'm sure. Let's go."

We had one more bad moment, when the coachman was helping us all into the carriage. "Where's Brianna?" he asked.

I was actually the one holding his hand when he asked the question, and my fingers involuntarily tightened over his. I wasn't well acquainted with the man; like the guards, he'd been hired to take us on this journey, since Lord Garvin couldn't bear the inconvenience of sending his own staff away for an entire month. But he was usually the one Lady Dorothea requested when she needed an extra driver, so he was frequently in and out of the servant's hall. He knew me—and he would know, as the landlady did not, that I wasn't the kind to take a tumble with random noblemen. There was no way I could communicate this information to Marguerite as I climbed inside and took my place beside her. I closed my eyes behind the veil and waited for doom to fall.

But Marguerite was proving to be an unexpectedly adept liar. "Brianna twisted her ankle when we went for a walk," she said. "I insisted she stay behind until she feels better. She can come in with the second coach."

That seemed to satisfy him. "Should I go tell the head groom to flag down the second coach when it comes by? They might not be planning to stop here."

"I've already asked the proprietor to speak to him."

"All right, then. We'll be on our way."

The four of us sat, rigid on our benches, until we felt the carriage rock with the weight of the coachman taking his seat, until we saw the two guards trot up on their horses, until we finally felt the vehicle jolt into motion and slowly pick up speed. Half a mile away from this accursed spot…a mile…five. Only then did any of us relax; only then did any of us take more than the shallowest breath. Marguerite doubled over and began sobbing silently into her skirt; Purpose and Patience did the same.

Not me. I sat bolt upright, one hand resting on Marguerite's back, and stared out the window with fierce concentration. It was only now sinking in that I had witnessed two murders and helped organize an elaborate scheme to conceal them. The horrors of this day would haunt me forever, whether or not anyone ever discovered what we had done. If we *were* found out, Marguerite's life could be forfeit, and possibly mine as well.

We would have to be very, very careful in Camarria if we hoped to make it home alive.

CHAPTER TWELVE

For the rest of the journey, Marguerite and I practiced lies and gestures.

I sat beside her in the coach, learning to watch her from the corner of my eye and to detect the small motions that signaled bigger ones she intended to make. For instance, her right hand would twitch slightly just before she raised and extended it to greet an acquaintance. Her chin would dip a fraction of an inch before she turned her head to peer over her left shoulder. Marguerite had always moved with a certain stateliness, but now she was slowing down to an even more deliberate pace in the hope of allowing me to match her, only one or two heartbeats behind.

Six days after we left Oberton, we arrived in Camarria, and we all took turns leaning out the window to get our first glimpses of the royal city. My overall impression was one of size. From what we could see from the carriage, it covered about three times as much land as Oberton, but it wasn't just bigger in terms of sprawl; it also claimed more height. In Oberton, the governor's five-story mansion was the tallest structure in the city. In Camarria, even from some distance away, I could see whole clusters of buildings that were even taller.

Even that wasn't the most impressive feature. Nico had mentioned Camarria's bridges, but I hadn't been able to picture what they looked like or how many there could be. But we passed dozens of them, all over the city, short ones linking one building to another, long ones arching over busy commercial districts. They appeared to have been constructed throughout the course of centuries because they came in all styles and materials. I saw a flat wooden walkway laid across the rooftops of two old commercial buildings; a short distance away arched a graceful construction of elegant white stone that incorporated decorative disks of black marble. When we got close enough to make out details, we could see the shapes of people hurrying across every span. Camarria appeared to be a city constantly on the move.

Despite the fact that the city was packed with carriages and pedestrians, traffic moved at a decent pace through the wide and well-kept streets. It wasn't long before we arrived at the palace, a magnificent building in the heart of the city. It was constructed of warm red brick accented with white stone and black wrought iron; the copper roof was green with verdigris. I lost count of the turrets poking up at every seam and corner, their roofs gathering into sharp points that pierced the afternoon sky. Two gently curving wings extended from the palace proper to create a paved courtyard enclosed on three sides. And the courtyard was overrun with horses, carriages, brisk soldiers, fine nobles, servants, and the occasional cat.

"Just looking out the windows as we drove in, I thought it would be easy to get lost in the city," Marguerite murmured. "Now I'm wondering if I might get lost in the palace."

"We'll figure it out," I said with more confidence than I felt.

She glanced at me as the carriage slowed in front of the massive doors. "Are you ready?"

I pulled my veil down to my chin, and the echoes did the same. Today we were all wearing simple green traveling dresses and headpieces wrapped with so much netting that it obscured our hair as well as our faces. "I better be."

She took a deep breath. "Me, too."

A minute later, the carriage came to a halt. A palace servant opened the door and helped us out, one by one. Marguerite made her way across the courtyard and into the grand foyer of the palace. I followed directly behind her, with Patience and Purpose on either side of me and one pace back. We moved in lockstep, our feet echoing on the polished marble of the floor, our heads lifting simultaneously to take in the high painted ceiling. Then we paused a moment to glance around the whole foyer, which was dotted with people—more servants, more guards, a smattering of visitors, and several ornamental suits of armor that *looked* like people, even though they weren't.

A tall, ample woman approached, holding herself with the self-importance of a high-ranking servant, and we all turned our attention to her. She was clearly well briefed on who might be arriving on any given day, for her greeting was a curtsey and a question. "Lady Marguerite Andolin?"

"Yes."

"Welcome to Camarria. I am Lourdes, the head housekeeper. You may send me word anytime you need anything."

"Thank you."

"I have set aside rooms for you in the east wing, where we are placing all the young ladies who are coming to visit."

"Are many of the others here already?"

"I believe all but two have arrived, and we expect them before nightfall."

"How many guests will be here altogether?"

"Twenty-two. Twelve women and ten men."

"It sounds very splendid!"

"Indeed, I believe it will be," said Lourdes. If she was anything like Constance, I thought, her sole goal in life would be to present her household, and the people within it, in the best possible light; she would see the royal family as extensions of herself, and their hospitality as wholly dependent on her management skill. In her own way, she was even more of a shadow to them than I was to Marguerite. "I will have one of the girls show you up to your rooms. Is your luggage outside with the coach?"

"Some of it. A separate coach will arrive in a day or two."

"Very good." I saw Lourdes's eyes flick from Marguerite to the three echoes and keep searching. "Is your maid outside with the coach as well?"

"Brianna had an errand to run for me when we arrived in the city, but she will be here within an hour or two," Marguerite said smoothly. We had debated this lie endlessly during the last two days. We had quickly decided to abandon the notion that I had run off or been dismissed; if Marguerite showed up without a maid, the housekeeper would undoubtedly offer to supply one, and we couldn't risk having a stranger around us. No, I must arrive as an echo, slip out as a stealthy stranger, and return as a maid, making sure that Lourdes or someone on her staff met me and knew I was on the job.

"Very well. I will have her shown to your rooms when she gets here."

"Thank you," Marguerite said.

"Dinner will be served in the dining hall at six," Lourdes went on, motioning to a passing serving girl. "Some of the visitors gather in the adjoining parlor beforehand, if you would like to join them there."

"Certainly. I look forward to it."

Lourdes gave instructions to the servant, and the four of us turned as one to follow the girl toward a wide doorway opening from the cavernous foyer. I was concentrating hard on synchronizing my movements with Marguerite's, so I couldn't say what sound or motion caused me to glance sideways at a shape that lurked near one of the suits of armor. And then I was so unnerved that I almost missed a step.

It was Nico Burken, and he had clearly witnessed Marguerite's arrival. From the corner of my eye, I could see his slight frown as he assessed the fact that I wasn't with her. I wondered if I could guess at the thoughts going through his mind right now: *Did Marguerite fire Brianna, or did she choose not to come? Did her mother fall sick—or did she want to avoid seeing me?*

He pressed his lips together and narrowed his eyelids as he watched us pass. I held my breath, but his gaze passed right over me without registering my face. Another few paces and we were out of his sight.

❧ ❧ ❧

Although the palace was enormous, it was methodically laid out, and it was clear Marguerite and I would have no trouble finding our way back downstairs at the dinner hour. Her suite on the third floor was elegantly appointed, with fine mahogany furniture and delicate silk hangings, though it was not nearly as large as her rooms back home. In fact, it consisted of only two connected chambers— a small but pleasant sitting room, and a large bedroom with four beds. One was wide and plush, covered with a dozen pillows and a lace duvet; the other three were comfortable but narrow, lined up in a row on the side of the room.

"The echoes don't get their own room?" I said stupidly.

Marguerite shook her head. "In most houses, they don't. Even my parents and my brothers have their echoes in their rooms with them. I created something of a stir when I insisted on the extra space. I think I was twelve years old."

"And you'd already learned their different personalities."

Marguerite perched on the edge of her bed, and Patience and Purpose and I each sat on our own. "Which I tried not to talk about. I can't remember how I finally convinced my father to give me an expanded suite. But my brothers made fun of me for weeks."

"Do you mind sharing a room with them?"

She shook her head. "No, I think I'll find it comforting that they're here. Although I'll keep thinking— I'll keep looking around and feeling like … like …" She pressed her fingers to her mouth and shook her head.

When I came hastily to my feet, she shook her head again and extended her other hand to hold me off. I stood there helplessly and said, "So how are you doing? You haven't been willing to talk about it much in the past two days."

"I'm doing—as well as I can, I guess," she said. She dropped her palms to the bed and leaned back in a half-stretch. "I keep feeling like I can't get enough air. I keep feeling like there's a patch over my eye, so I can't see everything that's in front of me. Like I've broken the heel off of one shoe and I'm limping along with one hip higher than the other. Like the world is incomplete, or my ability to comprehend it is incomplete. I'm not explaining it very well."

"Well enough," I said. "That's how I felt when Robbie came home married to another girl."

She smiled painfully. "So what I'm feeling is grief and loss."

"From what I know of both of them, they eventually heal," I said. "But I don't know how long it will take."

She dropped back so she was half lying on the bed, though her feet were still on the floor. "Maybe I don't want them to heal," she said. "Maybe I don't want to forget Prudence."

"Healing isn't the same as forgetting," I said, crossing the room to kneel by one of the trunks. "It's just a way to live with pain."

I unpacked one of my own plain dresses and shook out the wrinkles. "Time for me to make my appearance, I think," I said.

I changed clothes, then picked up a woven straw bag and stuffed a small square bundle inside. Jamison's clothes, still folded in the shape of a pillow. Marguerite watched me with shadowed eyes.

"What will you do with his things?" she asked.

"There will be a temple. Or a beggar. Someplace I can drop them off."

"Be careful," she said.

My only answer was a shrug. Too late for that. I said, "I'll be back in an hour or two."

Stepping into the hallway, I made my best guess as to where the servants' stairwell would be. The palace was so well organized that it was easy to find, and I headed downstairs toward the general direction of purposeful clatter. I only encountered a few other maids and footmen on my way—half in palace livery, half wearing the colors of the visiting guests—but I moved with such self-confidence that no one offered me assistance. I was able to slip outside through the kitchen and work my way around the outer edge of one of those great, curving wings of the palace without encountering anyone who asked my business. Only then did I take a deep sigh of relief.

I spent a few minutes investigating the streets nearest to the palace, admiring the well-kept facades of the buildings, which seemed to be a mix of commercial and residential establishments. Only the extremely wealthy would live this close to the king, I supposed, and all the shops in the vicinity would carry the highest-quality merchandise. Every person I passed was dressed at the height of elegance, even the maids and valets, who looked almost as fashionable, and even more arrogant, than the nobles they served.

About eight blocks from the palace, I came across the thing I'd been looking for: a wooden hut about the size of three large men huddled together, with a wide slit at the top of a padlocked door. A pauper's box, which I'd first encountered in Oberton, since no such amenity existed in the village where I'd grown up. Temple priestesses used the boxes to collect donations for the poor, Aunt Jean had told me, selling anything of value and distributing anything of use. I resisted the urge to glance around furtively, and just marched boldly up to the receptacle and slipped my bundle through the slot. I immediately felt as if I had dropped off an anvil; my heart felt lighter than it had in days.

Now I was free to wander with even less purpose, and I aimlessly crossed streets and picked my way across low bridges and peered through shop windows to see what items might be on display. I had been out for nearly an hour when I came across a small plaza with a pretty fountain, a ring of white stone statues, and three flower vendors. I had been wondering how quickly I would be able to get directions to a commercial district where fresh blossoms would be available, so I was delighted to stumble across these small-time merchants. They didn't have much variety and their prices were ridiculously high, but I was so pleased to be able to bring back flowers for Marguerite's first appearance that I didn't even care.

My hands full of dripping bouquets, I turned back toward the palace, debating my return strategy. I would like Lourdes to see me enter the building because she seemed like the kind of person who wanted to keep track of every soul under her roof, and I didn't want her hunting for me when I was pretending to be someone else.

Yet servants always entered through the back door, even when they were arriving someplace for the first time. Maybe I would get lucky and Lourdes would be patrolling the back regions of the palace when I walked in. Otherwise—

"You're so deep in thought," said a voice beside me, startling me so much I almost dropped the flowers. "Are you plotting a revolution?"

It was Nico. He fell in step beside me as I scowled at him and tried to calm my galloping heartbeat. "How long have you been following me?" I demanded. *Have you been trailing me ever since I stepped out of palace? Are you wondering why you saw me leave when you never saw me arrive? Even worse, did you see me drop Jamison's clothes into the pauper's box?* That last thought made my heart pound even harder.

"For about three seconds," he said. "I was off to run an errand when I spotted you buying flowers. Exactly what I would have expected you to be doing."

"Marguerite wanted something special for tonight, so I volunteered to go looking. I got out of the coach before we even arrived at the palace," I said, clumsily filling in details to our sketchy story. "I'd almost given up when I came across those vendors."

"Oh, there's a much better market not far from here," Nico said. "I'll take you there some morning."

"No, you won't."

"Why not?"

I was flustered. "Because I'm not speaking to you!"

"It *seems* like you're speaking to me."

"That's because you surprised me."

He grinned. "If that's all it takes, be prepared to be surprised on a regular basis."

"It's hardly a surprise if you're prepared," I snapped.

That made him throw back his head and laugh, which left me even more ruffled. "All right, then," he said genially. "I'll just surprise you with no warning. Forget I mentioned it."

All this time we had been continuing back toward the palace, but now I drew out of the way of the other pedestrians and came to a halt. "Don't you understand?" I exclaimed. "I'm *angry* with you. I don't *trust* you. I don't *want* you to pop up every time I turn around. I want you to leave me alone."

He stared down at me, now as serious as I was. "I understand that you're angry, but you're not being fair," he said. "If anything, I think I've proved that you *can* trust me."

"You lied to me!"

"I told you the truth when it mattered," he shot back. "Can you say the same thing to me?"

I opened my mouth, and then snapped it shut again.

Well, no. I couldn't. I hadn't lied to him yet, as it happened, but I was about to lie to him, to his master, to everyone at court. I would do so every day for as long as we were in Camarria. The fact that I was lying made it even more imperative to keep him at a distance because he was the very last person I wanted to discover the truth.

But maybe…

Maybe if I avoided him, he would just become more intrigued. He would be *more* likely to spy on me, trying to guess my secrets. Whereas if I relented, if I seemed to forgive him, he would be more relaxed. He would accept whatever time I had to give him, and not wonder what else I had going on in my life. Maybe I would be *helping* Marguerite, not harming her, if I kept Nico as my friend.

I had been silent so long that he started to grow amused. "What dark thoughts are tumbling through your head?" he asked. "Maybe you really *are* planning a revolution."

"If I was, you'd be the last person I'd tell about it," I said tartly.

"Well, I'd recommend against leading a rebellion," he said. "I know all you folks from Orenza want to rise up against the king, but that only leads to bloodshed and heartache. I'm sure you don't really want that."

"You're right," I said. "I suppose I'd better abandon my plans." I slipped back into the flow of traffic and started toward the palace again. Nico fell in step beside me.

"So we're agreed then," he said, as if we had actually talked out the tangle that lay between us. "Forgiveness on all sides, and no more lies. And friends again."

"We're *not* agreed," I said, "but I am willing to start over."

"From the very beginning?" He looked around, as if searching the streets for someone. "There's a promising urchin. Pickpocket, unless I miss my guess. Go see if he'd like to rob you and I'll come to your rescue again."

I was tricked into a laugh. "I rescued myself, thank you very much."

"Eh, maybe you did, maybe you didn't. If I hadn't come along, things might have turned out very differently."

I would have disputed that, except I was silenced by a sudden, vivid memory of Marguerite struggling in Lord Jamison's brutal embrace. It had taken five of us to vanquish him—and at such a terrible cost. I had to fight off a shiver.

"I suppose we can each have our own opinions on that score, but it hardly matters," I said in a frosty voice. "I don't think we need to go quite that far back."

"So let me guess where you think we should be in our timetable," he said. He seemed to be enjoying himself immensely. "Perhaps the second or third time we happened across each other in the flower markets?" He glanced down at me. "Unless you'd like to move ahead a few days. To after the kiss by the fountain but before the fight in the street. My very favorite moment, in fact."

He was outrageous, but I wouldn't let him see how appealing I thought he was. *Never forget how dangerous this man can be,* I reminded myself sternly. "The flower markets are the best you can hope for," I told him. "Be thankful for that much."

"Oh, I am. But I shall look ahead to the days when we might get better acquainted—again."

I shot him a dark look, which made him laugh. "So I suppose now I need to make polite conversation as we get to know each other," he said. "How was your journey to Camarria? Pleasant, I hope?"

Goddess have mercy on my soul. *Pleasant.* "It seemed like a very long trip," I said. "It was wearisome to be in the coach for so many days. How was your visit to Alberta?"

Nico grimaced. "More eventful than we were hoping."

"Why? What happened?"

"Lord Jamison—you remember him?"

I almost choked on my own saliva. "The prince's half brother. Of course I remember him."

"He was up to his old tricks in Alberta, and a young lady's brother took exception to his antics—and Cormac wouldn't defend Jamison. In fact, they had a huge fight. Cormac insisted Jamison stay behind to make amends, so the rest of us rode on without him."

I caught my breath. Merciful goddess, could we really be this lucky? How deeply had Cormac been disgusted? "Do you think the prince will complain about his brother to the king? Do you think Jamison might be banished from court?"

"I admit I entertained some of the same thoughts," Nico said, "but just today I heard Cormac say something about what he would plan 'when Jamison gets here.' I suppose Cormac has already forgiven him, but maybe Jamison will have learned his lesson from this. Maybe he will become a little better behaved."

I knew for a fact that not only had Jamison failed to learn his lesson, but now he would never have a chance to do so. Since I obviously couldn't say that, I merely replied, "I suppose we'll find out once he arrives. When did you and the prince get back to Camarria?'

"About a week ago. Visitors starting arriving in the city just a few days later. You can't turn a corner in the palace without seeing echoes scampering down the hallway. I think Cormac is enjoying himself so far, but I would imagine the novelty will wear off within a week or two."

By this time, we had arrived at the palace and were strolling through the enclosed courtyard, dodging carts and carriages and the occasional groom leading a restive horse. I had made up my mind: I would head to the servants' entrance and introduce myself to someone there and hope one of the maids or footmen let Lourdes know I had arrived.

"Well, I don't think the novelty will wear off for *me* for quite some time," I said. I made a big show of staring at the lovely brick walls and the many turrets, trying to strike just the right note between gaping yokel and admiring visitor. "It's so beautiful! I can't wait to see the inside."

"Oh, that's right. You just got here," he said. "Come in with me. I'll introduce you to Lourdes."

"Who's that?" I asked, all innocent.

"The head housekeeper. The most powerful person in the whole palace, not even excluding my uncle. You want to make sure she likes you."

I gave him a doubtful look. "Then maybe I shouldn't start out with an introduction from *you*."

He laughed and took my arm. "Nonsense, I have an excellent reputation. Much better than Lord Jamison's, at any rate. And she *does* like me."

I allowed him to lead me inside, where the scene was just as busy as it had been a couple of hours previously. Once more, I gawked at the high ceilings and pleasing proportions and sheer size of the great hall.

"It's so *big*," I said inanely.

Nico nodded. "Big enough to stage a battle. That was the original intent. If the palace was ever breached by enemies, the king's personal guards would have enough room to make a last desperate stand."

Now I looked around with even more awe. "And have they ever?"

"Not to my knowledge. But it could happen any day. Wouldn't that be an exciting development for your visit to the royal city?"

I had already had enough excitement for one trip. For one life-time. "Actually, I would prefer not to deal with invasions and war."

"Fine. But don't blame me if you're bored while you're here. Lourdes! I have someone you should meet."

The housekeeper had sailed up while we were talking, and she bobbed a polite curtsey to Nico. But she also smiled at him, which she hadn't done with Marguerite. "Good afternoon, Nico," she said. "I hope you're having a pleasant day."

"I am. Very pleasant. I ran into an old friend and I wanted to bring her to your attention. This is Brianna, personal maid to Marguerite Andolin of Orenza."

Lourdes fixed her eyes on me as if trying to judge my weight, strength, and general health. I felt a bit like a heifer at the market. "Ah, yes. She said she had sent you off to run errands."

I held up the bouquets. "She loves to be surrounded by fresh flowers. So I said I would find some, but I got a little turned around when I tried to make my way to the palace."

"Yes, Camarria is much bigger than Oberton. You must take care not to get lost," Lourdes said.

Nico glanced down at me, as if he'd just had the best idea. "I'll show you around some afternoon when her ladyship doesn't need you."

"Oh, would you?" I said, trying to sound grateful. "That would be so kind. But right now I think I must find her and help her get ready for dinner."

Lourdes gestured at someone behind me. "I'll have Annie show you to your room, and then to her ladyship's suite," she said. "Let me know if there's anything her ladyship needs."

"Thank you so much." I made a quarter-turn and bobbed the shallowest curtsey in Nico's direction. "And thank *you*," I said. "You've been so helpful."

It didn't seem to have occurred to him till right this moment that, with Lourdes listening, he could hardly press me to agree to meet him somewhere later. I saw a look of annoyance cross his face, but then he nodded and said, "I'm glad I could help. Let me know if I can be useful in the future."

I nodded in return and followed Annie out of the hall.

She led me first to my room, which was small, drab, and windowless, but at least I didn't have to share it with anyone. My trunk had already been delivered, but I didn't stay to unpack my things, just trailed Annie back downstairs two levels to Marguerite's suite.

I entered the room quietly, in case she was sleeping, and closed the door behind me.

No one was in the sitting room, so I crept over to peer in the bedroom, expecting to see three of the beds occupied. Instead, I found Marguerite, Purpose, and Patience huddled together against the far wall of the darkened room, anxiously staring back at me.

"My lady! What's wrong?" I exclaimed, stepping in.

Marguerite's body grew so loose with relief that I almost thought she'd collapse to the floor. "Brianna! Thank the goddess you're back! I was so worried—two servants have knocked at the door, but I wouldn't let them in. I can't have anyone see me with only two echoes! It would be a disaster! Everyone would know! Oh, why did we ever think we could carry off this insane idea—" She put her hands over her face and started sobbing. The echoes promptly burst into tears.

I hurried over and drew them all down onto the big bed in one wretched, weeping heap. I made soothing noises and patted their shoulders and stroked their hair and promised them everything would be all right. Eventually Marguerite sniffled and straightened up. The others did the same.

"I'm sorry," Marguerite said in a scratchy voice. "It's just that—every time I think about what we've actually done—I get so afraid. There are so many places to make a misstep—so many ways we can get caught out—and then—" She shivered.

"We won't think about 'and then,'" I said firmly. "We'll just think about 'and now.' And now I have to get you cleaned up and dressed for dinner. You'll feel better then. You'll see."

She looked unconvinced, but she nodded anyway. We spent the next hour readying ourselves for our first public appearance at the palace. Marguerite wore a rose-colored gown sprinkled with embroidered white daisies; it was accented by a swirling lace headpiece ornamented with tiny white petals. Patience and Purpose and I wore simplified versions of the same ensemble, though the lace of our own headpieces was thick enough to conceal my dark hair and long enough to cover our faces. We paused a moment to look at our group reflection in the mirror, and when Marguerite managed to summon a smile, we all conjured matching expressions. You could see the corners of our upturned mouths even through the pretty veils.

Despite the circumstances—the memory of murder, the fear of discovery, and an oppressive sense of impending disaster—I found myself feeling a growing sense of excitement. I was about to join a roomful of high nobles and eat my dinner in the presence of the prince. Whatever else I had expected my new life to bring me, it certainly hadn't been this. I had to make sure my smile was no broader than Marguerite's as I followed her out the door and down to the royal dining hall for our first meal at the palace.

CHAPTER THIRTEEN

It turns out that a servant isn't the most invisible creature in a nobleman's house. An echo is.

Marguerite and the rest of us first circulated through a large parlor sparsely furnished with chairs and stuffed full of people. So many people! It was impossible to count the numbers because they were all in motion, waving to friends or stepping over to greet new arrivals—and because they were all trailed by echoes who pivoted and bowed and curtseyed behind them. A simple maneuver, such as crossing the room to secure a glass of wine, created a churn in the crowd as big as a ship's wake passing through rough waters. Every movement created ripples of more movement. I could not imagine how everyone else was keeping their balance. I just fixed my eyes on the back of Marguerite's head and followed her everywhere, Patience and Purpose at my elbows.

From what I could tell, most of the people were about Marguerite's age or a few years older; most seemed somewhat acquainted with each other. Orenza was strategically important, but located a significant distance from any major trade routes, and few of these lords and ladies had visited Oberton in the past. Marguerite was almost a complete unknown. Some of the nobles in the room ignored her, but others made a point of introducing themselves.

"You're the girl from Oberton, aren't you? Everyone's been curious to finally meet you," was the careless greeting of a young woman with silky black hair and milky white skin. She wore a gown of the deepest shade of purple; clusters of amethysts hung from her throat, her ears, her wrists. My guess was that she was from

Alberta, which took amethyst as its traditional stone, and her next words confirmed it. "I'm Elyssa, you know. The one nobody likes." She threw her head back and laughed, and the two echoes with her did the same.

"Surely the prince likes you, or he wouldn't have invited you here," Marguerite answered.

"He likes the idea of keeping peace with Alberta," Elyssa said cynically. "He likes the idea of making my father happy."

I was a little shocked by the woman's plain speaking, but Marguerite merely answered, "Keeping the peace seems like an admirable goal."

"If you're not the one being sacrificed to achieve that goal," Elyssa said with the semblance of a sneer.

I thought Marguerite might have some sympathy with that sentiment, though she would never say so in a gathering such as this. Before she came up with a response, our little group was enveloped in a cloud of blue satin. That was really what it felt like, as if a small, spinning cyclone of sky-colored fabric started swirling around us. Elyssa and her echoes instantly decamped. Marguerite and the rest of us were left in a circle of a dozen identical women, all of them blonder than Marguerite and all dressed exactly alike. It took me a moment of quick study to determine that three were originals and the rest were echoes.

"You're Marguerite, aren't you? We've wanted to meet you forever," said one of the young women, extending her hand to Marguerite. Three of the others simultaneously reached out to Purpose and Patience and me. The hand of the echo felt cool and insubstantial on my skin, as if I had been touched by a ghost in a midnight dream.

"Oh—you must be the triplets from Banchura!" Marguerite exclaimed. "You're quite famous, you know."

All twelve of them laughed. "Yes, I'm Leonora, that's Lavinia, and that's Letitia," the first woman said. "But don't worry about it. You'll never be able to tell us apart. No one can."

"And your echoes—they're dressed just the way you are."

Leonora grinned. "Usually at home we put them in paler gowns or different accessories, but we thought, well, we're going to be so unusual here anyway, we might as well really play it up."

"Twelve of you—everywhere you go—that must be challenging," Marguerite said.

"Our father said that, when we were little, it was like having a huge litter of puppies tumbling through the house all day," said Letitia.

"That's still sort of what it feels like," Lavinia added.

"Do your echoes ever get confused?" Marguerite asked.

The triplets all shook their heads. So did their echoes. "No," said Leonora. "Though when we were little, the nursemaids sometimes made mistakes and put the wrong echo with the wrong baby."

"And then we would cry and cry and cry until someone came back in and switched the echoes around again," said Lavinia. "Finally our mother thought to tie different-colored ribbons on our wrists, *and* on our echoes. Three different shades of blue."

"That's still how we dress today, when we want to be helpful," said Letitia. "Leonora will wear navy, Lavinia will wear turquoise, and I'll wear sky blue."

"You never put on other colors?"

"Oh, of course," Letitia said. "But then we usually all match."

"Those are the days we don't want to be helpful," Lavinia said, and they all burst out laughing again.

"You make me wish I'd had a sister," Marguerite said. "I only have brothers, and we don't have much in common."

"We have two brothers, but neither of them has any echoes," said Leonora. At least, I thought it was Leonora. There had been some shifting around during the conversation, and I'd started to lose track.

"Well, you'd think they were each *other's* echoes, they're that close," one of the others replied.

"They banded together in self-defense," Leonora explained. "Not that we blame them."

"But I feel bad for anyone who doesn't have a sister," one of the others said. "Only brothers! That would be dreadful."

Marguerite sighed. "And now I feel even sorrier for myself!"

Lavinia turned toward her sisters and gave a brisk nod. All her echoes did the same. "I like her," she said. While her sisters murmured an agreement, Lavinia turned back to Marguerite. "We were determined not to, you know, but Cormac said we should give you a chance."

Marguerite drew back a little. "Why would you not like me before you even met me?"

"Because of Vivienne, of course," said Letitia seriously. "We have known her forever, and we've always been friendly."

"Thelleron is so close to Banchura, you see," Leonora explained. "There's always been a lot of visiting between our provinces."

"So when word came that Cormac had broken off his engagement with her so he could marry *you*—"

"We were very upset on her behalf."

Marguerite looked distressed. "But I'm not— There's been no engagement announced between us. I hadn't even *met* Prince Cormac until a few weeks ago—"

"We know," said Leonora, nodding wisely.

"We realized none of it was your fault," added Letitia.

Lavinia made a rather rude noise. "Politicians and their scheming," she said. "So we have decided to be nice to you after all."

"But of course we're still going to be friends with Vivienne," said Letitia.

Marguerite took a deep breath. I assumed she was having trouble keeping up with the rapid-fire conversation of the triplets; *I* certainly was. "Is she here?" Marguerite asked.

Leonora turned to take one quick glance around the room. "I haven't seen her yet, but I know she was invited. I can't even imagine how hard it will be for her to make an appearance every day and behave with some semblance of dignity."

"I hope she won't hate me," Marguerite said.

"Vivienne's too kind to hate anyone," Letitia said. "But I wouldn't be surprised if her heart was broken."

At that Marguerite looked even more distressed, but she quickly hid the expression as the group was approached by a knot of men— two lords with five echoes between them.

"As usual, the triplets find the most interesting person in the room and lay siege to her," said the one with three echoes. He was tall and slim, with light brown hair and a pleasant smile. On his left hand he wore a thick gold signet ring with small garnets studding the rim. As garnet was the traditional stone of Sammerly, I supposed that was the province he hailed from, but I didn't realize quite how exalted he was until he introduced himself. "Lady Marguerite. I'm Jordan. My family is so honored to have you come visit us, and I'm delighted to finally meet you."

"Prince Jordan," she replied, dropping a curtsey to Cormac's younger brother. Patience and Purpose and I curtseyed beside her.

"Please, just call me Jordan," he said. "I feel like I'm impersonating my brother whenever anyone uses my title."

"No one ever stands on ceremony with Jordan," said Leonora.

"He's the nicest member of the whole royal family," Lavinia added. "We like him a great deal."

The man who had strolled up with Jordan now showed us an easy smile. "I hope you like *me*," he said. He was shorter and stockier than Jordan, with skin the color of ground cloves. I thought he must hail from Pandrea, the central province of the Seven Jewels, where most of the population was similarly dark. I'd met a few Pandreans when they stayed at the Barking Dog, but they were even rarer than echoes in Orenza. "I'm just as nice as Jordan is."

One of the triplets linked her arm with his, and her echoes promptly did the same with his echoes; she had one extra, so two of her echoes attached themselves to one of his. "You're even nicer than he is because you're not already engaged to be married to someone else," she said.

Jordan looked alarmed and the Pandrean man laughed. "I'm not!" Jordan said. "There have been no formal agreements."

"Nonsense. Everyone knows a marriage between Sammerly and Alberta is eminently desirable," one of the triplets said.

"If not so desirable to be married to Elyssa," added another one.

"Nothing's settled yet," Jordan said firmly.

"I'm Dezmen, by the way," the Pandrean man said. When Marguerite accepted his proffered hand, Purpose and I took the hands of his echoes; Patience extended her arm but didn't seem to mind that no one was there to take it. I noticed that the echo who bowed to me never quite met my gaze before he stepped back behind Dezmen.

"Marguerite," she identified herself.

"Are you enjoying yourself so far, Marguerite?"

"I've only been here a couple of hours. I have to admit it is slightly—"

"Overwhelming," one of the triplets filled in. "We're used to big crowds of people because we *are* a big crowd of people, and even we are feeling a bit bewildered."

"The trick is to find one or two people you rather like, or at least can tolerate, and just attach yourself to them at every function," said Jordan.

"Like Elyssa will attach herself to you?" Lavinia said sweetly. At least, I thought it was Lavinia.

"I am sure she plans no such thing," Jordan replied.

"What makes her so bad?" Marguerite asked. "She introduced herself as the one everyone hates."

"Which is accurate enough," Leonora responded.

"She's just hateful," said another triplet, whom I decided was Letitia. Really, it was just as hard to identify them as it was to distinguish between Patience and Purpose. "She lies and she schemes—"

"And she mocks and insults—" added Leonora.

"She seems to enjoy making other people uncomfortable," said Dezmen more temperately.

"I wouldn't be surprised if she tortures animals for fun," said Letitia.

"So obviously, *she* shouldn't be the one I attach myself to," said Marguerite.

"No!" said Lavinia. "But the three of us are all quite amusing— and Dezmen and Jordan are each charming in their own way—so you could do worse than to make us your friends."

"I'm grateful to have the chance," she said. "I don't know a soul here. I don't even know who anyone else *is*."

"I can tell you that," said Jordan. "I know everyone here."

"Oh, yes, let's gossip about all the others," said Leonora happily. "Anyone in particular you're curious about?"

Everyone in our group shifted slightly so they could gaze out at the assembled company. "That beautiful woman in the gold dress," said Marguerite. "Who is she?"

That made all our new friends laugh. "Dezmen's sister Darrily!" Leonora exclaimed. "Isn't she ravishing?"

I had to squirm a little to peer over Marguerite's shoulder to see who she was talking about, but the woman was easy to spot. She was dark-skinned like her brother, but much more incandescently dressed, in a gown of stiff gold fabric accented with falls of antique lace at the bosom and elbows. Her black hair was combed back in a severe style, leaving the sharp bones of her face exposed. On her forehead was a single teardrop-shaped opal, held in place with a gold chain pinned into her hair. Against the deep tones of her skin, the gem seemed to burn with a living fire. She was followed by two echoes also dressed in gold and ornamented with opals. They were, by any measure, the most striking creatures in the room.

Dezmen gave an exaggerated, long-suffering sigh. "Do you think people ever go up to Darrily and ask her who her beautiful brother is?" he said. "No. I assure you, it gets very tiresome very fast."

"Marry her off," Jordan advised. "Then no one will trouble you anymore."

Leonora exclaimed with annoyance. "If you're saying that a woman simply vanishes once she's married, none of us will ever accept a proposal!"

He made her a deep bow. "I cannot imagine that, whatever else happens to you once you're wed, you will ever disappear."

"No," she said. "I don't intend to."

"Who else would you like to know about?" Dezmen asked. "Someone more interesting than my sister, I hope."

"I suppose you recognize Cormac," Leonora added. The prince had just entered the room, trailed by his usual entourage.

"Oh, yes! He was in Oberton just a few weeks ago."

"What did you think of him?" Lavinia wanted to know.

"You can't ask her that!" Jordan exclaimed. "She can't possibly say anything except polite comments about how much she enjoyed his company, especially since I'm standing right here!"

"No, but wouldn't it be interesting if she could?"

"Well, I for one am glad to see him," Dezmen said, "because that means it's time for dinner."

Indeed, not a minute later, one of the servants came in to announce the meal, and the whole crowd began to funnel through a door to an adjoining room. It turned out to be the largest dining hall I'd ever seen, and it was laid out in a unique fashion. In the center was one large rectangular table with eight place settings on the long sides and four on the shorter ones; it was laden with gold-rimmed china and heavy tumblers of sparkling leaded glass. Around this central board, on all four sides, were arranged two additional tables, one behind the other, set with plainer china and simpler goblets. I quickly realized that these secondary tables were meant for the echoes. If someone had only two echoes, one sat at the inner table and the other at the outer one; if there were three echoes, two sat at the outer one. As someone who had spent a fair amount of time arranging dinner tables for unwieldy groups, I was exhausted to think about the amount of effort that must have gone into calculating who would be placed where.

The nobles filed toward the main table, chatting amiably, and took their places according to gilt-edged place cards. For all the topics Marguerite and I had discussed during our days in the coach, we had never considered seating arrangements at formal dinners, so I didn't know if I should sit directly behind Marguerite or farther back. Fortunately, Purpose—who was never at a loss—went straight toward the inner table, leaving Patience and me to take up spots behind her at the outer one.

The meal was the most complex bit of choreographed action I had ever seen. Dozens of servants filed in, carrying steaming platters of food, and made every effort to serve the originals and their echoes at the same time. Whenever anyone at the central board lifted his fork or sipped from her wineglass, the appropriate shadows repeated the motions simultaneously. There was a constant ripple of motion, as if the main table was a colorful body of water and someone continually tossed pebbles into its depths, causing actions and reactions that spread outward from the middle.

I had thought it might be difficult to keep up, especially since I was several rows back from Marguerite. But she progressed through her meal in a slow and logical manner, and I was able to copy Patience even when I couldn't see what Marguerite was going to do next.

Besides, no one was watching me. I was invisible. I might have become very visible very quickly if I deviated in any drastic way from Marguerite's behavior, but for this night, at least, I didn't. I was so tense I barely tasted my food, and I couldn't have said if the liquid in my glass was water or wine. Judging by the slight giddiness that I started to experience halfway through the meal, it was wine; but Marguerite was careful to limit how much she drank. I imagined that, even more than I did, she knew how dangerous it would be to muddle her faculties this evening. Or ever, while we were in Camarria.

The meal seemed to last forever, and the evening was far from over. Prince Cormac came to his feet as it ended and invited everyone to follow him to the music room to hear some harpers considered the best in the Sammerly province. So we had a colorful parade through the halls—close to one hundred bodies jostling along as groups of three and four tried to stay together without stepping on anyone else's toes—but no one seemed to be anxious about the maneuver except me. And Marguerite, I supposed. I saw her glance over her shoulder a couple of times as if making sure I was still behind her. Of course, I never met her eyes, since I was glancing over my shoulder at the same time.

The ethereal, gliding sounds of harp music floated into the corridor, drawing us all in through a wide, arched doorway. Three slim young men sat on a low dais, practically embracing their instruments as they reached out to strum the stretched golden strings. Like the dining hall, the music room was spacious and arranged for guests with echoes. Clusters of chairs and sofas were surrounded by concentric rings of additional seating options that weren't quite as plush. The Banchura triplets commandeered a whole section of the room, joined by Lady Darrily and a couple of young lords whom we hadn't met yet. I saw Elyssa and her echoes trap Jordan in a corner of the room, and I had to discipline a smile.

Marguerite was glancing around for a place to sit when Prince Cormac approached and placed his hand on her arm. Through the fabric of my dress, I felt one of his echoes lay his fingers on my sleeve. His touch was much warmer and weightier than the touch of the Banchura echo.

"Come sit with me, onyx lady, and tell me about your journey," the prince invited.

"I'd be happy to," she said, and we all took our places in one of the clusters of chairs. Everyone in the room seemed to assume that Cormac didn't want to be interrupted because no one approached us for the next fifteen minutes.

If Marguerite was uneasy at being drawn into a private conversation with the prince, she didn't show it. She leaned back against her chair, seeming entirely relaxed, and she bestowed a friendly smile on the prince. Well—I was behind her, so I couldn't watch her face, but I saw Patience smiling through her veil, and I copied the expression.

"We were on the road nearly a week, which is the longest I've ever been in a coach," Marguerite said. "I don't know how people can bear it when they must travel all the time! Peddlers or couriers or merchants with businesses all over the realm. I found it exhausting."

"Yes, but if you never travel anywhere, you develop skewed notions about life," Cormac replied. "You think everyone looks like you or thinks like you, and you grow very comfortable with the notion that the world is a certain way. And then you find out that it's not, and it's likely to be an unpleasant discovery."

It was a piece of philosophy I happened to agree with. I hadn't traveled much until recently, but I'd certainly met my share of strangers from distant places whose attitudes and experiences in no way tallied with my own. Cormac was right that the interactions had been bewildering—but instructive.

"Having made the trip, I am quite determined to benefit from it!" Marguerite replied. "What places should I visit in Camarria that will give me another view of the world?"

"There are the markets, with merchandise from throughout the Seven Jewels and from countries across the sea. There are the ruins in the northern part of the city—the remains of buildings that were built by King Edwin, if our historians are to be believed. And, of course, there are the lords and ladies gathered in this room who will tell you stories about their daily lives that are much different from your own! You can learn something from each of these."

As he made that last observation, he gestured lightly toward those assembled lords and ladies. All of them appeared to be engaged in their own conversations, but I was pretty sure they were surreptitiously keeping their eyes on Cormac and Marguerite, wondering if the gossip was accurate. *Is it true? Will she be the one to marry the prince?* I imagined they wouldn't miss a single expression on her face—or his.

"There's one thing that I think must be the same from one end of the kingdom to the other," said Marguerite. "The presence of the triple goddess."

If I hadn't been trying to precisely mimic Marguerite's every move, my head would have jerked around at those words and my eyebrows would have shot up to my hairline. Marguerite hadn't mentioned the goddess since we set out on this trip. She hadn't even seemed to notice the temples we passed as we rode in this afternoon.

"Oh, yes, she is very much revered here in the royal city," said Cormac. "In fact, the oldest temple dedicated to the triple goddess is to be found in Camarria."

"I would like to visit it someday."

"Then we shall plan an expedition. What else would you like to see?"

"What else should I make sure not to miss?"

They talked sightseeing for the next few minutes, until a young man and his two echoes sauntered over. I thought I recognized him as one of the nobles who had accompanied Cormac on the visit to Orenza. "Do you mean to monopolize Marguerite's attention for the entire evening?" he demanded. "Surely you should be mingling with *all* your guests, not playing favorites."

"I scarcely need *you* to criticize my behavior," Cormac replied, but in a good-natured way. "Besides, I was very gracious to everyone else yesterday when Marguerite wasn't here."

"Yes, that's my point exactly," his friend replied. "Marguerite wasn't here! And I have had no chance to talk to her! Won't you come sit with me by the stage so we can enjoy the music? It seems pointless to pay so much money to hire the most accomplished harpists in the province and then ignore them completely."

Marguerite glanced at Cormac, but he made a dismissive gesture. "Fine, go sit with Nigel! Otherwise he'll be intolerable for a week at least."

Marguerite stood up and bobbed a quick curtsey, actions that her echoes and I repeated. "I do want to hear the music," she said, "but I've greatly enjoyed our conversation."

"We shall have many more opportunities to talk," he promised her.

The seven of us wound through the crowded room to take up places much nearer the dais, though Nigel had to roust out a few of his friends to open up enough chairs for all of us. Once we were seated, Nigel pulled his chair close to Marguerite's and began whispering a commentary in her ear. His two echoes similarly bent close to Patience and Purpose, their lips so close to the women's faces that

I almost expected them to press kisses against their cheeks. I had no echo to interact with, but I took up the same pose as Patience and Purpose, my body tilted toward an unseen presence, my face half-turned toward my missing companion. It might have been the oddest moment in an altogether odd evening.

And an altogether *long* evening. I hoped we were done when the music stopped, but no, that was just the signal for servants to return, carrying trays of wine and other refreshments. People drifted and shifted across the room, holding their drinks and exchanging light-hearted banter, before moving on to another friend, another conversation, another glass of wine.

It was the most pointless hour of my entire existence. These people did *nothing* useful with their time. I accepted that they weren't part of the laboring class who dedicated their lives to useful occupation—they didn't farm the land or work the mines or tend the livestock; they didn't cook, sew, garden, or clean—but I had thought they would at least engage in intellectual pursuits. Surely, if they had come together for no purpose but conversation, they would discuss politics, debate reforms, or dissect scientific papers published by the local scholars. But they did none of that. Instead they complained about the tedium of travel, they complimented each other on their clothing, they flirted, and they drank wine. And they all seemed perfectly happy not to force their brains to contend with anything more taxing.

Just from the incessant smiling and the staggering inanity, I was developing a massive headache. The wine didn't help, either. I had never in my life been so happy to see an evening come to an end.

The Banchura sisters were the first ones to make their goodbyes and slip from the room, leaving it noticeably emptier. Marguerite waited until another four or five guests had exited before she, too, headed for the door. I understood her logic; she did not want to call attention to herself by leaving too early or lingering too late. But if it had been up to me, we would have left even before the triplets did.

Just in case anyone happened to be watching us, we maintained our guise of mistress and echoes for the entire trek from the music salon to Marguerite's chambers. But as soon as we were safely in her room with the door shut behind us, the four of us practically fell apart. Marguerite cast herself into a chair, her head thrown back and her arm covering her eyes, while I dropped to a footstool and bent my head over my knees as if to fight off nausea. Patience and Purpose, released from Marguerite's control, just sat side by side on one of the sofas, their hands in their laps and their heads drooping with exhaustion.

"We have *how* many days here?" I demanded when I finally sat up again. Not until this moment did I pull off my headpiece with its gauzy veil. Finally I could see the world clearly again.

"Too many," Marguerite said faintly. "Hundreds. A lifetime."

"No, really. A month? I don't think I can bear it."

She sat up, smoothing back a lock of hair and rearranging her skirts. "No, but you were wonderful tonight! I mean, I could only get glimpses of you because you were usually behind me, but you were always so perfectly in tune. I actually forgot, from time to time, what a dangerous game we are playing."

"You should never forget that," I said soberly. "But I do think we pulled it off well enough, this first night at least. There will be plenty of new tests ahead."

Marguerite flopped back against the chair. "Yes! Because—I never thought of this until tonight—but there will be a ball at least once a week while we're here. And if you don't know the dances—well, I suppose I can say I've twisted my ankle or bruised my foot."

I smiled tiredly. "Oh, but I *do* know the dances. Most of them anyway."

"Truly? You can dance? You are a woman of infinite surprises."

I explained about the dancing instructor who had paid for her stay at the Barking Dog by giving lessons, and added, "But I might be a little rusty. We might want to practice here in your room before the first ball."

"Sometime in the next day or two," she promised. "Right now I'm too tired."

I came to my feet. "Let's get you ready for bed, then I'll go up to my room."

She and the echoes had also stood up, but at this she looked worried and uncertain. "Shouldn't you stay here? With me? In case one of the maids comes in to bring water or clean the room?"

I had already given this some thought. "Just keep your door locked and refuse to let anyone in. We need to establish you early on as an eccentric who doesn't like to be waited on by unfamiliar servants. I'll find a way to let Lourdes know that you only open the door when I'm in the room."

"I suppose that will work," she said doubtfully.

I managed to summon a tired smile. "*You* can get away with being a little odd. I can't," I pointed out. "If I'm not back in my room regularly, people are going to notice and comment on it."

Marguerite's face grew even more anxious. "But they'll notice if you never go downstairs to take meals with the other servants, either. And since you'll always be in the dining hall with *me*—"

"It will be tricky," I admitted. "Maybe some evenings you'll retire early to your suite and I can eat in the servants' hall. Or I'll make arrangements with the cook to swing by the kitchen after hours to pick up cold meals. Among the servants, we will paint you as fretful and demanding, always requiring my attendance, never allowing me a moment to myself." I shrugged. "It should work, though you will be viewed with some scorn."

"Better than being viewed as a murderer, I suppose," she said.

"Don't talk like that."

"I know. It does no good. It's just that—"

I came close enough to put my hands on her shoulders and give her a little squeeze. Shockingly familiar, I know, but she seemed to need the encouragement. "We can't change what happened. We can only go forward as best we know how. We will get through this. We will."

She nodded, took a deep breath, and attempted a smile. "I suppose I will feel more hopeful in the morning," she said.

"I'm sure you will."

Soon enough I had gotten her ready for bed, though I couldn't tuck her in for the night because she had to lock the door behind me. I was so tired that I staggered a little as I climbed the stairs to my quarters and I had to pause twice to remember the way. But finally I was in my own small space, with my own door and my own lock. Alone for the first time all day.

I leaned briefly against the door just to gather enough energy to step deeper into the room and unpack my trunk. Not until I had hung up my clothes and washed my face did I turn to the bed and prepare to pull back the covers.

That was when I spotted the small floral offering resting upon my pillow. A single white rose veined with the faintest pink. A man might have to search the entire city to locate that specific blossom at this time of year, might have to pay a small fortune to acquire it.

I blew out my candle, climbed into bed, pulled the covers up to my chin, and laid the smooth petals of the rose against my exposed cheek. Either Nico had bribed one of the palace servants to place this flower in my room—in which case at least one other person and probably every other member of the household staff knew that I had caught his eye—or he had the resources to discover which room was mine and the key to unlock this door. I couldn't decide which possibility was more alarming.

I didn't have the energy to worry about it. I closed my eyes and fell asleep within minutes, the rose still breathing its satin spell upon my skin.

CHAPTER FOURTEEN

"**I** want to go to the temple," Marguerite said.

I had been astonished, upon entering her room the next morning, to find her completely dressed, though she was wearing a simple gown and had barely bothered to style her hair. Patience and Purpose were similarly attired. But that astonishment was nothing compared to what I felt now.

"What temple?" I asked with a sense of foreboding.

"The one Cormac talked about last night. The old one."

"Why?"

She gave me a frosty look. "Why does anyone visit a temple? To seek the guidance of the goddess."

It was insubordinate, but I couldn't help my retort. "That's not why *you* generally go."

She flushed but didn't reprimand me, just lifted her chin in a defiant way. "Quickly. Before the other women start leaving their rooms. I believe they're all going off on some shopping expedition this morning, but I said I didn't want to go. But I don't want them to see me in the hallway and try to make me change my mind."

Wondering wildly, but not willing to argue about it, I reached for the door. "All right. Let's go."

"*Brianna,*" she hissed. "You have to change."

Now it was my turn to flush. One night of deep sleep and I had almost forgotten the role I had to play. "Of course. I'm sorry. Give me a minute. I—" I shook my head and scurried past her to root through the echoes' closet. It was a matter of a few minutes to swap my servant's clothing for an echo's dress and don a veiled headpiece that covered most of my hair. I kept my own shoes, since I assumed we would be walking some distance and Prudence's feet were just a little smaller than mine.

"Do you remember the way out?" I asked as Marguerite led us through the door. She merely nodded and set off down the hall.

I was not surprised, as we made it downstairs and began crossing the grand foyer, to find Lourdes there ahead of us. She struck me as the kind of person who almost never slept. Try to sneak through the halls at midnight to carry out some questionable errand, and you'd find her there before you, dusting the woodwork or checking the locks on the silver cabinet.

She glided up to us and offered a majestic curtsey. "Lady Marguerite," she said. "You're awake early. Is there something you need?"

"Good morning, Lourdes," Marguerite replied, proving the housekeeper was not the only one who could remember names. Her voice was a little plaintive, which I quickly realized was by design. "I woke with one of my headaches, and I thought a short walk might chase away the pain. It often does."

"I'm sorry to hear it. I could send someone for an apothecary."

"Perhaps later, if the exercise doesn't clear it up. Thank you." Marguerite turned to go—and then, as if suddenly remembering something, turned back. "Last night. The prince mentioned a temple nearby. I thought I might walk there, if it isn't too far."

"An excellent idea, my lady, and it's not far at all. Shall I have a footman escort you there?" I saw Lourdes's gaze briefly take in the echoes and look beyond us. "Since you seem to be planning to go out without your maid."

Marguerite didn't hesitate. "She's busy repairing the damage a few of my dresses sustained in transit," she said.

"I see."

"But I'll happily accept the attendance of a footman if you have one to spare."

A few moments later, a fresh-faced young boy in royal livery was leading us out through that magnificent palace courtyard. The place was already bustling with tradesmen who had probably been up even before Lourdes. Working folk were always at their jobs before the sun rose.

The footman helpfully pointed out key landmarks to Marguerite as we strolled down the wide streets. Maybe half of the buildings we passed were the same red brick as the palace, though none of them featured the verdigris roof; another quarter were white stone, and the rest were constructed of a wide variety of materials, from wood to plaster. I was impressed by how tidy everything looked. Back in Oberton, the governor employed a whole army of street sweepers, but Camarria was so clean that I thought King Harold must deploy street *scrubbers*. As with the palace itself, these buildings all showed evidence of great activity on the ground level, where servants and merchants were already at work, but all was quiet and curtained on the upper levels, where the wealthy and the idle still slumbered.

"There it is," the footman said as we rounded a busy corner. We hardly needed his announcement because the structure in front of us was so obviously a temple to the triple goddess.

It was situated on a small greenfield, a tiny verdant island in the middle of the busy city—and like an island, it could only be reached by a bridge. In fact, there were three, all wood, all arching over a merry little stream that encircled the temple; one bridge was white, one was black, one was red. The building itself was shaped like a three-leafed clover, each "leaf" the size of a small house and topped with a cone-shaped tower. The walls were made of piled gray stone worn smooth with age and blackened with lichen where they weren't striped with ivy. The whole complex exuded an air of ancient wisdom and hard-won peace, as if the building itself had endured so much turmoil and soothed away so much suffering that nothing could disturb it now, or anyone inside its walls.

From where we stood, gazing over the black bridge, we could only see the front of one of the round towers. It was set with a large door made of age-hardened wood that was banded with polished metal. On a pedestal before the door was a life-size statue of one of the goddess's incarnations—a woman with her arms stretched out to either side. Justice. My assumption was that the representations for mercy and joy could be found at the other two doors.

"What a lovely temple," Marguerite murmured. The boy smiled widely, as if she had directed the compliment at him.

"Shall I wait for you?" he asked.

"Oh, please don't. I don't know how long I'll be and I'm sure you're very busy."

"That I am," he said. He bowed smartly and set off back the way we'd come.

Marguerite led the rest of us across the painted bridge, and our feet made a pleasing, hollow sound as they struck the wood. But she strode right past the door for justice, and the three of us trailed after her. The next door we came to featured the goddess in her pose of joy, hands lifted over her head and her face wreathed in delight. Marguerite made a sound that might have been a snort, and we all kept walking. In the end, we entered through the door guarded by the spirit of mercy. Marguerite bowed her head, touched her fingers to her heart, and stepped inside.

This temple was even more dimly lit than the one in Oberton, since the windows were narrow slits in the walls and candles supplied the only other light. It took me a moment to clearly make out the arrangement of the interior of the tower, but it was simple enough. There was a series of pews set to face a small dais placed against the curved outer wall; on the dais was a statue of the goddess for mercy and a handful of flickering votives. The pointed ceiling overhead was lost to darkness. I assumed that the other towers were laid out in a similar fashion, though each chamber no doubt featured one of the other two incarnations of the goddess.

In the center of the tripart building was what appeared to be a walled chamber made of ornately carved wood. I supposed it served a prosaic purpose—hiding necessary supplies such as candles and cleaning materials—but the scrolls and whorls inscribed on its walls were so beautiful that it had a decorative function as well. More practically, it served to somewhat block a visitor's view, so that no one had a clear line of sight from one of the round towers to another. A way to further segregate the joyful from the troubled and the guilty, I thought.

There were about ten people already scattered through the pews in the tower where we had entered. "Let's sit for a while," Marguerite murmured, and we all slid into the very last row, Patience and Purpose between Marguerite and me.

The other three bowed their heads and seemed to fall instantly into a contemplative state. I mimicked their pose, but I was busy cutting my eyes from side to side, trying to take in more details. The other people sitting in this section seemed to represent all classes of society, from an elderly high lord to a serving girl who looked younger than I was. I could see two white-robed priestesses moving among them, offering comfort or absolution. Two of the supplicants left while I watched, and three more entered through our door and took seats near the dais.

One of the priestesses slipped into our pew and sat beside Marguerite. She was three people away from me, but I heard her ask in a soft voice, "Is there something that distresses you, my daughter?"

Which was the first time it occurred to me that Marguerite might think it was a good idea to confess to the sin of murder.

Before I could do more than go cold with horror, I saw Marguerite shake her head. "No. I mean, many things, but nothing more than the day-to-day troubles of the world."

"Sometimes it is those everyday worries that weigh most heavily upon our hearts," the priestess observed. "Life can be very hard even when it is completely ordinary."

"How do you bear it, then?" Marguerite asked. "Your own sufferings, as well as everyone else's?"

The priestess lifted her hands, palms up, then let them fall gracefully to her lap. "I deposit them in the care of the goddess," she said. "She makes all burdens light."

"So I am not praying enough."

"You are not trusting enough," the priestess corrected. "You pray, but you do not truly believe the goddess will lighten your load."

"I had a friend in Oberton. A priestess," Marguerite said. "She could convince me the goddess looked after me—looked after everyone—but I find it harder to believe now that I am in Camarria."

"You are a newcomer to our city, then. Will you be staying?"

"Just a short time. A month."

Which was enough to let the priestess know that Marguerite was one of the high nobles brought to the royal city at Prince Cormac's invitation—if she hadn't already figured that out by the escort of echoes sitting alongside her in the pew. "A month can be a long time when you're uneasy and sad," the priestess answered.

"A day can be a long time," Marguerite said. She glanced around the circular chamber, tilted her head back to look toward the tip of the pointed ceiling. Patience and Purpose and I copied her actions. I still couldn't make out anything above us except smoke and swirling darkness. "I thought I would feel better once I was here."

"Maybe if you come back tomorrow. And the following day, and the following days. You will feel a cumulative peace."

"I'll try that," Marguerite answered. "But I miss my friend."

"Write her a letter," the priestess suggested. "We send couriers daily between the temples of all the principal cities."

"You do?" Marguerite said, so artlessly that I instantly realized she had known this in advance. Taeline must have told her that all the temples were in constant communication. Marguerite had found a way to send secret messages back to her lover in Oberton without having to worry that anyone in the palace—such as an inquisitor or his nephew—would read her correspondence. "And you would be willing to include a note from me in your packets?"

"Certainly. Your friend will send her reply to us and you may pick it up here as well. Our couriers cover the ground much more rapidly than ordinary travelers—I believe the trek to Oberton takes only three days in each direction."

"Then I might hear from her within a week. Oh, that's marvelous! You've lifted my spirits immensely! So if I return here tomorrow with a letter—"

"Or I can bring you materials and you can write a note before you leave," the priestess offered.

"That would be so kind of you! Thank you! I would be so grateful."

"I will return in a moment," the priestess said, rising and exiting the pew.

I sat there seething, too far away from Marguerite to express my opinion of this particular development. Not that it was my place to express my opinion or to even *have* an opinion about my mistress's behavior. But our situation was perilous enough already without adding this element of intrigue. To be carrying on a forbidden dalliance while she was in the royal city as the top candidate to become the prince's bride—all while concealing her connection to a so-far undiscovered murder! Never, upon observing her heart-shaped face and gentle manners, would you guess this woman could be so breathtakingly rash.

The priestess returned to leave writing materials with Marguerite before she stepped to a nearby pew to minister to a new arrival. Marguerite spread the paper on her knee and scribbled a few hasty words before reaching into her pocket and pulling out a folded note—clearly something she had written back in her rooms late last night or early this morning. If I had had any doubts, they were now laid to rest. She had known before she left Oberton that this method of communication existed.

Maybe she had planned to be strong; maybe she had told herself over and over that she would not write her to her forbidden lover while she was in Camarria. But our terrible journey had weakened her resolve, or left her so confused and afraid that she reached for any kind of comfort. I found some of my anger softening as I realized how trapped and desperate she must feel, how alone and undefended. I only hoped she had been circumspect in whatever words she had committed to paper. Maybe Taeline and her fellow priestesses were too high-minded to peruse the letters of strangers—but maybe they didn't want to become unwittingly entangled in treason, either. If *I* were an abbess who had agreed to carry mail for any secretive parishioners, *I* would be reading the contents of anything that fell into my hands.

Then again, it had always been clear that I didn't have the necessary temperament to work in a temple.

In a few minutes, we were rising to go. Marguerite paused to hand her letter to the priestess, thanking her again in a low voice and receiving her three-part benediction. She paused again before the row of lit votives to speak a silent prayer. Along with Patience and Purpose, I bowed my head in imitation of Marguerite's pose, but I at least was formulating my own request. *Great goddess,* I beseeched, *keep her safe. Keep all of us safe. Do not let us make a single mistake.*

Too late, probably. We had already made so many.

We were barely across the bridge before someone fell in step beside us as if he was a favored and expected companion.

"Lady Marguerite," he said in a cheerful way. "May I escort you back to the palace?"

Nico. I was so surprised that I stumbled to a halt, which would have instantly betrayed us all if Marguerite hadn't also frozen in place. But her reaction was one of outrage and suspicion—unlike mine, which was mostly confusion and terror. "Who are *you?*" she demanded.

He swept her a bow that would do the prince proud. "Nico Burken. I work at the palace. Lourdes sent me to see you safely back, since you dispensed with the services of the footman."

"I do not require the services of a footman—or an inquisitor."

At that, he had the effrontery to grin. "So you do recognize me. I thought you might."

"I recognize your name. If I've ever seen your face before, I've forgotten it."

The insult made him grin even more widely. "No. Well, it's part of my job to be invisible."

"Then you might exhibit those skills and vanish now."

He laughed outright. "The housekeeper at Lord Garvin's mansion must be a much meeker creature than Lourdes if you think I want to risk incurring her wrath!" he exclaimed. "I can't possibly abandon you now. She'd have me executed."

"I feel certain that is an exaggeration," Marguerite said in a polite voice.

"I assure you, it is not."

"Then you inspire in me a desire to give you the slip so that upon your return to the palace, you are instantly arrested."

He crossed his arms and smiled at her, a coaxing expression. "I promise you, I am not as bad as Brianna would have you think," he said.

I had to muffle my gasp at his outrageousness. How dare he mention my name? How dare he think to discuss me with my mistress? It was unbelievable.

"If anything, she perhaps cast you in too flattering a light," Marguerite said.

"Well, that's good to hear! She's forgiven me after all!"

At that, Marguerite laughed. I realized to my chagrin that she had been playacting this whole time and that she was in fact greatly entertained by Nico's appearance. He had probably known it from the start.

"I would not be so sure of that," Marguerite warned him. "Brianna is fiercely loyal, and she will not forgive you if you harm me in any way."

Now his expression grew cynical. "It's the rare employer who can say that with certainty about a servant."

"If you doubt Brianna's loyalty, you don't know her well enough to be courting her."

He let his gaze wander past Marguerite's face toward the faces of her echoes, or what he could see of them through the netting. I tried not to hold my breath as he glanced in my direction and then behind me. I felt both melting relief and a peculiar sense of disappointment that he had looked right at me but failed to see me. "And yet, she has left you to walk a strange city alone," he said in a soft voice. "Not the behavior of a most devoted maid."

"I am not alone," she said, gesturing at the three of us. We all recreated her motion.

"You may as well be," Nico said. "If trouble came for you, the echoes would neither defend you nor run for help."

Well, he's wrong about half of that at least, I thought, and I was sure Marguerite was silently thinking the same thing.

"Is Camarria so dangerous, then, that a woman cannot walk abroad safely under bright sunshine?"

"I would wager your own city is not regulated so well that crime is unheard of," he countered. "I don't recall seeing too many high nobles traveling around Oberton unescorted."

Marguerite hesitated a moment, as if searching for an excellent retort, then shrugged and capitulated. She made another slight gesture, indicating that Nico should fall in beside her, and they began pacing slowly back toward the palace. Patience and Purpose followed closely behind them; I trailed after them all. "You might be right," Marguerite admitted. "But there are times I cannot think clearly when anyone is nearby, so I ordered Brianna to stay behind. I assure you, she was not happy about it."

"If I had been her, I would have snuck off behind you anyway."

Marguerite glanced over her shoulder, managing to catch my eye just before I turned my own head. Her face was prim, but I could tell she was laughing inwardly. "I hadn't thought of that. Do you think she's skulking around here somewhere?"

"No, as far as I can tell, she hasn't left the palace."

"Then again, there are a lot of doors," Marguerite pointed out. "You can hardly have been watching all of them."

He grinned again. "You'd be surprised."

"I hope you are not planning to stalk poor Brianna wherever she goes, every single day that we are in Camarria," Marguerite said. "She is quite independent, you know. I don't think she would appreciate being closely watched all the time."

This was even worse! Now *Marguerite* was prepared to talk about me, perhaps even give Nico romantic advice! I was so incensed I wanted to ball my hands up and howl. But I had to just stroll along behind Marguerite as if I didn't have a thought or a reaction of my own.

"I think perhaps no one realizes how closely everyone is watched—all the time," Nico said, his voice unexpectedly serious. I felt a chill shiver along my shoulder blades. He couldn't possibly realize we had been engaged in a perilous adventure that we could only pray had been witnessed by no one. "The king employs a band of inquisitors. Someone is always paying attention."

"I will strive to keep that in mind."

"Will you bring your maid with you the next time you decide to explore the city?"

"I cannot promise you that I will," Marguerite said.

He waited a moment, as if expecting her to elaborate on that. When she didn't, he finally said, "Why not?"

Because she has to shadow me all the time in another guise. Because I have to play a most hazardous game—and so far even you, clever inquisitor that you are, have not realized exactly what charade I must maintain. Of course she could not say either of those things. "I might have other tasks I need her to perform. I might have other days when I am craving solitude." She glanced at him. "I might have deeds to carry out for which I do not want a witness."

He snorted. "So you fear your 'fiercely loyal' maid might turn spy for your father or the crown?"

"Why, no," she said sweetly. "But perhaps I fear an overeager inquisitor might use blandishments—or torture—to induce her to tell tales on me."

He gave her a slow, sober look as he guided her across the street at a busy corner. I couldn't remember this particular intersection from our walk this morning. Nico must be taking us back by a different route. "You shouldn't say such things," he told her, "if you don't want me to start wondering just what sorts of activities you plan to embark on."

"Maybe I said it just to make you start wondering," she answered through a demure smile. "Maybe I thought it would be amusing to get you worked up over nothing."

"That's a risky form of entertainment," he said.

"There's something about Camarria," she murmured. "It makes me reckless."

Goddess save my sinful soul, I thought. I had been wrong when I'd thought this conversation couldn't get more appalling.

"Well," said Nico, "you're not the only country girl to say so."

Marguerite laughed—and a second later she gasped. The echoes and I all did the same. We had rounded the unfamiliar corner and come upon a scene of candy-colored delight. We were in a wide, open plaza filled with nothing but flower stalls, bursts of color so varied and so intense that the eye could hardly take them all in. The air was as sweet and heavy as honey. All around us was the muted roar of commerce as vendors called to customers, buyers bargained over prices, and dropped coins rolled and clattered in the street. Over the whole scene arched one of Camarria's famous bridges, a spun-sugar white stone with lacework balustrades. Over it a few couples meandered hand in hand, while groups of women paused to show each other their floral purchases.

"What a beautiful place!" Marguerite cried.

"Brianna has told me how much you love flowers," Nico explained. "This is the best spot in the city to buy them. It's a little farther from the palace than some of the other markets, but not so far that you can't walk it easily when the weather is nice."

"I wasn't even paying attention," she said, stepping deeper into the plaza and looking around as if trying to decide which stall to visit first. "I'm not sure I could find it again."

"I'll make sure to give Brianna directions," he promised. "Or I can accompany you the next time you decide to come."

"Surely you have more important tasks than squiring me around the city," Marguerite said.

He bowed again. "None more important or more enjoyable."

"Careful," she said. "Or I'll tell Brianna you were flirting with me."

"She would probably tell you that I was just trying to make you like me enough to lower your guard."

"Would she be right?"

He laughed. "Let's look at flowers."

They shopped for the next thirty minutes, Nico showing remarkable patience for a task that most men would find tedious in the extreme. He mostly refrained from complaining about the prices—which were shockingly high—but he did talk her out of buying a very expensive bouquet of orchids. He was right. The colors were gorgeous, but the blooms were already starting to wilt. They would hardly last another day.

The echoes and I were all laden down with bundles of paper-wrapped flowers when we finally left the market. By that time, I was practically exhausted with the effort of trying to copy Marguerite's every motion while eavesdropping on every word of her conversation with Nico—without once drawing his attention. I did find the energy to very sneakily glance around the plaza to see how many vendors carried a certain variety of pink-veined rose. I didn't see a single one on display.

"I think I'm done now," Marguerite said at last. "Brianna will believe I have gone mad."

"Nonsense. I've seen her buy twice this many flowers on your behalf," Nico said gallantly. "Are you too tired to walk back? There are wagons for hire just over there."

Marguerite hesitated. "Large enough to accommodate us all?" she asked.

I grew cold at the idea of sitting across from Nico in the close confines of a small vehicle, even for what was sure to be a relatively short ride. If he was staring straight at me for ten minutes, even through my veil, even as he had every reason to think I was someone else, I thought the chances were excellent that he would realize who I was.

I would have to sit beside him, facing Marguerite and Patience and Purpose. Though that would be even worse.

"I have errands of my own to run, and they're not in the direction of the palace," he said. "I would not be joining you."

"Then I think I would prefer to ride," Marguerite said. "Thank you."

Five minutes later, he had hired a wagon, helped us all in—not even seeming to notice how familiar my hand felt in his—and waved goodbye. I waited until he was completely out of sight before I slumped against the wooden seat as if my spine could no longer support me.

"Well, that was entertaining," said Marguerite. "I can see why you like him."

"I *don't* like him," I muttered.

"He certainly seems to like you."

I straightened up on the bench. I was on the backward-facing seat, next to Patience. "Or he's very interested in *you*," I said. "Trying to charm you into some kind of confession. I would think he's very good at that."

"I have been playing court games since I was a child," she said cynically. "Yes, and outmaneuvering my mother since I was born. I hardly think an inquisitor could trip me up."

"I hope not," I said. But I couldn't help but worry.

No surprise, Lourdes was prowling the magnificent foyer when we returned, and she approached us as soon as we entered.

"A coach has arrived with trunks intended for you," she told Marguerite. "I had them taken to your room, but I supervised their delivery myself." The implication being that she had made sure no impertinent maid or footman had had a chance to paw through Marguerite's things when no one was there to see.

"Thank you," Marguerite said. "Brianna is probably already unpacking everything for me."

"I didn't see her this morning, but I'm sure she's there now," answered Lourdes, sounding anything but sure.

"Indeed," was Marguerite's cool reply. She nodded to the housekeeper and swept toward the stairwell, the three of us at her heels.

Up in her suite, we found the additional trunks piled carefully in the main room. We unlocked them and began hanging up the clothes—all of which would need to be pressed before Marguerite could wear them—but I kept glancing with some distraction at the door. I didn't even realize I was doing it until Marguerite asked me what was wrong.

"Both Lourdes and Nico commented on my absence," I said. "I feel like I need to show myself belowstairs or start all sorts of rumors circulating. And yet there is much to do here."

"I can finish putting everything away," she said. "You go downstairs and do something to draw attention to yourself."

"It might involve casting you as a very persnickety and difficult mistress," I warned.

She smiled. "Describe me as if you were talking about my mother," she answered. "That should make me seem wretched enough."

"My *lady*," I said, but I had to muffle a laugh.

"*You* go gossip. *I* will make myself useful."

"Well, if you really want to be useful, you could mend that tear in your lavender gown," I said. "Although I don't know if you have any skill with a needle."

She made shooing motions to encourage me toward the door. "I can embroider very well, thank you, though I don't much like doing it," she answered. "I'll try my hand at mending."

"I was joking."

"Well, that will teach you to jest with me, won't it? Go on— downstairs with you."

I sighed and headed toward the bedroom, where my own clothes were laid out. "I have to change clothes, remember? I can't go about dressed like you, or it defeats the purpose of showing myself as me."

Marguerite's playfulness instantly disappeared. "Oh, Brianna, I'm so sorry. This whole thing is going to be just as hard on you as it is on me—"

"It's not," I said, pulling off my fine dress and reaching for my plain one. "And anyway, it doesn't matter if it's hard. We just have to do it."

"Yes," she said, "I suppose we do."

I spent the next two hours in the servants' domain, learning where the laundry rooms were, borrowing shoe polish, and joining the others for lunch. The arrangements at this meal were almost as highly choreographed as the ones at the prince's dinner, for we were all arrayed by our employers' stations, and furthermore the visitors' servants were somewhat segregated from the king's staff. I found myself sitting with the maids for Lady Elyssa and the Banchura triplets. As I might have expected, Leonora and Lavinia and Letitia seemed to be amiable and openhanded mistresses, and their maids were cheerful and hardworking, with very few complaints to offer. That wasn't the case with Lady Elyssa's serving woman, who sighed and complained throughout the whole meal.

"Why do you stay with her then?" asked Letitia's maid.

"The money! I'll be able to retire in five years, if I can last that long. But I probably can't. The rumor is that almost no one's stayed with her longer than a year since she turned eleven years old."

Leonora's maid turned to me. "What about Lady Marguerite? From everything I hear, she's a likable sort."

I couldn't bear to paint her as mean-spirited and underhanded, so instead I shook my head. "She's kind enough, but she's so fretful. 'Should I wear this? No, I don't like it, let me put this on instead.' Pretty soon she'll have tried on every gown in her closet and end up back in the very first one! She can be merry one minute, then dark and glum five minutes later, and she's always coming down with some ailment. Her head hurts. Then her stomach is queasy. And then it's, 'Oh, Brianna, can you massage my back? It aches so much.' She'll send me off to buy powders from the apothecary, and then never use anything I bring back. When she's gone, she wants me in the room so I can *take care of things*—though everything's already washed and pressed and hung up—but when she's back she sends me away so she can have privacy. And she doesn't want any of the palace maids to make up the bed or straighten the room—I have to take care of all those chores, too, because she's so particular about how everything is done." I rolled my eyes. "So I don't know how often you'll see me down here over the next few weeks."

"That sounds dreadful," said Leonora's maid.

"It sounds wonderful," sighed Elyssa's.

I shrugged. "It's like every other situation. It has its good points and its bad points. But I'm used to hard work and I love living in the city, so the job suits me for now."

Talk turned to other topics then, which was fine with me. I figured I had dropped just enough information to make my erratic behavior seem credible without complaining so much that people started wondering if I was telling the truth. I had to confess I found it difficult to believe Lady Elyssa could be as bad as her maid was saying, and by the way the Banchura women glanced at each other, I could tell they were thinking the same thing. Then again, Lord Jamison's valet probably had equally terrible things to say about *his* employer, and I was sure all of them were true.

Or, well. Used to be true.

After the meal, I made up some reason to cross the foyer just so Lourdes could get a look at me. I stayed alert in case I unexpectedly ran into Nico on the stairs or in the hallways, but he must still have been on his own errands because I didn't encounter him anywhere in the palace. I told myself I was relieved.

I finally returned to Marguerite's room to find that she not only had put away all the new clothes, but also had made good on her promise to mend the lavender gown. She'd done an excellent job of it, too, with stitches as small and fine as my own.

"You can take a job as a seamstress if your parents ever turn you out of the house," I told her.

"If they turn me out because I'm a murderer, I'll probably be in a dungeon somewhere," she said lightly.

"Maybe they'll turn you out because of your inappropriate liaisons," I said. I had been so flummoxed by Nico's appearance that I hadn't even had a chance to question her about our visit to the temple this morning.

Her face showed a mulish expression, but she didn't say I had no right to comment on her behavior. Neither did she say something patently untrue, like *I haven't done anything wrong!* What she actually said was, "I am trying to be discreet."

"If you end up married to the prince," I said, "I don't think you can ever be discreet enough."

"I'm not married to Cormac yet," she answered.

"No," I said, "but couldn't you use your time away from Oberton to try to get over this other person? You said yourself that it was time to end the relationship. Take this opportunity to leave the past behind."

"And how long did it take you to get over Robbie?" she snapped.

"That's the thing," I said. "I came to Oberton so I had something else to think about. So you're in Camarria. Think about something else."

"It's more complicated than that."

I shrugged. Maybe it was. In my experience, it was easy to make things more complicated than they had to be. Making a decision and sticking to it usually took care of the messy details. But maybe that wasn't as true for someone in Marguerite's position.

"Then let's do something simple," I said. "Let's get you ready for dinner."

CHAPTER FIFTEEN

O ur second dinner at the royal palace was even grander than
the first because it took place in a very large, very formal dining hall and included the king, the queen, the young princess, and a
handful of other high-ranking visitors, in addition to Prince Cormac
and all his guests. I was unsophisticated enough to be thrilled by
the notion of seeing the king in person, though the arrangement
of the dining hall worked to my disadvantage. The room held six
long tables for the nobles, and twelve for their echoes, and it was
difficult to see through all the clusters of people that separated me
from the royal family. I did get enough glimpses to note that King
Harold looked a good deal like Cormac, though his handsome
face was wearier and sterner, and his smiles less frequent; Queen
Tabitha looked clever and cold. Princess Annery, who might have
been twelve years old, rarely looked up from her plate and never
spoke to anyone except her mother. Her two echoes, seated behind
her, seemed equally listless.

By contrast, the echoes belonging to the king and queen had
more color and substance than most others I'd encountered, as if
the responsibilities of ruling the realm weighed almost as heavily
on them as on their originals. I wondered if their hands would be
warmer to the touch, their gazes more direct. I remembered Nico's
story about King Edwin, whose spirit was able to flow from his own
body to that of his echoes. I wondered if that was a trick mastered
by everyone who wore the crown. I would never want to witness
a regicide, of course, but that magical transference was certainly
something I would like to see.

After the meal, which seemed endless, the whole mass of diners adjourned to another huge hall—again, more formal than the salon where the prince had entertained his guests the night before. The ceiling was high and covered with glinting gold leaf; the walls were panels of dark wood interspersed with panels of maroon wallpaper decorated with the royal crest limned in gold paint. Two gilded thrones had been set up on a velvet-covered dais; behind them were less ornate chairs clearly designed for echoes. There was nowhere else in the room to sit.

It was quickly clear that the visiting nobles had been brought there to pay their respects to the king and queen, and that no other entertainment was to be had. Footmen moved through the room, issuing soft-voiced instructions, and slowly everyone drifted to one of two camps—diners who were familiar visitors to the palace, who had no need to seek an audience with the royal couple, and newcomers who would be expected to make their obeisance to the throne.

Obviously, Marguerite was in the second group, along with about half of Cormac's guests. I wasn't surprised to see the Banchura triplets in the first group because that province lay closest to Sammerly. Nigel and a few of the other men also turned out to be familiar to the king. Now that I knew Elyssa was expected to marry Prince Jordan, I understood why she, too, was able to stand with the visitors who had been to court before. She must have traveled here many times in the past—or at least often enough to allow Jordan to realize how much he disliked her. But perhaps she had only visited Camarria once or twice; I didn't think it would take too much contact with her for anyone to reach that conclusion.

Lady Darrily and her brother, Dezmen, were standing with the people who were already acquainted with the king. She looked just as stunning tonight, in a dress of burnt orange accented with falls of lace; again, she wore an opal pendant against her forehead, held in place by a golden chain. Even in the muted light of the high-ceilinged room, it glowed with a wicked light.

"Her affectation is so much better than mine," Marguerite breathed. I was standing right next to her, Patience and Purpose on my other side.

I risked a reply, trying not to move my lips. "Yes, but her affectation isn't calculated to save her life."

"As far as you know," Marguerite retorted. "Everybody has secrets."

Unfortunately, I knew this to be true.

If there was any particular order to how people were being invited to approach the throne, I couldn't discern it. My guess was royal whim. King Harold would whisper to a footman, who would approach someone in the crowd and lead that person back to the dais. After a short conversation with the king and queen, the individual would bow or curtsey, then join the group on the other side of the room. Given the number of people still awaiting an introduction, I figured this whole process could take close to two hours.

It seemed like an exceedingly tedious way to spend an evening.

We had been standing there for about fifteen minutes when the young woman standing closest to Marguerite looked over with a friendly smile. She was short and a little plump, with curly brown hair and a pink complexion. She was attended by two echoes, and all three of them wore necklaces of sculpted amethyst. Probably from Alberta, then.

"We haven't had a chance to talk yet, but I'm Cali," she introduced herself. "You're Marguerite, aren't you?"

"Yes."

"I was very excited to be invited to Camarria, but I wish this part of it was over," Cali confessed. "I'm a little nervous about meeting the king."

"So am I," Marguerite replied. "What are we supposed to say?"

"Elyssa told me that he will just ask a couple of simple questions," Cali said. "He does not expect deep conversation. He is merely showing kindness by taking the time to meet us all. Though I'd rather he was kind from a distance, frankly."

"I think I agree with you."

Cali gave her a quick appraisal. "He'll want to talk longer to *you*, I expect. I mean, if you're really going to marry Cormac—"

"Oh, that has not been decided yet," Marguerite said easily. "I'm just in Camarria visiting, like everyone else."

At that exact moment, the footman arrived to summon Marguerite to the throne. She nodded a quick farewell to Cali, then followed the footman with her usual grace, not displaying any nervousness at all. Purpose was right behind her, and Patience and I a half step behind. My hands were both cold and sweating; I was as anxious as I'd been since we arrived at the palace. This was the one time I had to play my role perfectly. To be caught out in a deception right in front of the king...

I kept my eyes fiercely focused on Marguerite's back and dropped into my curtsey right along with her. The king extended his hand so Marguerite could kiss his ring; Patience and Purpose and I all leaned forward, pursing our lips, before settling back on our heels and tilting our heads up to gaze at him with reverence.

"Marguerite Andolin of Orenza," Harold said in a rumbling voice. "It is good to finally meet you. Your father and I have been having some very profitable conversations lately."

"I'm glad to hear it," Marguerite said.

"He seems most eager to develop a warm relationship with the crown."

"I don't doubt it. I would think all your subjects desire such a thing."

"Indeed, I would welcome closer ties between Sammerly and the western provinces. Perhaps you will help me work toward that goal."

"Happily, sire."

The queen leaned forward. Her eyes were almost as green as the emeralds she wore around her wrist, a reminder that her earliest loyalty was to Empara. Her expression was one of intensity as she surveyed Marguerite, but her words were conventional, even a little banal. "You reside in the city of Oberton, do you not?" she asked. "I have never been there. What is it like?"

"In terms of landscape, its most striking feature is the mountain range to the north, where the onyx is mined. The mountains are particularly beautiful at sunset, when they look purple against the evening sky."

"You can hardly go wrong when there are mountains on the horizon," the king answered.

"I was born in Empara, where the lands are mostly forest," Tabitha said. "I confess I never find the prairies and flatlands to be very interesting."

"I agree," said Marguerite. "Give me mountains or woodlands any day over fields and farming."

Just as the inanity of the conversation was starting to make me relax, Harold spoke again. "I wonder how my son Jamison enjoyed his recent trip to your city. He had never been there, either, and was quite looking forward to visiting."

Marguerite hesitated just an instant too long before replying in a voice that was almost steady. "We didn't have many opportunities to talk, but he did seem to enjoy himself."

Perhaps I was wrong, but I thought the queen sent her husband a look of pure loathing when he introduced Jamison's name to the conversation. Her tone was exceedingly dry. "Yes, Jamison always seems to—enjoy himself—wherever he goes," she said. "Court has seemed so quiet with him gone. But we expect him back any minute now to liven our days."

Now Harold returned Tabitha's venomous look with a measured stare in her direction. "And we are, as always, happy to have him in our midst—because we love him a great deal."

"Despite his flaws," Tabitha added icily.

"I suppose we all have plenty of those," Marguerite said.

Unexpectedly, Harold laughed. "I suppose we do. It was good to talk with you, Lady Marguerite. I will let your father know that I have met you and found you most charming."

"Thank you, sire," she murmured, curtseying again. We all curtseyed behind her as a footman appeared to lead us to the other side of the room.

As we walked, I fixed my eyes on Marguerite's back. I was sure she was trembling. Once we were far enough from the thrones, I brushed past Purpose so I could hiss encouragement through my veil. "You handled that very well. Don't be so worried."

She couldn't answer because we were suddenly enveloped by the Banchura triplets. They surged around us in a wave of foaming blue, all friendly smiles and reassuring pats on the arm.

"See? It wasn't so bad, was it?" said the one I decided to consider Leonora for the evening.

"But isn't the king the dullest man you've ever talked to?" demanded the one I took for Lavinia. "I realize it's impossible to have an interesting conversation at a formal audience, but he takes *boring* to a whole new level."

It was clear this Banchura noblewoman had never had a conversation with the king that included guarded allusions to her possible marriage to his oldest legitimate son as well as protestations of affection for his bastard child—whom she had murdered. *Boring* didn't seem like the right word.

But Marguerite played right along. "That was fine by me," she answered. "I was so overwhelmed that I would have been incapable of witty remarks. I'm still probably incapable of rational speech."

Leonora patted her arm again. "That's fine, we'll just rattle on with silly gossip."

Jordan approached us just then, making a big show of pushing through the triplets' nine echoes to join the originals in the center of the group. "Gossip? Oh, please, do share," he said. "Standing around watching my father make labored conversation with noble guests is not my idea of entertainment. I need a distraction."

Lavinia jerked her head in the direction of Lady Elyssa, who had fallen into conversation with an older man who had been seated near Harold at the dinner table this evening. I pegged him for a high-ranking councilor or confidante of the king, though he only had a single echo. And I didn't see a woman nearby who might be his wife. He didn't seem to share the general dislike of Elyssa; at any rate, he was smiling somewhat fatuously at whatever she was saying. I had to fight to keep a sardonic expression off my face. A beautiful young schemer and a powerful old man. It was the oldest story in the history of relationships.

"Notice anything odd about the hateful Elyssa?" Lavinia asked.

Jordan glanced quickly her way and back at Lavinia. "Someone appears to be enjoying a conversation with her?"

"That *is* remarkable," Leonora agreed. "But something else."

Jordan turned to study her more closely. "She's missing an echo!"

"Precisely," Lavinia said.

"*And* she was missing the echo last night, too. Though almost nobody noticed because the room was so crowded," Letitia added.

"What happened to her?" Marguerite wanted to know.

Leonora spread her hands. "She *says* the echo tripped over a shoe left lying in the middle of the room. Twisted her ankle, and won't be able to walk for a few days."

"You don't believe her?" Marguerite asked.

"It's just so odd," Lavinia said. "Are there ever any shoes lying around in *your* room? Is your maid that careless?"

"No."

"And then, when I said something nice, like, 'You poor thing! You must miss your echo so much,' she said the most awful thing," Letitia went on.

"Just dreadful," Leonora confirmed.

"She said, 'It's actually been something of a relief not to have three of them dragging behind me the last couple of days,'" Lavinia told us. "'I feel ten pounds lighter,' she said."

"'Twenty pounds' is what she said," Letitia corrected.

"Well, ten or twenty, it's still unfathomable," Leonora said.

Jordan was still studying Elyssa. "She said that?" he demanded. "And she meant it?"

"She certainly sounded like she meant it!"

He shook his head. "It's unbelievable. There was this time— we'd been out hunting, and one of my echoes took a spill when his horse shied at a snake. He broke his leg in three places and had to stay in bed for four weeks. And that whole time—" He shook his head again, as if he knew he could not possibly put his emotions into words. "For every minute of those four weeks, I felt like my arm had been amputated. I felt like my lungs wouldn't fill up with air. And my leg wouldn't stop aching. I knew exactly where every fracture was in his bones—I actually walked with a cane for the first week, and I limped for the next three. Being without my echo *hurt* me."

The triplets were all nodding. "When we were younger, there was some expedition, I can't even remember where—" Leonora began.

"The old mill," Letitia interjected.

"That's right, the mill. For some reason, there was limited space in the carriages, and our mother decided each of us would only get to bring two echoes."

"We screamed and sobbed and threw such tantrums that she had to turn around and take us home," Lavinia finished up.

"It's not that we were trying to be difficult," Letitia said earnestly. "In general, we were very happy and well-behaved children."

"We were just so *miserable*," Lavinia said.

"It was *painful*," Leonora added.

"It was *wrong*," Letitia said.

"So it just doesn't make sense that Elyssa would be happy to leave an echo behind," Leonora finished up.

"I agree," Marguerite said. "It does make you wonder about her—her sympathetic tendencies."

Letitia turned to Jordan. "So you see," she said, "you can't marry her."

He smiled in a somewhat guarded fashion. I supposed that if the king really wanted the marriage to go forward, Jordan wouldn't have much choice in the matter. "Nothing has been settled yet," was all he said.

Lavinia was looking off in the direction of the thrones. "Thank the goddess!" she exclaimed. "The last poor soul has had the last uncomfortable conversation with the king and now this interminable evening can finally be over."

She was right—the whole mass of people had started to drift toward the door and those who were farthest toward the back had already made their escape. We allowed the motion of the crowd to edge us closer and closer to the exit, until we were finally in the hallway and headed toward some of the smaller and more intimate spaces of the palace.

"What now?" Marguerite asked.

"Bed for me!" Leonora exclaimed, and her sisters and all of their echoes nodded in vehement agreement.

"There will be cards, conversation and cognac in the small parlor where we were last night," Jordan said. "But it is an entirely optional gathering."

"Then I think it will be bed for me as well," Marguerite said. She put a hand to the back of her skull, and Purpose and Patience and I did the same. "I am starting to get one of my headaches and I don't want it to get worse."

"Oh, you poor thing," Letitia said. "We'll hope you're feeling completely recovered in the morning."

Jordan peeled off once we reached the foyer, while the triplets and Marguerite climbed the stairs to the third level. Another round of goodbyes and then the triplets continued on down the hallway while the four of us ducked quickly inside Marguerite's rooms.

I had barely locked the door behind us when Marguerite doubled over as if in agony. She had not released the echoes yet, so they too were bent in half, their heads practically touching their knees, their hands lifted to cover their eyes.

"My lady!" I exclaimed, hurrying over to put my arm around her shoulder and pull her upright.

She was almost gasping for air. "Sweet goddess! To hear a man talking about how much he loves his son—when I know his son is dead! When I know *I killed him!*"

"You didn't kill him," I began, but she flung her hand in the air to stop me.

"My echo is the one who beat him to death, but I *am* my echoes! My echoes are me! It is my fault he is dead. And there is no chance that his murder will go unpunished!"

"They might note his absence and they might even find his body, but that doesn't mean they'll figure out how he died," I said, urging her over to a sofa and sitting beside her. Patience and Purpose followed us, still mimicking Marguerite's every move.

"But they will! They'll keep looking and looking—they'll keep asking and asking—"

"And they'll find a corpse in a lake and think he must have tumbled in the water after he drank too much wine," I said firmly.

"Brianna, I'm so afraid," she moaned.

I put my arms around her again and pulled her into a reassuring embrace. "I know. I am, too. But we don't have any choice. Unless you want to confess now, tell Cormac or his father exactly what happened—"

She jolted away from me. "No!"

"Then you have to keep playing the game."

She was still for a moment, then took a long, shuddering breath. She nodded. The echoes nodded, too, and then slouched back against their cushions as she finally thought to release them. "Then I'll keep playing the game," she said.

I folded my hands in my lap and gave her a searching look. "Those things the triplets were saying tonight—and Prince Jordan—about losing an echo. Were they right? Is that how it feels?"

She nodded again, wearily this time, and slumped against the back of the sofa. "Worse. It's there all the time, this—this hole in my life. As if part of me is missing. As if someone has put a hand over my eye and I can't see clearly out of the other one. I don't know how to explain it."

"It's grief. You don't have to explain it. Everyone who's ever felt it knows what it feels like," I said softly.

"Does it ever get better? Does it ever go away?"

"It gets better. It doesn't go away, not entirely," I said. "You just get used to it."

"I don't think I'll get used to it," she said.

I patted her on the shoulder. "Maybe not," I answered. "So then you'll just have to learn to work around it."

CHAPTER SIXTEEN

In the morning, it seemed best for Marguerite to suffer from one of her fictional headaches. I had errands to run and she wasn't feeling very social, so she liked the notion of spending a few hours alone in her room. I swung by the kitchen to assemble a plate of food and grumble a little.

"I couldn't even go back to my own bed to sleep last night because she wanted me nearby every minute!" I exclaimed to one of the Banchura maids. "And now she'll lock herself in her room and refuse to let anyone in till I've returned. I can tell you right now, this visit can't be over fast enough to suit me."

I offered a much calmer version of the same story to Lourdes when I paused in the foyer to ask directions to an apothecary's shop. She offered to send a footman to fetch anything I needed, but I shook my head.

"I think it will do me good to walk around in the fresh air for a while," I said, knowing the housekeeper would understand very well what I was attempting to convey. *It's my one chance to get away from this demanding monster, and I am not going to give it up.* She might even have been sympathetic.

I enjoyed my trip through the bustling city streets, which had a fresh, damp smell from a rainstorm that had moved through the night before. The apothecary's shop was in a completely different direction from the flower market we had visited with Nico, and nowhere near the clover-leaf temple, so I had to mind my landmarks to make sure I would be able to find my way back. I ended up in a thriving commercial district with dozens of small shops crammed together on narrow, cheerful streets that were thronged with people. Working class, mostly, though I spotted a number of individuals I took to be tradesmen's sons and merchants' daughters—rich enough to have money to spend, but not so wealthy they could turn all of their chores over to servants.

I spent twenty minutes in the apothecary's place just because I liked it. It was bigger than any similar shop I'd visited in Oberton and lined from floor to ceiling with wooden shelves holding boxes of mysterious herbs and powders. The young man working behind the counter looked to be a year or two older than I was and eager to pass the time, so he opened half the containers in the store to show me the contents. I now knew where to come if I needed to cure a cough, dissolve a wart, settle my stomach, enhance my memory, improve my eyesight, or stop an itch. I suspected he probably stocked darker potions, too, but I didn't inquire about them. If any inquisitor was going to follow after me and ask what I'd wanted to buy, I didn't want items like *poison* to be on the list. In the end, all I bought was a simple powder that would ease Marguerite's supposed headache.

Once I was back outside, I began a quick and purposeful stroll along the streets, glancing at every shop window I passed. Here was a milliner, here a boot maker, here a boutique that specialized in gloves. I had had no need of an apothecary, but I had reasoned that it was likely to be located near dozens of other enterprises that catered to the rich and the near-rich. And I definitely wanted to find—

There it was. A wig maker's shop. I went right in.

I was the only customer at the moment, though the cramped space at first seemed overfull of bodies. Or rather, it was full of bodiless heads set on counters and tables and shelves and staring sightlessly toward the door. Each bust sported a carefully styled coiffure and the occasional jaunty hat besides. Through a small door I spotted a workroom where three women were bent over long tables, swatches of hair spread out before them like so many bolts of silk.

One of them looked up, saw me, and came out into the shop to greet me. Her silver hair was so perfectly combed and curled that I had to wonder if it was real or fake. "Are you interested in buying a wig?" she asked.

Indeed, I was.

I'd brought a lock of Marguerite's hair so I could match the color as closely as possible, and I knew exactly the texture and length I needed. The wig maker had three completed samples to choose from, none of them perfect, but all of them sized well enough to fit my head. She offered to make me a custom product, but I didn't want to wait. So far I had managed to conceal my own darker hair under elaborate headpieces, but I needed to be able to expand my accessories. And I was tired of taking chances.

Well. I would continue to take chances the whole time we were in Camarria. But at least I could minimize this hazard.

Actually, there was a second, more immediate risk, and I wanted to mitigate that one, too. Once I'd examined the blond wigs, I began to look at the options in brown. In the end I bought two, one in each color, and made sure that the fair one was carefully wrapped and laid in the bottom of my straw bag, with the dark one on top.

I stepped out of the shop with the frowning air of someone who was trying to remember if there was anything else she needed to accomplish, and I paused to glance around. Were there any other items in this particular district that might prove useful to a pair of women engaged in a dangerous charade?

"What's next on your shopping list?" asked a voice in my ear, and I made a creditable show of jumping in surprise. In truth, I had been expecting Nico to appear ever since I left the palace.

"You startled me!" I exclaimed. "You shouldn't leap out at people like that."

"I don't know why not. It's very entertaining," Nico said. "So what else do you need?"

"I think I've gotten what I came for. Right now I'm just looking around."

He nodded at my woven basket. "So you bought a love potion at the chemist's—"

I had to strangle a laugh. "Headache powder! For Marguerite."

"And—" He cocked his head. "A wig?"

I nodded vigorously.

"Also for Marguerite?"

This time I did laugh. "No! It sounds so silly, but before I left Oberton, my aunt Jean asked me to buy a wig for her. Apparently she once knew someone—a romantic rival, I think—who had the most beautiful hairpiece, and she'd bought it in Camarria, and my aunt Jean had always been jealous. So when she heard I was coming here—" I shrugged, to indicate that I thought it was ridiculous, but I had been trying to humor an old woman. What Aunt Jean would say about this story I didn't even want to imagine. "Here, let me show it to you."

I brought out the brown wig, leaving the blond one concealed in the bottom of the bag, and held it out for his inspection. Nico tried to summon polite interest. "It looks very fine. I hope she likes it as much as she expects to."

"I guess we'll find out when I return to Oberton," I said, tucking the wig back in my bag.

"So you're finished with your errands? Are you heading to the palace?"

"Yes, if I can retrace my steps."

"No need. I'll take you."

I frowned, like someone who had suddenly remembered that she was angry with the scamp who had just showed up in her life again. "Maybe I don't want your company."

"Sweet goddess," he muttered before saying in a normal tone of voice, "Didn't we go through all this already? You're angry—I'm sorry—we'll start over."

"That was before you started trailing behind Marguerite, spying on *her*!"

He shrugged. "I thought it was no bad thing for her to realize from her earliest days here that people are closely watching her movements. If the prince intends to take her as his bride, her behavior must be completely above reproach."

"She was at a *temple*."

His expression was serious. "I think we both know that Marguerite can get in trouble at a temple just as easily she can anywhere else."

I flounced a little and started walking, picking a direction at random. Nico easily caught up and gently took hold of my arm to set me on a slightly different course. "So tell me," I said in a voice of great annoyance. "Are you running behind all of Prince Cormac's *other* guests and advising them to watch their behavior? Surely one or two of them has engaged in activities you do not approve of."

"I am not," he said cheerfully. "All of them can sell state secrets and befriend smugglers and visit illicit lovers, and I wouldn't so much as whisper a warning."

"Then why are you so concerned with Marguerite's well-being?"

He glanced down at me. He still hadn't released my arm. "Because *you* would care if she came to harm," he said, his voice unwontedly serious. "And perhaps come to harm alongside her. Surely you don't even need to ask me that?"

I met his gaze and for a moment we walked on blindly, too engrossed in each other to pay any attention to where we were heading. Fortunately, we didn't trip over any impediments in the street or stumble into anyone blocking our way.

"You don't know me well enough to care what happens to me," I said.

"I might not know you very well, but I care what happens to you."

"I'm only going to be in Camarria for a month," I answered.

"Unless the prince marries Marguerite."

Silence again, and another moment of staring, then I pulled my gaze away and concentrated on my feet. "Well," I said, and nothing else.

His grip on my arm changed as he tugged me in another direction. "I want to show you something. How soon do you have to be back at the palace?"

"Within the hour, I suppose. Marguerite has a headache and I don't think she'll leave her room until I'm back."

"That's enough time," he said. "Come this way."

I didn't say yes but I didn't say no, and pretty soon he had guided me out of the crowded shopping area and onto quieter streets watched over by taller and more ancient buildings. "The financial district," he explained. "Every merchant who owns a ship or has a stake in a mine has an office in one of these places. If you wanted to strike at the heart of the Seven Jewels, you'd come here and set the whole block on fire."

"I have no such ambitions," I said. "So this is what you wanted to show me? These old buildings?"

"No. This."

He guided me around a corner and into a scene of lovely chaos. We'd arrived at a broad, crowded square that seemed to be the very center point of the financial district, with clerks and lawyers and merchants and servants crossing in all directions with purposeful, hurried strides. No horses or carriages, though—this particular plaza seemed to be reserved for pedestrians. Over it all arched a long, elegant bridge built from honey-gold stone. Inset into its supporting architecture were carved faces alternating with ancient heraldry. They stared out over the busy plaza like watchful guardians.

"The bridge at Amanda Plaza, named after our first queen," he said. "I thought you'd like to see it."

"Gorsey," I said, like any yokel, staring at the site. "I think I would."

His hand slipped down my arm to twine with my fingers, and he pulled me after him. "Come on, then."

Handfast as any lovers, we climbed onto the smooth arch of the bridge as it rose higher and higher above the city. People passed us in both directions, the professional-looking ones moving with determination and speed, while the young couples and the nannies and the first-time visitors dawdled even more than we did. Near the midpoint, we stopped and gazed down at the sight below. From this perspective, I could see the pattern in the brickwork of the plaza, a complex arrangement of straight lines and herringbone angles, brighter in some spots than others where new bricks had been laid in over the decades to repair broken sections. I could also see that five different boulevards fed into this one central spot and that each street was lined with more of those tall, stern buildings that looked older than any structure I'd ever seen in Oberton.

When I said as much, Nico nodded. "This is the oldest block in the oldest city in all the Seven Jewels. They say that before the plaza was laid down, and before the buildings around it went up, this spot was the center for trade between the lands across the mountains and all the small communities on this side of the divide. King Edwin set up court here partly for that reason and partly because he said having the mountains at his back gave him a defensible position. He was more worried about uprisings in his own provinces than attacks from his neighbors."

"You seem to know a lot about history."

"I like it. I like to know what happened before I was born. Makes me wonder what will happen after I'm gone."

I'd never had the time for such philosophical musings. Or maybe I'd just never had the interest. I placed my basket at my feet and pointed with the hand I had just freed up.

"Those statues over there—who are they supposed to be?"

"Queen Amanda and her echoes. Can you tell that the echoes are carved from lighter stone? Other than that, they're identical."

"What's that in the center of the plaza? A shrine?"

It was another grouping of statues, this time featuring the three incarnations of the triple goddess, standing with their backs to each other and their arms extended in the traditional poses. In the brickwork behind them, in the triangle of space created by their bodies, was a metal grate that might have been two feet square. While we watched, I saw three different people approach the statues and toss coins into the grate by pitching them over or under one of the goddess's outstretched hands.

"Something like that," Nico answered. "Except for the main temple, it's the most famous holy spot in the city. It's considered lucky to drop a few coins in when you're hoping for the goodwill of the goddess. Wedding parties often come here on their way to the ceremony. Families whose loved ones are sick will throw in a few coppers. People awaiting trial." He shrugged. "Anyone, really."

I leaned over the railing, trying to get a better look. "Is there a way to get the money *out*?"

He nodded. "There's a small tunnel that the priestesses use to gather the donations once a quarter or so. Rumors always abound about thieves who've found ways to break into the tunnel and clean out the money, but in my experience that's never happened."

"And you would know."

I picked up my bag and tugged him to the other side of the bridge, so we could examine any interesting features on that side of the plaza. The first thing that caught my eye was a small dais large enough for about five people to stand side by side. "What's that?"

"That's where the king sends his herald when he has some important proclamation to make. For instance, when Cormac was born, the news was announced here. If we ever go to war, this will be where the public finds out about it." He glanced down at me. "When Cormac gets engaged, here's where the announcement will be made."

"So some lucky random passers-by who came to the plaza to throw money at the feet of the goddess will be the first people to find out that the prince is taking a bride."

Nico laughed. "Well, usually there's already a sense throughout the city that something important is about to happen. I've heard stories about the days right before Cormac was born. Everyone knew that the queen was about to give birth, so people flocked to the plaza to hear the news. Some of them camped here for days, bringing commerce to a virtual halt. One story is that the king asked the midwives to hurry her labor along just so the city would go back to normal. People usually know when to expect a big announcement and they come here for the details."

"Do you think people are already gathered here hoping to learn about Cormac's engagement?"

"I suppose there might be a few," he said. "But no one expects an announcement till the end of the month, right before the visitors are supposed to leave. *Then* you might see the crowds start to form."

"What if there's no announcement?"

"Then the crowds go home disappointed. But most people seem to think the prince will be betrothed by that time—and to Marguerite."

I knew Marguerite both dreaded that thought—and dreaded what it might mean for the kingdom if the betrothal did not go forward. I couldn't think of anything noncommittal to say, so I remained silent.

"I liked her," Nico said. "I didn't think I would."

I turned just enough to give him a mock curtsey. "Since she values your opinion so highly," I said, "I'll share your approval with her."

He grinned. "She's uncommon," he went on. "I would say she's both sharp and gentle, with an unexpected sense of humor."

"Not a bad description," I admitted. "I can't imagine I'd ever find anyone else to work for that I liked half so well."

"So you don't contemplate leaving her service. For any reason. Whether she returns to Oberton or moves permanently to Camarria."

He didn't specify what the reasons might be. Such as forming a romantic attachment to someone who lived in a city that Marguerite had left behind. "Not at the moment," I said, staring out over the bridge instead of meeting his gaze. "I suppose that could change."

We spent a moment silently contemplating the scene below us, though the hurrying clerks and laughing lovers seemed much less intriguing to me now. I let my eyes travel over other points of interest—a high brass gate that sat between stone posts but didn't seem to be guarding anything; a lone tree growing out of the only patch of ground that wasn't completely bricked over; and a blank stone wall, maybe eight feet high and ten feet wide, that anchored one corner of the plaza.

I asked about each one in turn. The gate was symbolic; King Edwin had installed it to signify that Camarria was the entrance to the Seven Jewels. The tree, which was nearly one hundred years old, had been a gift from the queen of Ferrenlea, across the ocean; it was supposed to represent the flowering of friendship between the two nations.

"Though apparently it has never actually flowered," Nico added. "In Ferrenlea, such trees put out big white blossoms in the spring, but this one never has."

"What about that wall?"

Nico turned his head to contemplate it. "That's for public executions."

"*What?* That's gruesome."

He shrugged slightly. "Execution is reserved for serious crimes. The idea of making it public is to give other miscreants pause before they commit the same kinds of acts."

I stared somewhat fearfully at the wall of mortared stone, which took on a sinister aspect now that I knew how it was used. And because I was closely affiliated with someone who had committed a serious crime. "How are they— What method is used to kill them?"

He glanced down. "I wouldn't have expected you to be so bloodthirsty."

"I'm horrified. But I feel compelled to ask."

"The guilty parties are lined up against the wall, facing a team of archers—two for every criminal. There's a signal, and all the archers shoot at the same time."

"Why two archers?"

"In case one misses the mark. To make sure the death is quick."

"Who gives the signal?"

He was still looking down at me, his face very serious. "The inquisitor."

"You?"

"My uncle."

"How many executions do have you in the average year?"

"Since I have been in the city, only three."

"What were their crimes?"

"Two attempted treason, and one committed murder."

"In this whole city, you've only had one murder in two years? I'm impressed."

I could tell he didn't like the note of sarcasm in my voice because a slight frown pulled down his eyebrows. But he answered readily enough, "It was a scandalous case in which one nobleman plotted against another in an elaborate scheme designed to ruin an entire family. The whole city followed the investigation and was interested in the outcome, so the sentence had to be carried out for the whole kingdom to see. For crimes of passion or accidental killings in bar-room fights, justice tends not to be so severe." He shrugged. "Or so public."

I took a deep breath. "Ah. So there are some instances in which criminals are punished in secret, quietly disappearing from their shops or houses instead of being shot through the heart for the entertainment of the masses."

"It's not entertainment," he said quietly. "A civil society cannot endure if there aren't rules—and if there aren't consequences when the rules are broken."

"Well, make me a promise," I said, wriggling my hand free from his hold, where it had rested comfortably all this time. "If you ever have cause to arrest me, and you think I might end up in front of your squad of archers, slit my throat quietly in some alley instead. I would much prefer that ending."

His face was even more serious now. "Why would you ever have cause to be arrested?"

"I can't think. I certainly hope I'm not. But I can't imagine a worse way to die than being paraded through the streets and shot in front of the whole city."

"I don't think you need to worry," he said. "Nothing's going to happen to you."

I bent over to pick up my straw bag. "Time to get back, I think. Marguerite will be waiting."

We followed the bridge to the other side, just so I could say I had traversed the whole thing, then cut through the middle of the plaza with the rest of the pedestrians. Our route took us past the goddess statues and Nico paused just long enough to toss a few coins toward the grate. I saw them glitter as they arced through the air before passing soundlessly through one of the narrow openings. He had offered the goddess real gold, then. I looked at him with my eyebrows raised, as if to ask, *What did you wish for?* He only smiled and shook his head. But he did take my hand again as we continued on toward the palace, and I let him hold it the whole way back.

CHAPTER SEVENTEEN

When I finally returned to Marguerite's rooms, I found her almost as fretful as I had painted her to the servants below-stairs, and it took me a few moments to calm her down. I didn't think the detour with Nico had added more than thirty minutes to my outing, but apparently it had seemed like hours to her. I hardly liked to say that I had been dallying with the king's inquisitor while she was pacing through her suite, wracked with nerves, so I told her that the shopping district was farther than I'd thought it would be and I'd gotten lost on the way home.

"I'm sorry you were so anxious," I said in a gentle voice. "But I only see two choices. Either I never leave to run errands or you try not to worry when I'm gone."

"I know—you're right—it's just that when you're not here I start thinking of all the things that can go wrong."

"They haven't gone wrong yet," I said. "We'll get through this."

She cheered up as I showed her the blond wig, and we spent a few minutes admiring how it changed my look once I put it on and arranged the false hair in exactly her style.

"Look at that," she said, as we stood side by side before the mirror and gazed at our reflections. "You hardly even notice the differences in our faces. You might not need to wear a veil at all."

"I still think a veil is a good idea," I said. "But I admit this makes me feel better about the whole deception."

She showed no inclination to join the other nobles in their afternoon activities. In fact, she'd already told a housemaid—speaking through the closed door—that she didn't plan to leave her rooms until dinnertime. So I fetched a tray of food from the kitchen and brought it up so Marguerite and I could share a luncheon with the echoes.

We spent the rest of the afternoon dancing.

There was to be a ball the following night and Marguerite wanted to make sure I was as good as my boast. All four of us took off our shoes so we would make a limited amount of noise, then we lined up for a waltz. Patience and Purpose made up one pair, Marguerite and I another. As Marguerite hummed a simple song to give us the beat, we swung into the measures of the dance. Truth to tell, I was a little worried that my technique wouldn't be as refined as that of a noblewoman's, but apparently my dancing mistress had been as good as she claimed.

"Whoever taught you the steps did an excellent job!" Marguerite exclaimed after we'd practiced two numbers. Patience and Purpose spun and twirled beside us, their blank, pretty faces wearing faint smiles. Hard to know, but it seemed as if they were enjoying themselves. "Let's try some of the reels and the other dances. If there's anything that's unfamiliar to you, let me know. I can always sit those out."

There were only two that I didn't recognize, though Marguerite said they weren't very popular and might not even be performed. "But you'll do just fine," she said. "I'm so pleased."

"What's going to be the entertainment for tonight, do you know?"

She made a face. "Cards."

I felt a flicker of apprehension. "Uh-oh. I only know the simple games, the ones children play. I don't know any of the rules for the fancier games."

She laughed. "Don't worry. You won't need any skill for this. But I think you'll find the evening deadly dull."

In fact, as I had during our first evening at the palace, I rather enjoyed myself. Again, everyone gathered in one of the salons before dinner to laugh and flirt and gossip. Lady Elyssa's injured echo was still too incapacitated to join her, but it didn't seem to bother her. In fact, when Nigel tried to express his sympathy, she said in a sweet voice, "But, Nigel, I so much appreciate the chance to see how dreadful life always must be for the unfortunate people who only have two echoes to begin with."

He made a strangled sound of displeasure and stalked off, his two echoes hurrying behind him. Elyssa turned her smiling face toward Marguerite. "It's so easy to ruffle him," she said. "It's hardly even fun."

Marguerite didn't have to answer that because they were joined by two young men accompanied by three echoes each. Elyssa, who grew quite lively at their approach, greeted them enthusiastically and introduced them to Marguerite. One was from Banchura and one from Empara, and their triple echoes marked them as highly eligible. No wonder Elyssa was excited to see them.

"Shall we make a pact now that the four of us will sit together for the card games tonight?" she suggested.

"I don't care about the games—I'm more interested in securing your promises that you'll dance with me tomorrow. Both of you," said the one from Banchura, a dark-haired fellow with a deep scar through one eyebrow. Probably a souvenir of a childhood accident. As discreetly as I could, I let my gaze wander to the faces of his echoes, to find them all similarly marked. If this young man had fallen and cut his face open, had the echoes all fallen at the same time, with the same results? Or had he received a singular blow to the head, an unfortunate slice on the face, that wasn't repeated on his echoes? Had the wounds just magically opened up in their own skin, even if no harm was visited upon their bodies? I would have to ask Marguerite.

"I'd love to dance with you—half the night, if you like," Elyssa replied.

"I'm not sure I can spare half the night, but I'd be happy to be your partner as well," Marguerite said.

"And mine," the other noble interjected. Even without a scar, he wasn't as attractive as his friend, though he wasn't exactly homely;

merely, he had a somewhat nondescript look about him. If it would ever be possible to overlook a man trailed by three identical shadows, he was the sort of person it would be easy to ignore. "I might not be as smooth as Deryk in extending invitations, but I'm more likely to be sober."

"That's true," Elyssa said to Marguerite. "But Deryk is funnier, so it all evens out."

"Funnier and meaner," Deryk answered. "Let me tell you what I learned today about that ghastly girl from Thelleron."

"Vivienne?" said Elyssa in a mocking voice. "Oh, yes, *please.*"

"You'll have to tell me some other time. I must go say hello to Darrily," Marguerite spoke up, waving at someone across the room. My guess was that she didn't like Deryk's tone, or the fact that he seemed to enjoy Elyssa's company. I admired the neat way she extricated herself from the conversation.

We were only halfway across the room when a footman came in to announce dinner, so Marguerite didn't get a chance to talk to Darrily. We all filed into the dining hall we'd used the first night, and dinner was served as it had been that night as well. I felt more at ease this time and better able to enjoy my food, which was delicious.

Afterward we convened in a long, well-lit room set with a couple dozen small four-person tables. I followed faithfully behind Purpose while I tried to figure out the layout. I quickly realized that the center of the room held six of those four-person tables, lined up in two rows of three, and that was where all the nobles would sit. For each one of the nobles' tables, three echoes' tables had been set up in one straight line. I watched in fascination as the card players gradually settled into their chairs, all the echoes sitting in the exact same spots as their originals, just one or two or three tables away.

As always, I was in the outer ring, which meant I had a good view of the entire room—and even more important, a clear view of Purpose's back, so I could mimic her movements. There was one empty chair at my table, meaning one of the men at Marguerite's table had only two echoes. But one of the other echoes was a perfect replica of Prince Cormac, who apparently had chosen to seat himself to Marguerite's left. At some signal I missed, the prince's echo picked up a deck of cards from the center of the table and began to shuffle.

I tried not to rub my palms on my dress, but my hands were a little sweaty; this might be even more difficult than eating a meal, when everyone else was somewhat occupied with their own cutting and chewing. Here, I was in a small group and we were all staring at each other. A miscue would be more readily noticed.

Except echoes didn't really stare. Or notice things. And they couldn't speak up to question me if they did.

The echo dealt seven cards to each spot at the table, even the empty place. I waited for Purpose to pick up her cards before I reached for my own. And then it was all I could do to keep from laughing. They were blank. These were special decks, manufactured simply to allow echoes to play games with the exact same props and gestures as their masters. Who would ever have thought up such a thing?

Cormac's echo laid a card down in the middle of the table, and the female echo across from me did the same. I waited until Purpose put down her own card before I put mine down as well. All three of us paused for the length of time it should have taken our fourth player to select a card, then the female echo gathered up the hand. Then it was her turn to lead.

It was the most bizarre experience of my life to date.

It was tempting—so tempting—to play out of order, to refuse to deal when it was my turn, to gather up a hand even if Marguerite hadn't won it. Would the echoes look at me askance, tilt their pale faces toward me in puzzled wonder? Would they be bewildered, thrown off their rhythm, incited to a level of uneasiness so great that it caught the attention of their originals? I didn't do it, even though I suspected the echoes would not respond in any way. But there were servants moving among the tables, filling water glasses and offering plates of sweets, and *they* might notice if I behaved out of character. We were so much at risk that it would be suicidal to do anything that might draw attention to me or to Marguerite. But I did wish I might have the chance.

We had been playing for maybe a half hour when all the men—originals and echoes—came to their feet. I sat back in slight alarm, but it turned out they were merely moving to the next table so that, by the time the night was over, all the men would have had a chance to play in company with all the women. I had to suppress a groan as I quickly calculated that, if they spent thirty minutes at each table, we would be playing cards for three hours.

Marguerite had been right after all. I was beginning to be as bored as I'd ever been in my life.

Things got a little more interesting, and a little more unsettled, when Lord Deryk's echo took his place on my right. While the other lords had been animated and friendly, judging by the behavior of their echoes, Deryk was in exceptionally high spirits. He went through two glasses of wine before the first two hands were dealt, chugging them down so quickly the servers had to scurry over to refill them. My guess was that he had been imbibing pretty heavily ever since the game began—and so had his echoes. The one sitting by me seemed completely intoxicated. His gestures were broad and careless, his smile loose and wide, his whole demeanor unsteady. Pretty soon I was forced to pull half my attention from Purpose and focus it on Deryk's echo just in case he did something outrageous.

He didn't, but he did grow increasingly sloppy, with the result that when he shifted positions in his chair, he accidently kicked me in the leg. I thought I heard Marguerite's soft gasp of pain, Deryk's hastily muttered apology, and then his echo was grabbing my hand and planting a wet kiss on my knuckles. I was so annoyed I wanted to wrench my arm away, but Marguerite and the echoes merely endured the unwelcome touch in what seemed like frigid silence, so I let my hand lie listlessly in his grasp. A moment only, then he released me, and play resumed.

I thought perhaps Deryk would now display a bit more decorum, but that didn't prove to be the case. Five minutes later, when a footman came by with wine, the lord was quick to request more. I was glad to see Purpose shake her head in the negative when the server offered to refill her glass. Like me, I was certain Marguerite was wishing this night would soon come to an end.

Five minutes later, it almost did. At the main table, Deryk had hitched himself forward in his chair to tell a story that required a great deal of gesticulating and laughter, and naturally his echoes all did the same. One swipe of their hands knocked over their wine-glasses, and I instinctively leapt to my feet to spare my dress.

No one else was standing.

Not Purpose. Not Patience. Not Marguerite.

I stood there motionless for the longest moment of my life, while the echoes at my table stared at me and footmen throughout the room stared at me and the nobles at their gaming tables stared at me. An independent echo. A creature who did not exist. We were exposed. We were doomed.

The room was utterly silent. Not a whisper of conversation, not a clink of glassware, not a flutter from a shuffled deck of cards.

Then slowly, deliberately, Purpose came to her feet, brushing at the front of her dress, which was stained with a few drops of wine. A moment later, Patience stood up, making no attempt to replicate either my pose or the one that Purpose held. Finally, Marguerite rose and glanced around the room.

Now everyone was staring at her.

"Your echoes," said the lady sitting at the table with her. Her voice was thick with awe. "They have minds of their own?"

"Hardly that," Marguerite said in an easy, offhand way. "They are capable of some individual motion, but only when I choose to release them. Mostly I control them—" She snapped her fingers, and the three of us instantly adopted her exact stance. "But when I'm alone, or when I'm very tired, or when I'm upset—" Here we all paused to turn accusing looks on Lord Deryk and his shadows. "Sometimes I let them go."

"I've never heard of such a thing," someone else said.

Rescue came from the most unexpected quarter. "Then you've been living in some unsophisticated backwater," said Lady Elyssa. She came to her feet in a graceful surge of glittering gold satin, tossing back her black hair and smiling contemptuously. Her two echoes kept to their seats, their hands folded before them on the table, their eyes gazing downward. "It's a common enough thing among people who have particularly fine command of their thoughts."

Now she made a sharp gesture and her echoes leapt up and instantly, seamlessly, began copying her again. "But generally speaking, I find life less tedious when I don't have to wonder if my echoes are behaving themselves," Elyssa added with a throaty laugh. "So I usually don't give them freedom."

She and her echoes sank back to their seats, and after a moment of strained silence, the nobles returned to their card games. But there was a great deal of whispering around the room, a good number of surreptitious glances thrown in our direction. I spent the next hour scrupulously following every move that Purpose made, but I was relieved beyond description when Prince Cormac and his echoes pushed back from the table and stood up.

"This has been a very instructive evening," he said, in a tone that indicated it was now concluded. "Thank you all for a most enjoyable time."

The rest of the nobles were dropping their cards, standing up, and starting to mill around as Cormac made his way over to Marguerite. "I wanted to offer my apologies on Deryk's behalf," he said. His echoes all showed faces of grave regret to Patience, Purpose, and me. "His spirits are often high, but he is usually more entertaining than disruptive. I am sorry if he made you uncomfortable."

She offered him a composed smile. "I assure you, this is not the first time some inebriated noble has spilled a little wine on my dress," she said. "I am entirely recovered from the incident."

"That's gracious," he replied. "But I hope you fare better tomorrow night at the ball, and that your evening is one of unalloyed delight."

Her smile widened. "I hope so, too."

He bowed over her hand, she curtseyed, and all their echoes played along. He turned to make goodbyes to a few of the other guests, and she said her own farewells to her particular friends. Finally, we were out the door, heading down the hallways and up the stairs to the safety of Marguerite's room.

The minute the door was locked, we all loosed soft wails of horror and collapsed into each other's arms. We stood there the longest time, huddled together, rocking back and forth, and trying to hold back tears.

"I'm so sorry. I'm so sorry," I said over and over again, while Marguerite clutched my cold hands with her own icy fingers and said, "It's all right. It's all right. It's all right."

At last, I straightened up and wiped my dripping nose. "I almost ruined everything," I said. "After all the times I've told *you* to be strong, to be careful, *I'm* the one who behaved stupidly."

She shook her head. She flicked a hand at the echoes and they moved over to sit on one of the couches. Marguerite and I still stood by the door, taking deep breaths and trying to calm our nerves.

"We're both going to make mistakes," she said. "We know it's going to happen. We just have to recover quickly, like we did tonight."

"Releasing the echoes. That was brilliant," I said. "I was so stunned I never would have thought of it."

She turned her head to look at the echoes. Patience had slumped against the cushions and was half asleep, but Purpose was bent forward, picking at the stain on her dress. "I didn't," she said.

"What?"

"I didn't let them go. Not consciously. *Purpose* is the one who figured it out. She's the one who saved us all."

Now I was the one to turn and stare. Purpose gave up trying to rub away the stain; now she sagged next to Patience and closed her eyes. "How is that possible?" I whispered.

Marguerite shook her head. "I don't know."

CHAPTER EIGHTEEN

I slept badly and woke in my own small room feeling worried and unrefreshed. To my surprise, Marguerite seemed to have passed a better night than I had, for she was oddly cheerful when I arrived at her door. She and the echoes were already dressed, but in their simplest clothes; clearly, she intended to skip the morning's social events, as had already become her habit in three short days.

"Let's go to the market," she said, "and buy flowers for the ball."

The last time we had been there, Nico had showed us the way and a hired conveyance had carried us back, but the route was fairly straightforward and I was pretty sure I could find the place again. But we hadn't been walking for more than three blocks when Marguerite said, "Let's go to the temple first."

I was behind her, so she couldn't see the reproach on my face. But she could hear it in my voice. "My lady. There hasn't been time for Taeline to send a reply yet."

"I know," she said. "I just want to go."

So we changed course and headed to the three-towered temple instead. Once again, we crossed the bridge, circled the building, and entered through the door for mercy, taking our seats near the back of the round room. Once again, I tried to maintain a pious expression as I surreptitiously glanced at the other penitents gathered in this wing of the sanctuary. I wondered if any of them could be praying for absolution for crimes that were as heinous as ours. The young woman with the sleeping baby on her lap—did she feel guilty for cuckolding her feckless husband, or had she poisoned his soup because he beat her when he was drunk? Perhaps the elderly

217

man with the palsied hands had pushed his demented wife down the stairs because he was no longer hearty enough to care for her and death seemed preferable to a precarious existence. I stared for some time at a handsome professional man who might have been twenty-five. He looked strong enough to strangle a rival and smart enough to embezzle funds. It was impossible to judge from their faces what secrets they carried in their hearts.

Which was a comfort to me, if we were equally as difficult to scan.

One of the priestesses paused at the pew and asked if we wanted her to pray with us. Marguerite surprised me by shaking her head and looking down at her hands. The priestess walked on, but we sat there for another twenty minutes while Marguerite continued to meditate, her fingers methodically stroking the onyx disks of her bracelet. So she truly had come here this morning just to soothe her soul by laying her troubles at the feet of the goddess. Even I was beginning to feel the peace of the temple seep into my bones by the time Marguerite lifted her head. She touched her fingers to her forehead, breast, and lips, and the three of us quickly followed suit. Then we all rose to our feet and quietly exited the building, not having spoken a word since we stepped in.

"Can you find the way to the market from here?" Marguerite asked once we were back in the sunlight and crossing one of the bridges.

I glanced around because this was the point at which Nico generally came bounding out of the shadows, but he was nowhere in sight. Of course, that didn't mean we hadn't been followed by some *other* member of the inquisitor's crew. I was just as glad our errands today all seemed to be completely innocent.

"I think so. Last time we walked there from the temple and first we took this street, to the right—"

Between the two of us, we remembered the way well enough, and the one time we had to ask a stranger for directions, he confirmed that we were on the correct route. As before, the flower market seemed to burst onto our senses in one glorious riot of color and scent the minute we turned the final corner. I practically gasped, and I heard Marguerite laugh.

"It's just so *beautiful*," she said.

"It really is."

We browsed slowly, almost sensuously, pausing at stalls where the arrayed blooms possessed particularly intense shades, and sniffing at the air as if color produced its own weighted aroma. Tonight, Marguerite would be wearing a deep-dyed gown in a hue somewhere between red and purple; it was almost too vivid for her pale complexion, but I knew the right headpiece would draw attention back to her face. So we gathered bunches of lilacs, stems of roses, sprays of azaleas, and handfuls of violets, each petal just a tint away from the actual color of the dress.

"I can hardly wait to get started putting these together," I said as we headed over to the carts-for-hire and paid for passage home.

"Do you have time to make four of them before tonight?"

"I do—but it will take me the rest of the day."

Marguerite patted the back of her head. "Then I think I feel another of my headaches coming on."

She said as much to Lourdes, who was naturally lurking in the foyer when we returned to the palace. "Shall I have lunch sent to your rooms?" the housekeeper offered.

"Oh, that would be so kind of you! Enough for Brianna, too, since I will want her to stay by me in case I need something."

"Certainly, my lady."

As soon as we were in her suite, I hastily switched to my workaday attire. "If I ever leave your service, I think I'll join a theater group," I observed. "Not only am I getting a great deal of experience as an actress, I've become adept at quickly changing my appearance, which is something I understand actresses must do between scenes."

"Why would you ever want to leave my service?" Marguerite asked from the bedroom, where she had retired with the echoes.

I laughed. "Well, I wouldn't. I can't imagine even a theatrical troupe could live a life as exciting as *this* one is proving to be."

I accepted the tray when the maid arrived, thanking her in a whisper to reinforce the notion of Marguerite's headache. The minute the door was shut, the other three leapt up, and we all had a hearty meal, since the morning's walk had left us hungry.

"Now," I said, spreading the blossoms on a center table, "let's get to work." It took me nearly five hours—even with the help of Marguerite and the echoes—to create the four headpieces, but I was absurdly pleased with how well they turned out. Marguerite's was the most elaborate, a confection of wire and net and flowers that fit closely over a sleek chignon. The updrawn hairstyle left her delicate neck exposed; the deep décolletage of the dress accentuated the whiteness of her skin, which we had left bare of any jewelry. The effect was striking. Her cheeks and her throat were so pale, so still, between the vivid variety of the flowers on top and the rich darkness of the dress below, that your eyes were instantly drawn to her face.

"Everyone will want to dance with you," I predicted.

She stood in front of the mirror, admiring her reflection. She wasn't particularly vain, but it was clear she liked the way she looked in this ensemble. "I hope dancing is more fun than playing cards," she said.

"I'm sure it will be," I answered, but inwardly I was feeling a certain trepidation. More chances to make a mistake during a ball, I thought. More opportunities to trip, take a misstep, fail to imitate Marguerite perfectly. Last night's revelation that she could release her echoes would excuse a certain amount of clumsiness on my part, maybe, but I still saw a lot of places for this evening to go badly.

But Marguerite could be right. It could be fun.

In fact, Prince Cormac and all his guests seemed to think the ball would be the best of good times. No one lingered in the drawing room before the meal or took much time over dinner, and soon we were assembling in a charming room of high ceilings, glittering chandeliers, mirrored walls, and polished wooden floors. A quartet of musicians was already in place, playing soft music with a lilting beat. A thrill of excitement hummed through the air.

Nothing quite like the chance to twirl about in the arms of an attractive partner to make it seem like the world was rife with possibilities.

I saw the Banchura triplets whispering together and heard Elyssa's tinkling laugh before I realized exactly why everyone was so on edge. All the women were wondering: *Who will Cormac dance with first?* Everyone knew the rumor that he would be taking Marguerite as his bride—but it was still only a rumor. They could all still make plays for his attention, and a ball was an excellent place to pursue romantic intrigue. It was hardly a surprise that most of the ladies lingered near the doorway, hoping to be the first to catch his eye when he strolled into the room.

Marguerite was about as far from the doorway as she could get when Cormac stepped across the threshold, and I saw him pause for a moment, looking around the room. It seemed to me that he noted her position and didn't want to cause a stir by crossing the entire width of the floor to speak to her, so he turned to one of the women more conveniently nearby. It happened to be Darrily of Pandrea.

"Would you honor me with a dance?" he asked, offering her a bow.

She laid her hand in his and curtseyed so gracefully that the opal pendant against her forehead didn't even quiver. "Majesty, I would be delighted."

Everyone else quickly paired up once the prince had made his selection. Since there were twelve men and twelve women present, no one was left to sit on the sidelines to feel sulky and unattractive, as had happened at every country dance I had ever attended.

I was certain Marguerite was not best-pleased when Lord Deryk was the first man to solicit her hand. But he seemed somewhat chastened and much more sober this evening.

"You must allow me a chance to apologize for my boorishness yesterday," he said. "If you refuse me now, I'll simply follow you around all evening, growing increasingly desperate in my attempts to win your forgiveness."

Her face showed neutral politeness. "No need for such extreme behavior," she said. "I was not harmed by a few drops of wine."

"Of course not," he said, apparently unable to suppress a roguish smile. "When did a little wine ever hurt anyone?"

Marguerite laid her hands in his, and Patience and Purpose and I joined up with his echoes. "Still," she said, "I would prefer not to be doused again tonight."

He laughed and pulled us onto the floor to join the other waltzers. For the first few measures, I was shaky and nervous, knowing that the dips and turns of the dance would prevent me from always keeping Marguerite and her echoes in sight. How could I copy her steps if I couldn't even watch what her echoes were doing? But I quickly realized that dancing might be the easiest imitation of all, since my *partner* was mimicking his original's movements exactly. All I had to do was relax and follow his lead. Perhaps my head might tilt at an imperfect angle or my expression might not mirror Marguerite's, but I would spin and sway just as she did as long as I followed my partner's cues.

I began to enjoy myself.

Deryk, despite his flaws, appeared to be an excellent dancer, and we all skimmed along the floor with great energy and flair. Marguerite even consented to take a second turn with him; in the glimpses I got of her face, I could see she was smiling. I didn't think she was sorry, though, when another lord solicited her hand as soon as the second dance concluded.

It was a little trickier for me to copy Marguerite as she partnered with this fellow because his echo was more reserved than Deryk's. His arms around me were almost weightless; his cues were so subtle that now and then I had trouble telling which way I was supposed to turn. Some of my nervousness returned, and I made more of an effort to watch Patience and Purpose when I couldn't see Marguerite.

Nonetheless, I managed to make it creditably through the dance, and I started to relax again. But Marguerite had barely pulled her hands free from his clasp before she was approached by a new partner—Prince Cormac.

"Would you honor me with this dance?" he asked formally, and she formally accepted. The music started up again and I stepped into the embrace of one of his echoes.

It was like dancing with an ordinary man. His hands were warm through the fabric of my dress, his arms were muscled and powerful, and he led me through every spin with decisive firmness. Even more unnerving, he looked me straight in the eyes, as the other echoes had not, with a gaze that was almost unblinkingly direct. I practically expected him to open his mouth and ask how I was enjoying my visit to the royal city.

Except. The dark eyes might be direct, but they weren't expressive. Even through the scrim of my veil I could tell that he wasn't actually focused on me. There was a blankness to the firm lines of his handsome face, an empty, waiting look. The closest comparison I could come up with was the expression you sometimes see on the face of a man who's sleeping. This creature wasn't fully alive—but he might be, someday, if something woke him up.

I thought again of the story of King Edwin, of the essence that flowed from his original body into the shells of his echoes. This echo looked perfectly ready to receive Cormac's spirit if the situation arose. Though I did not think tonight would be that occasion.

The three sets of echoes spun in a slow orbit around Marguerite and Cormac, as I assumed all the other echoes circled their originals. I found myself wishing I could have a seat somewhere above the dance floor so I could see the splendid sight. I risked a few glances at the high walls, looking for places where the molding seemed thick enough to mark a hidden door. Surely there were peepholes behind some of the wainscoting; surely there were undercooks and upstairs maids clustered in secret alcoves, peering down at us and sighing in envy. I wished I could trade places with one of them for five minutes, just to enjoy the magnificent choreography of the ball.

But, of course, I couldn't slip away. And, of course, I needed to pay attention to what was happening right around me, where the motions of the dance sometimes took me close enough to Marguerite and Cormac to overhear snatches of their conversation.

"I remember this," Cormac said the first time I caught some of their words.

"Remember what? I've never been to Camarria before." Like his, her tone was light, flirtatious. I knew she was capable of pretending, but she *sounded* like she was having a good time.

"Dancing with you. There was a ball at your father's house."

"Indeed, there was."

"You wore a white dress with red ribbons."

"I'm flattered that you can still call it to mind."

"I'm not sure I'll ever forget it."

"But you've seen so many girls! In so many dresses!"

"And you wore a lovely necklace. All white and black stones, except for one drop of red, right—" He freed a hand so he could touch a fingertip to her chest, just above the neckline of her dress. I could feel the echo's warm finger press for a moment against my own bare skin. "Here."

"A necklace of onyx," she said, sounding a little breathless. "To show how proud I am of the city where I was born."

Prince Cormac took her hand again, and the echo took mine. "Yes," he said, "but there are other cities in the Seven Jewels where you might find yourself equally at home if you gave yourself the chance."

I couldn't hear her reply to that, since a swell of the music indicated a change in our pattern, and the echo swept me into a series of complicated steps. By the time we were back within earshot, Cormac and Marguerite were discussing less heady stuff and she was perfectly in command of her voice.

I hoped Cormac didn't flirt so broadly with all the other women at court—although, from what I could tell, *all* the nobles flirted with each other all the time. I couldn't imagine what any of them would talk about once they were actually married, since they didn't seem to have any conversations of substance beforehand. Although I supposed that marriages between nobles were ultimately about property and possessions, and those topics would dominate their discussions once they had joined their estates. Probably not that different, when you came right down to it, than the conversations Robbie and I used to have about the improvements we would make to his father's farm once we inherited it.

I stifled a sigh.

Marguerite accepted a second dance with Cormac, but it was a reel, so energetic that there was no breath left for conversation. After that, everyone took a short break to sample refreshments and whisper bits of gossip they'd managed to pick up during the evening so far. The musicians were just retuning their instruments, signaling that the dancing was about to start again, when Dezmen came over and offered Marguerite a friendly bow.

"Are you free for the next number?" he asked. "So far you've been besieged by suitors."

Marguerite set down her empty glass and smiled. "Free and happy to dance with you!" she said. "Perhaps you can explain *why* Prince Cormac thinks I would be interested in going on an excursion to see some ruins on the far edge of the city."

Dezmen chuckled and held out his hand. "Oh, but they are very *special* ruins!"

I lost the rest of his answer as his echoes also extended their hands and Marguerite's shadows responded. But Dezmen had only two echoes to Marguerite's three. I had to assume that Cormac had hired extra men and women to fill in when the numbers were unequal, so I was not surprised when a masculine shape materialized in front of Purpose just as I allowed one of Dezmen's echoes to take my hand. The newcomer wore all black, with no ornamentation at all; clearly, he was trying to make himself as unobtrusive as possible. But as far as I was concerned, he might as well have been wearing scarlet and gold—and having his appearance announced by blaring trumpets. Because it was Nico.

I was as nerveless and free of volition as any echo when Dezmen's shadow first pulled me onto the dance floor. *Nico!* He had told me himself that he sometimes filled in for missing echoes at the king's balls—how could I possibly have forgotten? It was by the sheerest chance that he had been closer to Purpose than to me. It so easily could have been my hand he grasped, not hers. And the minute he'd looked me in the eye, he would have recognized me. Even through the veil. Even not expecting to see me. Or, I don't know— maybe he was so used to dancing with echoes that he wouldn't have bothered glancing down at my face. He was so accustomed to their blank expressions, their averted eyes, that he wouldn't even have bothered to check whether this one might be different.

But as soon as his hands closed over mine, surely he would have noticed something amiss. Expecting an echo's cool fingers, he would have been surprised by my warm ones. He would have glanced down—he would have identified my face—he would have—

What would he have done?

Cried out in astonishment, come to a sudden halt, caused Dezmen and the other dancers to crash into him, demanding to know what was wrong? Or would he have played along—crushed my hands in his, maybe, fixed his fierce gaze on mine, and hissed out angry questions under his breath? If Nico ever found out about our deception, he might not expose me, not right away, but he would require an answer, and at the moment I couldn't think of any story that would satisfy him. I could certainly tell him that one of Marguerite's echoes had died, but that would be a tragedy; that would be something that would earn her the horrified sympathy of everyone in this room. He would want to know why we had con- cealed such a thing, and there was no explanation that made sense except the truth—which I obviously could not share.

My brain was in such a whirl that I was almost unaware of the first few measures of the dance. Not until I almost stumbled into Patience did I realize that Dezmen's echo was trying to steer me into a turn and that my body was not properly responding. Then a flood of adrenaline turned my skin prickly and my hands clammy, and I turned almost *too* quickly. I had to concentrate. I had to play this precisely right. Nico might not be my partner for this number, but he was only a few feet away. If I stumbled, if I missed a step, he was close enough to see. He was near enough to recognize me even if he wasn't holding me in his arms.

I took a deep breath and focused on the echo's dark face. His eyes didn't quite meet mine; his smile was rote and remote. But I could follow his movements well enough. I could survive this dance. I concentrated ferociously on the music, on the subtle shifts of the echo's body.

But for every step, every beat, I was tinglingly aware of Nico, dancing with Purpose just a few feet away from me.

Purpose. Had it really been sheer luck that she was standing where she was, the farthest away from Dezmen's two echoes? Or had she deliberately positioned herself there, realizing that one of us would be paired up with an ordinary man, and that *I* should not be the one to have that man as a partner? But the echoes were incapable of independent reasoning. Weren't they? Even I hadn't thought the situation through that thoroughly. Even Marguerite had not. How could an echo have analyzed the danger and moved so subtly to avert it?

It had been chance. It must have been. Nothing else made any sense.

The dance with Dezmen finally came to an end and, to my relief, he did not ask Marguerite for a second one. But as the nobles and their echoes churned through the room, looking to partner up again, I started mentally reviewing where the next risk might lie. Of the twelve men on the dance floor tonight, there were four who had only two echoes, and any one of them might solicit Marguerite to dance at any point. I had to stay alert; I had to make sure that, whenever the numbers were unequal, I always paired up with an echo. I could not risk even a single dance with Nico.

Though I couldn't help a brief, wistful speculation about what it would feel like to waltz with the inquisitor's apprentice.

The next few dances held no particular terrors, but by that time I was too tightly wound to completely relax. If any of my part-ners had been human and capable of speech, they would certainly have asked me what was wrong because I was jumpy and frequently clumsy. My hands were as cold as theirs. I never quite focused on their faces because I was constantly trying to glance around to assess if we might be in danger. By the time the third hour of the ball came to a close, I had developed a real version of one of Marguerite's imaginary headaches.

It was probably midnight when the crowd paused to take another refreshment break. Marguerite had snagged a glass of lemonade and joined the Banchura triplets on a set of sofas, so our mulberry-colored gowns provided dark contrast to their cascade of aqua and teal and cobalt.

"Have you noticed?" Leonora murmured with her goblet against her lip. "Elyssa's injured echo is *still* missing."

"That poor creature has been confined to Elyssa's room for the entire time they've been here," said Letitia, the sister who appeared to have the kindest heart. "She must be absolutely wretched to be separated from all the others."

"Do you think Elyssa should have brought the echo downstairs anyway, but made her sit out the dances?" Marguerite said curiously.

"A very good question!" Lavinia exclaimed. "I suppose Elyssa was right to leave her upstairs because I'm sure the echo would try to dance if she was here with the rest of them. The impulse to conform would be too strong to allow her to sit, even if her leg is broken, don't you think?"

"What would *your* echoes do?" Leonora asked.

It was a serious question now that Marguerite had revealed herself as someone with unconventional echoes. She thought it over before replying, "I'm not sure. Even when I release them, we're never more than a few feet apart. If I was halfway across a ballroom? I'm not positive one of them would sit quietly and wait for my return."

"We could experiment," Leonora suggested. "Have Dezmen dance with you and *don't* allow that dancing master, or whoever he is, to pair up with your third echo. See what happens."

"I don't think so," Marguerite said, sounding amused. "It would be just my luck that she would grow agitated and start *throwing* herself through the crowd, determined to find me. Think how embarrassing for poor Dezmen! And for me!"

"Maybe some other time. *Not* at a ball," Lavinia said. "We'll all go walking in the garden and see what happens when you try to leave one of them behind."

"Maybe tomorrow," Letitia said. "The weather is supposed to be fine."

Marguerite's attention had been caught by a disturbance at the door. I saw the way her body grew still as she trained her eyes in that direction, and I saw Patience and Purpose grow equally focused, so I looked the same way. At first I didn't understand what had made them so uneasy. A man stood just over the threshold, his gaze flicking across the crowd as if he was counting bodies. He wore severe black and was almost as expressionless as an echo. From this distance, it was hard to tell his age or station, but I put him in his middle fifties and supposed him to be an employee of the crown. Not a servant—perhaps a secretary or a financial advisor...

Or an inquisitor.

On the thought, I felt my stomach clench. Yes, of course. He had that still, coiled look of latent power that I had seen in Del Morson, the governor's inquisitor back in Oberton. He was about the same height and build as Nico, so this could very well be Nico's uncle. During the short time that we had been in the palace, he had not bothered to show himself to Cormac's guests, though I had assumed he was observing all of us from some invisible lair. I couldn't imagine what had drawn him out of hiding tonight to make a very public appearance at a very frivolous event.

Or rather, I could. The thought made my stomach knot even more tightly.

"Who's that?" Marguerite asked.

"Can you be a little more specific?" Leonora replied gaily. "There are dozens of people here."

"At the door. He just arrived."

The triplets and all their echoes turned their attention that way. Marguerite took the opportunity to glance briefly at me. Her eyes were filled with dread, and I was sure she could see me very properly mimicking her expression.

"Ooooh, I don't know, but he's a dour one, isn't he?" was Lavinia's irreverent response.

"He doesn't look friendly at all," Letitia agreed.

"He looks like he's got bad news," Leonora observed.

"Well, now that's a shame. I wonder what news would be so bad that he couldn't wait until after the ball to deliver it?"

"I hope nothing's happened to the king," Marguerite said in a worried voice. I was pretty sure she had no fears on that score, but the triplets instantly took up the thought.

"Oh, no! That would be awful!"

"I saw him at breakfast this morning, and he seemed just fine."

"How old is he? I don't think he's even sixty yet. He's a young man still!"

"Well, maybe it's something else."

"But what else could it be?"

It was clear, by the rumblings of the crowd around us, that others had noticed the arrival of the inquisitor and were also starting to speculate about what his appearance might mean. Prince Cormac seemed to be the last person in the room to realize that doom stood on his doorstep, but eventually even he felt the weight of the inquisitor's gaze and turned to see who had come calling. By that time, everyone else had stopped whatever else they were doing to watch the drama unfold. No one raised a glass or took a step or spoke a word as Cormac made his way through the frozen crowd to the black-garbed figure waiting at the door. His echoes trailed behind him.

We all held our collective breath as the inquisitor murmured something into Cormac's ear. The prince started back with a look of mingled anger and horror. "Are you sure?" he demanded. The inquisitor nodded and spoke again. His voice was too low for anyone but Cormac to hear him, though we all leaned forward in mute anticipation, straining to catch a syllable.

Cormac half-turned from the inquisitor and looked wildly around the room, but the person he sought was already headed his way—his brother Jordan, clearly deducing that something dreadful had happened to the family and bracing himself to learn what it was. The minute Jordan arrived at Cormac's side, the inquisitor repeated his news, and the younger prince looked just as appalled. The three of them conferred quietly for another moment while the rest of us stared and fidgeted and exchanged wide-eyed glances. Then, without a backward glance, Cormac and his brother strode out of the ballroom, their echoes and the inquisitor closely following.

Those left behind practically exploded with exhaled breath and then instantly began firing off questions. *What happened? Was that the inquisitor? Did you hear what he said? When are we going to find out what's wrong?* We joined most of the dancers as they drew into a tight pack in the middle of the room, nobles in the center, their echoes arrayed behind them.

"Someone's dead—I heard him say *that* much," one fellow reported.

"They found a body, that's what I thought he said," a woman replied.

Other voices took up the tale, added their own queries and observations. "Whose body? Who's dead?"

"I thought I heard a name. I thought he said 'Jane's son.'"

"'Jane's son'? You mean *Jamison*?"

"What? Jamison? The king's bastard? Is he dead?"

"They found Lord Jamison's body?"

"Jamison is dead?"

"Jamison is dead!"

I wanted to sag to the floor with guilt and fear. My heart had grown huge and unwieldy, and now it was trying to blunder its way out of my chest. How much worse it must be for Marguerite! But she couldn't faint. She couldn't break down.

Now was not the time to draw attention to ourselves. Now we must be as shocked and surprised and bewildered as anyone.

I supposed we could do no better than to follow the lead of the Banchura triplets. "What dreadful news," Leonora said, touching her hand to her forehead, her heart, and her lips. Many others in the crowd did the same. "I confess I didn't like him, but it's always a miserable day when someone so young comes to an early end. May the goddess have mercy on his soul."

"But how did he die?" someone asked.

"I suppose we'll find out in a day or two," Lavinia answered. "But I for one don't feel like dancing anymore. It seems too heartless. I'm going up to bed."

Most of the women murmured agreement and gathered up their skirts to follow her out the door. Most of the men shook their heads and collected into a smaller, more compact group to discuss the implications a little longer.

Marguerite followed the rest of the women out the door and through the hallways toward the guest suites. "Terrible," someone would murmur after every few steps, and someone else would answer, "I know. Unbelievable."

"Well, I for one might celebrate," Elyssa said loudly as we were all climbing the stairs. When a few of the others cried out in reproach, she sneered. "He was a miserable, wretched man."

"But he's *dead*!"

"That doesn't change who he was when he was alive."

"I will say a prayer for him," Darrily answered, "and let the goddess choose how to judge him."

The general assent to that generous sentiment saw us safely to Marguerite's door. Marguerite bid everyone a quiet goodnight, and we quickly slipped inside.

Once again—as seemed to happen almost every time we stepped across that threshold—the four of us fell into each other's arms. This time we were all trembling so hard that we couldn't even keep to our feet, but sank to the floor in one shivering, sobbing pile.

"They've found him," Marguerite managed to gasp out. "Oh, Brianna, I am so afraid!"

I was afraid, too. Terrified. But I tried to steady my voice. "We only have two choices. As we've always had two choices," I said, gulping back tears. "We stay, or we run. I will do whichever one you want."

"There's nowhere to run," she whispered.

"Then we stay. And we continue to play the masquerade."

CHAPTER NINETEEN

It was hard to know who would be able to glean the most information the next day—Marguerite the noble or Brianna the maid. We decided that I would go belowstairs early in the morning to grab a quick meal and learn what the servants were saying. Then Marguerite would dispense with her habit of morning isolation and join the other guests for a late breakfast. One way or another, we should find out just how much the inquisitor already knew.

I slipped down the servants' stairwell and was headed for the kitchens when I heard a soft voice call my name. I whipped my head around and found Nico loitering in the hallway.

"I thought you must come down this way," he said, still speaking very low. "Come walk with me."

I could hardly find a better source of news, but I didn't dare leave Marguerite alone too long while I engaged in a dangerous dalliance with the inquisitor's nephew. I glanced back toward the stairwell. It took no great acting skill to appear willing but worried. "I can only be gone a few minutes. Marguerite—" I shivered. "She's so upset. I imagine everyone is."

"I don't believe I've ever seen the court cast in such uproar," Nico said.

Well. I had to hear the details. I glanced at the stairwell again and nodded. He took my elbow and showed me down a back passage that led to a side exit. It fed into an ornamental garden that—as I was leading a double life—I had had no time to explore. It was only a couple of acres, planted with low, flowering bushes and stands of ditch lilies; painted white benches provided quaint seating areas beside a pond that glittered with fish. A wooden bridge arched over the tranquil scene, offering a pleasant view—and the assurance that no one could be hiding near enough to eavesdrop on a conversation.

We didn't speak until we were in the center of the bridge, our elbows resting on the wooden railing and our gazes directed at the water feature below. For the first time since I had met him, Nico appeared entirely serious. There did not seem to be a single laugh left within him.

"The gossip is that Lord Jamison has been found dead," I said, my voice low even though no one but the fish could overhear us. "Is that true?"

He nodded. "True. The royal family is shattered. Harold is in a rage, but Cormac is half wild with grief and remorse. He and Jamison quarreled when they were on the road, you know, and Cormac is now asking himself if it is his fault that Jamison is dead."

"How did he die?"

"Drowned, apparently. Although the details are—puzzling."

I turned to face him. "Drowned where? And what do you mean about the details?"

He continued staring down at the garden. "There's a small lake on a property about a day and a half from here, just off the Charamon Road. Some children were swimming there a couple of days ago, and they found his body."

"How gruesome for them."

"I imagine so."

"Did he fall in and drown?"

"It seems likely. Although, as I say, it's puzzling."

"How so?"

"His body was stripped to his underclothes."

"Huh," I said in a thoughtful voice, as if I was trying to puzzle out what might have happened. "Well—perhaps he went swimming, but he didn't want to get completely naked in case someone else happened along. And then he tired and he went under."

Nico nodded. "Right. That's probably how it happened. But then, what happened to his clothes?"

"His clothes?"

"His trousers and jacket and shoes and rings. They're all gone. Wouldn't he have left them on the shore if he'd taken them off to go swimming?"

"Oh! I see what you mean!" I exclaimed, as if I was much struck by the observation. "Although—well—in some neighborhoods, if the locals found a pile of fancy clothes just lying on the ground, they wouldn't ask too many questions. They'd just quietly gather up the goods."

"That was my thought, too. The same is probably true of his horse. Which is also missing."

"I think it seems even *more* likely the horse found a new home right away. Any farmer I know would have considered such a find a gift straight from the goddess."

He nodded again. "But other things are odd. For instance, the body was lying on the bottom of the lake."

I opened my eyes wide. "Should it have been floating instead? I'm sorry, I don't know how these things work."

He gave me a brief glance before resuming his study of the pond below us. "I don't know much about it, either, but my uncle says if a body has been in the water long enough, it will rise to the surface. Unless there's something holding it down."

"Was there?"

He looked at me again and didn't answer. I hesitated a moment and then summoned the sort of irritation I figured I would show if I was absolutely guilt-free. "Nico, either tell me what you're thinking or stop dropping little hints and then shutting your mouth! *You're* the one who invited *me* out here, so I think you must want to talk about it, but it's fine if you don't. I'll just go back inside and try to keep Marguerite calm."

"It's just that there are so many details that don't make sense," he said. "My uncle has sent a whole team of men to the lake to find out what they can."

"What details?" I asked. "Don't be so mysterious."

"There were a couple of rocks and branches. Stuffed down his underclothes as if someone had shoved them there. Weighing him down. As if to make sure he *didn't* float to the top of the water."

I allowed my eyebrows to shoot up in astonishment. "That *is* suspicious. Unless—"

"Unless what?"

"I never met the man, so I can't judge. Was he the kind who might want to kill himself? If he wanted to make sure he drowned, maybe he weighted *himself* down."

Nico stared at me. "It doesn't sound like the Jamison I knew."

I shrugged. "You said he'd had a fight with Cormac. Maybe he thought the king would be angry with him as well. Maybe he thought there had been a rift with his family that he couldn't repair. Maybe he had done something shocking and someone was about to reveal it. I can think of a lot of reasons a man might end his life."

"Maybe, but I'm far from convinced. And it still doesn't explain—" He shook his head.

I crossed my arms and just waited. The pose of an annoyed women who was *not* going to ask for something again.

"There were welts and bruises on his face and back. As if he'd been in a fight," Nico said.

I tried to give the impression of trying not to snort. "Well, if what I've heard is true, there were probably a lot of fathers and brothers who would have been happy to beat him up. So that doesn't surprise me."

"No, but it does raise questions," Nico said. "It's one of the pieces that doesn't make sense."

I sighed. "Put the pieces together for me, then."

"Maybe he got into a fight—probably, as you say, over some girl he treated badly. Maybe this person knocked him unconscious and threw him into the lake, first stopping to strip off anything that might identify him. And piling him up with rocks for good measure."

I stared. "You think he was *murdered*?"

"I think it's a good possibility. And my uncle is almost certain of it."

I wrapped my arms around myself as if, on this lovely summer day, I was suddenly cold. It took no effort at all to tremble with horror. "That's dreadful. Surely it can't be true."

"I hope it's not," he said. "But we're proceeding as if it is."

"I find myself wondering," I said slowly. "Are you sure the body you found is Lord Jamison's? If you didn't find his clothes or jewelry—and if he'd been in the water for a few days—" I shivered delicately. "Did he even look like himself?"

Nico nodded. "I asked exactly the same question when the courier arrived last night, and that's one of the things my uncle is going to verify. But many things point to the body being his. His hair and beard are such a distinctive color, that's one clue. Plus, the height is about right for Jamison. But I think the first reason everyone thought it was him is simply that he's missing. If this isn't Jamison, where is he?"

"Has the king been looking for him?"

"Yes. That's why the news arrived so fast upon the discovery of the body. Harold already had men traveling the Charamon Road, trying to find out what happened to him. This dead body seems to answer that question. But, as you say, we cannot be sure just yet."

I sighed. "Well, for the sake of the king and his sons, I'll hope it isn't Jamison. But then that means some other poor man has lost his life, and he, too, has family and friends who will mourn him! It's very sad no matter who it turns out to be."

"It's more than sad," Nico said grimly. "If it turns out that someone did murder Jamison, there will be a manhunt that will turn this kingdom upside down. Harold won't rest until the killer is found and brought to justice."

"Justice," I said, my voice as steady as I could make it. "You mean shot by archers in Amanda Plaza."

Nico nodded. "That's exactly what I mean."

"I hope I'm gone by then," I said. "No matter how much someone may deserve to be executed, I wouldn't enjoy seeing it happen."

"I've never enjoyed it, either," Nico said, which surprised me a little, since he was such a passionate defender of the crown. But it was some comfort to know that he wouldn't relish the experience if he had to stand there and watch an arrow pierce my breast.

I gathered my skirts in both hands and said, "I must get back to Marguerite. She'll be worried sick. How much of this may I tell her?"

"All of it, if you like. The news will have spread through so many channels by now that none of it will be a secret for long."

I turned to go, and he fell in step beside me, though neither of us moved very quickly. Even though this had been one of the most unsettling and worrisome conversations I'd ever had with the man, I was still fool enough to wish for more time with him, another ten minutes, another five. Apparently, I had neither a brain nor a sense of self-preservation.

"So will your uncle send you out to this lake so you can help look for clues?" I asked as we stepped off the bridge and headed for the side door.

"No. He wants me here, conducting investigations from this end."

I gave him an inquiring look. "What can you learn in Camarria?"

"The state of Jamison's finances, for one thing, in case you're right. In case he was in difficulties one way or the other. I'll also find out if anyone in the city had a grudge against him and had a reason to track him down. I might turn up nothing—but I might find the final piece that makes the whole picture make sense."

That didn't sound so bad; Marguerite and I hadn't done anything in Camarria that would tie us to Jamison, so Nico's investigations would do us no harm. "Well, I hope someone learns something very quickly," I said as we slipped back inside the palace. Naturally, I hoped for no such thing.

"So do I," he said. "But I also hope—"

I didn't get a chance to learn how he might complete that sentence because another figure glided through the shadows of the passageway, heading in our direction. It was a man in his late thirties, thin and nondescript. If I had had to guess his occupation, *inquisitor's assistant* would have been my first supposition. "Nico," he said. "I've been looking for you."

Nico nodded at me and turned away without another word. They hurried off in one direction, and I went in the other. My heart was so heavy that I wondered that I had the bodily strength to haul myself up the stairs, but my veins were laced with so much prickling unease that I felt spurred to faster motion.

We hadn't been discovered yet. Our actions still might never come to light. But for the first time, I was truly afraid that they would.

The rest of the day, and the entire one that followed, were as somber and tense as any I had passed in my life. Cormac's guests gathered for meals and organized outings to some of the local attractions, but neither Cormac nor Jordan joined any of the activities and no one had much heart to enjoy them. It seemed unfeeling to laugh and flirt when a man you knew had recently been murdered, but it was intolerable to do absolutely nothing. So the nobles played cards and strolled through the gardens and visited Amanda Plaza, where everyone took turns tossing a few coins through the grate behind the statues of the triple goddess. I thought it would be fascinating to find out what particular grace everybody prayed for, whether it was mercy or justice or joy. I didn't even have to ask what Marguerite was hoping for when she dribbled her coins through the narrow openings.

Though if there was a goddess who would promise to keep secrets, that was the one I would have prayed to for the rest of my life.

"This is so utterly wretched," Leonora groaned that afternoon as Marguerite and Darrily took tea with the sisters in their expansive suite. "I feel so very much in the way! Surely the king is wishing every one of us gone."

"Should we leave then?" Marguerite inquired. "Just go back home?"

"I asked Jordan that very question when I came across him in the hallway this morning," Letitia said. "He looked very serious and pale, but he was willing to stop and talk to me for a few moments."

Letitia glanced around the room with her eyes at their widest. "He said that his father had made it clear that none of us would be *allowed* to leave until the mystery of Jamison's death has been cleared up."

Darrily's dark brows pulled down in a frown. "Why? I agree with your sister, we must all be a great nuisance at this time."

Now Letitia leaned forward, dropping her voice to a whisper. "The inquisitor wants us to stay."

Darrily started backward as if she had been stung. "'The inquisitor'! But— Does he think any of us could have been involved in Jamison's death?"

Letitia spread her hands. "I don't know! But I was under the impression that anyone who tried to leave would appear suspicious."

Lavinia's eyes took on a mischievous sparkle. "Oh, it's enough to make me want to pack up and head out of town, just to see what would happen."

"You can't do that!" Marguerite exclaimed. "If you catch the attention of the king's inquisitor—"

"Gorsey, what could the bad man do to me?" Lavinia drawled.

"Arrest you, for one thing," Darrily said drily.

"Oh, this is ridiculous!" Leonora exclaimed. "None of us hunted Jamison down and knocked him senseless and threw him in a lake! The king—or his sinister inquisitor—is being melodramatic. There is no reason we shouldn't be allowed to leave this dreary palace where we can only be an annoyance to our hosts."

Darrily's expression was sardonic. "I agree," she said. "I, too, would be happy to leave. But *I* do not want to be the one who catches the inquisitor's eye because I am impatient to be gone."

"Nor I," Marguerite said in a soft voice. "But it certainly would be good to go back home."

Oh, it certainly would.

For me, the brightest moments of both those days—and simultaneously the most terrifying ones—were the chances I had to snatch quick conversations with Nico. This situation had rattled him; he seemed eager to talk to someone as a way to make sense of the unfolding events. More than once it occurred to me that he was just pretending to be disturbed by the discovery of the body and the possibility that he might be hunting a murderer. More than once I thought perhaps he was trying to trick me into an unwary admission—that he and his uncle had already figured out who the killer was and they were hoping I would unwittingly supply them with more evidence.

But I didn't think so. He might be an inquisitor's apprentice, but he was also a young man, not a hardened investigator. Not so many years ago, he had been an impoverished low noble living off charity with his widowed mother. There was something boyish in his reaction to Jamison's death, I thought. Maybe it was just that he had never before known someone who met his end through violence.

Or maybe he realized that *I* was rattled by the situation and that *I* wanted constant updates and reassurance, and he was seizing every opportunity to be with me when I was at my most vulnerable so he could provide a little comfort.

At any rate, we both wanted to talk to each other every day, and we quickly formed the habit of meeting on the white bridge that overlooked the small side garden. He had no fresh news for me that first night after the ball, but the second night he did.

"We've found Jamison's clothes," he said almost without preamble.

I felt a jolt of terror that I tried my best to hide. "You did? Were they buried somewhere near the body?"

He shook his head. "Not even close. They were here in the city."

"I don't understand. Here where?"

He gestured vaguely toward the south. "Someone dropped them off at a pauper's box run by one of the temples. Except the clothes were so fine that the priestesses set them aside, thinking they had been donated in error and the owner would come looking for them. Instead, *I* found them."

"How clever of you!" I said admiringly.

"I kept thinking. If his things weren't at the lake, where would they be? If someone really did kill Jamison, he could hardly risk keeping the clothes with his own possessions."

"He could have burned them along the side of the road," I suggested. "That's what I would have done."

Nico nodded. "Me, too. But maybe he was traveling in a public conveyance, or in company with someone who would have found such behavior suspicious."

"Couldn't he have burned them in the fireplace of an inn where he stopped for the night?"

"In the middle of summer? A fire would be suspicious."

"Oh! You're right."

"Much as I hate to think it, I believe the discovery of the clothes is even stronger evidence that his death was murder."

"I'm not sure why."

"It's like you said. A rural freeholder who found fine velvet and satin lying on the ground—and a leather belt with a silver buckle, set with garnets, no less—well, that person would have kept the items to sell or use. Only someone with a crime to cover up would have tried to hide them."

"That makes sense," I admitted. I knew that all too well. As casually as I could, I asked, "Do the priestesses have any idea who left the clothes behind?"

"No. The collection box is unattended, and they only check it every few days. So not only do we not know *who* dropped them off, we don't know *when*."

"Have you found out any more about Jamison's finances? Any reason someone might have wanted to kill him?"

"Nothing suspicious yet, but I imagine every tailor and cobbler in the city would have liked to see him dead," Nico said with a hint of humor. "He ordered only the best, but he frequently forgot to pay his bills. The city tradesmen only did business with him because of his connection to the crown."

"It would be kind of the king to settle some of those debts," I said.

Now Nico's expression was cynical. "Expedient, more like. I am going from shop to shop, offering to pay whatever Jamison owed— and encouraging all the tradesmen to confide in me about anything they know."

"I hope you discover something useful." Though I knew he wouldn't. "But it seems like all of this could take a very long time."

"It certainly could."

"Have you considered that you might *never* discover who killed him—if he was actually murdered?"

Nico was silent a moment, and then he shook his head very slowly. "Oh, we'll find out," he said in a low voice. "Malachi—my uncle—will never stop looking."

I swallowed around the sudden tightness in my throat. "Why? Was he that fond of Jamison?"

He glanced at me with narrowed eyes. "Not fond of Jamison. Fond of the queen," he said.

I was sure my face reflected my bewilderment. "What? How is she involved in this? And why would that matter to your uncle?"

He stared at the water again as he answered. "You know Tabitha is Harold's second wife. Perhaps you don't know that they are completely at odds—they hate each other as much as any two people can. She has no fondness for Cormac or Jordan, either, and she absolutely despised Jamison. When Malachi first broached the notion that someone had murdered Jamison, the very first thing Harold said was, 'Did *she* kill my son? If so, you won't have to execute her in Amanda Plaza because I will strangle her with my bare hands.'"

This was a complication that hadn't even occurred to me might arise. "Oh dear," I said faintly. "How awful. For everyone."

Nico nodded. "Indeed. Fortunately, I can't see any reason she would have tracked him down on the Charamon Road to do away with him, so I don't think she's a serious candidate for murder. But if there's the merest hint that the queen might be suspected of the deed, Malachi will search every corner of the kingdom to bring the true criminal to justice."

"Why?" I said again.

"He's an Empara man—like me, like the queen herself. It was one of the conditions her family imposed before they agreed to the marriage. The king had to agree to hire Malachi as one of the inquisitors for the crown. That was more than twenty years ago. Since then, he's slowly worked his way up to the top of the ranks. There are many who suspect his loyalty is more to Tabitha than to Harold, though he's been so vigorous in carrying out his duties that it hasn't really mattered." Nico blew out his breath. "Till now."

"If the queen *is* guilty—though I could hardly believe such a thing!—will your uncle be willing to show the evidence against her?"

"A question Harold is already asking," Nico replied. "You see why Malachi will not rest until this crime is solved."

"Yes," I said, wishing very much that Malachi did not have such a powerful incentive. "I can only hope he starts finding answers very soon."

"I think we all hope that."

"Marguerite said something this afternoon. Lady Letitia of Banchura told her that none of Cormac's guests will be allowed to return home until you've learned what's happened. Is that true?"

Nico nodded. "Although it seems just as unlikely that any of them could be guilty of murder, my uncle wants to make *sure* of it before they are scattered to the corners of the kingdom. But naturally, nearly two dozen high nobles cannot be held prisoner in Camarria for weeks and weeks. Although—"

I waited a moment before prompting, "'Although' what?"

He glanced down at me, his expression softening from the grim lines it had held from the moment we met on the bridge. "Although I would not be unhappy if there were some reason you could not go home by month's end," he said softly. "I certainly wouldn't have arranged for a murder as the circumstance that kept you here—but if that is one of the consequences, I cannot be entirely sorry."

I tried to suppress a smile as I gave him a quick sideways glance. "I hardly think this is the time for dalliance," I said primly.

Before I knew what he was planning, he swung me around so that my back was pinned against the bridge and his hands were gripping the rail on either side of my body. He crowded closer, pressing against me, dropping his head so his mouth was only inches from mine.

"Maybe it's exactly the right time," he murmured. "When better to remember what it feels like to be alive than when you're faced with the stark reality of death?"

I tried really hard not to wish he would kiss me. "I thought we were starting over," I said breathlessly. "Getting to know each other again. Getting to trust each other again."

"By my count, we've already known each other just about as many days as we did in Oberton."

"But they've been such hectic days."

"My days are always hectic," he said, leaning even closer, but still not quite touching my mouth with his. I could tell he was giving me time to offer a strong counterargument or to struggle in his hold; I could tell he was making sure I was willing. Goddess save me, I *wanted* to protest—but not as much as I wanted him to kiss me.

All I could come up with was, "Well, then."

It wasn't an invitation, but it wasn't a refusal, and he interpreted it as acquiescence. He dropped his mouth on mine with a heavy pressure, brought his hands around to squeeze me against his chest. I felt flushed with guilt and delight and madness and sensation. I pulled back just so I could lean forward again and press my mouth to his with even greater urgency. I felt one of his hands move from my shoulder to the back of my head, holding me in place so I couldn't easily break the kiss again. He held me even tighter, bending me backward over the railing, so I was even more dizzy and off-balance. My foot slipped as I shifted against his weight, and then I did break free, laughing as I clutched his arm to keep from toppling over.

"Eek! I'm going to go tumbling off the bridge!" I exclaimed.

He cradled me closer and dropped a kiss on the top of my head. "No, you won't," he said. "I won't ever let you fall."

I rested my forehead against his chest, taking a moment to steady my breathing. "That's a nice promise."

"I mean it."

I could think of so many potential answers to that, from *You won't mean it when you learn the truth* to *Why have you decided to give your heart to me?* I couldn't decide what to say, so I just shook my head and remained silent.

"Unfortunately, I can't stay out here much longer and prove it to you," he went on. "I have more work to do for my uncle."

I freed myself from his arms and made a great show of smoothing down my skirts and patting my hair in place. "Perhaps I will run into you sometime tomorrow or the day after," I said in a demure voice.

He grinned at me and took my arm in his, turning me toward the palace and walking me down the arch of the bridge. "Count on it."

CHAPTER TWENTY

Nothing of any significance happened the next day, unless you count a few more kisses shared with Nico, but the following day just cascaded with disaster.

It began innocently enough, when Marguerite announced her intention to visit the temple instead of joining the other nobles as they went off to inspect some new bridge that was under construction. I had started to hope that anyone spying on Marguerite had just decided that she was extremely devout; at any rate, I was clearly never going to be able to convince her to curtail her visits to the temple. So Patience and Purpose and I donned plain dresses and tried to match Marguerite's pious expression, and off we went.

I walked beside Marguerite, my head bowed at the same angle as hers, while the echoes followed a pace behind. This allowed the two of us to converse in low voices while we walked, though we tried to make sure our lips hardly moved so no one realized we were talking.

"Do you expect a letter from Taeline already?" I asked.

"Maybe. If the courier was as fast as the priestess implied."

"I wonder if the news about Jamison has made it all the way to Oberton."

"Oh, I'm sure it's traveled to every city in the Seven Jewels by now."

"But she probably had to write her reply to you before she found out about him."

"No doubt. I wish so much I could talk to her about all this, but—" She shrugged. I copied the slight movement as I tried to guess what Marguerite hadn't bothered to say. *But she's too far away and no part of this story can be committed to a paper that anyone might read.*

I had always assumed Taeline was more of a go-between than a spiritual counselor, but now I thought perhaps the priestess fulfilled both roles for Marguerite. "If she was here, would you tell her? What really happened?"

Marguerite was silent a moment. "Probably."

"She wouldn't report you to an inquisitor?"

"As I understand it, it is safe to confess to priestesses. I suppose now and then one of them has betrayed a confidence, but I'm sure Taeline never would."

I couldn't think of too many people, including all the priestesses I had ever met, that I would be willing to trust with the knowledge that I had committed murder. "Maybe once you're home," I said. "You can talk to her then."

Marguerite was silent a moment. "Sometimes I wonder if I'll ever make it back to Oberton," she said, her voice even softer than before. "Don't you? Sometimes I have this feeling that something will happen—here—" She swept her arm out to indicate all of Camarria. I belatedly made the same gesture. "I might be engaged to Cormac and pressured to stay here for the duration of the betrothal. I might be arrested for murder. Either way, I'll never be able to go home."

"Don't talk like that," I said.

"I try to be as brave as you are," she said. "But I'm really just a coward."

"I'm not brave," I said. "I just don't know what else to do."

By this time, we had arrived at the temple of the triple goddess. As always, once we crossed the bridge, we circled around to enter the door guarded by the representation of mercy. We all paused before the statue and touched our fingers to our hearts, then stepped quietly into the sanctuary.

The place was more crowded than usual, so we couldn't all sit together. Marguerite took a place on the aisle of the second-to-last pew, while the echoes and I settled in the row behind her. As always,

I tipped my head down just as the others did, but I kept my eyes open and let my gaze dart all around the room, just to watch what everyone else was doing. There were six priestesses—more than usual—moving among the penitents, so I figured the crowd would empty out relatively quickly. And indeed, within twenty minutes, everyone sitting in Marguerite's row had already risen and departed.

So she was sitting by herself, her head bowed and her hands clasped, when one of the white-robed priestesses entered her pew from the other side and slid soundlessly down the bench to sit beside her.

"May the goddess have mercy on your soul," the priestess said in low tones. "What brings you to the temple today?"

Marguerite started so violently that Patience and Purpose jerked upright on either side of me. I didn't react quite so spasmodically, but I admit I was staring. I recognized that voice.

"Taeline!" Marguerite exclaimed. "But how are you— What are you doing here? Did you get my letter?"

Taeline nodded. "I had planned to write you with my news, but it was faster to bring it myself."

"What news? Good or bad?"

"I hardly know. I'm being transferred to the main temple in Thelleron. Though I will spend ten days or twelve days in Camarria for training before my transfer is complete."

"Thelleron! You're being transferred! But you're—that means— you won't be in Oberton anymore?"

"That is indeed what it means."

I thought Marguerite might say, *I'll miss you, if I ever make my way back to Orenza.* Or, thinking ahead to how she would manage her covert communications, she might ask, *Are there any other priestesses in Oberton I can trust?* Or even, in the spirit of friendship, *How exciting for you! Does this mean you are rising in the ranks?*

But she didn't say any of these things. She put her hand to her mouth (the echoes and I did the same) and turned her head away. I caught a glimpse of tears glittering in Patience's eyes. Marguerite must be crying.

"I'm sorry," Taeline said. "It's why I wanted to tell you myself."

Now Marguerite bowed her head even lower and covered her face with both hands. She tried to keep her sobs silent, but I saw her shoulders tremble and heard her draw a ragged breath. Beside me, Patience and Purpose were equally shaken.

I tried to manufacture tears of my own, but in truth I was dumbfounded. I knew that Jamison's death had left Marguerite on edge and that every small setback assumed magnified significance, but surely this was an overreaction. There were other priestesses Marguerite could turn to for spiritual comfort. There were other methods Marguerite could use to communicate with a secret lover—

A secret lover.

And then, of course, I knew.

Taeline hadn't been carrying messages for Marguerite; she had been receiving them and sending them in return. It was *Taeline* Marguerite loved, not some impoverished tradesman or married noble. And this was the most disastrous romance Marguerite could possibly have embarked on. There was no hope of happiness there. Assuming she didn't make a match with the prince, her parents might have allowed her to marry a disgraced noble and found a way to make him respectable, but she would never be allowed to set up household with a woman. People among the professional and working classes did it from time to time, though they always suffered some prejudice for it, but neither high nor low nobles were allowed to admit such affinities existed. Not only was Marguerite likely to be married off to a man she didn't love, she would be married to a *gender* that she didn't care for. I could hardly imagine a situation that would be more wretched.

"I'm so sorry," Taeline said again. "I didn't think—perhaps it *would* have been better to put this all in a note. But I just thought at least I'd get to see you from time to time while you're in Camarria—"

"Yes— I'm really— I'm glad for that," Marguerite choked out. She still had her head turned away and was still trying desperately to control her weeping. "It's just that—once I'm back in Oberton— if I ever am—"

"'If'? What does that mean?" Taeline asked.

Marguerite shook her head. "It's been so dreadful here. I can't even tell you."

"Now you have to tell me," Taeline said.

Marguerite shook her head even more vigorously. "No. It's so awful—and anyone might overhear—"

Taeline hesitated a moment, then rose to her feet. "Come with me."

We all gazed up at her with our tearstained faces. "Come where?"

"There's a private space where we can talk."

Moving with the heaviness of despair, Marguerite pushed herself up and the rest of us stood as well. We followed Taeline to the middle of the temple and halfway around the ornate room that sat at the center of the three towers. I noticed that the sanctuaries dedicated to justice and joy were practically empty at this hour of the day. Or maybe they were always almost empty and I just hadn't noticed. Maybe people always needed mercy more than they needed the other benedictions.

Taeline glanced around to make sure no one was watching, then she twisted a decorative knob on the ornate paneling. I was not the only one who gasped when a hidden door opened to reveal a small, shadowy room—which was actually, it turned out, the head of a staircase spiraling downward.

"A secret passageway?" Marguerite breathed, sounding as if intrigue had jolted her momentarily out of her grief.

"An underground complex," Taeline corrected, ushering us all quickly inside then pulling the door shut after her. The five of us barely fit in the small space, so Marguerite and Purpose climbed down the first two metal steps and waited. I could see the stairwell curving down for maybe another twenty feet. It appeared to end in an arched corridor dimly illuminated by torches or candles or something else with a restless flicker.

Taeline said, "Apparently in the temple's early days, the priestesses were quite fierce in their commitment to justice. They hid any number of political refugees here until it was safe to spirit them out of the city."

Marguerite and I exchanged quick looks. "Is the complex used for the same reasons today?" she asked.

Taeline laughed and brushed past the four of us to take the lead as we descended. The metal stairs were slick under our feet and portions of the railing rusted under our hands, so caution was in order.

"I imagine the king's inquisitor knows all about the compound, and it would be the first place he looked if some prominent criminal went missing," she said. "But the priestesses keep the rooms clean and well stocked in case there's ever a need for them. Some women will retreat here for a few days when they crave solitude. And it continues to be a place where it is safe to hold private and dangerous conversations."

By this time, we had arrived at the bottom of the stairwell, where we clustered as we looked around. The passageway branched off in three directions, which I guessed ran under the three towers. Two of them were short, relatively well-lit hallways lined with five doors apiece. The third one tunneled off into darkness and gave the impression of continuing for a very long distance. My geography was weak underground, but my sense was that it pointed in the direction of Amanda Plaza. This might actually be the route the priestesses took to collect coins tossed into the grate at the feet of the statues.

In which case, Taeline was right. The inquisitor certainly knew about this place.

"A few of these rooms should be empty," Taeline said, leading us into one of the shorter hallways. "Let's find a place to sit and talk."

We passed two rooms whose open doors showed priestesses either in silent contemplation or earnest conversation, but the third door we tried opened onto a dark and empty chamber. Taeline found an unlit torch, ignited it from one of the wall sconces, and used it to light three fixtures in the room. There were more furnishings than I'd expected—a plain wooden table and a half dozen wooden chairs, a severe cot shoved up against one wall, a small cedar chest in the corner. Still, the whole place had a distinctly cavelike feel. The stone floor was smooth but uneven; the walls, hacked from the bedrock below the city streets, were rough and imperfect; and there was the slight, pervasive smell of mold. I didn't think this would be the place I would choose as a retreat if I wanted to meditate myself back into a state of peace.

On the other hand, if I was hiding from an inquisitor? I'd hole up down here and be grateful.

"Now," said Taeline, taking a seat at the table and watching the rest of us settle in place. Her expression was expectant but unconcerned. I wondered what kind of iron nerve it took to maintain that level of calm all the time. "Tell me what's happening."

Marguerite folded her hands in front of her on the table, and the echoes and I did the same. In a flat voice, she said, "I killed a man and I'm afraid I'm going to be discovered and arrested."

Taeline's chair screeched on the stone floor as she started backward. So much for boundless calm. "You *what*? What *happened*?"

Marguerite had gotten the first sentence out with no trouble, but now the words seemed to stick in her throat. "Lord Jamison— you remember, I told you about him—"

Taeline nodded. "The king's bastard son. He had quite a reputation."

"We encountered him on the road when we were four days out from Oberton. He came across us as we were walking along a pretty path—some distance from the road—no one else was nearby. He *attacked* me. He tried to—tried to assault me. The echoes helped me fight him off, and one of them hit him with a rock and then he—then he fell to the ground and he—he was dead."

"Goddess have mercy on your soul," Taeline said, fluttering her hands across her body in a benediction. She was staring at Marguerite. "And *his* soul. What did you do?"

"We threw his body in a nearby lake and hoped no one would ever find him."

"'We'? You and your echoes? Was anyone else with you?"

Marguerite glanced at me and nodded. I shifted in my chair, adopting my own pose, and said, "I was."

Taeline's reaction was almost as violent this time as the last. "Who are *you*?" she demanded. Her eyes narrowed as she focused on my face, noting all the ways I did not resemble Marguerite. "You're not an echo," she said slowly.

"My maid. Brianna. She helped me fight off Lord Jamison."

"But why is she—" Taeline's voice trailed off as Marguerite broke down crying, dropping her head to rest on her folded hands. "One of your echoes died in the struggle," she guessed. "Oh, no. Oh, I'm so sorry."

"We thought we would raise less suspicion if Marguerite still appeared to have three shadows," I explained. I leaned over to put my arm around Marguerite's shoulder and hug her tightly. "But it's been a dangerous masquerade."

"Everything about this situation is as dangerous as can be," Taeline agreed in a grim tone. "But you must tell me the rest. No one knows what happened, except the two of you—and now me?"

Marguerite attempted to pull herself together, lifting her head and swallowing her sobs. "No one knows," she said, trying to keep her voice steady. "I didn't think— I was sure no one would believe my version of what had happened."

Taeline passed a hand over her face. I could tell she was struggling to absorb the horrible details and all that they might mean for Marguerite, while summoning the serenity of a spiritual counselor. "Perhaps they would have," she said, "if you had come straight to the temple to beg for intercession by a priestess of justice. But now—so many days after the event…"

"Had he been an ordinary man, I might have done so," Marguerite said. "But he is the king's son. His murder cannot be overlooked."

"More than that," I spoke up. "The inquisitor has a special interest in this case." I filled them in on Nico's observations about Malachi and the queen. "I do not think this is a situation in which justice will be tempered by mercy," I finished up in a regretful voice.

Marguerite nodded. "So now I cower in Camarria, hoping no one discovers my crime. But since his body was found a few days ago—"

Taeline reached across the table to take Marguerite's hands in a comforting clasp. "My poor dear," she said quietly. "How very terrible this must have been for you."

Marguerite stared back at her intensely. "I did not want him dead. You must believe me. When I saw what had happened—when I could bring myself to believe it— Oh, Taeline, you have no idea! And now! If the king's inquisitor learns the truth—I would run away, as far as I could, but where would I *go*? I am so afraid and so sorry and so guilty, but I don't know what to *do*."

"I don't know, either," Taeline said. "But I will think about it very hard!" Still holding Marguerite's hands in hers, she glanced around the interior of the room. "Maybe this place could provide a refuge for you after all. I could ask the abbess if she would allow you to stay here—"

Marguerite shook her head. "I am closely watched. We all are. If I were to suddenly disappear, they would look for me."

"And Nico and his uncle know that you consider the temple a safe haven," I said. "They would come here immediately."

Marguerite slumped back in her chair. "There are no safe havens," she said in a weary voice. "Not for me."

Taeline squeezed her hands more tightly, then released her. "We will find one," she promised, coming to her feet. "We will discover a way out of this mess."

The rest of us stood up as well, though I didn't make my usual effort to mimic Marguerite's movements. I was trying to decide if I should offer to leave them alone so they could talk in private, but I couldn't think of a casual way to phrase it. There wasn't time, anyway—we heard voices in the hallway and it was clear a group was arriving.

"We have to leave," Marguerite said. "I fret if I'm gone from the palace too long, in case there's news while I'm away." Her voice broke a little as she added, "But it was so good to see you and to share this terrible burden! I know you're leaving in a few days—I know you might not be able to help me—but just being able to tell you all of this..."

Taeline threw her arms around Marguerite, and for a moment the two of them rocked together like lost sailors who had finally found solid ground. I turned to face the wall—and Patience and Purpose followed *my* lead, not Marguerite's, so the three of us had our backs to the two of them. "I'm so glad I'm here," I heard Taeline whisper. "I wish I had been here sooner. I don't know what I can do for you, but I promise you, I will not make you endure this alone."

There was a moment of silence—there might have been a quick kiss—and then the sound of the door opening. I turned around to see Taeline exiting into the hallway, Marguerite at her heels. The echoes and I followed.

We had only taken a few steps toward the stairway when we encountered a woman whom I immediately took to be the abbess of this temple. She looked to be in her late fifties or early sixties, with thick gray hair piled on top of her head in a neat bun. But it was more the expression on her face that led me to guess her station. It was hard to describe it—a cross between kindness and implacability, I thought. This was someone who knew how rough the world could be, who had seen every imaginable transgression, yet still believed that there were unshakable moral principles that would guide all of us along the rocky path. She would forgive, I thought, but she would not yield. I wondered what she would say if she knew all the particulars of Marguerite's situation.

It seemed unlikely she would learn them today, though Taeline did pause to introduce Marguerite, and Marguerite did bow her head to receive the traditional benediction from the formidable woman.

"How much longer do you plan to be in Camarria?" the abbess inquired civilly.

When she answered, Marguerite's voice was as steady as if she hadn't been sobbing just a few minutes ago. "About three weeks. Perhaps longer if the prince invites any of us to extend our stay."

The abbess bestowed a shrewd glance on her at that answer; my guess was that court gossip made its way to the temple with commendable speed, so she was aware that Marguerite was considered the top candidate to be Cormac's bride. "If you are here through the end of the year, we will expect to see you on Counting Day."

I knew about Counting Day, of course. Once a year, early in winter, all the nobles with echoes were commanded to appear at the nearest temple so the goddess could get a complete record of all the echoes in the kingdom. It was said that if any nobles failed to comply, their echoes would simply disappear the following day. As Nico had told me, the echoes were considered gifts from the goddess, and what she had given, she could also take away. I had no idea if any of the nobles had ever ignored the directive and, if so, whether their echoes had really vanished. I knew that if *I* had been a noble, I wouldn't have taken the risk.

"If I am here that long, I will certainly do so," Marguerite answered. "I have never been outside of Oberton on Counting Day, so it will be strange to observe it at a different temple."

"Come early," the abbess advised. "It will be crowded."

Taeline spoke up. "I have never been outside Oberton on Counting Day, either, but there are only a few dozen nobles with echoes in all of Orenza. Are there so many more in Sammerly?"

The abbess nodded. "When I was a young priestess, more than thirty years ago, the numbers of echoes had dwindled to the lowest point in history. It was quite easy to count them, since there were so few! The kingdom had been at peace for so long that there seemed to be very little reason for the goddess to continue producing echoes for their original purpose—that is, keeping the leaders of the country safe from harm. But lately—" She paused and gave a little shrug.

"You have seen an increase in echoes?" Marguerite prompted.

"We have. Family after family coming to the temples with newborn babies and their attendant shadows. This has caused me to wonder if there is some threat to the kingdom in the making, and the goddess is preparing for it."

"Although I don't know how much help babies will be in defending the country," Taeline said practically.

The abbess smiled. "No. Of course not. But some of those echoes are adults by now, since their numbers started rising about twenty-two or twenty-three years ago. So perhaps the threat—if there is a threat—is almost at hand."

Marguerite's face showed a faint alarm. "I don't like to gainsay you, but I *hope* there is no danger in the offing!"

"I hope the same, naturally," the abbess said.

Behind us, we heard a woman's voice call out, and the abbess nodded to us formally. "I must go. I enjoyed the chance to meet you, Lady Marguerite. Perhaps in the future we will have the opportunity to speak again."

A few moments later, the five of us had climbed the metal stairwell and emerged into the sanctuary. Taeline carefully closed the door behind us, and once again the central column looked like nothing more than a highly decorative closet in the middle of the temple.

"Peace follow you and the goddess rest your soul," Taeline said, touching her fingertips to Marguerite's forehead, heart, and lips. "We will stay in touch. Something will occur to us to get you out of this trouble."

"Thank you," Marguerite whispered. "Just for being here."

Taeline turned to me and I bowed my head for my own benediction. "Goddess watch over you," she murmured, and then, even more softly, "and please, you watch over Marguerite."

"I will," I replied, my voice as quiet as hers. Then I followed Marguerite and the echoes out of the building and into the sunshine.

Once we crossed the bridge, I fell in step beside Marguerite, while the echoes trailed behind. Marguerite had seemed very calm as she spoke to the abbess but now, as we walked along, her breath would occasionally catch, as if the memory of grief had caught her unaware. This time we didn't detour through the flower market, but headed straight back toward the palace.

We had traveled in silence for about ten minutes before I asked, "How long have you loved Taeline?"

Marguerite gave me a quick sideways look, but seeing no judgment in my expression, her own face relaxed. "For years, I think. Before I even knew what love was. I met her when I was sixteen because it had become fashionable for the nobles of Oberton to give their daughters a religious education. Taeline was twenty and still an acolyte, but she came to the palace once a week for a year to teach me about the goddess. We talked about everything. We stayed in touch once my studies were done, though we didn't get together as often. At first, I didn't understand why I was so unhappy in the weeks when I didn't see Taeline. I didn't even know it was possible for a woman to fall in love with a woman. I didn't know what love felt like." She gestured. "And then I did."

"And she loves you, too?"

Marguerite nodded. "For all the good it will do either of us."

I shrugged. "I don't know. Even if you can't be together—even if you know it won't have a happy ending—you have to be grateful for love every time it's in your life. It's so rare and precious. It's something you share with one other person, and no one else understands how you feel or what you have. It's like a language that only two people will ever know, and you can't ever be sorry you learned it, even if you never get a chance to speak it again."

Out of the corner of my eye, I could see the small smile on her face. "I like that description," she says. "I have just been used to thinking it is such a great and terrible tragedy of my life, that I cannot be with Taeline."

"How much more terrible would it be if you'd never known her?" I said. "Now you'll have this memory forever to carry with you wherever you go. To warm you on cold nights and give you strength when you're feeling weak. I think that's what love is supposed to do, even if you can't have it as long as you like."

Marguerite took a deep breath. "Yes. You're right. I will hold on to it like a jewel and wear it against my heart the rest of my life. Even if my life isn't very long."

"Don't say that."

She was silent for a moment, thinking something over. "Did you hear what the abbess said? About the echoes?"

"Counting them, you mean?" I replied cautiously. I knew that wasn't what she referred to.

"No. About how there have been so many more echoes born in the past few years. About how the goddess knows the kingdom is heading for trouble." She took a deep breath. "Headed for war, maybe. War that will happen because *I* did a terrible thing and so *I* could not marry the prince and *I* failed to unite the provinces—"

An echo would not have done it, but I briefly laid my hand on her arm in a comforting gesture. "That's not the way I interpreted her comment."

"There's no other way to interpret it!"

"Oh, yes, there is. When did she say the echoes started increasing in numbers?"

Marguerite frowned. "I don't remember."

"Twenty-three years ago. What was happening at that time?"

"I was born! And all the goddess did was look at me and she realized I was dangerous."

I couldn't help laughing, but I shook my head. "Twenty-three years ago, King Harold married Queen Tabitha."

She glanced over at me, an arrested expression on her face. "Why would that have put the kingdom at risk?"

I shrugged. "Nico told me they hate each other. The king thinks she might have killed his son."

"But she *didn't*."

"No, but if Harold believes she's capable of murder, what else does he think she might do? What would he do to stop her? If the goddess is trying to prepare the country for war, I think she's looking at events that happened long before you encountered Jamison on the road."

She dropped her gaze to the road before her and walked on for a while in silence. "Maybe," she said at last. "I can't judge. I'm having a hard time thinking about anything beyond my own situation."

"I don't blame you," I said. "But we'll get through it. We just have to be careful. And clever. And brave."

"And lucky."

"And lucky," I repeated. That was the attribute that worried me most. So far, we'd been clever enough to make it through, even when we weren't careful; so far, we had managed to summon courage when we had to.

But you never have any control over your luck. You never know when it will gather you close with a reassuring whisper or fling you away with a jeering laugh. And the longer we were in Camarria, I feared, the more fickle our luck would become.

CHAPTER TWENTY-ONE

The afternoon was quiet, but a few of the nobles had exerted themselves to make the evening agreeable by organizing an impromptu musical evening. There were no paid musicians on hand, but it turned out that a number of the royal guests could play an instrument or hold a tune. And so could their echoes. I was surprised and impressed when Nigel and his two shadows each took up small stringed instruments and settled themselves on the low stage to play. From what I could tell—not being a musician myself—they all produced identical notes, all at the same time, but the addition of the echoes' instruments gave the piece resonance and depth.

A performance by the Banchura triplets was even more impressive. They ranged themselves on the dais, the sisters in front, their echoes behind them, and proceeded to sing a wistful ballad in close three-part harmony. Their echoes did not sing, of course, but they hummed along with their originals, note for note; their unearthly, inhuman voices gave the entire piece a haunting, unsettling quality. Even the bored nobles in the audience were moved by the presentation, and everyone applauded madly once it was over.

"I'm glad I have no pretensions to musical ability," Marguerite remarked to Darrily when it was over, though I was sure she was really letting *me* know that we would not be the next ones up on that stage. "I would not like to try to follow such an act."

Elyssa, sitting with Deryk a row behind, was close enough to overhear. "No, indeed, they are quite talented," she said in her usual hateful way. "If their father ever loses his fortune, they could go on the road and sing for money. I'm sure they would be quite popular."

Darrily gave her one brief, cool glance. "Let's hope *your* father is never impoverished," she said. "Since I can't imagine how *you* would earn your keep."

Marguerite never enjoyed such sparring, so I was not surprised when she soon made her excuses and headed up to her room. I helped her undress and get ready for bed, even though it was relatively early. The emotional stresses of the day had left her drained.

"I think I'll swing by the kitchens and see if I can learn anything new from the servants," I said casually. This was a partial lie, since I had not been entirely truthful with Marguerite about how much time I was spending with Nico. She knew that I had spoken to him a few times, but not how long the conversations had lasted or how often they had ended in a kiss. I didn't want her worrying that I might be tricked into an indiscretion; she had so much else to worry about.

"You'll stay in your own room tonight?" she asked.

I nodded. "I must do so sometimes. I'll be back early in the morning."

"All right, then. Goodnight."

I did stop by the kitchens, but just long enough to see if the cook had any gossip to share. Not ten minutes later, I was out the side door and hurrying toward the garden. Night had fallen some time ago, but the air was still warm with the sticky heat of late summer. Between the moonlight and the faint illumination spilling from the palace windows, I had just enough light to see my way down the path and up the sloped wooden arch of the white bridge.

Nico wasn't there and I was more tired than I'd realized, so I sank into a sitting position and rested my back against the latticework supporting the railing. It was the first moment of solitude I'd had all day, and I spent it thinking over Marguerite's relationship with Taeline. Despite my encouraging speech to Marguerite, I could see no way that situation didn't end in heartbreak, particularly if Marguerite married the prince. I thought perhaps Taeline had requested the transfer to Thelleron with the hope that starting a new life would help her endure the heartache once Marguerite married Cormac or some high noble. It wouldn't surprise me to learn that, among the priestesses, romances were fairly common. Taeline might have realized long before Marguerite that she was falling in love where she had little chance of happiness. But that didn't mean she was any more prepared to endure the pain of its inevitable ending.

I drew my legs up and rested my cheek against my knee. *And how will she endure the pain of her lover being arrested for murder?*

But that wouldn't happen. We would be clever and careful and lucky and brave...

I saw no one exiting from the palace, heard no footsteps approaching, but I felt a slight vibration in the bridge as someone began to climb it. I lifted my head and saw a shadow moving through the darkness. "Nico?" I called in a low voice.

"So you *are* here," he said, finishing the climb and dropping down beside me. "I didn't see you, but I thought I would come up and wait for a few minutes anyway."

"I was too tired to stand," I said. "Lately, every day seems three days long."

"It has been a hard stretch," he agreed. He slipped an arm around my shoulders and leaned in for a quick kiss before settling back against the bridge. I liked the casualness of the kiss, the fact that it seemed natural and expected. I liked that he pulled me against him almost absentmindedly, and took my hand in his free one, and played with my triskele ring as if these were all just normal parts of his day. I liked thinking that this was what my life could be like.

If my life was utterly and completely different than it was going to be.

"Did something happen to make today particularly hard?" I asked in a sympathetic voice.

He hesitated, then nodded. "They've found another body."

I scrambled to a more upright sitting position, but managed not to dislodge my hand from Nico's light grip. "Another body? Another *murder*? Oh, no! Where?"

"In the lake. Where they found Jamison."

Goddess have mercy on my soul. They'd discovered Prudence. "I don't understand," I said. "Is some crazy person just killing people and throwing them into the water?"

"It's certainly a possibility," he said. "But my uncle believes the deaths are related in some fashion."

"Why?"

"The bodies seem to have decomposed at about the same rate. Meaning they were probably placed in the water at about the same time. And therefore killed around the same time."

"Maybe they killed each other," I suggested. "Although I don't know how they would have ended up in the water, then."

"It's possible," he said. "There's a bridge over the lake—small, sort of like this one—but they could have been standing on it together. Gotten into an argument and started to fight. They both could have tumbled over the side."

I felt relief pour through me like a rising flood. It was such a logical explanation. "How very tragic that would be."

"Not as tragic as murder," he said dryly.

"What could you tell from this other man's body?" I asked. "Did he look like he'd been in a fight, too?"

"It wasn't a man."

"It was a *woman?*" I exclaimed as if shocked. "Then— What do you suppose happened?"

Nico passed his hand over his face as if weary from too much thinking. I doubted he could be as weary as I was, though, or thinking any harder. "The scenario could have been much the same," he said. "They were on the bridge. They struggled. Jamison tried to force himself on her and she resisted hard enough to send them both into the water."

"That's awful. Just awful," I said. "Though it does seem to fit with everything I have heard about Jamison."

"It does," Nico agreed. But he sounded dissatisfied.

I tried to read his face in the dark. What was he not telling me? "Do they have any idea who the girl is?"

"Not yet. We're asking around to see if any local women have gone missing. So far everyone seems to be accounted for."

I let a note of doubt creep into my voice. "I suppose Jamison could have picked up a woman during his travels. Some country girl who was impressed by his fancy ways. He could have told her he would bring her to the city and set her up in a big house. But the more time she spent with him, the less she liked him." I allowed myself a delicate shiver.

"Right. I have to admit that was my first thought, too."

"And now you don't think so? What changed your mind?"

He was silent a moment. He started playing with my hand again, toying with my ring, sliding it up to my knuckle, then pushing it back in place. "My uncle must have sent ten people to investigate Jamison's drowning, and one of them is a man who studies dead bodies to learn how they died."

"That's gruesome."

"I know. What must the conversations be like at *his* house in the evening? But he believes the corpse isn't that of an ordinary woman. It's an echo."

For a moment, I absolutely could not breathe. *Dear goddess, sweet holy spirit, have mercy on my soul.* They knew. They knew. "Well, then, your mystery is solved, isn't it?" I asked, fighting to speak in a normal voice. "If you can recognize her face—but how can you be sure she's an echo and not an original?"

He nodded. "That's the thing," he said. "And I didn't know it until now, either. When echoes die, they revert to some—the investigator called it some 'primal undifferentiated state.' Their faces become blank and their hair falls out and their bodies just become a torso and limbs. You can't even tell if they're men or women."

I drew a sharp breath of relief, though I hoped he would think it was astonishment. "That's unbelievable."

"That's what I thought. But my uncle confirmed it with two coroners in the city. So we have no idea who this echo belonged to."

"Then how can you be sure it's a woman?"

"Apparently the whole process of—of—reverting happens much more slowly if the body is in water. So her body is still that of a woman, but her features aren't very defined. My uncle has decided this means we can't be *positive* she's an echo, and we still must look for other possibilities. But the investigator seems very sure."

I shook my head, as if I couldn't quite take in all the details. In truth, I was trying to figure out what to say. "Well. So. If she *is* an echo. And if she and Jamison killed each other—I can't even think up a story that might explain how that happened."

"I can," Nico said, "but I don't like it."

"Tell me."

Then he described what had happened that day as accurately as if he'd been standing there watching. "Jamison encounters a noble-woman and her echoes. He assaults her, she resists, and in the fight, he's killed and so is one of the echoes. The others dispose of them in the lake and hope nobody notices."

"It certainly sounds plausible," I admitted, hoping he could not hear the pounding of my heart. "But I would think that would make your task very simple! Find the fine lady who's missing one of her shadows."

"Yes, and my uncle plans to do just that," Nico answered.

I felt a sudden flicker of hope. "Your uncle must be pleased at this turn of events."

"Pleased? Why?"

"If Jamison was killed by a noblewoman and her echoes, surely the queen had nothing to do with his death. Perhaps he will not feel so compelled to solve the crime."

"Unless the noblewoman who quarreled with Jamison was a particular friend of the queen's. Unless Tabitha *asked* this woman to pick a fight with Jamison. It's unlikely, I'll admit, but Malachi hasn't lost any of his zeal for the case. In fact, he's sending men to every corner of the Seven Jewels, checking on the well-being of every noblewoman with an echo."

"That could take some time."

"It certainly could."

I remembered the conversation in the temple. "Although I suppose you could wait till Counting Day. *Then* you'd know who was missing an echo." Naturally, I did not expect this to aid in his investigation at all, since I would accompany Marguerite to the temple in Prudence's place. But—would the deception serve on that holy day? Did the goddess empower the priestesses to discern which echoes were authentic and which were merely pretend? I had to control a shudder as I quickly abandoned that line of thought. We had so many more pressing and immediate worries.

"I don't think we need to wait until Counting Day," Nico replied. "I think we have an answer much closer at hand."

I sat up straighter, as if puzzled but trying very hard to understand. "What do you mean?"

He gestured toward the palace. "There are twelve women here who have echoes of their own. Most of them would have traveled along the Charamon Road on their way here. Most of them had some reason to dislike Jamison. Maybe one of them is the guilty party."

"But—they've been here a week and everyone's always been accompanied by the proper number of echoes. Haven't they?"

"I don't know. Who pays attention to echoes? Do *you*? Everyone just assumes they're there, where they're supposed to be. Do you go around counting every time you see a noblewoman? Do you even know how many echoes someone is supposed to have?"

"I—I've never really thought about it," I said. "Until I started working for Marguerite, I was hardly around echoes at all."

I was thinking furiously. He might be right—I had realized for myself that no creature in this city was more invisible than an echo. Since we had arrived at the palace, I *had* been counting echoes, but mostly because we were in such strange circumstances and I was trying to pay attention to every critical detail. But most nobles (with Marguerite being a notable exception) practically ignored their own echoes, at least in public venues. How closely were they monitoring those belonging to other people? The footmen who served the dinner tables paid more attention to the echoes than anyone else in the palace, but only because they had to synchronize when they poured wine and filled plates. Could they have said how many echoes any specific noble should actually have? Would they have given it a second thought if a noble who was supposed to have three echoes was suddenly down to two?

"I'm sure Cormac could tell you how many echoes everyone on his guest list ought to have—but I doubt he's made sure that that's how many showed up every night," Nico said. "I mean, look at those girls from Banchura! Nine echoes between them. One of them could have been missing this whole time and no one would have noticed."

"That's true!" I exclaimed. I didn't feel guilty for casting suspicion on the triplets because I knew for a fact they hadn't killed Jamison. "I've seen them walking out the palace doors like some kind of *mob*. No one could ever keep track of how many of them are together at one time."

"And Lady Elyssa. I heard that one of her echoes has been missing ever since she arrived. Elyssa claims she was injured, but maybe she's actually dead."

Even less did I mind throwing suspicion on Elyssa. "Yes! How dreadful if Elyssa turned out to be a murderer, but—that does seem very odd."

"Then there are the guests who showed up at the palace with only two echoes to their names," Nico went on. "Maybe that's all they ever had. But maybe they were supposed to have three, and everyone else failed to notice—or was too polite to speak up."

"So that's what you're going to do now," I said. "Investigate every one of Cormac's guests."

He nodded in the dark. "Quietly and carefully, not rousing anyone's suspicions. We don't even plan to let anyone know about the other body." He kissed my fingers. "So don't tell Marguerite."

Once again, I was flooded with a terrible fear that he was laying an elaborate trap for me. *He knows what we have done. He knows about our charade. He is trying to trick me into a confession.* As casually as I could manage, I said, "Your uncle will be angry if he learns you have told me all this."

"Probably," he agreed. "But I walked from the temple to the flower market with Marguerite, and I *was* counting echoes, and I know there were three. So you're the one person I feel I can trust."

A delicate lure designed to make me relax? An honest and oh-so-sweet declaration of faith? Either way, I had to play along. My gut twisted as I thought of how bitterly I was deceiving him, how absolute my betrayal was. But my only other choice was to betray Marguerite.

I lifted my free hand to touch his cheek, slightly rough from a day's growth of whiskers. "I'm glad you trust me," I said softly. "I wish you didn't have to spend your time thinking about such dreadful things."

He captured my hand, brought it to his mouth, and then pulled it aside so he could kiss me on the lips. I bent into his kiss, my mouth as hungry as his own, my desire rising just as rapidly. Did I simply want to forget all the impossible tangles of my life, take a few moments to replace thinking with feeling? Did I want to complicate his emotions, cloud his thoughts, bind him to me with the oldest and most powerful of ties? I needed him to trust me, to believe in me, to want to protect me. I needed to seduce him.

Did he need to seduce me?

Or were each of us half in love with the other, drunk on the possibilities of passion, ready to tumble into blind infatuation? Was any of this real, or were both of us modeling love as a new costume in a dangerous masquerade?

He had nudged me down into a reclining position and shoved my skirts up around my waist. He was swiftly unknotting the strings of my underclothes, but I was just as busy with the laces of his trousers. I stroked his hard body through the thin layer of fabric, and he hissed with pleasure. Then he abruptly sat up and leaned back on his hands as if trying to make sure they weren't free to come roaming back to my body.

"Really? Here?" he said in a breathless voice. "I thought you needed four walls and a bed."

"It's my preference," I answered, plenty breathless myself. "But I can't possibly let you follow me all the way up to my room, and I don't know where *you* sleep, but I have to think fifty people might see us on the way there—"

"A hundred."

"So I'm willing to compromise."

I sat up and stretched forward for another kiss, but he pulled back. "It's not right," he said, more seriously than he'd spoken all night, and we'd been talking about sober topics, indeed. "Not that I've never had a girl in a hallway or a garden, but it's not right. Not for *you*. You're more special than that."

He must have seen the look of devastation that crossed my face because he leaned in to give me another deep kiss, more reassurance than passion. Then he resettled himself and pulled me into his arms, my back against his chest. He locked his arms across my ribs, where no doubt he could feel the hammering of my heart, and bent forward to nuzzle my neck.

"I want to lie with you all night," he whispered. "Love each other, then make each other laugh, and love some more. We'll find the time for it, and the place. Just not tonight."

I let him rock me against his body and drop kisses on my cheek, and I pretended I was pleased that he thought so highly of me. But part of me was terrified. Part of me thought he was holding back because he didn't trust me; that he didn't think his heart would be safe within my care. And all of me knew that he was right.

CHAPTER TWENTY-TWO

Naturally, the first thing I did the next morning was tell Marguerite every word of Nico's revelations and speculations. She sat on the sofa and shivered with an internal chill, but she didn't break down and weep. I wondered if her visit with Taeline yesterday had fortified her unraveling spirit. Or if Taeline's announcement that she was moving to Thelleron had broken her so completely that she had no tears left to shed.

"Let's go to the temple," she said quietly when I was done. "And then the flower market. We can't change the past or direct the future, so we must try to get through the days the same way we always have."

The visit to the temple was surprisingly soothing—to me, certainly, and I think to Marguerite as well. Patience and Purpose and I again sat a row behind Marguerite, and Taeline eventually took a seat beside her. They talked in low voices for nearly an hour, and I hummed softly to myself so I would not be tempted to listen. From where I was sitting, I could not tell if their fingers touched as their hands lay on the bench between them, but I hoped with all my heart that they did.

Marguerite seemed at peace as we crossed the city to the flower market, and she picked out only blossoms of white and red. "I want to wear the colors of Oberton tonight," she said, toying with the bracelet on her arm. "A white dress and a black shawl and my beautiful onyx necklace. I want to remember where I come from and who I am."

We spent the afternoon making headdresses—I did most of the designing, but Marguerite insisted on setting some of the stitches, and the echoes helped by feeding out rolls of ribbon and holding stems steady when something needed to be tacked in place. We kept to our color scheme but changed the gown Marguerite planned to wear when word filtered down that Cormac and Jordan would join the nobles for dinner.

"A black dress and a red scarf, then," Marguerite said. "So we can show honor to the dead."

Indeed, all the visiting nobles, and their assorted echoes, attended the dinner in similarly somber colors accented with their own favored jewels. As always, they first gathered in the drawing room to visit before the meal. Darrily looked magnificent, her dark skin and dark dress lightened only by the trapped fire of the opals she wore draped around her throat and braided into her hair. The Banchura triplets and their echoes were all arrayed in deepest blue, every gown an identical shade; the sapphires sewn into their bodices matched the fabric so perfectly the gems were only visible because they glittered when any of them moved. It was impossible to tell how many were actually present because they constantly shifted position as they whispered to each other or addressed the other guests or flagged down a servant to request a glass of wine. I tried to count the total of originals and echoes, but I kept losing track. I had no reason to suspect that there would be fewer than twelve on hand—but I was glad that it wasn't easy to be sure.

After we had all been in the drawing room about twenty minutes, Cormac and Jordan stepped through the door, followed by their echoes. There was a moment of absolute silence while everyone turned to stare at them, and then, in a murmurous rustle of lace and silk, every noble dropped into a deep curtsey or a low bow. It was an acknowledgment not of royalty, but of grief—heartfelt on the princes' behalf, I thought, if not on Jamison's.

Jordan merely nodded in response, but Cormac addressed the room. "Thank you," he said. "I'm sorry I've been so preoccupied. I haven't forgotten that you are all here at my request and deserve my attention."

I thought the word *attention* was more of a threat than an apology, but that was probably because I felt nervous and guilty. Everyone else seemed to take his greeting as an invitation, and the nobles surged forward to cluster around the princes with soft words of welcome and condolence. There was a slow shift and churn as one or two people spoke to Cormac, then drifted away to address Jordan; others stepped forward to take their places. Jordan was far enough away from me that I couldn't hear anything he said, but I caught the rhythmic litany of Cormac's voice speaking the same words over and over: *"Thank you... Yes, it is dreadful... No, we've learned very little... but thank you..."*

I had to assume Cormac was at least as well informed about the situation as Nico. So the prince was lying to all his guests with as much cool nerve as Marguerite had been lying to him for the past week.

I decided that for the rest of my life I would always just assume that no one was telling the truth. Judging from my recent experiences, I would be mostly right.

When it was Marguerite's turn to offer Cormac her hand and her sympathies, he managed to summon a smile. "You are wearing my favorite necklace, I see," he said.

"It seems like such a minor thing," she said. "But I thought if one small piece of beauty could lift your heart just the tiniest bit, I was duty bound to make the effort. I had no choice but to wear it."

"A subject who is both loyal and kind," Cormac replied. "That is a rare combination."

"Oh, surely not. There must be thousands who match that description."

Cormac's smile widened a little. I thought perhaps this mild flirtation might be the first respite he'd had from rage and sorrow since the news about Jamison arrived five nights ago. "Loyal, kind, beautiful, and noble," he corrected himself. "Shall I pile on more adjectives? Soon you will find yourself in a category of one."

Marguerite's laugh was light, but it caused a dozen heads to whip around in her direction, since no one else had managed a mirthful exchange with either prince this evening. "I do not desire to be so singular," she said. "Merely to be of some comfort to you in this dark time."

At that moment, a footman stepped through the door to announce that dinner was ready. Cormac drew Marguerite's arm through his and turned toward the door. I found myself instantly linking arms with one of his echoes.

"Sit with me tonight," he said, leading her from the room. "Make this whole evening almost bearable."

Goddess have mercy on my soul.

I don't know how much food Marguerite managed to choke down that night. As always, I tried to emulate Patience and Purpose, and they appeared to serve themselves just as heartily as they would on any other occasion. For myself, I could hardly swallow a bite. I felt exposed, anxious, and afraid. Yet, judging by the expressions on the echoes' faces, Marguerite was relaxed, entertained, sympathetic, and amusing in turn. *If you're not careful, he's going to want to sit beside you every night for the rest of this visit*, I thought as I stared at her back. *How many days can you keep up this pretense?*

Could she keep it up forever, if Cormac and the king could tear their thoughts away from Jamison's death and bend their attention once more to the question of who should be the prince's wife?

The interminable meal had moved on to its third course when the footman serving my table made an awkward turn and almost dropped a tureen onto the head of one of Cormac's echoes. A titter of amusement swept through the nobles, while the other footmen in my line of sight looked mortified; a loud and public mistake was every servant's worst nightmare. After a shaky recovery, the clumsy one moved slowly down my table, dishing out portions with a steady enough hand.

But I noticed something odd about his technique. He wasn't paying close attention to the footman who was serving Cormac and Marguerite and the other nobles at their table; not only was he not well synchronized with his colleague, he didn't even seem to be *watching* the other man. As a result, I had my soup as soon as Marguerite did, and I started eating when she sampled her first mouthful—but there was no soup in Patience's bowl. Yet she, too, picked up her spoon and lifted it to her mouth, so that her movements were exactly timed with Marguerite's.

I tried not to frown, since Patience's face remained serene, but this had never happened in the past week. The echoes were always served as soon as the originals were, specifically so they could consume exactly the same amount of food. Obviously, Patience wouldn't starve to death if she missed a few bites, but I couldn't imagine that any royal servant would make such a gross error.

Trying to be discreet about it, I studied the footman as he moved down the table, sloppily dishing out food. Come to think of it, he had done a poor job of serving the earlier courses as well. He'd given me a much larger piece of bread than he'd given Patience, but my helping of fruit was smaller.

Have half the footmen in the palace come down with illness and been replaced by untrained workers? I wondered. *This is what I get for spending all my time with Marguerite instead of dining in the kitchens, learning the gossip!*

The graceless footman finished his task and turned toward the serving door to carry his tureen away. I watched him out of the corner of my eye and saw the other footmen trailing behind him.

One of them was Nico.

My hand clenched on my spoon and I had to hope no one heard my sharp intake of air. Nico was wearing a servant's livery and a neutral expression—as were the rest of them—but now that I was paying attention I could tell that at least four of them were not truly footmen. Inquisitor's men, I supposed. There to thread their way through the tables of echoes and see if any of them were missing.

This would be the best opportunity to count them, as they were arrayed behind their originals and likely to stay in place for at least an hour. Even the echoes of the Banchura triplets would be easy to tally, since they were all finally sitting still.

I wondered what Nico and his uncle would think once the meal was over and they realized that every echo was accounted for.

Would they decide that none of Cormac's invited guests could be responsible for Jamison's murder? Would they focus their attention on other suspects? How could they not? My first reaction had been fear, but maybe it should have been relief.

Nico already knew Marguerite had three echoes with her in Camarria, but let that fact be confirmed by someone a little less biased in my favor. Let the inquisitor himself come stealing through the room, counting bodies and matching up faces. I would smile as widely as Marguerite, eat just as much food, gulp down just as much wine. Let him be convinced that Marguerite could not possibly be a murderer, and let him turn his eyes away.

Let us take one long, slow breath of relief.

I made it to the bridge that night only ten minutes before Nico did, but I had dropped down to a seated position again and pretended to be drowsing. I stirred sleepily when he sank beside me and stretched his legs out before him. His dark clothing made him look like a spilled shadow against the whiteness of the painted wood.

"There you are," I said through a faked yawn. "I was hoping you could get here sooner. I'm usually in Marguerite's room while she's away at dinner, mending clothes and making sure everything's ready for the next day, but tonight I was done early." I turned my head to accept his quick kiss. "But I suppose you were busy."

I thought this was a brilliant lie. He couldn't possibly disprove it, since I knew exactly where he'd been the whole time I *wasn't* patiently waiting for him on the bridge. And it would make it seem that I had a life apart from Marguerite's—in case it might have occurred to him that I didn't.

"Busy, though I don't know if we've discovered anything useful," he answered, putting an arm around my shoulder and drawing me close enough to nestle against him. "Trying to count all the echoes and make sure everyone has the right number."

"Did Cormac give you a list of how many belong with each guest?"

"He did."

"And did you find any that were missing?"

He was silent a moment, and I felt a spurt of fear. I turned my head to gaze up at him with what I hoped was an expression of innocent inquiry.

"Nico? You found a missing echo?"

"Or two. Maybe."

I pushed myself to an upright position, and his arm fell away. "But how exciting! And how terrible! What did— What can you tell me? I don't want your uncle to be angry with you but—I really want to know!"

"Well, you know Elyssa has been missing an echo practically since the day she arrived. So it was no surprise to see that there was an empty chair by her place at dinner tonight."

"At dinner? You spied on everyone during the meal? That was clever."

He smiled briefly. "Glad you think so. It was my idea."

"So Elyssa is your suspect?"

"Probably not. The palace maids have confirmed that there is, indeed, an injured echo in Elyssa's room. But so far we haven't confirmed that anyone has seen the two healthy echoes *and* the injured echo at the same time."

I gasped. "You mean—one echo could be dead. And sometimes the remaining two are with Elyssa, and sometimes one of them pretends to be the one that's hurt."

"Exactly. Although that would require the echoes to be capable of a level of sophisticated acting that I doubt any of them could manage."

I spared a moment to think Purpose could probably pull off such a deception, but, of course, I didn't say so. "But Elyssa's echoes possess a certain amount of independence, don't they?" I said slowly. "That's what Marguerite told me. Maybe they *could* manage such a performance."

"Yes—well—we will quickly find out," Nico said. "Even my uncle is not prepared to go bursting into a noblewoman's room at night unless he is positive she is guilty of a heinous crime. But someone will follow her in the morning, counting how many shadows trail her, and someone else will enter her room to see whether or not an injured echo inhabits it. So we should know very soon whether or not Elyssa is our culprit."

"I hope she is," I said. "Everyone dislikes her so much."

"It would make for a very tidy ending," he agreed.

Then I remembered. "But you said—there was a second echo missing?"

He nodded slowly. "Lady Vivienne of Thelleron. Cormac says she's supposed to have three, but there were only two behind her at dinner. However, Cormac doesn't remember if she ever had three with her at any point in the past week. Apparently, he has avoided her as much as possible."

"Lady Vivienne—wait, she's the one who used to be betrothed to Cormac, isn't she, until he broke it off?"

"That's right."

"I can see why she might want to kill *Cormac*, then, but not why she would want to murder Jamison."

Nico shrugged. "If she was hurt enough, or angry enough, those emotions could extend to everyone else in Cormac's family, I suppose. And if Jamison taunted her or provoked her—as he very well might have—"

"Then she could have attacked him," I finished up. "And she just showed up in Camarria, hoping no one would realize she was missing an echo."

"As I said, Cormac didn't notice. And I didn't dance with her at the ball, so I couldn't tell you how many echoes she had with her that night."

I arched my eyebrows. "'Didn't dance with her at the ball'?" I repeated. "You were invited to that event? The prince must value you highly."

Nico grinned. "No, don't you remember? I told you I sometimes fill in as one of the 'extra men' when a nobleman only has two echoes and he wants to dance with a woman who has three. That's what I was doing the other night at Cormac's ball."

"Then you're the wrong person to ask," I said practically. "Who were the 'extra women' at the ball? *They're* the people who could tell you if Vivienne was one echo short."

He flicked my nose with a finger. "What a clever girl you are! I should consult you every time I'm trying to solve a mystery!"

I laughed back at him. "So you already thought of that."

"Indeed, I did. But two of the young women who had that role said they didn't fill in for Vivienne, and the other one has left the city for the week. So, instead, we will spy on the lady for a day or two and see what we can discover."

I frowned and settled back against his shoulder. "Lady Vivienne," I repeated. "I don't think Marguerite has had many dealings with her. At any rate, she hasn't mentioned her to me, whereas she's *always* talking about Leonora and Letitia and Lavinia."

"Apparently Vivienne has kept to herself a great deal since she arrived. Which perhaps argues a guilty conscience."

Marguerite had kept to herself a great deal, too, and for exactly that reason. I hoped he didn't make the connection. "Or a broken heart," I said. "If she truly loved Cormac, this situation must be almost unendurable for her."

"I don't think it has been easy for Cormac, either," Nico said. "Even before all this happened with Jamison."

I heaved a sigh of sympathy, which was only partly manufactured. I found myself wondering what Vivienne's story was. Had her echo disappeared under mysterious circumstances that she would not easily be able to explain? Would Nico and his uncle consider her responsible for Jamison's murder on no more evidence than that? What would Marguerite do if someone else was accused of the crime she had committed? Would she smile with relief and return giddily to her own life? I couldn't think it of her, but if she did? What would *I* do? Could I allow an innocent woman to face those remorseless archers in Amanda Plaza?

I had been saying it over and over these days, it seemed, but the words rose unbidden to my mind. *Goddess have mercy on my soul.*

It was my turn to say something, but the best I could come up with was, "If Vivienne and Elyssa are able to produce all their echoes, what will you do then?"

"I'm not sure. Expand the search, I suppose. But that could take weeks."

"Would you expect all of Cormac's noble guests to remain in the city while you kept looking?"

He turned swiftly to draw me into his arms. "I don't know what Malachi plans, but that would be my preference," he said huskily. "To have you here for months."

"Even if it meant the mystery was never solved?" I whispered against his mouth.

"Even then."

He kissed me and we stopped caring about the murdered bastard, the missing echo, the grieving king. I even stopped worrying about whether or not he was laying a trap for me and how much he would hate me if he learned I was lying to him. I just kissed him and shivered as he ran his hands along my body; I just reveled in the way my skin and breasts and mouth and heart responded to his eager touch. I pressed myself against him, silently asking for a deeper kiss, a more intimate caress. I had pulled up the tail of his shirt and now I ran my hands along the smooth warmth of his back. It was a delight to feel his muscles straining beneath the supple skin.

Just as he had the night before, he abruptly pulled back, panting with thwarted desire but looking very determined. "Not here," he said.

"Nico—"

He kissed my forehead. "That's another mystery we must both attempt to solve," he said. "How we can find an hour alone together without too many people knowing about it."

"*You're* the one who's familiar with the palace and the city," I pointed out. I very huffily straightened my bodice and tugged down my skirts, making it clear that I wasn't happy with the turn of events. "Tell me a place to meet you and I will."

He brushed a hand across my cheek. "I just don't want you to be sorry," he said.

I stretched up to kiss him hard. "Do I *act* like I'm going to be sorry?"

"Sometimes people change their minds. Sometimes people wish something undone, but it's undoable."

Well, *that* had a certain resonance. "And sometimes they don't care about consequences," I said.

"You could stay in Camarria, you know."

"What?"

"If Cormac and Marguerite don't become engaged. If Marguerite returns to Oberton. You could stay. Plenty of work here for someone who's as smart as you are."

My heart was racing, but I attempted to answer playfully. "Becoming an inquisitor for your uncle."

"He does have women working for him, if you were interested in that life. But there are plenty of nobles who could use an excellent maid."

He was serious. That made it harder for me to catch my breath. "If Marguerite goes back to Oberton, I have to go with her. She needs me."

"She could hire *five* people to take your place."

"Yes, but—you don't understand. Her life has been—it seems she has had so many advantages, but in many ways—it's just that she's so alone."

He shrugged. I wasn't sure in the darkness, but I thought he might look a little hurt. But the tone of his voice was sardonic. "In my experience, a noble will get rid of a servant at any time without a second thought. You're far more loyal to her than she would be to you."

"Maybe," I said. I allowed a touch of desperation to creep into my voice. "I wish I didn't *have* to choose. I didn't realize this was going to be so hard."

Nico pushed himself to his feet, then held out a hand to help me up. "Well, there's only one solution," he said. "We have to hope Cormac and Marguerite make a match of it, after all."

I laughed as gaily as I could and held the crook of his arm as we strolled off the bridge. "That would be perfect," I said. It would be horrific. "I will suggest that to her every chance I get. So *you* keep whispering *her* name in Cormac's ear."

"I will do so at every opportunity."

We had just stepped off the final plank when a shape moved toward us through the shadows. I had scarcely registered it as the body of a man before Nico dropped my arm and shoved me behind him, apparently ready to defend me to the death. I hadn't even seen him pull a weapon, but clearly the person approaching us had.

"Put away your dagger," said a deep voice, silky and amused. "I am completely harmless."

I felt Nico relax and straighten, and he sheathed his blade. "Hardly that," he retorted. "Though I'll believe you mean *us* no harm."

"In fact, my mission here is purely social. I would so much like to be introduced to your young lady."

The man's stealth, his purring voice, his complete command of the situation, had given me a few clues as to who he might be. But it didn't make me any happier to be right. Nico touched my arm to urge me forward.

"Brianna, this is my uncle Malachi, the inquisitor of King Harold's court. Uncle, this is Brianna, who serves as maid to Lady Marguerite Andolin of Oberton."

I didn't know the protocol of conversing with an inquisitor—I mean, unless he was torturing you, and then I imagined you just told him everything you knew, whether or not it was relevant to the topic at hand. Should I curtsey? Address him as "my lord"? Or should I remain silent until he gave me permission to speak? And while all these questions were chasing through my brain, more frightening ones crouched at the back of my mind. *Why does he want to meet me? What does he know about my masquerade? What does he know about Marguerite?*

He was probably used to people being paralyzed around him because he quickly took command of the conversation. "Hello,

Brianna," he said, reaching for my hand and holding it in a strong grip. "I understand you've set out to fascinate my nephew."

Nico laughed, and I blushed. Even though it was dark, I was sure the inquisitor could see the flushing of my cheeks. He seemed like a man who didn't require daylight. "I have been enjoying his company and hope he has been enjoying mine," I said, because the answer could seem both genuinely demure and a little coy.

"He likes country girls," Malachi said. "He's never been interested in city women who put on airs and lie to a man's face."

Gorsey. "I've never been very fancy, I'm afraid," I said. "But I find I love living in the city more than I ever thought I would."

"Oberton or Camarria?"

"Both."

"I spent some time in Oberton when I was younger," Malachi said. "But I like Banch Harbor and Empara City better. Have you traveled much?"

I shook my head. "No. This is the first time I've left Orenza."

"You should visit Empara City at least. Beautiful place."

"Maybe Marguerite will go there someday."

"What's she like?" the inquisitor asked with casual curiosity.

Though I knew it was anything but casual. This was a man who collected information with the single-minded focus of a fanatic; he would hoard his snippets and confidences like a miser hoards treasure, picking through them to find the perfect jewels.

I knew I had to be careful. If I sounded fawning and overly pleased with my situation, he would think I was lying, perhaps covering up some indiscretion of my own. If I was brief and unhelpful, he would think I was withholding information about Marguerite. I settled for a version of the story I had told in the kitchens.

"She's a good mistress, but she's fretful," I said. "Delicate. Has a lot of headaches and other ailments. The first time I met her, she threw up on my shoes."

"Yet you still wanted to work for her?"

"Well, I've dealt with worse than vomit."

Malachi made a motion with his head, indicating that he wanted to walk, so I nervously fell in step beside him. Our feet made crunching noises on the gravel of the path, which led us toward the formal gardens behind the palace. Nico came behind us, close enough to hear every word. I wondered what he thought about Malachi's sudden appearance and gentle (so far) inquisition. Did he think his uncle just wanted to get to know the girl his nephew was spending so much time with? Or did he expect the inquisitor to conduct a subtle interrogation? Had Nico perhaps even arranged this meeting? *We will be on the garden bridge the hour before midnight. I will shower her with kisses and talk to her of love, and she will be so dizzy that she will tell you anything you ask.*

The moon threw just enough light to show me the shapes of trees and hedges that lined our path; I couldn't see the colors of the flowers in their tended beds, but their sweet, heavy perfume drifted around us as we walked. Behind us, the palace loomed as a massive shape of darkness, lights showing in only a few scattered rooms. It must have been later than I had realized if most of the world was asleep.

It seemed like forever before Malachi spoke again. "They say that if you want to know the true measure of a man—or a woman—watch how that individual treats those who are in a lower station," he said. "If he cheats the tradesman or she berates the maid, well then. You know all you need to know."

"Oh, I've never seen Marguerite be rude to anyone."

"How does she treat her echoes?"

Obviously, not an idle question. I had to assume he had been present—or had had a man present—at the card game the other night. He already knew Marguerite's echoes had some volition of their own, so it would be safe to make that admission.

"Differently than a lot of the other nobles, from what I've observed," I said. "She gives them a little more freedom. I can't exactly describe it."

"That's interesting," Malachi said. "Can she tell them apart, one from the other?"

I hesitated a moment—and when my hesitation grew noticeable, I faked a laugh. "I'm afraid you'll think her very strange," I said.

"I assure you, I will not."

"She has named them. And she says she knows which one is which."

He glanced down at me, and I was pretty sure I could feel astonishment emanating from him, though he kept his voice satin-smooth. "Named them," he repeated. "I have not heard of that before."

"I thought it must be unusual."

"Can *you* tell them apart?"

Yes. "No."

"Would I be able to?"

I turned my head as if to give him a critical appraisal. What could I discern in the moonlit darkness? He was about Nico's height and a little heavier, though his black clothing hid his frame. He was bald and clean-shaven, as if he had long ago dispensed with any of the softening effects hair and a beard might provide. I couldn't clearly make out his features, though his nose was prominent and his eyes seemed deep-set and dark. "Maybe," I said candidly. "You seem like the kind of person who can do anything he wants."

That made him laugh; even Nico chuckled behind us. "I have been around echoes, one way or another, my whole life," Malachi said. "And I have never once thought I might want one of my own."

"I've come to the same conclusion," I replied. "There is a whole additional level of calculation you must make, from what clothing you should wear to how much food you need to whether there's enough room in the carriage."

"Although I suppose, if you have been attended by echoes since birth, these calculations become habitual," Malachi speculated.

"It seems to be that way with Marguerite," I agreed. "But I still think that if I had shadows behind me all the time, I would find it tedious—when it wasn't downright inconvenient."

"Well, yes," Malachi purred, "I can think of *several* situations in which having an audience would be inconvenient indeed."

Of course I could only call *one* such situation to mind, and my face flamed again. I decided to take a saucy tone. "Well, you're the inquisitor," I said. "I'm sure you *usually* don't want an audience."

"Very true," he said, sounding amused. "I often think I would have chosen a much different profession if I had been a man with echoes."

I remembered the story Nico had told me the very first time I met him—about an ancestor who killed off his own echoes so he could take a dangerous job for the crown. Nico had said the story was about his great-grandfather, but I wondered now if he might have been describing Malachi. Just five minutes in his company convinced me he would be capable of such a thing.

"I would have had a different life myself," I said. "Because I would have been a rich lady living in a fancy house!"

"I hear stories now and then," said Malachi, "of a gardener or a milliner or some workingman who's got an echo trailing behind."

I was genuinely surprised. "I always thought they only appeared to high nobles."

"Or those who have dallied with them."

My third blush of the night. "Oh! Of course!"

"But I myself have only met echoes within the walls of the very best homes," Malachi finished up. "So maybe the tales are fabricated."

As he spoke, we followed the gravel path around a sweeping turn, and now we were facing the back of the palace. Over the uneven horizon of trees, trellises, and statuary, I could see its entire silhouette, a thick rectangle topped with a whimsical skyline of turrets and towers. Now there were even fewer windows showing light from within. The windows at the very top, the servants' quarters, were all dark. Maids and valets always went to bed at the earliest opportunity, since their days usually started well before dawn.

"Funny when you think about it," Malachi went on. "How comparatively few people in the kingdom have echoes—and how many of them are here right now. If you wanted to ask all of them a single question, you could get a good start on your work in one place."

I tried not to shiver in the warm night air, since I was sure he would notice. He probably noticed that I was making the effort. Boldness seemed my only course. "What would you ask them all?" I said.

I felt him glance down at me, but I kept my eyes fixed on the palace walls. He spoke in the softest voice he had yet used. "What would you do if you lost an echo?"

Ten minutes later, I was safely in my room, wondering if anyone else was in the back garden to notice the faint light coming from my window. I thought the only other people awake at this hour were probably guards and inquisitors, and my guess was that they would be looking for trouble in much different places than the servants' quarters.

I hadn't known what to reply to the inquisitor's final question, but he hadn't had much else to say to me, either. Almost as soon as he spoke the words, he turned to Nico and said, "It's late and I have something I need you to do for me. Let's see this young lady inside." So the three of us marched in a straight line for the back of the palace. I didn't even have a chance to kiss Nico goodbye because as soon as I put my hand on the door, they veered off in another direction. I felt a little resentful and a little bereft—and exceptionally uneasy. What had Malachi wanted from me, and had he obtained it?

I changed into my nightclothes and climbed into bed and opened my eyes as wide as they would go. I was so tired that I knew I would fall asleep within seconds, but I wanted to think for a moment. I had considered swinging past Marguerite's room on my way to bed, but I hadn't decided how much to tell her about the interlude with Nico and my conversation with Malachi. She already knew that the inquisitor was looking for missing echoes. Did she need the details about Lady Vivienne? She knew that I was flirting with the inquisitor's nephew. Would it add to her worry if she thought I was falling in love with him? Would she become afraid that I would choose him over her? Would Malachi's sudden appearance ratchet up her fear? Would I be kinder to her if I simply withheld much of the truth?

I was lying to Nico about Marguerite. Should I start lying to Marguerite about Nico? Would that make me the most loyal or the most untrustworthy person in the kingdom?

I honestly didn't know what to do.

CHAPTER TWENTY-THREE

The following day unfolded only slightly differently than the previous two.

In the morning, Marguerite and I walked to the temple, flanked by the echoes; once we were seated inside, she whispered with Taeline while I silently prayed to the goddess, asking for guidance. We had planned to head for the flower market, but we unexpectedly encountered the Banchura triplets and their comet's-tail of echoes, so we joined them for an impromptu tour of one of the historical districts. Our way took us across three famous city bridges, each distinctive.

The first was an ancient passageway of crumbling mortared stones topped with a splintery wooden roof; it stretched over an old, empty arena that used to be a public slaughterhouse, so Letitia told us. We could still see the narrow drains sunk in the slate of the floor. The second was a contraption of ropes and boards slung over a sewage canal. It swayed so alarmingly with every step we took that Marguerite and I were convinced it would collapse with all of us still clinging to the hemp handrails. But the third was a lovely affair of wooden beams and painted plaster that carried us from a rather grim, workaday neighborhood into a charming collection of elegant houses, discreet hotels, and expensive shops.

"We've been here ten days now, and I think I've only seen a few small corners of the city," Leonora said. "If Cormac isn't going to provide us with more entertainment, I'm just going to go out on daily expeditions until I've explored every mile of Camarria."

"Oh, yes, let's all go," said Lavinia. "Marguerite, will you join us?"

"As often as I'm able," Marguerite said. "Unless I have one of my stupid headaches."

Letitia leaned over and rubbed her forefinger in a circular motion on Marguerite's temple. "No more headaches," she said. "I forbid it."

The evening ended with a subdued dinner, which Cormac attended. Once again, he asked Marguerite to sit beside him and chase away his melancholy. I saw the looks that passed between some of the visiting nobles as she accepted his arm and stepped toward the dining room. Were the rumors true? Was Cormac about to propose? Would he be able to push past his grief long enough to think again about the future of his country?

Marguerite played her part to perfection, but we were barely back in her suite when she said, "I think I'm going to throw up. I can't stand all this *lying* to everyone!" Indeed, her hands were cold but her face was damp with perspiration as I helped her out of her clothes and into a silken robe. She tied her sash and began to pace across the room.

Purpose and Patience secured their own robes and fell in step behind her, their own faces set in similar lines of worry and remorse. I settled onto one of the sofas and watched them, tucking my feet up to keep out of their way.

"Is there anything I can do to help you?" I asked quietly.

"No one can help! There's nothing *to* do! But things would be much better if I didn't have to listen to Prince Cormac go on and on and *on* about his poor brother whose life was tragically cut short! First I want to scream and then I want to beg for mercy." She shook her head. "And then I want to start sobbing.

"But you handle yourself so beautifully," I said in admiration. "I am constantly listening for signs of strain in your voice, and I never hear it. You seem relaxed and sympathetic and delightful."

She threw herself onto a seat across from me, and the echoes dropped onto their own chairs. "Don't you find it a little horrifying that I am none of those things?" she demanded. "Yet perfectly able to appear as if I am? Do you not wonder if every single person you have ever met in your entire life is showing you a false face?"

"In the past, I didn't," I admitted. "But these days—yes, very often."

She closed her eyes and leaned her head back. "Don't bother wondering," she said. "Just assume they are."

"My lady—"

She jumped up again, and Patience and Purpose surged to their feet. "I wish I could outrun my thoughts," she flung at me over her shoulder. "I wish I could outrun my memories. How far do you think I would have to go?"

"Farther than the world stretches, I'm afraid."

She groaned and kept pacing. I was beginning to think she would not calm down for some time and I didn't want to leave her while she was in such a state. If Nico arrived at the bridge, looking for me, he wouldn't find me.

Maybe that was just as well.

For the next hour, Marguerite alternated between striding through the room, bitterly repeating some of Cormac's comments, and collapsing on one of the chairs, looking tired and defeated. When I suggested that she would feel better if I cleaned her face and got her ready for bed, she rounded on me in anger.

"*Nothing* will make me feel better! But you can leave me if you want to! I wouldn't blame you. *I* would leave me, if I could find a way to break out of my own skin." She gestured wildly at the echoes. "*They* would leave me, if they could. Go ahead! Do it! Abandon me!"

She dashed across the room and flung open the door. When they followed her, running closely behind, she grabbed Patience's arm and tried to shove her across the threshold. The echo bleated and twisted in Marguerite's hold, looking frightened and confused.

"Go on! I know you want to!" Marguerite cried, pushing even harder. She grabbed Purpose's arm with her other hand, and tried to force both of them through the door at the same time.

I was so stunned it took me that long to scramble up from the sofa. "My *lady*! Stop that! Shut the door! Anyone could be out in the hallway—"

She was still wrestling with the echoes when she started to weep. "I don't care! I don't care! It's better for *them* if they go—!"

By now I had crossed the room. I reached for her, but she fended me off— first with her elbows, then with her hands—dropping her grip on the echoes to do so. I managed to dodge her flailing arms while inching near enough to the door to shut and lock it. Then I took a deep breath and set my back against it. Was she finally going to succumb to nearly two weeks of stress and uncertainty? How could I calm her down?

But I could see at once that that wasn't going to be my task. Purpose and Patience had linked arms and made a gentle cage around Marguerite, pressing closer, giving her struggling body no room to maneuver. I could see Patience leaning in, making *shh-shh-shh* noises of comfort, could see Purpose urging them all to move toward the bedroom in one straining knot. Marguerite was still crying, harder now, uttering phrases like *"I can't"* and *"Just go,"* but her motions were slower, more leaden, as she lost the will to fight. Step by step, the echoes took her to the bedroom; whisper by wordless whisper they soothed her lacerated heart. I followed behind, feeling both helpless and full of wonder, ready to do my part when I got the chance.

The echoes eased Marguerite to the bed and sat beside her on the lace duvet. Patience rubbed her hands and Purpose drew Marguerite's head down onto her shoulder, then looked at me in a clear directive. I hurried to get a damp cloth and a glass of water, and I drew a stool over so I could sit beside the bed.

"Here, drink this," I murmured as I wiped her face. "Wouldn't you like to lie down now? You must be so tired. It's been so hard. I know. But you'll feel better in the morning."

Marguerite sipped the water and nodded her head and tried to say thank you, but she was too exhausted to do more than mouth the words. It took me another twenty minutes to exchange her robe for her nightdress and tuck her under the covers.

"Can you sleep now? Shall I blow out the candles?"

"I want them with me."

"The echoes? They're right here."

"*With* me."

"What—"

But the echoes knew. They climbed under the covers next to her, one on either side, shields against despair forged from her own blood and bone. I heard her sigh with something that was almost contentment. Or maybe just relief.

"Should I go to my own room or stay here tonight?"

"Stay, please."

"Happily." I didn't have to manufacture the yawn or the slight laugh that followed. "I'm so tired myself I'm ready for bed right now, too."

"Tomorrow will come too soon," she said drowsily. "It always does."

In the morning, Marguerite didn't have to pretend to have a headache. And this time she actually looked as bad as she usually pretended to feel, her face pale, her eyes bruised, her mouth pinched.

"I'll fetch you breakfast and spread the word that you'll be keeping to your room today," I said. "Are there any errands you'd like me to run? It looks like this could be a very productive day for Brianna."

She smiled wanly from her seat before the window. "You could bring me back some flowers."

I couldn't resist patting her on the head, for all the world like a sick child. "I will."

Purpose followed me to the door and I heard her set the lock behind me. After a quick stop in my own room, I swung by the kitchens, where I sighed loudly over Marguerite's poor state of health and gobbled down a meal before carrying a tray up to Marguerite's suite. Once I made sure all was well there, I was back downstairs and out the palace doors.

The morning was sunny and fine, not too hot, as befit a day when summer was about to ease into autumn. I had plenty of stops to make before I headed to the flower market because I had had very little time to myself since this masquerade began. I posted a letter to my mother, purchased a few trinkets for my siblings, and picked up sewing supplies to mend a couple of Marguerite's gowns, as well as hairpins to replace the ones we were continually losing from our headdresses. We had spent enough time strolling through the city that her walking shoes had become scuffed, so I needed polish, and I wanted more ribbon for the next set of head-pieces I planned to design. When I passed a confectionary shop, I couldn't resist going in to buy a bag of hard candies in assorted flavors, since Marguerite and all her echoes loved sweets in any form.

Naturally, Nico was waiting for me when I stepped back outside. Truth to tell, I was a little surprised that it had taken him that long to materialize. Of course, he had probably been sneaking along behind me ever since I walked out of the palace, waiting to see if I would visit any suspicious locations so he could report back to his uncle.

"Good morning," he said.

"And good morning to you. Would you like a piece of candy?"

"I might," he said. "What kind did you get?"

I opened the bag and held it out so he could see. "Four flavors," I pointed out. "Everyone has a preference."

He was carrying a lumpy sack in one hand, but he slung it over his shoulder so he could tuck his hand in the candy bag. But now he paused to look at me, eyebrows raised. "'Everyone'?"

"Marguerite and her echoes. As I told your uncle, they all have slightly different personalities."

He pulled his hand slowly from the bag and popped a red candy in his mouth. "I thought you couldn't tell them apart."

"I can when they're reaching for their favorite flavors." I shook the bag to redistribute the contents, peering in to search for a piece that was green. "Marguerite always wants lemon. Purpose likes grape. Patience likes cherry. I like lime."

He waited for a beat. "And the third echo?"

Goddess save me, I had forgotten about Prudence. She was always disappointed if there wasn't orange in the mix. My stomach clenched into a hard ball, but I managed a light laugh. "Prudence. *She* will eat anything. So she's easy."

"Malachi found your story extraordinary, you know. Echoes with their own names. Their own attitudes. He said he's never heard of that before."

I shrugged. "I can't help it if the inquisitor has limited experience."

He grinned, resettled the sack on his shoulder, and took my arm. He set off in a direction I had not intended to go, but I acquiesced without protest. "I'm sorry if he frightened you," he said.

"I imagine he frightens everyone. I imagine he *wants* to."

"Some truth to that," he admitted. "But I hoped you would be too brave to give in to such fears."

Now I was the one to give him an inquiring look. He grinned down at me and said, "Last night. When you didn't show up at the bridge. I thought probably Malachi had scared you away."

I wondered if I should be honest about some of the things I'd been thinking. *It wasn't Malachi who made me uneasy. It was you, inviting Malachi to come meet me. Did you want to show me off to your uncle? "Look, here's the girl I've been seeing. I think she's special." Or did you want him to question me, to pry out the secrets you've been unwilling or unable to learn? Was he there at your invitation? Or was he drawn there by his own curiosity—or suspicion?*

But I had started lying to Nico so long ago, I didn't know how to be truthful now.

"I *wish* I had stayed away last night because of your uncle," I said. "But, in fact, Marguerite had a bad night. She was sick to her stomach and a little feverish, and I didn't feel like I could leave her."

"I'm sorry to hear that. I trust she's better this morning?"

"Yes, but cranky enough to want solitude. So I slipped out as soon as I could—and I plan to stay away half the day! She'll be very contrite this afternoon, however. She's always sorry if she thinks she's said an unkind word."

"Well, I'm glad to hear that she treats you so well—but the sentence that caught my attention was 'I plan to stay away half the day.' Do you really?"

Now I was laughing. "No. But I might dawdle on the way back."

"For an hour? For two?"

I eyed him. "Why, exactly?"

"Because there's a place you might like to see. I thought of it yesterday and I was going to tell you about it last night—but then you didn't make an appearance. I would be very sorry if I never got a chance to show it to you."

"Well, this is most intriguing! How far away is it?" I glanced around, just now realizing that the buildings we were passing were made of old stone and crumbling mortar. "Have we been in this district before?"

"Nearby. We're headed toward Amanda Plaza, though we're coming in by a different route."

"We can throw coins into the grate."

"Well, we *can*, but that's not why we're going there."

"Why, then?"

He smiled and shook his head and, to make himself even more provoking, began pointing out various buildings with historical significance and unusual architectural features, even though it was clear I had no interest in these things. It was probably another ten minutes before we made it to the plaza, where we hung back before approaching the goddess statues because a wedding party was there before us. They were all laughing and joking as they dribbled their coins into the grate, guessing out loud at the wishes their friends might be making. They were watched benevolently by three priestesses all wearing the red robes of celebration. I reflected that, since I had come to know Marguerite, I had almost forgotten that the temple servants wore any color besides white.

"They look happy," I said, my voice wistful.

"They should! Or I don't have much hope for their future together. But they're very slow. Come on. We'll offer our coins on the way home."

He drew me in the direction of a building that stood on one border of the plaza. It was tall and narrow, five precarious stories high, and it looked like it had been abandoned some years ago because of structural instability. There was a padlock on the thick wooden door that was set somewhat crookedly into an iron frame, and the grime on the bottom-story windows was so thick that I couldn't see inside.

"*This* is what you wanted to show me? I'm guessing it's the oldest building in the city, and you wanted me to see it before it gets torn down. Tomorrow, I'm hoping."

He laughed as he pulled out an ornate old key and fit it into the lock. He had to expend some effort to get the key to turn, and I could have sworn I saw flakes of rust drift down. "One of the oldest," he corrected, "and currently owned by the crown. Not in daily use. But my uncle finds it handy from time to time."

We stepped inside and looked around. We were in an open space that constituted the entire bottom level, although it didn't feel particularly roomy because the windows were so dark and the ceiling was so low. There was a faint smell of mold and the occasional skitter and scurry from small creatures I didn't want to look too hard to identify. From the layer of dust on the floor, I surmised that Malachi hadn't found the place to be *handy* any time in the past year. Across from the entrance, I spotted a stone stairwell built into the wall and spiraling sharply upward through a shaft that I guessed led, level by level, to the top floor.

"I've changed my mind," I said. "It's so much more inviting than I expected."

He paused to close the door and drop a bar in place to keep anyone from wandering in off the street. "I was sure you'd appreciate it. Come on, we're going upstairs."

"Oh, good. I'd have been disappointed if we didn't."

I took the first step somewhat gingerly, but the stairs seemed so solid they might have been hewed out of a mountaintop, and I followed the ascending spiral with Nico close on my heels. I glanced into the successive levels as we passed them, but they were all the same—single open rooms with streaked windows and dusty floors. However, each story grew lighter as we climbed, as if the mud and dirt from the street couldn't reach high enough to cloud the glass, and by the time we arrived on the top floor, the space almost had an airy, sunny feel. It was a little too warm, however, and had a musty odor, though that was an improvement from the scent of mildew downstairs.

I was a little breathless from the climb—although, from what I could tell, Nico wasn't winded at all—but I wandered around the perimeter of the room, pausing to glance out of each window. The building was high enough to give me an unobstructed view of the plaza, with its tree and well and executioner's wall, as well as the honey-colored stone bridge that arched over it. I could see the clerks and nobles and servants and petitioners crossing the square in a constant, busy exchange. But I was so high up, and the old glass panes were so thick, that everything seemed silent, remote, and unreal, somewhat like a painting come to life.

"I can see why your uncle would like this place," I said, and this time I meant my words. "It seems a most excellent place for spying."

Nico joined me at the window. "Yes, the first month that I worked for him, we had someone stationed here day and night for a week, watching for a man we believed would be meeting a friend in the plaza below. They were planning—well, I'm not supposed to talk about it. But a crime against the crown."

"Sounds exciting."

"Tedious, mostly. But the man did eventually show up, and we arrested him, so the long hours paid off."

I turned away from the glass, leaning my back against a stone wall that stretched between two of the windows. "So? What did you want to show me here?"

He dropped the sack he carried and spread his hands. "Just the view."

I tilted my head. "I've seen the view, or one very like it, from the bridge."

"That's right. I'd forgotten."

Of course he hadn't forgotten. I nodded at the floor. "What's in the bag?"

"Just some things I thought might be useful as I went about my day." When I maintained my silence, he went on, "A blanket, in case I wanted to sit somewhere and the ground was dirty. A jug of water. In case I got thirsty."

I let my eyes travel around the room before I fixed my gaze on him. "Both of those items would seem to be useful in this particular setting."

"That's just what I was thinking. So if you'd like to sit down—and perhaps have a sip of water—"

I had been trying very hard to keep my smile from showing, but I could feel the corners of my mouth turning up. I settled my back more comfortably against the rough stone of the wall. "Nico, I simply have to ask. Do you have seduction on your mind?"

He stepped close enough to touch me, but he didn't. Instead he placed his hands on the wall on either side of my head and leaned in. "Well, I didn't, but if *you* were bent on seducing *me*, I don't see how I could stop you."

"Oh, now, you must think me a wanton," I murmured, lifting my face toward his. "The kind of woman who's always trying to catch a man."

"Not that so much, no, but I believe you could snare any man you set out to catch."

"I'm sure you've had many more girls than I've had boys," I scoffed.

"Not me. I've been much too busy to pursue romances."

I affected great surprise. "So then—you're completely untutored in the ways of a man with a woman?"

"Well," he said with a grin, "I wouldn't put it quite that way."

"I suppose you wouldn't mind gaining a little more experience, though."

"Experience is always good."

"I think you should kiss me," I murmured, pushing an inch away from the wall.

But he didn't bend closer. In fact, he shook his head. "I'm not going to take advantage of you—here, in a locked building, where no one would come running if you called for help. You have to be the one to start. I have to be sure. *You* have to be sure."

I lifted my arms to twine them around his neck and stepped in so close that I could feel the length of his body against mine. "I *am* sure," I whispered. "I am tired of standing in a high place and looking down on the world. I want to live life, not watch it."

I pressed my mouth against his and held him tight, feeling his body gather and harden in reaction to mine. He kissed me back with a building fervor, never initiating a new kiss, only responding to mine. He finally did put his arms around me, but so loosely that it would take me no effort to break away.

I was still wrapped around him when I pulled my head back just enough to say, "Where's that blanket?"

"The floor will be hard," he warned.

I laughed. "I think I'll manage."

He dropped his arms. "Let me get it from the sack."

He knelt on the floor to spread out the blanket, and I began discarding items of clothing, one by one. My shoes, my stockings, my overdress, my underdress, everything, methodically stripping them off and folding them neatly and setting them aside. I made sure to do this while standing right before Nico, who was still on his knees. I was directly in front of one of the windows, so the sunlight washed over my body and illuminated every inch of my skin. I wondered if people from the streets or neighboring buildings could see in through the dusty glass. If so, they were getting quite a show.

Nico just stared up at me, his lips slightly parted, his hands completely stilled in the fabric.

"Maybe none of those other girls told you this part, but it's much better if you get undressed, too," I told him. "Or is that something else you expect me to do for you?"

He instantly rolled to his buttocks and kicked off his shoes. His jacket and shirt came off so fast I didn't even see him touch the buttons. "Just waiting for the invitation," he said. His pants and underclothes were shucked off just as quickly, and then he was kneeling again.

I dropped to a crouch beside the blanket, balancing myself with one hand on the floor, and took a moment to study him in the daylight that was just as interested in his body as in mine. Nico was far more muscular than Robbie had been, with admirably defined arms and a sculpted torso edged with dark hair. What I saw between his legs was more impressive than Robbie, too.

"You should be posing for artists who want to carve statues out of stone," I said.

"I think you've already turned me to stone," he said. "I can't move. I can just stare at you."

"That would get boring very quickly."

"Not to me."

"Well, it would to me," I said, crawling forward onto the blanket, not stopping until one of my knees was between both of his. I set my hands on those beautiful arms, running my fingers up the smooth flesh. Then I scooted even closer and embraced him again, pressing my breasts against his chest. Sweet goddess, the feel of skin against skin, warm, sleek, intimate. I have never known another sensation that compared.

I brushed my lips over his. "You're still waiting for invitations?" I asked.

"Yes," he breathed.

"Then kiss me. Put your arms around me first."

He complied with both requests.

I was the one to pull him down to the blanket, the one to run my palms with a sensuous delight over his hips and thighs and backside. I was the one to take his hand and lay it on my breast, then to pull his hand away and draw his mouth down instead. Then I began to give commands, which he faithfully obeyed. I told him to kiss me again, and he did. I told him to love me, and he did. And when I demanded that he tell me what he was feeling, he laughed and said, "Joy."

❧   ❧   ❧

Afterward, Nico and I lay entangled on the very thin blanket on the very hard floor and simply talked. I had pillowed my cheek on my folded dress while he propped his head up with one hand so he could gaze down at me. His other hand was resting on the curve of my hip, while I had one hand pressed flat against his chest. I couldn't remember the last time in my life I had felt so much at peace.

"I think next time I come here, I'll bring a down comforter," Nico said. "Something to put between the blanket and the floor. Or maybe even a feather mattress."

"How about a bucket and a mop?"

"That might come in handy."

"Curtains for the window. A chair. A brazier, in case you wanted to cook something."

"Or in case it got cold," he said.

I laughed lazily. "It's still practically summer."

"Well," he said, "if I was coming back here for months and months. Through the fall and winter."

I was silent. He waited a moment for me to speak, then drew his hand from my hip, closed it over the hand I had pressed against his body, and carried it to his mouth. "Although I suppose, by winter, any number of circumstances might have changed," he said softly.

"I could very well be back in Oberton," I said.

"Perhaps," he answered. "But perhaps Cormac will have proposed to Marguerite and she will still be in Camarria, planning her wedding."

Perhaps Cormac will have had Marguerite arrested for treason.

Or, more truly, executed for treason. And me right alongside her.

It was hard for me to envision any future that allowed me to live happily in Camarria. But I had to pretend. "Perhaps," I agreed. "He has been most attentive to her the past two nights. He seems to find her company restful in the midst of all his grief."

"Will she marry him if he asks her?"

"How could she say no? He will only propose if her father and the king come to an agreement. If she believes the stability of the realm depends on her marriage, she could not possibly refuse him."

He folded his arm and dropped his head onto his bent elbow so his eyes were on a level with mine. He still held my hand in his. "And if the king and the governor come to no such agreement? If Marguerite returns to Oberton? Would you stay in Camarria—if I asked you to?"

My heart started to pound. He was serious. He was not merely flirting, he was not pretending to court me simply to gain information about Marguerite. He was in love with me. He hadn't said it, but I knew that expression. I had felt it on my own face. It was the visible transcription of the heart's deep secret.

Sweet beyond reckoning and disastrous beyond telling.

"I don't know," I said.

The truth was, I didn't know what choice I would have made if I had been free to choose. I couldn't leave Marguerite *now*—absolutely not—I could *never* leave her if we couldn't come up with some reasonable explanation for the loss of an echo, an explanation wholly disconnected from a summer journey up the Charamon Road. But if we were just ordinary women, just mistress and maid, not bound together by terrible circumstances? Would I leave her then to follow my heart? I couldn't imagine having a better job than serving her—but could I have a better life? If the situation had been different, would I have been willing to leave her so I could be with Nico?

It would have been a difficult choice. But I thought I might have bid her goodbye.

Now I would never know.

Nico's eyes were still focused unwaveringly on mine. "What would help you make up your mind?" he asked.

"I don't know," I said again.

"I love you, you know. I'm not just playing."

My smile felt a little lopsided. Or maybe just sad. "That's good to hear, though I don't know why."

He kissed my fingers again. "Why I love you?"

"There are so many girls just like me."

He laughed softly. "Are there? Funny, I've never met any of them."

"Well, I don't know what might make me special."

"I like that you're strong, and you're not afraid, and you just wade in and *do* things, instead of hanging back and waiting for someone to show you the way," he said. "I like that you laugh even when you're angry. I like that you try to be fair-minded even when you're sure you're right." He dropped my hand, but only so he could reach up and touch my hair, my cheek, my shoulder. "I like your face. I like your smile. I like the sound of your voice. I just like *you*. I don't know a better way to explain it."

My heart was breaking, but I forced myself to smile. I wondered if he would like *that* about me as well—my ability to lie to the people who cared about me the most. "So now I should list all the qualities I find appealing about *you*?" I said.

His answering smile was warm. "I wouldn't presume to make such a demand."

No reason not to tell him, though. Maybe my words would give him something to hold on to once he realized how deeply I had betrayed him. "I like that you're a sophisticated man with a country boy's heart," I said. "Just when I think, 'Oh, he's too fine for me,' you say something that reminds me where you came from. I like that you make me laugh even when I don't want to laugh. I like that you know so many things, but you still want to learn new ones. I like that you mention your mother in conversation—most men don't, you know."

That amused him. "They don't?"

"They pretend they were hatched in a cave or something, and are wholly responsible for their own raising."

"I'll have to pay more attention to my conversations with men."

Now I was the one to reach out and touch his face, his arm, his body. "I like the way you look," I said softly. "I never thought I would be with such a handsome man."

I really thought he might be blushing. "I have some muscles, I suppose."

I laughed. "You're very attractive," I assured him. "Any girl would say so."

"I'll take your word for that."

I lifted my hand to gesture at the room around us. "And I like that you brought me here—that you thought about how you wanted to be with me, and you schemed to make it happen." I brushed my fingers against his lips, then nestled my hand inside his again. "And I like that you didn't want to push me or persuade me. That you wanted me to be certain."

"And are you certain?"

I leaned in to kiss him. "I'm sure I wanted this to happen," I said very low. "But I'm not sure what I want to happen next."

"You'll think about staying? If Marguerite goes back?"

I hesitated, but what did one more lie matter? One way or the other, his heart would break even more completely than mine. "I'll think about it," I said. "I promise."

CHAPTER TWENTY-FOUR

Not until dinnertime did I realize I'd forgotten to engage in what was arguably my most important task—uncovering any new information Nico had about Jamison's death. Maybe he wasn't *trying* to distract me from this goal, but he had done a good job of it nonetheless.

I *had* remembered to stop by the flower market, and I'd returned to the palace laden down with armloads of fragrant blossoms. Marguerite was feeling more cheerful, though she wasn't able to manage lively, and she buried her face in one of the bouquets as if inhaling the scent of absolution.

"I want to wear dark colors again, as the court is still in mourning," she said. "Perhaps the wine-colored dress with the black net overlay? And my onyx necklace."

"Two days in a row?"

She shrugged. "Darrily wears her opals every day."

"Then let's get started on the headpieces."

My design for the night was a simple clip that held three roses and a gauzy veil. By the time I had stuffed my own hair under the blond wig and carefully set the clip into the artificial curls, I felt like I had half the world balancing on my head; I wasn't sure I would ever design another headpiece that was intricate and ornate.

"Well, we look sober but attractive, I'd say," was Marguerite's verdict once we were all dressed and observing ourselves in the mirror.

"Let's hope the prince approves."

Marguerite grimaced and led the way downstairs. I saw Cali and a few of the other women send speculative glances her way as she entered the salon, and it wasn't hard to know what they were thinking. *Is it really going to be you that Cormac marries? Do none of us even stand a chance with him?* But Marguerite made her way across the width of the room, as far from the doorway as possible, as if to leave the field clear for any woman who wanted to set herself up as a rival. I saw Elyssa and Darrily casually position themselves by the door, turning their backs to it as if they didn't even care who might step through next. I wondered if anyone was fooled.

Marguerite took a seat next to a dark-haired woman who might have been in her mid-twenties. She had a woebegone expression intensified by the severe navy color of her dress; the two echoes sitting behind her looked like they might burst into tears at any minute.

"May I sit here?" Marguerite asked politely. "Or are you waiting for someone?"

The woman gave her one long, considering look that held so much sorrow it could hardly be considered rude. "Please. Sit," she said at last, and Marguerite settled beside her.

"I'm Marguerite. I'm not sure we've ever been formally introduced."

"No. I'm sure Cormac felt it was best to keep us apart if he could. I'm Vivienne."

My attention immediately sharpened and I had to be careful not to stare. So this was the ill-fated Lady Vivienne of Thelleron. Not only had she lost the right to Cormac's affection, she had showed up at court mysteriously missing an echo. One way or the other, she had had a hard time of it lately.

"I'll understand if you tell me you'd rather not sit and talk with me," Marguerite said.

Vivienne made a hopeless gesture. She seemed so dispirited that I had the reprehensible thought that she never would have had the nerve or energy

to kill a man. *As nobody should,* I reminded myself.

"When I set out for Camarria, I was angry with everyone," Vivienne said. "Angry with the king for breaking my engagement, with Cormac for not standing up to his father, with you for simply existing. With my father, for making me come here when I knew, when *he* knew, that everyone would stare and point and say, 'Poor Vivienne.' But he insisted it would be worse if I didn't come, that everyone would think Thelleron was out of favor. Maybe Thelleron *is* out of favor, I don't know." She shook her head. "But none of that matters now."

"Why not?" Marguerite asked, her voice soft and sympathetic. "Has something changed?"

Vivienne caught her breath sharply as if she was fighting back a sob. She gestured over her shoulder. "You might have noticed—or maybe you didn't—but I'm only attended by two echoes."

There was just the slightest tremor in Marguerite's voice. "And you should have three? Forgive me, I don't know the details about everyone in the room."

"I *do* have three," Vivienne said, "but while we were on the way to Camarria, something terrible happened."

It couldn't possibly be as terrible as what happened to us, I thought. My guess was that Marguerite was thinking the same thing.

"Oh, no! What was it?"

"A wheel came off the carriage, and we tumbled into a ditch and we all got jostled around. My maid broke her arm, but one of the echoes, she—she broke her neck. The coachman and the guards pulled us out of the wreckage, but she—she couldn't *feel* anything and she couldn't *move*, and it was the most terrifying thing you can imagine."

Very well, this was *almost* as bad as wrestling with Jamison and causing his death. I saw Marguerite shiver. Which would be worse—to have an echo that died, or an echo that lived, but in a paralyzed state?

"What did you do?" Marguerite asked gravely.

Vivienne put her hands to her cheeks. "I didn't know what to do! I knew I had to complete my journey—I had to show that Thelleron has not been rejected by Sammerly, even if I have been rejected by Cormac." Vivienne shook her head. "But when my echo got hurt—"

Marguerite reached out impulsively to take Vivienne's hand. "I'm so sorry. I didn't mean to upset you. You don't have to talk about it. We can discuss—I don't know—fashion instead."

"No—I *want* to talk about it," Vivienne said. She pulled herself free from Marguerite's hold, but calmed down a little. "No one else has noticed, or at least they haven't asked me about it. They give me sideways glances, and they look away without speaking to me. Do they treat me so oddly because I've been spurned by the prince or because I'm missing an echo? I don't know. I've felt so alone."

"Well, you can talk to me," Marguerite said. "What happened to your echo? Where is she now?"

"I had to leave her at the first inn we found," Vivienne said, trying very hard to control the tremor in her voice. "The inn-keeper and his wife promised they would care for her until help could arrive, and they sent their own son back to my father's house with a desperate message. Of course, I paid them almost every coin I had! It was the hardest thing I've ever done to walk out of that inn and climb back in the coach. I could feel her eyes on me as I left the room. I could feel her straining to follow me. But—but—she couldn't move." Vivienne shook her head. "It was so terrible."

"I can scarcely imagine anything worse," said Marguerite. Though I was sure she could think of *one* thing. "And is she with your parents now? Has she made any progress?"

"Yes, she is with my parents. She has recovered some slight abil-ity to move her hands and feet, but she cannot sit up on her own and she cannot walk. They think—perhaps once I'm back— There is some thought that she *can't* move independently of my actions, that she doesn't know *how,* but once I return—well, I can only hope so. I can only pray." She glanced around the room as if she was in a prison cell. "If only Cormac would let us go home!"

"Yes," Marguerite said. "I am looking forward to the day we are allowed to leave."

Just then, Cormac entered, creating his usual stir. Elyssa and Darrily and their echoes crowded around him, barely allowing him to get three paces into the room, and a half dozen others moved as close as they were able. Marguerite continued her quiet conversation with Vivienne, not even glancing in the prince's direction. When the servant announced dinner, Darrily was the one who went in on Cormac's arm.

The meal passed easily enough, though I did pause to marvel at how quickly I had become accustomed to playing the part of an echo. I knew just what cues to expect from Purpose in front of me and Patience beside me. I knew how Marguerite would hold her fork and how often she would touch her napkin to her lips. I knew that I would remain completely invisible unless I did something to draw attention to myself. *I could play this game forever,* I thought.

If only I didn't have to.

As the meal ended, Cormac and his echoes stood up, extending their wineglasses in an impromptu toast. "I know these have been somber days here at the palace, and I appreciate all your patience and sympathy," he said. "Even in my time of grief, I have not forgotten that I am your host, and I will attempt to provide some gaiety in the coming days. Tomorrow evening, we will hold another ball, and the day after that, I shall lead an outing to our botanical gardens. For tonight, I hope you will all join me for a musical evening in the green salon."

Some of the nobles applauded, others raised their own glasses in response, and all of them seemed to grow lighter in spirit. I could tell everyone was thinking more or less the same thing: *Are we done mourning the death of Jamison? Can we move on to our usual occupations of gossip and flirtation?*

I was not deceived. Cormac might pretend that he was once more focused on entertaining his guests, but Malachi was still investigating each one as a potential murderer; the balls and botanical expeditions were merely attempts to distract the lords and ladies from that unpleasant reality. Not that it would matter to anyone in the room but Marguerite.

And me.

❧ ❧ ❧

It was late before I made it to the bridge rendezvous, but Nico was still waiting. After our encounter earlier in the day, I had thought I might feel shy around him, uncertain, worried about what he might be thinking. But instead I ran up the wooden arch with my arms extended and cast myself into his embrace.

"It's been so long since I've seen you!" he exclaimed as he covered my face with kisses.

I laughed through the pounding of my heart. "Barely twelve hours!"

"A lifetime."

I nuzzled his throat. "I was so very busy all afternoon," I said, "and yet I kept thinking, 'I wonder when I can meet Nico in that old building again?'"

"How extraordinary," he said. "I was thinking exactly the same thing. Every minute of every endless hour."

"But I don't know that I can get away much in the next few days." I sighed. "Marguerite is feeling better, so there is much she needs me to do."

"Yes, and my uncle has a long list of tasks for me as well. But just in case—" He dug into a pocket and produced a key. Even in the dark, I could tell it was a match for the one that had opened the padlock on the building we had visited this morning. "I had a copy made. Anytime you want to go there, you can get in. We could meet there, even if our schedules don't allow us to walk there together."

"Most excellent," I said, slipping the key into my own pocket. "And then, if you fail to arrive, I can amuse myself by cleaning the place so that it has a more welcoming atmosphere."

He kissed me. "I thought it was the most welcoming room I had ever been in."

My laugh was accompanied by a blush. "Indeed, it has rapidly become one of my favorite places in the city."

"But unfortunately, it might be a day or two before we can return," he said on a sigh.

I glanced up with an assumption of hopefulness. "But tomorrow night—perhaps you could get free then?" I asked. "Cormac is having another ball, so Marguerite won't need me for a couple of hours."

I knew he couldn't, which was the only reason I had been rash enough to make the suggestion, because I certainly wouldn't be free, either. He sighed again.

"No, I must attend the ball as well, remember?" he said. "Playing substitute echo. A very dismal chore."

"That's right. I forgot. Are you still trying to determine if everyone has the proper number of echoes? Oh, but, Nico! I've learned something important!"

His voice sounded amused. "Have you? What?"

"Lady Vivienne—she's the one who is missing an echo, right? Marguerite talked to her this evening, and she told me that Vivienne's echo was injured in a carriage accident. She was paralyzed, isn't that awful? Apparently they sent the echo back to Thelleron to be cared for by Vivienne's parents. So she can't be the murderer, can she?"

"She can't be if the story is true," he agreed. "We're checking it out."

I let disappointment seep into my voice. "You already knew."

He kissed the tip of my nose. "I did. But I am impressed by your investigative skills. Do you interrogate Marguerite every time she comes back from a meal?"

I laughed. "No! But she is often in the mood to talk, and she can't really have a conversation with her echoes. When she mentioned Vivienne, I started asking a few questions—very casually!—like, 'How many echoes does she have?' And then she told me the story. She said Vivienne was extremely upset, which makes me think she's telling the truth."

"Or she's a good actress. We'll know soon enough."

"If it's not Vivienne—what about Elyssa?"

"Sadly, she *is* telling the truth. We have confirmed that she has one injured echo and two healthy ones."

"So—then—that's everybody, isn't it? Everybody who's here, at any rate."

"Yes."

I looked up at him. "What are you going to do next? Is Malachi still determined to find the killer?"

"More determined than ever," he said. "There is an inn near where they found Jamison's body, and we think the woman who owns it might be able to tell us more about the passengers who traveled through recently. Unfortunately, she's been gone for the past week, off to see a daughter who has most inconveniently gone into labor. She might have some information for us."

I felt my breath turn shallow as my chest tightened up. Yes, the innkeeper had talked with us when we returned from that disastrous outing—she had even commented that Marguerite's maid was missing. She seemed like the sort of person who would remember every detail about any noble who paused under her roof—and would be only too happy to share everything she knew with anyone who asked.

She would be able to describe Marguerite, certainly. But surely, in the entire kingdom, there had to be more than one fair-haired noblewoman with three echoes. We would be in desperate straits only if the woman knew Marguerite's identity. Had I addressed her by name? Had the coachman mentioned it to the innkeeper's groom? There were so many ways we could be brought down.

Nico put his hands on my shoulders and peered down in the dark. "You've grown so quiet," he said. "Is something wrong?"

I shook my head and manufactured a yawn. "No, I'm just so tired I've forgotten how to have a conversation," I said ruefully.

Nico turned me toward the palace. "Time for you to go to bed, then."

I resisted. "No! I want to talk to you."

He pushed me firmly toward the foot of the bridge and I couldn't help stumbling along beside him. "You can talk to me tomorrow."

"I keep feeling like we're going to run out of time."

"We won't. I promise. We have days and weeks and months and years ahead of us."

I wished I could believe it. We paused outside the palace door, glanced around quickly, and allowed ourselves one long, last fervent kiss before stepping inside and heading our separate ways. My heart was leaden in my chest as I hurried up the empty stairwells and crept through the quiet hallways.

We didn't have years or months ahead of us; we probably didn't have weeks. We probably only had days before the innkeeper came back and whispered Marguerite's name to Malachi.

In the morning, not at all to my surprise, Marguerite wanted to visit the temple. As before, the echoes and I sat behind Marguerite and waited for Taeline to join us. As before, I hummed quietly to myself to block out any chance of overhearing their conversation, but I could tell that Marguerite was pouring out a passionate tale of the past two days and that Taeline was listening in grave concern. I thought, but I was not sure, that their hands were locked together in the only type of contact they could allow themselves in public. There were so many other things to fret about that I was surprised by how sad it made me to think they could never have more of each other than that simple touch.

As we left, Taeline blessed us each with the traditional benediction. It was the first time I noticed that she wore a bracelet identical to Marguerite's. Well. Marguerite had told me it had been given to her by someone who loved her; I should have guessed that the person was Taeline. I nodded my thanks to receive the goddess's blessing and Taeline nodded in return. I thought she looked weary, though she tried to hide it under her usual serene expression. I knew she was supposed to move on to Thelleron within the next week and I wondered how difficult that transition would be for her.

Naturally, the next place Marguerite wanted to go was the flower market. As we sorted through roses and gladiolas and azaleas, I stood shoulder to shoulder with her and held a whispered conversation.

"I know a place you could go if you—if you wanted to be alone with Taeline."

She glanced at me sharply, as did Patience and Purpose, but I did not look away as an echo should. The flower sellers were dashing from customer to customer, trying to keep up; they were not paying attention to how closely one echo was mimicking her mistress. "It's not even proper to discuss such things," she said.

"I know. But I can help you if you want."

"How do *you* know of such a place?"

"Maybe I've been there."

"Maybe with the inquisitor's nephew?"

I felt the color rise to my cheeks. "I know I should have told you."

She held a spray of violets to her face, but they looked wilted and sad. I shook my head.

"I had hoped you were seeing him," she said. "But I didn't like to pry."

"Hoped? Why?"

She selected a single peach-colored rose from a tall vase. Its petals were still closely furled but starting to loosen; it reminded me of the face of a sleeping child just about to awaken. "*Someone* should be wringing some happiness from this wretched situation. And I liked him." Now she held the rose to my face as if to test it against my complexion—what would have been her complexion, if I had truly been an echo. "So you like him?"

I grimaced. "More than is good for my peace of mind."

"Does he want you to stay with him if I go back to Oberton?"

I forced a laugh and produced a lie. "Gorsey! We haven't talked about anything so serious. Anyway, I wouldn't want to."

She dropped the rose into the basket of blooms she meant to buy. "Don't think you have to come back to Oberton on my account."

"I would come back for my own sake," I said. "I would *never* find a situation that suits me so well. I'll stay with you till you set me out the door."

"Well, then," she said. "You will be in my service forever."

After that, we didn't speak much until we were in a hired cart, rolling smoothly along Camarria's well-kept streets. Then Marguerite said, as casually as if she was asking about a shoelace or a hair ribbon, "So this place. Where is it?"

"Near Amanda Plaza."

"Private?"

"Yes."

"Is there any time of day it cannot be used?"

"Not that I'm aware of."

"Then I'll see what she thinks."

I smiled at her, and for the first time in days, Marguerite smiled back.

Everyone rushed through dinner in their haste to get back to the ballroom. The women were all dressed in the darkest versions of their brightest colors, so as to look both festive and properly respectful of the dead. As soon as we were inside the ballroom, I glanced around, hoping to spot Nico, but I didn't see him. Perhaps his uncle had found a more important task for him than squiring echoes around a dance floor. I told myself I was relieved.

The musicians were already in place, and as soon as Cormac bowed to Lady Elyssa, inviting her to be his partner, the dancing started. Prince Jordan was the first to solicit Marguerite's hand, so we all paired up. Jordan's echo was almost as forceful and assured as his older brother's, which I found unnerving. I kept expecting him to speak—perhaps to ask me why *I* seemed unlike any echo he had ever encountered before. He didn't, but I felt like he watched me through the entire dance.

I was glad to move on to the next partner, though I was certain Marguerite was less than thrilled when Lord Deryk took her in his arms. "Don't worry, I'll behave" was his careless greeting, and for the most part, he did. Judging by his echo's arm around my waist, Deryk didn't hold Marguerite too tightly, though he did spin her vigorously into the dance's dips and whirls. When she made a breathless protest, he merely laughed and spun her again.

Marguerite stumbled, and so did I. His echo grinned down at me, wholly unrepentant. I wondered if Marguerite felt the same desire I did to deliver a hard slap. We both repressed the urge.

Deryk sued for a second dance, but Dezmen had been hovering nearby, awaiting his turn, and he stepped forward before Marguerite had even risen from her curtsey. "Don't take another turn with him—I haven't seen you in days," Dezmen said, holding out his hand. It was a ridiculous exaggeration, since they had been seated across from each other at the dinner table, but Marguerite was not about to correct him.

"Dezmen—dear man—I'll be *delighted* to dance with you," Marguerite responded, making Deryk scowl and Dezmen laugh. She took his hand, and Patience and Purpose paired up with his echoes.

I found myself partnered with Nico.

My violent start was covered by the opening steps of the dance, a skirling reel with a lively pace. I thought my heart would hammer its way out of my chest, and I could barely breathe, making it a challenge to get through the energetic figures of the dance. But this was the best number I could have hoped for—we would have limited contact, clasping hands and breaking apart to romp through the prescribed steps. He might never even realize who his partner was. Like any good echo, I kept my gaze slightly averted from his, but I watched him from the corner of my eye. He never looked down at me, but ceaselessly glanced around the room, watching for trouble, looking for oddities, searching for clues.

He was a splendid dancer, muscular and trim. Every time he caught my hand to give me a twirl or placed his palm against my back to propel me forward, he did it with such instinctive grace that he hardly seemed to be aware of his motions. I followed his cues without deviation, not even paying attention to Marguerite's movements. In this particular instance, it was far more important that I respond to him than copy her.

Never since the day I was born had I been so happy to have a song come to an end. I was next to Marguerite as she and her echoes offered curtseys to thank Dezmen and his companions, and the men all bowed in response.

"That was a great deal of fun," Dezmen said, holding his hand out again as the musicians chose this least propitious moment to segue into a waltz. "Won't you honor me with a second dance?"

Marguerite placed her hand in his. "My lord, I would be honored."

Dezmen bowed again and kissed her fingers.

Nico kissed my fingers.

His hand tightened on mine so sharply that I thought the bones would shatter.

I was still wearing my triskele ring.

CHAPTER TWENTY-FIVE

Now I really couldn't breathe.

We all stepped into the daring embrace required by the waltz and began moving much more sedately around the dance floor. I had no idea how tightly Dezmen was holding Marguerite, but Nico pulled me so close against him that I felt flattened against his chest. *Now* he wasn't glancing around the room, making sure he didn't overlook anything interesting; now he was glaring down at me, his face wearing a complex expression of fury, bewilderment, and dawning horror.

"What. Are. You. Doing?" he hissed. "Why. Are. You. *Here*?"

I wondered if I could brazen it out. *Dancing with you,* I might say. *I knew you would be partnering with the extra echoes and I persuaded Marguerite to let me play this role.* But I couldn't draw in enough air to speak.

And I knew he wouldn't believe me.

So I just stared up at him, my expression stricken, my eyes beseeching. *Please, whatever you do, please don't expose us here...*

"You can't be— How long have you—? What's going on?" he said. His whispering voice was weighted with dread.

I still said nothing. I shook my head, the tiniest motion. *I can't explain.*

He dropped his voice even more. "Where's her third echo?"

Now I closed my eyes, unable to bear the look in his. I couldn't say the words. *At the bottom of the lake, next to her murderer, until your uncle dredged her up.*

"Brianna," he breathed.

The music swelled around us; Dezmen guided Marguerite through such a wide circle that her skirts belled out and she laughed with pleasure. Nico and I hastily tried to copy them, a beat behind. Nobody seemed to notice. I hoped our fumbling mimicry didn't catch Marguerite's attention because I didn't want her to glance over and recognize Nico. She would instantly realize that disaster had struck, and she might fall apart, right there in the middle of the ballroom, with no hope of escaping to safety.

There still might be no hope. As soon as Nico recovered from his stupefaction, he might pull me to a halt right in the middle of the waltz, cause the other dancers to crash into us and careen off to the sides or to stop in their tracks and stare at us while the whole world fell into a gaping silence...

Marguerite and Dezmen executed a lovely maneuver, and their shadows circled around them, stately and precise. Nico's arm around my waist had loosened enough to allow me to breathe, but he still had my hand crushed in his. I managed to lift my eyes to his face again and saw that his fierce expression still persisted. But now it was modulated by a frown, and I imagined he was reviewing everything that had happened in the past ten days—his banter with Marguerite at the flower market, his dozens of conversations with me. Everything he had told me.

Everything I had not told him.

The music built up again, and again we spun gaily around, like colorful tops on a playroom table. Still Nico didn't speak, not to ask me questions, not to shout accusations. Still we stared at each other, while he remade the picture of me he carried in his head and I waited for the world to end.

The music ended first. I had thought this waltz would go on for the rest of my life, so I was confused when the last notes sounded and were replaced by the light buzz of laughter and conversation. All the women curtseyed and all the men bowed, and Nico practically mangled my hand between his fingers.

"Meet me at the bridge tonight," he murmured. "Don't tell her."

Dezmen had already released Marguerite but Nico kept his grip until I nodded. Then he finally let me go. I had been leaning back so hard for the past ten minutes that I almost tumbled over when I no longer had to resist him. I watched him stalk off the dance floor and thought he looked uncharacteristically awkward, twice bumping into other people and not seeming steady on his feet.

Goddess have mercy on my soul, I thought. *What have I done to him?*

I both longed for the ball to end immediately and wished the musicians would play until dawn. I couldn't bear to keep up the masquerade for one more second, but I didn't think I could face Nico and his blistering inquisition. I thought I might be sick. I thought I might faint.

I smiled and aped Marguerite's every movement and danced for two more hours.

Lady Vivienne was one of the first to announce that she was weary and ready to seek her bed. I hadn't paid any attention before this, but now I was convinced that she had been among the first to leave every gathering since we had been in Camarria. I saw Marguerite glance longingly for the door, but she never wanted to draw attention to herself by being too quick to end any activity. But when she heard Nigel say, "If enough of the women retire early, we can get up a game of cards," she laughed in his face.

"Well! I thought you would be disappointed if too many of us slipped off while the night was so young, but now that I realize it will make you *happy* to see us go, I shall bid you goodnight."

"Nothing of the sort! I would dance all night with you," Nigel protested.

"Too late! I'm heading up to my room." She dropped him a quick curtsey, half mocking and half sincere. "But I thank you for a *most* pleasant evening."

She was in a good mood as she climbed the stairs and moved through her room, pulling off accessories and stepping out of her shoes and making idle observations about the behavior of the others at the ball. I tried not to hurry her into her nightclothes or seem too eager to leave for the night, but I must have been quieter than usual because she remarked on my silence.

I forced a laugh. "Just tired, I think," I said. "There's not much time to sleep when you're leading a double life."

She yawned and lay back on her pillows. "I suppose not. But you manage it with such aplomb that I sometimes forget this is even more wearing on you than on me."

I drew the covers to her chin and blew out the candle. "I doubt that," I said. "I think it's wearing on both of us."

"I think you're right," she said with a sigh. "Well, I'll see you in the morning. You go straight to bed now."

Of course what I did was go straight to the garden bridge.

Nico was waiting for me, his elbows resting on the railing, his gaze fixed on what he could make out of the shadowy pond below. He didn't turn to look at me when he heard my footsteps on the wood, didn't take me in a hungry embrace and rain kisses on my skin. He had obviously spent the last two hours thinking, and he didn't like any of his conclusions.

I stood beside him, not close enough to touch, and leaned my own arms on the railing. For a very long moment, we stood there in silence.

"So tell me what happened," he said at last in a level voice.

"You have already guessed it," I said in the same tone.

"Tell me anyway."

"We had stopped at the inn because our horse threw a shoe. The landlady showed us a path that we could follow to a little lake to get a break from the tedium of travel. Jamison came upon us there. He insisted on walking on alone with Marguerite because he had something— He said he had something to tell her. Once they were out of sight behind some trees, the echoes started getting agitated. Then we heard Marguerite cry out."

I paused a moment to steady my voice. "The four of us ran to her right away and found her struggling in his arms, both of them on the ground. He had her skirts up and his pants undone, and he—" I paused for a moment and shook my head before going on. "So we kicked him and hit him, and he fought back. He flung Purpose away so hard I thought she was unconscious. He cut Patience with a knife. He grabbed Prudence and slammed her against the ground, over and over and over. Then he reached for Marguerite again— but Purpose was on her feet, and she hit him with a rock. On his head. Hard enough to make him fall."

I risked one look at Nico but he was still staring at the water below. "We first realized Prudence was dead, and we were devastated. It was a few minutes later that we realized Jamison was dead, too. And then we were terrified."

"And this scheme—this insane notion to dress you up as Marguerite's dead echo—how did she convince you to agree?"

I lifted my chin. "It was my idea. *I* had to convince *her*. And it seems to have answered very well. No one else has guessed, at any rate."

"How long did you intend to try to carry it off? Forever?" Now he turned to me, but he didn't reach for me. There was anger in his voice and in the taut set of his shoulders. "You would be willing to sacrifice *the rest of your life* to play at being a noblewoman's shadow?"

"Maybe. I don't know," I answered quietly. "My only thought was to get us through this visit. And then perhaps we could have concocted some tale of disaster that befell us on the road home."

"Most disasters still yield a body. How did you propose to get around that inconvenience?"

"I don't know," I said again. "We were *desperate*, don't you understand that? We still are."

Now he was glaring at me. "Why didn't you tell me?"

"Really? Tell you? That Marguerite and her echoes had killed the *king's son*? Marguerite was convinced that, even if she told the story exactly as it happened, she would be shown no leniency, and nothing you've told me about your uncle's investigation has led me to think otherwise. But *you* think she could confess the whole and emerge unscathed?"

"No," he snapped. "I think very likely she will be tried for murder, if she is ever discovered, and the consequences will be dire.

But you could have told *me*. If you trusted me enough. Which you obviously do not."

"How could I put you in such a position?" I demanded. "You are bound by duty and honor and family ties to tell your uncle everything you know! How could I ask you to lie for Marguerite?"

"You could have asked me to lie for *you!*"

There was a long moment of silence as we studied each other in the dark. I could see so little of his face, but his voice was threaded with anger—and a great deal of hurt.

"I have been lying this whole time, and it makes me hate myself," I said quietly. "I did not want you to have to make the same choice."

"You didn't trust me," he said again.

"With my own life? I think I would have risked it. With Marguerite's life? No!" My own voice was starting to rise. I gestured toward the palace. "How do I know you won't go straight to your uncle tonight and tell him everything you've learned from me? How do I know you haven't done so already?"

"I won't. I haven't."

"But you *should*. And if he discovers *you* have been lying to *him*—" I shut my mouth and pressed my lips together and shook my head. Turning to stare down at the garden again, I slipped my hands around the rail and gripped as tightly as I could. "There is no end to the number of people I care about who will be hurt by this," I said.

"That is the way of murder," he said shortly.

I gave him one quick, bitter glance. "So you blame her? Think she was at fault—think she deserves to *die* for protecting herself from assault? If that's so, you have a terrible notion of justice."

He sighed and squeezed his palms briefly against his temples. "Maybe if it had been some random lord who attacked her—some low noble with no direct connection to the crown—there would have been room for clemency. But the king will not be able to forgive anyone for killing his son."

"Then Marguerite has no choice but to pretend that nothing happened. And pray to the goddess that your uncle never discovers the truth." I silently added, *And that you never betray us.*

"He will discover it, though," Nico said in an urgent voice. "Malachi will keep looking and digging and prying—he will not rest until he is able to prove that the queen had no involvement in Jamison's murder."

I didn't answer, and Nico laid a rough hand on my shoulder, forcing me around to face him. I shook him off and demanded, "What do you expect me to *do*? Should we run? Where should we go? I cannot imagine a place of safety."

"Not for Marguerite, perhaps. For you."

I gaped at him in the dark. "You want me to *abandon* her—"

"I could get you out of the city—there are a couple of places you could go—"

I shoved him in the chest. "I *won't*! I can't believe you would *ask* it of me! To leave Marguerite when she needs me most—"

He grabbed my shoulders again and gave me a hard shake. "There is no hope for you otherwise, Brianna, do you understand?" I heard anguish in his voice. "If you were present, if you assisted at the murder—*all* of you could be put to death, Marguerite, the echoes, you. They will make no distinction between mistress and maid. But if you're gone—if Malachi's eye doesn't fall on you—"

Now I put both hands against his chest and pushed hard. It rocked him briefly off-balance, but not enough to make him release me. "I am *not* leaving her. I *was* present at the murder! I *did* assist, and I'm glad he's dead! And I see no choice but to play this charade out till the end."

"You're an idiot," he said.

"Just because I'm loyal? I thought that was one of the things you liked about me."

"I'd like you a lot better disloyal and alive than faithful and dead," he shot back.

I shook my head. "I don't know what else to do."

Again, he stared down at me in the dark, so long and so silently that I started to get nervous. "All right," he said finally. "Here's what we'll do. Marguerite will announce that she's received bad news from home and she'll ask permission to return to Oberton, which the king will regretfully refuse. She will fail to come to the break-fast table one morning and everyone will assume she has returned home, so the search parties will be sent off along the Charamon Road." He drew a deep breath. "But she'll have headed east instead. Toward Banchura. There will be ships at Banch Harbor that can take her to a hundred destinations."

My head was spinning. I had never been past the borders of Orenza until we left for Camarria, and now I was to sail away from the Seven Jewels entirely? "And once we get to Banch Harbor?" I asked. "What country should we book passage to?"

Nico shook his head. "I've never left the kingdom myself. But my mother had a cousin who visited a dozen countries, and he always spoke highly of Ferrenlea. It would be a place to start."

"We'll need—money—a carriage, or at least horses—"

"You should pawn whatever jewels you can before you leave Camarria," he said. "You won't get as good a rate anywhere else along the road. I'll hire a conveyance for you. And a driver."

"You *can't*," I said. "Because once your uncle discovers that Marguerite is missing, he will investigate her disappearance, and if he finds that you helped her—"

Nico was almost laughing. "I have a bit more discretion than that! I will make the arrangements through another party. The trail will be very cold."

I took a deep breath. "How soon should we leave?"

"As quickly as possible. If not tomorrow, the day after. I can arrange to have the carriage meet you somewhere. You will not be able to bring any baggage with you, I'm afraid."

"Maybe Taeline will be able to gather some things for us—"

"Taeline— Oh, Marguerite's priestess friend?" I could hardly be surprised that he knew her name. "No. Marguerite can't tell her. She can't tell *anyone*."

I held my peace. There was no possibility that Marguerite would leave the city, leave the *kingdom*, without letting Taeline know she was going. "And then—? For the rest of our lives, we will live in some foreign place, surrounded by strangers?"

"Maybe only a year or two. If Malachi believes Marguerite to be the murderer, and he believes her to be out of his reach, he will eventually stop looking for her. You'll let me know where you are, and I'll write to let you know when the situation here changes. You'd never be able to return to Oberton, but you could live in Empara or Thelleron. It could be a good life."

It sounded impossible. I wasn't sure we could assemble the cash to pay for four tickets to a foreign destination, and I wasn't sure Marguerite could summon the energy to attempt the flight. How would we live once we were in Ferrenlea? Could I get employment? Could I learn to speak the language? Would I be able to understand the local customs?

Could I leave my family behind, with only a scribbled word of explanation—explanation that would, perforce, be yet another lie? Could Marguerite leave hers?

Could we do it if it was our only hope of survival?

"I'll ask her," I said, my voice very soft. "But I'm not sure she'll agree to go."

"But then … Brianna—"

"I know," I said. All the fight was gone out of me; all the anger had drained from him. I leaned in, lifting my head up, and for the first time this evening he drew me into his arms, though his hold was loose as if wasn't sure he really wanted to cradle me to his heart. Still, I snuggled against him, inhaling the scent of his clothes and skin, wishing I could curl up in his embrace and stay under his protection forever.

"So," he said at last, speaking over the top of my head. "Was any of it real?"

I knew what he meant, but I pretended I didn't. "Any of what?"

"Us. The talk. The kisses. The … everything. Did it matter, or were you just trying to find out what I knew?"

"I didn't want it to matter," I told him honestly. "I wasn't sure that *I* could trust *you*. I remembered how we met in Oberton—when you were spying on me for the crown—"

"Just that once," he interrupted. "Just that first day."

"I thought maybe you already knew what had happened to Jamison. That you were laying a trap for me. And that *you* were only pretending to care."

"I wasn't. Not a minute of it." I felt his chest expand as he took a deep breath. "But all this time. When I told you about the investigation. When I repeated everything my uncle said. Is that all you wanted from me? Information?"

I pulled back just enough to scowl up at him. "I *tried* to keep away from you," I said sharply. "At the beginning. Remember? The first time I saw you in Camarria, I told you to stay away from me. At first I was afraid of what *you* might find out from *me*. Then I was afraid—afraid of this very thing! That you would discover I'd been lying to you, and you'd hate me forever."

"I don't hate you" was his instant reply.

"Well, I wouldn't blame you if you did," I said, my voice muffled as I looked down toward his shoes.

He lifted my head with a hand under my chin. "You didn't answer me," he said. "Was it real?"

"Will you believe me if I say it was?"

The slightest note of laughter in his voice. "You might have to convince me."

I lifted my arms to wrap around his neck and he drew me close for the first time this evening. "So real," I whispered. "So impossibly good. Now you understand why I can't leave Marguerite—but you made me want to. I never thought I would have any desire to move from Orenza, to live far from the people and places I know, but I started imagining a life in Camarria with you. I will never stop wishing it was possible."

Now his grip tightened so abruptly I could barely breathe. "It might be possible."

"I can't abandon her. Don't ask me to."

"No. But you'll come back someday. I have to believe that. This won't be a permanent exile."

"You'd wait for me?" I breathed.

The answer to that was a hard kiss and an embrace that lifted me off my feet. "Brianna," he groaned against my mouth. "As long as you're alive in this world I don't think I'll have a choice."

My feet still dangling a couple of inches above the bridge, I kissed him back with a reckless passion. He set me down but only so he could use his hands for other purposes; my own hands were busy as well. It was dark, it was late, and I had contravened so many other social covenants that I discovered I didn't have any deep-seated principles left about the proper place to make love with a man. Rash criminal wanton that I was, I stripped down, I covered his body with mine, I thrashed about with no cover but the shadows and no roof but the stars.

And was glad to do so. And willing to do it again any chance I got.

CHAPTER TWENTY-SIX

At first Marguerite said no. Then she said yes. Then she said she had to consult Taeline.

"You're not supposed to tell anyone," I said, because I'd promised Nico I would, but she just gave me a single expressive glance.

"I won't tell anyone *else*. But I'm not leaving without talking to her."

It had been a difficult morning. Marguerite had sat in frozen silence as I haltingly confessed what had happened last night, at the ball and afterward. She didn't rail at me and demand to know how I could have been so stupid, though I apologized so often during my recital that maybe she felt it would have been pointless. She just seemed to grow smaller and more brittle with every word I spoke. "Then we're doomed," she said quietly when I was finished, and put a hand over her eyes.

But I shook my head. "No—listen—Nico thinks we could sail away. Live abroad for a couple of years, maybe in Ferrenlea. He'll help us get to Banch Harbor. We could escape. We could *try*."

"*I* could try," she said, dropping her hand. "*You* would stay here."

I was affronted. "I'm not leaving you!"

"Well, you should."

"You couldn't possibly make that journey by yourself," I scoffed. "You don't even know how to comb your own hair."

"No, but I can speak a few words of Ferrenlese," she retorted.

"Really? That will be handy!"

"If we go. I don't know. I don't know."

There wasn't much time to discuss it because we had to dress for the prince's expedition to the city gardens. "I could skip it. I could say I have one of my headaches," Marguerite said, but I shook my head.

"Maybe there will be some other outing planned for tomorrow or the day after," I said. "*That's* the one we'll skip. We can disappear while everyone else is gone."

"If we decide to run away."

"If we do."

The visit to the gardens was complicated and time-consuming, involving dozens of carriages and a great deal of muttered complaining, mostly by the women. But the gardens themselves were spectacular, acres and acres of rosebushes, flowering trees, and plant beds interspersed with fountains, statuary, and reflecting pools.

"I should have brought my sketchbook," Letitia said.

"Oh, too much work," Leonora answered. "I just want to gorge myself on color, not try to reproduce it."

"I want to pick armloads of flowers to take home with me," Marguerite observed. "But I feel certain the gardeners would disapprove. I would be banned from ever returning."

"Well, they could hardly begrudge you one little blossom," Lavinia said, snapping off a single white rose and tucking it behind Marguerite's ear. "You just don't look right without flowers in your hair." We had left the palace without creating any elaborate floral headpieces, since it seemed likely the components would wilt in the sunshine. The echoes and I were wearing our veils, but they were tacked to simple hair clips.

The sun was relentless, my blond wig was causing my scalp to sweat, and by the time we had been in the gardens twenty minutes I was wishing Marguerite might faint from the heat so I, too, could collapse on the path. But we spent another hour soaking up the color and scent before Cormac finally turned us all back toward the street where our carriages were parked.

"There's a light lunch laid out in the dining hall," he informed us once we made it back to the palace. About half of the ladies declined the treat, saying they wanted to retreat to their rooms to freshen up. It was no surprise that Marguerite was among this number.

"You need to take a message to Taeline," she said as soon as we were back in her suite. "Ask her to meet me tomorrow morning—in the place you told me about."

"Gladly," I said.

"And then—and then I'll decide."

I ate a quick meal in the kitchen before setting out for the temple, half-expecting Nico to appear at my side before I had gone very far. But he didn't. He hadn't been on the outing to the garden, either, so clearly Malachi was keeping him busy with some project. I wondered how he was strangling his conscience as he began the endless task of lying to his uncle about Marguerite. About me. I didn't think he would have hesitated to tell Malachi the truth if I hadn't been involved.

I found the temple fairly empty as I stepped in through the door for mercy. I didn't see Taeline among the white-robed priestesses and wondered if she'd given up on the notion that Marguerite might come to visit this day; usually we were there before noon if we came at all. I paused before the statue of the goddess with her arms reaching down before her as if to offer absolution to a groveling miscreant, and I said a short prayer. *Goddess, have mercy on my soul.*

Then I wandered over to the circular tower set aside for justice. Each of the three supplicants in the room was deep in conversation with a priestess dressed in black,, but none of them were Taeline. I paused in front of this representation of the goddess, too. She stood so calmly, so implacably, with her arms stretched out to the sides as if she fought for balance in a shifting world. *Very well, then, I'll plead for justice,* I thought. *Because in a just society, Marguerite would not be punished for saving herself from that terrible man. And if there is any righteousness in you, you will know that, and you will protect her.* As prayers went, it was a bit accusatory, but I felt better after letting the goddess know how I felt.

In the third chamber, I didn't even look around; I went straight to the statue at the front of the room. Her arms were lifted above her head and her carved face was bright with a smile. *Yes, please, goddess, grant me joy,* I begged silently. *Joy for me, joy for Marguerite. Maybe we don't deserve it. Maybe we can't have it for very long. But couldn't we have it for a short time, just enough to keep our hearts warm for as long as we have memories?*

She didn't answer, but her smile didn't waver. I couldn't tell if she'd heard me.

When I turned to scan the pews that faced the dais, I found Taeline standing at the end of one row, watching me. She was wearing the red robes of celebration, and they threw a rosy tint into her pale cheeks, but otherwise she looked the same as always. I nodded at her, found a seat in an unoccupied bench, and waited for her to join me.

She slipped in next to me and whispered, "Has something happened to Marguerite?"

"Nothing new," I said, and gave her the update as succinctly as I could. Before I'd left the palace, I'd asked Marguerite how much Taeline knew. *Everything* had been her response. So at least I didn't have to spend time explaining anything.

"She has to go," Taeline said as soon as I was done. "If it is her only hope of survival—and if he will truly help her—" She paused for a moment to study me. "You trust him?"

"It hardly matters if I trust him," I said. "He knows everything—and as soon as someone questions the landlady, the inquisitor will know everything, too. But I believe that if Nico planned to betray us, he would have done so already. So I believe he will supply a guide and a carriage that will take us to Banch Harbor, and not to the Camarria dungeons."

"Then she has to go."

"She wants to see you one last time. In private." I took a deep breath. "I know a place you can meet."

There was a long silence while Taeline first studied me, then dropped her gaze to stare at her folded hands. Maybe she was wondering if Marguerite was right to trust *me*. Maybe she was reviewing her vows to the goddess and trying to decide if such a meeting would break them—and if she cared. Maybe she was just trying to hold her hope and fear and sorrow in check.

"When?" she said at last.

"Tomorrow morning. If all goes well, we will be gone the day after that."

She nodded, as if that made sense, though it hardly made sense to me. One more day in Camarria? One more night, maybe two, to lie beside Nico and whisper of love? One more day before I abandoned every detail of the life I had known and flung myself into unwanted adventure? I could scarcely make myself believe it.

"Where?" she asked.

"There's an abandoned building near Amanda Plaza. I have the key."

"Describe it."

Within a few sentences, she was nodding again; she undoubtedly spent a great deal of time at that square, and it was a distinctive building. "I'll be there," she said, and rose to her feet without saying another word. She didn't even offer me the traditional benediction before she stepped away and slipped into another pew and greeted the petitioner with a restrained smile.

I took a moment to collect my thoughts, then hurried back to the palace.

That evening as we dressed for dinner, Marguerite and I laid our plans. We would skip the morning's planned outing to some ruins on the edge of town so that she and Taeline could keep their assignation. Once we returned, I would resume my maid's clothing and make a discreet circuit of the city, pawning jewels for cash. Marguerite would attend the evening dinner and any social function that the prince planned, but she would admit to feeling unwell. That way no one would be surprised when she didn't join whatever outing the prince had planned for the following day.

After the rest of the guests had gone off on their excursion, we would make our way downstairs wearing plain gowns and sturdy shoes and, in Marguerite's case, the wan expression a woman might assume if she was plagued by a severe headache. "I always feel better if I visit the temple," she would say to anyone who expressed concern, and off we would go. But we would head to some other meeting place that we had determined beforehand. Assuming that Nico really would supply us with a carriage and driver, we would instantly begin our perilous journey. Constantly starting with fear every time we heard carriage wheels behind us. Incessantly wondering if we had made the right choice. Trying unsuccessfully to hide our broken hearts.

"One thing," I said. "It will be easy to track four identical women as they move through the city. We must find some way to make ourselves look different. We will dress the echoes in gowns of different hues, and we'll bring accessories to change our appearance, slowly, as we stroll along. I'll take off my wig. Purpose will remove her veil, but Patience will leave hers on. Someone will put a red scarf over her shoulders."

"That's a good idea."

"And we'll split up, just a little. I'll walk with one of the echoes on one side of the street, you'll walk with the other one a few feet back. Release them, so they don't move the way you do. We won't be so noticeable."

"All excellent notions. I would think you had been a runaway your whole life." She sighed and made a minute adjustment to the red flower pinned in her coiled blond hair. "I wish we could manage just *one* change of clothes, though. It will be very tedious having a single dress and one set of underthings for the foreseeable future."

"I've thought about that, too," I said. "I'm going to pack a small bag with absolute necessities and leave it with Nico. He'll find a way to get it in the carriage."

"Brilliant!" she exclaimed. "Then I think we're all set. What else is left to do?"

"Get through dinner and tomorrow."

Dinner was simple enough, though I frequently caught myself gazing around the room when I should have been glancing down at my plate or pretending I was talking to Jordan's echo, seated beside me. *One more dinner in this room,* I was thinking. *How long will I remember exactly how it looks? How long before I have another meal even half as good as this one?* As fugitives with a severely limited budget, we would find ourselves scrambling to buy food and to find shelter and to replace our woefully limited wardrobe.

You'll manage, I told myself fiercely. *You'll find work. The customs may be different in Ferrenlea, but someone will always need a maid or a cook or a seamstress. You'll survive.*

Please, goddess, let us survive.

After the meal, the prince provided an evening of musical entertainment, but as far as I could tell, the nobles paid very little attention to the performers. Instead, they clustered together in their chairs, flirting and repeating gossip. Vivienne was the first one to excuse herself and seek her bed; Marguerite was the fifth.

An hour later, I was on the bridge with a portmanteau at my feet, impatiently awaiting Nico. He laughed when he arrived ten minutes later.

"Aren't you the smart one, always thinking ahead?" he said in an admiring voice.

"There's no money in it, if you were thinking of stealing it," I joked. "I'll do my pawning tomorrow. Is there a place you recommend that I go?"

"I'll do better than that—I'll have Chessie meet you in the morning and take you to one of the more reputable establishments. Chessie is one of my, um, professional contacts."

"Sounds interesting," I said, wondering if I was about to meet a criminal. "But I can't do it until the afternoon."

"All right. Can you be under the stone bridge at the Amanda Plaza by one?"

I nodded. "I think so. How will I recognize Chessie?"

"She'll find you."

"And are you sure *she* can be trusted? What if she goes straight to Malachi?"

Nico laughed softly. "He's the last person she'd tell a secret to."

"Sounds like a story there."

"Yes, but it's not mine to tell," he said, his voice abruptly changing as he took me into his arms. "We're making all these plans and then I suddenly realize— What I'm doing is sending you away from me. I can't believe it. Tonight and tomorrow and then you're gone." He shook his head. "It seems impossible."

"You could come with us," I said into his shirt. "Don't just hire a carriage. Take us to Banch Harbor yourself—and sail with us to Ferrenlea."

"I've been thinking about it," he said.

I pulled back. "You *have?*"

He kissed me. "What, it wasn't a serious invitation?"

"No, it was! It would be wonderful to have you along! It would seem much more like an adventure than a headlong flight. But—" Reality swept in to dampen my sudden delight. "Oh, but we couldn't have you give up your whole life for us! You have a respectable position here, and an uncle who trusts you, and a mother who relies on you—"

"These are the very things that I am weighing," he admitted. "And if I am gone from the city, I won't know what happens with Malachi's investigation. I won't know when it's safe for you to return."

"You have to stay," I said stoutly.

"I don't know," he said. "I'm still thinking it over."

I sighed and leaned my head against his chest. "We don't seem to have been very good influences on each other," I said. "We've showed a shocking lack of morality—we've lied to our closest friends on the other person's behalf—and now you're thinking about throwing away responsibility and setting off on a vagabond's life, all for my sake."

"Well," he said, "being moral and telling the truth and staying behind all seem like they would make me unhappy. So I might choose to do what makes me happy."

I lifted my head. "So I've made you selfish, too."

He kissed me. "I was always selfish," he said against my mouth. "I'm just enjoying it more."

I laughed, and then I sighed again, and then I kissed him a second time. And a third and fifth and tenth and hundredth time. Because he might not come with us after all—*shouldn't* come with us, and I would make that clear as soon as I had an opportunity to speak—and I needed to collect as many memories as I could while I still had the chance.

It is strange enough to slip out of your room and look nervously over your shoulder and feel your heart race as you set off on your own forbidden tryst. It is doubly strange to go through all these motions as you escort someone else to her illicit rendezvous. Lourdes seemed to watch us with a sharper stare than usual as we crossed the immense foyer. The footmen offered to accompany us if we wanted an escort. Every serving girl we passed in the street, every merchant we glimpsed through a shop window, seemed to gaze at us a little too long, as if committing our features to memory, as if preparing to give testimony about when we had passed and what we were wearing.

I was betting that tomorrow's journey to the designated meeting point would be even more fraught with imagined dangers. Or real ones. This short heart-stopping trek across the city was just a rehearsal.

Taeline was waiting for us, idling across the street from the abandoned building. I had to look twice to realize it was her, for she was dressed in an ordinary gown of navy blue, and her dark hair wasn't pulled back in its usual knot, but loose around her shoulders. She looked both younger and less serene in her everyday attire—or maybe it was the excitement of the desperate romance that caused her face to flush and her lips to tremble.

My key opened the rusty padlock with no trouble, and the five of us were soon inside. We all paused when we were just across the threshold and listened for a few moments, waiting to see if anyone had followed us and planned to object to our arrival. But all we heard from the street outside were the normal noises of horses and carts and people.

Life going by outside. A different kind of life being explored inside.

"There's a blanket on the fifth floor, and better light," I said. "I'll wait down here. And the echoes—" Well, I didn't know about Patience and Purpose. I presumed this would be a situation in which Marguerite would want to release them, so they were not mimicking her every move—but I honestly could not predict how close Marguerite would want them or how exactly they would behave.

"I'll leave them on the second floor," Marguerite said. "We will all have a sort of privacy."

She took Taeline's hand and led her up the stairs, Patience and Purpose following. I heard two sets of footsteps stop at the first landing, and two sets of footsteps continue.

After that it was quiet, or at least whatever noises that were produced on the top story and drifted down to the ground level could not be heard through the sound of my soft humming. I moved slowly around the perimeter of the room, trying to find spots on the grimy windows that were clean enough to give me a glimpse of the outside world. I could only see pieces of the people and animals passing by—a crest on a carriage door, the long nose of a horse, a woman's bonnet. It wasn't quite enough to allow me to assemble an entire picture in my head.

Maybe an hour after we arrived, the others descended carefully down the stone staircase. Marguerite and Taeline were holding hands, and so were Purpose and Patience. All four of them looked as if they had been weeping, for their eyes were red, their cheeks were wet, and their faces were flushed. But at the same time, they all looked rested and tranquil, as if the emotional storm that had passed through them had left them exhausted and at peace.

Marguerite came straight to me and kissed my cheek. "Thank you," she said. Taeline hung back, but she nodded soberly in my direction. I wondered what color she would pick to wear when she returned to her temple duties.

"We have to get back," I said. "I have a lot to get done this afternoon."

"I can't believe we're leaving tomorrow," Marguerite said.

"It's good you're going," Taeline responded.

Marguerite sighed. "Yes. But I can't bear it."

She paused to kiss Taeline one more time—sweetly, as if just touching her lips to the spray of a sacred fountain—and then headed out the door. I secured the padlock once we were all out on the street. And then, with no more than a single long, searching look at Taeline, Marguerite turned and began walking back toward the palace. The echoes and I fell in step behind her. I could tell she was crying again because, beside me, Purpose and Patience were weeping silently.

Well, and because I was crying, too.

I managed a quick lunch down in the kitchen and shared a lament with Vivienne's maid.

"Is *your* mistress always so full of sighs and tears?" I demanded. "She's the kindest woman, but gorsey! Lady Marguerite is so despondent sometimes it just makes my heart sink to my shoes."

"Lady Vivienne didn't used to be that way," replied the maid, a heavyset middle-aged woman whose round face showed great kindness. "She was always rather a happy girl. But first there was the break with Cormac, and now this business with the echo—" She shook her head. "I'm not sure she'll ever be her old self again, even once we're back in Thelleron."

"Marguerite is having such a bad spell with her headaches," I declared. "She didn't go with all the others to visit the ruins this morning, and I'll be surprised if she gets up tomorrow before noon."

"That poor woman. I hope the goddess takes pity on her and sends her some relief."

Once I had advanced the idea that Marguerite would be prostrate tomorrow, it was time to go. I had a satchel full of jewels—everything Marguerite owned except the onyx necklace, which she planned to wear at dinner tonight, and the onyx bracelet, which she never took off. Would this be enough to fund our flight? It had better be.

The streets of Camarria had never seemed so crowded as I made my way down busy boulevards and across two bridges on my way to Amanda Plaza. Today there was no wedding party clustered around the goddess statues in the center, so I paused before each one as I dropped three coins into the grate and spoke the briefest of prayers. *Goddess grant us mercy. Goddess mete out justice to those who wrong us. Goddess bring us joy.*

Then I headed for the shadow that, an hour past noon, lay in a squat, straight line almost directly under the arching stone bridge. A few people were already loitering there, as it was one of the few places in the plaza that offered shelter from the sun. At least two looked like pickpockets; one was a frazzled young mother holding a whimpering baby; and one was a young woman about my own age. She was dressed like a boy, though the clothes were loose-fitting and nondescript. Most of her hair was tucked under a soft cap, but a few tendrils of auburn peeked out from the edges. She was a little taller than I was, a bit more slender, and alert in the way of a feral cat. Her delicate features were a little too sharp to be beautiful, but she was certainly arresting. I found myself wondering how well Nico knew her and feeling a little depressed because she was clearly a *much* more interesting person than I was. My guess was that she had seen me the minute I stepped into the square and had already formed her own distinct impressions about *me*.

Just in case I was wrong, I didn't approach her, but the minute I paused in the shadow, she stepped over to me. "I believe we have a friend in common," she said.

Nico had told me we wouldn't be using names, but that this would be the phrase to expect from his contact. I nodded. "I'm sorry if I kept you waiting."

Chessie's smile was quick and attractive. "There's always plenty to see at Amanda Plaza. I wasn't bored at all."

I couldn't help smiling in return. "I guess we should get started."

She nodded and turned toward the southeastern corner of the plaza, setting off toward a quadrant of the city I hadn't had had occasion to explore. Within a dozen blocks, it was clear this was a rather disreputable district that I probably *never* would have had a reason to visit under ordinary circumstances. Most of the buildings were shabby or abandoned; those still in use appeared to be taverns, gaming salons, moneylenders' offices, or brothels. At this bright hour of the day, business was slow, but there were still patrons at every establishment. I didn't feel like I was in danger, precisely, but I did hold my satchel of jewels very firmly to my chest, and I did pay close attention to my surroundings.

"I think there's someone following us," I said quietly to Chessie as we turned a corner onto a street that looked marginally more respectable than the last two.

She gave me a sideways grin. "Two, actually. They're with me. Most people don't notice them. I'm impressed."

I smiled tightly. "I've developed my powers of observation greatly in the past couple of weeks."

"That's what catastrophe will do for you."

She paused in front of one of the more prosperous-looking buildings, held up a hand to tell me to stay in place, and ducked inside. I tried not to look nervous as I stood with my back to the covered window and kept watch on the street. I could still spot only one of Chessie's confederates, a slim youth loitering before an empty storefront a few buildings away. I couldn't tell if it was a man or a woman. I wasn't sure if the extra protection should make me feel safer or more at risk.

After a moment, Chessie opened the door and motioned me inside. The interior of the shop was nothing to look at—a plain room featuring a wide table bolted to the floor, two chairs, and a locked door heading to a back room. Hardly any light sifted in past the heavily curtained window, but a row of lit lamps provided excellent illumination, at least over the table. I assumed anyone who was buying stolen jewelry needed good light to be able to judge the quality of the gems.

The man standing behind the table was short, bald, and wholly forgettable, with indistinct features and a medium build. Even his eyes were an indeterminate gray, though I thought their expression was shrewd as he sized me up.

"No need for names," he said, "but I'm pleased to meet you. I understand you have some goods to sell."

"I do."

"Well, show me what you've got."

"Honest prices for my friend, please," Chessie said.

"Of course."

I set the satchel on the table but kept a firm grip on it in case the proprietor had any notion of grabbing it and running from the building. It seemed like a good idea to show him only one piece at a time and agree on its price rather than to dump everything out at once and have him make me one comprehensive offer. He didn't seem to mind the strategy. He picked up each ring, each necklace, and surveyed it through a jeweler's loupe before naming a sum. The offers were on the low side of fair, but I accepted all but two of them without comment. On those two, I negotiated and had my way. I thought Chessie looked approving.

"That's it," I said when the satchel was empty.

"What about the ring on your finger?" he asked.

My hand closed involuntarily into a fist. "It's not for sale. Anyway, it's just a bauble."

"A rare piece," he argued. "Only seen two rings like that before and both of them fetched a pretty price."

I felt a brief flare of curiosity. My grandfather had given it to my grandmother when they were courting, and he'd been a glamorous figure who met a mysterious end, so there *could* be some wild romantic history to the ring. Maybe he'd stolen it from a high noble or won it in a card game with a sailor or had it bestowed upon him by the king for an act of great valor. But it hardly mattered. I wasn't giving it up—no, not though we starved halfway between Camarria and Ferrenlea. My mother had said she was giving me the ring *to remind you that, wherever you are in the world, someone loves you.* I was about to wander deeper into the world than it had ever occurred to me to go, and I would need that reminder every day of my life.

"It's not for sale," I repeated.

He stared at my hand for another moment, then shrugged. "Too bad. Let me get your payment for the rest of this stuff."

"Small coins," Chessie said softly.

His expression was derisive. "All I carry."

He unlocked the door and carried the jewels to the back room, returning with a heavy cashbox. Chessie watched him unblinkingly as he counted out my payment, and I refilled my satchel. *This is all we have to pay for our freedom,* I thought as I slung the strap over my shoulder. *I'm not sure it feels heavy enough.*

"Come back someday if you ever change your mind," the pawnbroker said as we turned for the door.

"I will," I said. *I won't.*

The sun hardly seemed to have moved at all when we stepped outside. The whole transaction had been quicker and more painless than I'd expected, though I was pretty sure it would have been a different story without Chessie at my side. "Thank you," I told her sincerely. "Do I owe you anything?"

She flashed that pretty smile again. "No," she said. "I'll do anything for free if it gives Malachi more trouble."

Under any other circumstances I would have been dying of curiosity, but it seemed pointless to wonder about Chessie when I would never see her again. "Then I'll just be heading back."

"Would you feel safer if I was with you?" She nodded toward my bag. "That's a lot of cash to be carrying."

"If you've got the time and the inclination, I wouldn't mind," I said honestly. "At least until we get to the more respectable parts of town."

She set off with an easy stride and I fell in beside her. "Ah, that's where all the *real* crimes are committed," she said. "By the nobles and the royals."

I gave her a sideways glance, and she laughed. "But you're probably less likely to be robbed on the street," she conceded.

We made it across town without incident, and finally parted a few blocks from the palace. I thanked Chessie again and she nodded and melted away. I did turn to watch her for a few paces, and I thought I picked out her second companion from the busy throng, though I couldn't be sure.

I'll have to ask Nico her story, I thought. Although if I only had one more evening to spend with Nico, I probably wouldn't waste it talking about lost-waif girls and how he happened to know them.

The big brick courtyard seemed busier than usual, crammed with carts and horses and people standing around in groups, whispering to each other as they stared at the wide doors. I cast them a few curious glances as I hurried past them and slipped around one of the long, curving wings to enter the palace from the back. The first person I encountered as I stepped through the door was Lourdes, and she stared at me with as much astonishment as she would show if I'd returned from the dead. "Brianna!" she exclaimed.

I felt my heart bound with fear. "What's wrong?"

"You're not with Marguerite?" she said, a question so stupid that even she shook her head at it. "I mean— Then you don't know..."

I didn't even pause to demand *Know what?* I gathered my skirts and raced up the back stairs. I could hear a buzz of conversation that grew louder as I ascended, and when I burst onto the third story, I found a crowd of people gathered in the hallway. I saw Elyssa, Cali, the Banchura triplets, Nigel, Dezmen, and Darrily—all their echoes—with a handful of palace staff lurking at the edges. There were so many of them that it was hard to tell which door was the focal point of their attention, but I had a terrible conviction that it was the one to Marguerite's room.

I began pushing my way through the onlookers without the slightest attempt at gentleness. "Let me through— Excuse me, I need to get past— *Let me through!*"

Three soldiers were posted at Marguerite's door, facing outward and standing shoulder to shoulder to prevent anyone from entering. I strained to see past them to the scene inside.

It could not have been worse. Marguerite and her two echoes stood with their backs to the window, the afternoon sunlight creating halos of their blond hair and picking out the embroidered patterns on their blue dresses. More soldiers were scattered through the room, some rummaging in closets and cabinets, others merely standing at attention to make sure their quarry didn't sprint for freedom. Malachi Burken, the king's inquisitor, had planted himself in front of Marguerite and was reading doggedly from a paper in his hand, pausing with every sentence to glance at her and ask, "Do you understand?" Nico stood off to one side, watching his uncle recite the charges, his hands balled up at his sides, his face a stony mask.

Malachi appeared to be finishing up his accusations. "And for these reasons, a charge of murder has been leveled against you, for which the punishment is death. Do you understand?"

Marguerite's face might have been sculpted from ice. "I understand."

I couldn't help myself. *"No!"* I wailed, and struck at two of the men guarding the door. They were so surprised that they both recoiled, and I was able to slip in past them. "Marguerite! *Marguerite!*"

Out of the corner of my eye, I saw Nico start toward me, but two of the soldiers in the room had me in their custody before he could take three steps. I struggled in their hold and called out her name again.

Her calm, pale face flushed with anger and she took a hasty step away from the glass. "You," she said, her voice cold with contempt and loathing. "You sniveling bitch. I *trusted* you, and you *betrayed* me." Patience and Purpose wore matching looks of fury and hatred. Then abruptly, all three of them turned away, as if they couldn't bear the sight of my face one more second.

"Get her out of here," Marguerite flung at Malachi as I collapsed in a howl of pain and denial. "Or I won't speak another word."

CHAPTER TWENTY-SEVEN

They had to drag me from the room, frantic and despairing. I saw Malachi gesture at Nico, and he strode over to follow my captors out the door. "I'll take charge of her," he said to his uncle as he stepped into the hallway.

I had sunk to my knees, forcing the soldiers to haul me along as a deadweight, and I continued to moan and fight and plead. All the spectators gathered in the hallway pressed back against the walls to allow us passage, and I caught glimpses of their avid faces and snatches of their whispered speculation. *"Is that the maid? What did she do?"* I wanted to spit in every one of their faces.

"Where should we take her?" one of the soldiers asked as he yanked at my arm, trying to force me upright.

"Let's just put her in my chambers for now," Nico answered. "I'm sure the inquisitor will want to talk to her later and make more permanent arrangements."

The guards jerked me to my feet and I stumbled along with them, twisting around to try to see Nico. "I didn't! She knows I didn't!" I cried. "*Tell* her!"

His eyes burned into mine as if he was trying to convey a message, and he gave his head one quick savage shake. But his voice was cool as he replied, "I think it's best that you don't say anything else until the inquisitor is present."

I continued to plead but Nico said nothing more as we completed that long, humiliating trek down the stairs, across the gleaming foyer, and through an unfamiliar hallway where I assumed high-ranking palace staff must have their quarters. Nico unlocked a door and the soldiers dumped me unceremoniously inside. We appeared to be in a two-room suite outfitted with spare but expensive furnishings and so heavily curtained that very little afternoon light sifted through the windows. I scarcely took time to glance around. I was more interested in lunging for the door after the soldiers, but Nico shut it and threw the lock before I could reach the threshold.

"Noooo!" I wailed again, pounding my fist on the obdurate wood. Nico grabbed me roughly by the arm and dragged me into the second room, kicking that door shut as well. Like the outer chamber, this one had more shadows than furniture, though it was hard to miss the large bed that took up most of the available space. But he pulled me right past it and practically flung me against the far wall. Then he took me by both shoulders and started to shake me.

"Are you *mad?*" he hissed, his face barely an inch from mine. "Marguerite has bought your life with her accusation!"

"She thinks I betrayed her!" I sobbed.

He shook me again. "Don't be a fool," he said, just as furiously. "She knows there is no hope for her, but she refused to bring you down with her. If she hadn't pointed the finger at you, you'd be in that room with her, facing an execution. She *saved* you. She wouldn't have done that if she believed you turned informant."

I struggled to free myself from his bruising grip. "I have to go to her," I said. "I can't let her face this alone."

His fingers tightened even more. "You'd throw away this treasure she's given you—the last thing, the *only* thing, she'll ever be able to give you—your life?" he demanded. "Do you think she wants you to die at her side? Or do you think she wants you to live?" He shook me again and the tone of his voice was urgent. "Brianna! What do you think she wants?"

I forced myself to stare at him, forced myself to think about what he was saying. If he was right—if Marguerite didn't believe I had betrayed her—then there was no question that she was trying to protect me. There was no question that she was trying to save me from the anger of the king, the vengeance of the inquisitor. If Marguerite trusted me, if she knew that I was faithful, she would not want me anywhere near her.

The realization made me sag to the floor with despair, pulling Nico down with me. Now I started sobbing, covering my face with my splayed hands, struggling to contain uncontainable grief and fear. He drew me into his arms and cradled me against him, murmuring my name and rocking me back and forth.

It was a long time before I cried myself out, and by then we had shifted positions several times. Now Nico's back was against the wall, and I lay across his lap, my head against his chest, and one of my hands caught in his. Some time ago he had slipped the strap of the satchel over my shoulder and laid it aside, and he had dried my cheeks with the sleeve of his fine linen shirt. I felt both a tightness and a burning in my chest, as if some great fire had charred through my rib cage and roasted my internal organs, but I was finally calm enough to speak.

"What happened?" I croaked.

"The landlady at the inn returned yesterday morning. She not only described Marguerite, she not only recalled her name, but she remembered that the maid had mysteriously gone missing. Every detail she supplied confirmed Malachi's theories—and pointed him in an unambiguous direction. Couriers arrived this afternoon with the news."

"Has he told the king?"

"Only minutes before he went to arrest Marguerite."

I stirred on his lap but did not pull away. "What will happen next?"

"There will be an examination of evidence tomorrow or the day after. Two of Harold's trusted advisors will hear the case as Malachi lays out the facts and presents testimony. Then the advisors and the king will decide her fate."

I gazed up at him, mutely asking what that fate might be.

"It will be execution," he said reluctantly. "She killed the king's son. It is not a situation that invites clemency."

I tried to swallow against my tight throat. "How long before the sentence is carried out?"

"Most likely the following day."

I sat up. "But that is not enough time! Surely the king will need to inform her family! How can he think to kill a high noble of Orenza and not expect the western provinces to mutiny in response? He must wait. Surely he sees that."

Nico looked grave. "I believe one or two of his advisors are with him right now, making that very point. But Malachi said Harold was in such a rage that he was in no mood to listen to reason. I think Harold will insist on carrying out the punishment without giving Lord Garvin a chance to negotiate."

It was too awful. I could hardly take it in. I buried my face against his shirt and tried not to dissolve into tears again. "If only I could go to her," I whispered. "If only I could show her that some-one still cares about her, that she is not wholly alone in the world—"

He pressed his mouth against my hair. "You can't," he said, his voice as quiet as my own. "And she is."

I couldn't bear the thought of encountering any other residents of the palace by making a trip up to my own room—and anyway, Nico didn't seem too certain that I would stay away from Marguerite if he let me out of his sight for one moment. So he sent someone to my room to fetch all my belongings and bring them back neatly packed in my single trunk. I tried not to imagine what the young man had thought as he gathered my clothes and folded my under-garments. "That's Daniel," Nico said as the slim, nondescript youth dropped off my luggage and exited with no more than a nod. "He's more or less permanently assigned to me in case I need someone to run an errand. You'll probably see him around a lot."

I had managed to scrub my face and comb back my hair and try to force myself into a more civilized appearance, and now I glanced around the room. We had moved back to the outer chamber and I had insisted on opening the curtains in the faint hope that sun-light might make the day a little less bleak. But the view from Nico's window showed the refuse pile from the kitchens, though hardly any stink made its way past the glass. I could understand why he mostly kept the curtains shut.

"So. This is where I'm to stay for now," I said.

Nico made an indeterminate gesture. "You don't have to," he said. "Though I'd like to keep an eye on you. And if you're not with me, I'm pretty certain Malachi will assign a soldier to watch over you. At least until—" His voice trailed off.

I tightened my lips and moved half blindly around the room, touching a finger to the leather armchair, the ebony armoire. Nico stood in the middle, turning slowly to keep me in his sight.

"You don't have to— I don't expect you to— I realize everything between us has changed," he said, uncharacteristically awkward.

I came to a halt with my hand resting on the polished surface of a wooden desk and stared at him across the room. "What is it you're not saying?" I asked straight out.

He met my eyes without attempting to look away. "I keep waiting for you to ask me the question."

"What question?"

"Did I tell Malachi about Marguerite? *You* didn't betray *her*, but did *I* betray *you*? That's what you're thinking—or you will be, when you can think about anything but her."

I gave a short, sharp nod and resumed my aimless blundering around the perimeter. "You could have, I suppose," I said. "Though I don't know why you would have waited until today."

"Because I knew you'd be gone from the palace?" he suggested. "Because you were out with Chessie?"

"Oh, right. That makes sense."

"Or because I was still trying to decide whether or not I was going with you."

I shook my head. "You were never coming with us. That was just a dream." I glanced at him, but kept walking. "A good dream, though. I liked it."

"I didn't tell him, though."

"I know," I said.

"How do you know?"

I shook my head again. "Because I know you. Because I love you. Because I know that—"

"Wait a minute," he said.

I stopped and gave him an inquiring look.

"You haven't said that before. *I've* said it, but you haven't."

I actually had to think about it a moment. "What? That I love you?"

"Yes. That."

"Well, what did you think?"

He spread his hands as if to say, *How can you ask me that?* "It's one of those things that a person can't just presume."

I crossed the floor, went straight up to him, and put my arms around his neck. "I love you," I said seriously. "But I don't know that it will do either of us any good."

He kissed me. "Speak for yourself. I think it will do *me* unutterable good."

I leaned my head against his chest. "But I can't think of anything else. Not right now. Not while Marguerite—" I couldn't finish the sentence.

"There's something else you should know," he said.

I lifted my head with a new sense of apprehension. "What?"

"I'm sure Malachi's going to want to question you."

I felt a surge of panic. "What should I tell him?"

Before he could answer, there was a firm knock and a man called, "Nico? Are you in there?" As if Nico's words had summoned him, the inquisitor had appeared at the door. I had had only one brief conversation with the man, but I would never forget his voice.

"Stick to the truth as much as you can—but lie about yourself," Nico breathed. Then he released me and called back, "Yes, we both are! Hang on. The door's locked."

In a moment he had ushered Malachi inside and the three of us had seated ourselves on a set of straight, uncomfortable chairs. "Do you always keep it so dark in here, Nico?" Malachi asked, letting his eyes roam around the room.

Nico pushed himself to his feet to fetch lamps and matches. "Brianna had much the same reaction," he said. "I suppose I'm here so rarely I don't mind its gloom."

I was sure it wasn't the gloom Malachi wanted to chase away; he wanted to banish all the shadows so he had a better chance of interpreting the expressions on my face. I folded my hands in my lap and tried not to be nervous. I reminded myself that I had perfected the art of lying during the past two weeks. Now I would see if I had gotten good enough to deceive the inquisitor.

"So, Brianna. I need to ask you some questions," Malachi said, his rich deep voice sounding almost avuncular. *He wants me to trust him,* I thought. I doubted that he took this tone with most of the people he interrogated.

"Go ahead."

"From what I understand, you were present on the afternoon that Lord Jamison met his death at your mistress's hands," he said. "I've heard Lady Marguerite's accounting of that day. Now I'd like to hear yours."

I hesitated a moment, trying to think how Marguerite would have told this story. Our versions had better match in most details or he would be more suspicious than no doubt he already was. Marguerite would have had no reason not to tell the truth—except as it related to me. That tallied with Nico's advice. I took a deep breath.

"Our horse had thrown a shoe and we stopped at a posting house. The proprietor told us there was a lake nearby if we wanted to take a stroll. Lord Jamison came upon us as we were walking and said he had something he wanted to discuss with Marguerite. In private."

I paused, and Malachi waited without comment. His bald scalp and beardless face were smooth and pale, but his eyes were layered and dark. He seemed to have limitless patience. I took another breath.

"Marguerite told me to wait on a bench overlooking the lake, so I sat down. She told the echoes to wait, too, but they followed her when she walked off with Jamison. I watched them until they all disappeared into a patch of trees. It wasn't too long after that when I heard yelling and screaming coming from that direction. I jumped up, but I didn't know what to do. Marguerite had told me to stay behind." I let a little agitation creep into my voice, and then took a moment to visibly calm myself. "So I just stood there another minute or two. The yelling got louder—until all of a sudden it stopped. Then Marguerite called my name. So I ran toward the trees, and that's when I saw the bodies."

"Bodies?" he said, seeming surprised by the plural.

I nodded. "Lord Jamison and Prudence."

"Ah. The echo."

"They were both dead. Marguerite was crying. It was horrible."

"What did you do?"

"I started crying, too."

He maintained his calm. "After you and the lady and the echoes all pulled yourselves together. What did you do?"

I whispered, "We threw the bodies in the lake so no one would ever find them."

"Whose idea was that?"

Mine. "Marguerite's."

"Who came up with the plan that you should masquerade as her dead echo?"

I did. "Marguerite."

"What did you think of that idea?"

"I thought it was terrible!" I burst out. "I thought there was no way I could do it! How could I possibly copy every move she made? But she told me no one would notice. She told me that no one ever looks at echoes—that they're practically invisible."

"Did you find that to be true?" "Mostly," I said. "But it was still really hard."

"I imagine it was," Malachi said in his smooth voice. "I imagine there were days you wished you'd never agreed to do it. Days you wondered when you'd ever have a chance to be yourself again."

"Plenty of those," I said, but I eyed him warily. I sensed another bad question coming.

He hitched himself closer, fixing those bottomless eyes on my face. I wanted to glance over at Nico, who had been utterly silent and utterly motionless during this whole interview, but I couldn't look away from the inquisitor.

"So tell me this," Malachi said. "You knew we had discovered Jamison's body, did you not? That news surely must have filtered down to the servants' hall."

I nodded.

"And you were aware that my nephew was helping me investigate the death, were you not?"

I nodded again.

"Yet you didn't come forward with any information." I shook my head. "Why is that?"

I bit my lip, glanced at Nico, and clasped my hands even more tightly. "I was afraid."

"Afraid of Nico? I have formed the impression he would have been most sympathetic to your plight. Why didn't you tell him anything?"

I felt a blush color my cheeks, and I couldn't help indulging one brief, happy realization: *So Nico really didn't tell Malachi what he knew.* I brushed the thought aside. I didn't have time for it. I was trying to guess what answer Marguerite would have given when the inquisitor asked her why I hadn't betrayed her to the king. "I was afraid of Marguerite."

"I understand that she is a rich woman with a powerful father, and you would not want to cross her," Malachi said. "But surely you realized that once she was arrested, she would have no more power over you. So why were you afraid?"

I remembered the first day of our journey, when we had gotten no farther than the Barking Dog. I remembered how my brothers and sisters had lined up to stare at the governor's daughter and her echoes, how Marguerite had charmed them all with her warmth and liveliness. I remembered the weight of the baby sleeping in my arms. "My family," I whispered. "We spent the night at my mother's posting house, and Marguerite saw how much I loved them all. She told me if I didn't do *exactly* what she said, she would have them all arrested. She said they would survive only as long as she did." I twisted my triskele ring on my finger and looked up at the inquisitor as tears spilled out of my eyes. "Did she have time to send a letter?" I choked out. "Please tell me they're safe."

I thought I saw a hint of compassion come to the inquisitor's face. "She has sent no messages today, at least," he said. "I could send a courier to make certain they have not been harmed."

"Don't alarm them," I begged. "Don't tell them I'm in danger."

"You're not in danger," Malachi said. "And my messengers are most discreet."

I dropped my head and stared at my folded hands. "Thank you."

Malachi put his hands on his knees. "Thank *you* for finally telling me the truth," he said. "I wish you had spoken up sooner, but I understand why you did not. I am sorry that you have had to go through such an ordeal—witnessing a murder, and then being forced to protect the murderer. But things will be easier now."

I squeezed my hands together more tightly and nodded, but I could not bring myself to look at him. Easier? *Easier?* I could not imagine how they could get any harder. "What will happen next?" I asked.

Malachi pushed himself to his feet. "A swift trial and swift justice," he said. "This is almost over."

Nico rose and walked his uncle to the door. "Let me know what you need me to do next."

"I will," Malachi said, "But for now all you need to do is watch over this one. Not a particularly onerous task for you, I would imagine." He laughed and disappeared into the hallway.

CHAPTER TWENTY-EIGHT

Nico and I slept in the same bed that night, curled up together like exhausted lovers, but we shared nothing more intimate than a few kisses and a chaste embrace. I was too sad and weary to summon passion. But I was unutterably grateful for the comfort of his arms.

I slept badly, woke early, then lay there for more than an hour while Nico slumbered beside me. The room appeared even more stark and impersonal by the faint morning light that managed to sneak past the heavy curtains. This might as well be a chamber in some roadside inn, blandly waiting for the next indifferent occupant to arrive. If I were going to spend more than a day or two in this suite, I would want to do some extensive redecorating.

Would I stay here? What did my life hold if Marguerite died?

She can't die, I thought. *There must be something we can do.*

My brain darted here and there, trying to come up with ideas that qualified as "something." Could we smuggle her from the room disguised as a servant? Bribe the guards who watched the door? Provide a rope that she could use to climb from the window? Each possibility seemed less likely than the last.

Nico snorted, started, and opened his eyes. I lay on my left side, facing him, watching him shake himself to full wakefulness. I saw the moment he remembered that I was in the bed with him; he quickly turned onto his right side and smiled at me across the pillows.

"Hello, love," he said, taking my hand.

"We have to do something to save Marguerite," I said.

His smiled faded and he just looked tired. "I wish we could," he said. "But we can't."

"We can. We have to," I insisted.

"Brianna. She is guarded by the inquisitor's men and will be scheduled to die within a few days. I am so sorry. I know how terrible it is. But I cannot change what is."

I stared at him. "If it was me. If I was the one locked in that room. Would you just sit back and say, 'It's terrible but there's nothing I can do'?"

His expression intensified and he reached over to take my face between his hands, bringing his head so close to mine our noses almost touched. "If it were you in that room? I'd plot a daring escape. I'd murder the guards in the middle of the night and spirit you down the stairs. I'd have a coach and six horses waiting in the courtyard, and we'd ride out so fast we'd be halfway through the city before Lourdes even had time to raise the alarm."

"Then—"

"But we probably wouldn't make it to safety," he said, raising his voice to drown me out. "Malachi would expect me to behave so rashly, and he'd have soldiers stationed just outside the palace, and more soldiers stationed on every road we might take to freedom. I'd fight them all, you understand, anyone who tried to stop us— I'd leave a trail of blood and bodies behind—but eventually I'd be overcome. And you'd be caught and returned to your little room and you'd die anyway, just as you were scheduled to."

"But—"

Now he rested his forehead against mine. "I'll die for you, Brianna, but not for anyone else. I want to *live* for you. You're the one I want to keep safe. And that means I can't risk myself for anyone but you."

I stared into his eyes, just inches from mine, and could feel my own fill with tears. "But they're going to execute her," I whispered.

He lifted his hands from my face just so he could gather me close, squeezing me even tighter when I shivered under the covers. "I know," he said. "It's terrible. I know."

We lay that way for a few moments, until I could force myself to stop crying. *Maybe there's someone else who can rescue her,* I thought. I lifted my head.

"Can Taeline see her?"

"The priestess?" Nico rested his chin on the top of my head and thought about it. "Normally prisoners aren't allowed any visitors," he said. "But that much I *can* do for her. I can get dispensation for the priestess, and make sure all the guards know that they must let her in."

I sat up, pulling myself free of his arms, though he protested. "Then I'm going to talk to her." I glanced down at Nico, who looked like he never wanted to get out of bed. "At least—am I free to leave the palace? Or am I still under suspicion?"

"I think Malachi believed your story. Well, I'm sure he did, or you'd already be locked up beside Marguerite. But I wouldn't be surprised if, perhaps, you found yourself trailed by a guard or two."

I jumped out of bed, already unlacing my nightgown. "I don't care. They can follow me across the whole city of Camarria. All I'm doing is going to the temple."

He just lay there watching me, though his expression grew appreciative as I pulled the nightgown over my head. "I would accompany you, but I'm sure Malachi wants me to attend him this morning."

I paused to kiss him before I headed to the other room, where we had left my trunk. "That's all right," I said. "I know the way."

I entered the temple through the door for justice and walked up to the first priestess I saw. "I need to talk to Taeline," I said baldly.

But Taeline had already spotted me because I saw her thin, graceful shape hurrying my way. She was wearing red for celebration and I tried to see that as a hopeful sign. But in reality, she probably had been assigned to meet with a bridal couple later in the day.

"Brianna," she exclaimed in a low voice. She sounded even more distressed than I was, impossible though that seemed. "We have heard some news—is it true?"

I glanced around. "Is there somewhere we can talk in private?"

A few minutes later we were seated in one of the small underground rooms, huddled around a scarred wooden table and trying to come up with a plan. Our best idea seemed unlikely to work, but so far we hadn't devised better alternatives. When Taeline went to visit Marguerite, she would wear a second robe under her outer one, and this she would leave behind. Marguerite would position herself at the door, listening closely, and when there was a change of guards, she would don the priestess's clothing. Then she would knock on the door from the inside and demand to be released. We were going on the hope that the fresh guards wouldn't realize that the priestess had already left.

"But her face," Taeline said.

"The guards don't know what Marguerite looks like," I said. "There are so many visiting lords and ladies, I'm sure the guards can't keep them all straight."

"Well, she looks just like her echoes!" Taeline exclaimed. "So all the guards have to do is glance at them!"

"The echoes can pretend to be sleeping. She can even shove some pillows under her covers so it looks like her body is in her bed."

"Maybe," Taeline said in a doubtful voice.

"We have to *try*," I said fiercely.

"Oh, yes. We have to try."

"One thing," I said. "They won't let me see her. So I can't tell her—I can't let her know—I can't find out for *sure* that she knows I didn't betray her."

Taeline laid a comforting hand on my wrist. "She never doubted you."

"Yes, but I want her to *know*," I said. I pulled my triskele off my finger and dropped it in Taeline's hand. "She'll recognize this ring. She knows what it means. I want you to give it to her."

"But, Brianna," Taeline said in a very quiet voice, "you realize you'll never get it back."

"I *will*," I said. "Marguerite will give it to me when she escapes."

Taeline hesitated, then nodded and pocketed the ring. "Yes. When she escapes. Where shall we have her go?" She glanced around the room. "I don't think she can come here, since Malachi Burken is very well aware of the existence of these hidden chambers."

"The empty building by Amanda Plaza?" I suggested. "I could bring you the key and you could make sure the door is unlocked. I would unlock it myself," I added, "but I think the inquisitor is having me followed."

"Doesn't your friend Nico know about the building? Can we trust him?"

"Yes. And yes."

"It might not be ideal, but I can't think of a better place," said Taeline. "And we'll still need to find some way to get her out of the city."

I wished I knew how to contact Chessie. I was certain she would help us spirit Marguerite out of Camarria if it meant the slightest disgrace or inconvenience for the inquisitor. Maybe I could ask Nico how to find her.

Or maybe it was best to leave him out of any schemes in case everything fell apart. I wasn't sure what the punishment would be for aiding a condemned woman to escape, but I had to think it was severe. I could risk myself; Taeline was obviously prepared to put herself in harm's way. But I didn't want to endanger Nico.

Besides, he had already said he had no intention of saving her. This was something we had to do without him.

"I have money," I said. "Yesterday I pawned all her jewels so we could pay for our trip to Ferrenlea. I'll bring the money here and she can use it to go—somewhere."

"Ferrenlea after all?" Taeline asked with a twist of her lips.

"I don't know. Maybe. Maybe Marguerite will have some ideas."

Taeline nodded. "All right. It's a crazy plan, but I don't know that we can do any better." She came to her feet and so did I, though I had to rest my hand on the table to keep my balance. I was so tired.

"When will you go to her?" I asked.

"Why not now?" She eyed me a moment. "Would you like to wait for me here? Is there something else you need to do?"

In fact, since I was not allowed to see Marguerite, I had no occupation at all. It was an odd feeling. "No," I said. "Nothing. I'd be happy to stay, if that's allowed."

"This place has always been a sanctuary for outcasts," she said. "You'd be welcome."

In a moment she was gone. I sat back down at the table, wishing I had a book or a sewing project to help me pass the time. I kept glancing at the narrow bed pushed up against a wall. I had slept so poorly the night before that even that meager mattress looking inviting. There didn't seem to be any reason not to lie down and close my eyes, and let my anxious, questing mind try to settle for just a few moments.

I probably fell asleep within five minutes. My dreams were chaotic and troubled, and I woke feeling both panic and disorientation. Where was I? Why did I feel so weighted with dread? What terrible thing had happened, lying just beyond the reach of memory? It was only a few seconds before the details all came rushing back to me, and then I wanted to bury my head under the flat pillow and take refuge in sleep again.

But there was a stir outside of my room—the sounds of women's voices raised in eager questions and quick responses. I forced myself to stand up, smooth down my hair, and open my door.

Just down the hallway, right where the spiral staircase ended in an open space, Taeline was standing within a circle of priestesses. There were seven or eight of them, some in black robes, some in white or red. Taeline waved me over and they all turned to appraise me. I approached somewhat warily, but I saw welcome in all their faces. Several of them patted my arm or shoulder as I joined the group. I gathered that they all knew Marguerite's situation and believed that she had had no choice but to defend herself against Jamison.

"Did you see her? What did she say?" I demanded.

"I saw her. There were three guards outside the door and more stationed up and down the hallway," Taeline reported. "One of them came in with me and stayed the whole time, but he let us go into the second room and close the door."

"How is she doing?" It was a stupid question, of course—how *could* she be doing?—but I couldn't stop myself from asking.

"She is surprisingly calm," Taeline said gravely. "She knows what's coming, and she's afraid, but she seems reconciled to her fate. Relieved, almost, that the lying and pretending is done. And so grateful that you have escaped the inquisitor's net. She asked me over and over if you were truly safe. The knowledge that you are seemed to give her great peace."

"How have they treated her?"

"Well enough. She says they've brought food for her and the echoes—plain but decent. She's been allowed no visitors except me."

"You say you were able to see her in private," I said. I glanced around at the other priestesses, wondering how much they knew. "Were you able to—give her anything? My ring, for instance?"

Taeline nodded, her face briefly lightening, though she wasn't able to muster a smile. "Yes. She recognized it instantly and put in on her finger right away. She said, 'I know I should give it back to her, because it means so much to Brianna, but it means so much more to me, right now, in this place.' She was crying."

The priestesses murmured their approval, even though they couldn't know the whole story behind the ring. One or two of them patted me again on the arm and the back.

Taeline took a deep breath. "And I was able to slip off the extra robe and hide it behind her clothes in the armoire. But she doesn't think she'll be able to use it. She doesn't think she'll be able to leave because the guards are watching so closely. Indeed, when it came time for me to go, the guard stepped inside the bedroom and counted to make sure there were three women remaining behind—Marguerite and two echoes. She said a guard accompanies every maid who brings in a tray of food or a pitcher of water, and each time he counts how many women are left in the room. But she was willing to keep the robe anyway. Just in case."

"Maybe she'll get lucky," I said. "Maybe the next set of soldiers won't be so vigilant. Maybe they'll be corrupt. I'll bring you all her money, and you can take it to her tomorrow, and she can use it to bribe the guards. I'll ask Nico to make sure the soldiers who are watching her tomorrow have a streak of greed."

Taeline looked very tired and very sad. "Maybe," she said.

The other priestesses closed around her, putting their arms on her shoulders and drawing her into a communal embrace. "You can't lose hope," one of them said. Another one added, "The goddess is merciful." At different times, they each found a moment to touch their fingers to their foreheads, their chests, their lips. I found my hands automatically moving through the same ritual. I wasn't sure I trusted the goddess to be merciful—or just or joyful—but I was willing to solicit help from any source. We needed so much of it.

"I'll be back in the morning," I told Taeline. "With the key. Just in case."

She pulled free from the temple women long enough to give me a hug. Her arms felt so thin around my neck, as if grief had already started to whittle her away. "Just in case," she repeated. "I'll look for you then."

I had no reason to hurry back to the palace, so I wandered through the city, visiting the few places I knew and finding my way to new ones. I crossed a dozen bridges I had never encountered before, several of them so old and crumbling they seemed to have fallen into permanent disuse, others busy with foot traffic even as the evening hours approached. At the apex of each one I paused to look down at the scene below, viewing rooftops, flower gardens, storefronts, warehouses, public squares, and private offices from my high vantage point. All these people, living lives I would never know anything about. All these people, utterly indifferent to my own triumphs and tragedies, my wildest hopes, my darkest fears. *What connects us to other human beings?* I wondered. *Why do we choose to love some and wholly ignore others? What is it that leads us to care?*

Knowledge, I decided. Experience. If I worked in that little fabric shop, if I lived in that house with the tidy garden, I would be friends with my fellow shopgirls and on good terms with my nearest neighbors. I would celebrate their happy news and weep at their losses, as they would cheer and mourn with me. I wouldn't be viewing them from a cool, remote distance; I would be beside them, shoulder to shoulder, arm in arm.

If something happened to Marguerite—if the king carried out his vengeful punishment—would I find a community to be part of? Where would I go, where would I belong? Could I make Nico my whole world? How could I stay at the palace, in Camarria, if the king condemned Marguerite to death?

I didn't know. What I *did* know, because I had done it before, was that it was possible to recover from grief. It was possible to build a fresh life around different people, new routines. It was possible to start over. But I thought this second blow would be even more devastating than the first one. I wasn't sure how much strength I would have if a third one came along.

I passed through the flower markets on my way home, not intending to stop. What was the point? I was sure Marguerite would be unutterably grateful to receive a bouquet of fresh blossoms, but I wouldn't be allowed to deliver them to her—and besides, since everyone thought I had betrayed her, it would seem odd if I brought gifts to her door.

But as I passed a stall where the owners were packing up for the day, one of them called out, "Half price if you buy now!" and I couldn't help stopping. They had a fine selection of roses in almost every available color, but I was drawn to the ones so pale they looked white. They were miniatures, their petals clustered so densely around their yellow hearts that they had a weight and toughness. *These would last a few days if I tacked them into a headband,* I thought. All of my sewing materials had been brought to Nico's room, along with my clothes and personal items, so I could actually embark on such a project tonight. And I needed a task, something to occupy my hands as well as my mind.

"I'll take some," I told the vendor. "These roses—and these— Oh, and a bit of that baby's breath. No, none of those pink ones. Only white will do."

The evening passed in a blur of thread and fabric and flowers because I had to make *three* headpieces, even though the ones for Patience and Purpose were much simpler than the version I made for Marguerite. Nico checked in on me once to see if I needed anything. He seemed bemused by my determination to complete the project but, on the whole, relieved that I found a distraction.

"Malachi wants me to come back, but I thought I should see if you made it safely through the day," he said, pausing to kiss the top of my head and finger a length of tulle. I batted his hand away from the fabric.

"Dinner, if you could provide it. I haven't eaten all day."

"Why not?"

"I didn't think to ask the priestesses for food. And when I got back to the palace, I went to the servants' hall but—" I just shook my head. I didn't want to relive those moments of hostility by describing the expressions I had seen on the faces of the abigails and maids.

"Of course," Nico said quietly. "They all believe you betrayed your mistress."

"Most of them despise me for it," I said. "A few of them looked as if they admired me, instead. Those are the ones," I added, "that *I* find the most disgusting."

Nico nodded. "I'll send Daniel to fetch you a meal. And make sure you're fed in the morning."

"I'm going back to the temple tomorrow," I said.

He eyed me for a moment. "Plotting something?" he finally asked.

I held up one of the completed headpieces. "I want to give this to Taeline so she can give it to Marguerite."

"*And* you're plotting something."

I shrugged. "It wouldn't hurt if the guards stationed at Marguerite's room tomorrow were open to earning a little extra cash."

Nico shook his head. "I'm not saying all the inquisitor's men have the highest moral standards, but colluding in the escape of the woman who murdered the king's son? No one would risk the consequences of something so rash."

"Well, then," I said, bending over my task again, "I suppose I'm not plotting anything after all."

CHAPTER TWENTY-NINE

I slept a little better that night but still woke very early, my mind already restless. I lay there more than an hour, thinking about the day at hand and the days to come.

When Nico opened his eyes, he yawned, turned on his side, and took me into his arms. "I like this," he said, speaking into my hair. "Waking up next to you."

"It's the only good thing to come out of this situation."

"Once Marguerite—once the king decides what should become of her—have you thought about what you plan to do next?" he asked. He was speaking carefully, I thought, trying not to sound opportunistic. *You said you couldn't stay with me because you were loyal to Marguerite, but you'll be free once she's dead. Will that change your mind?*

"I'm having a hard time thinking beyond the present moment," I confessed. "But I do know I want you in my future."

"Well, that's good to hear."

"I love you," I said straight out, "but I don't know if I'll be able to stay in Camarria. If Marguerite is put to death and everyone thinks it's because I lodged information against her, I certainly can't stay at the palace."

He drew me even closer and kissed the top of my head. "Maybe not," he said. "But maybe. People forget things after a while."

"*I* won't be able to forget," I said quietly.

He kissed me again and let that be his only answer.

"So. This afternoon is the trial," I said.

"More like a reading of the accusation, a summation of the evidence, and the king's disposition."

"Is it a public event? Can I be there?"

He shook his head. "There will just be a few people in the room, including the councilors and the accused. But typically people who have an interest in the proceedings will gather in the hallway outside so they know the judgment as soon as it is handed down."

"I want to be here for that."

"I thought you were going to the temple."

"I'll make sure I'm back. What time will it be?"

"Three o'clock."

I sat up. "Then I'd better get going."

It didn't take me long to return to the temple and hand over all the things I had gathered—the key to the empty building near Amanda Plaza, the satchel of money, and a woven sack where I had carefully layered the headpieces I had made for Marguerite and the echoes.

"If she doesn't want the money, I'll bring it back with me to the temple," Taeline said, "and you can have it."

"Why wouldn't she want it?"

"If she thinks it won't do any good. If she thinks it won't buy her freedom."

"If she doesn't want the money, just keep it. Use it to help a widowed mother or a starving child."

Taeline nodded. "What will you do—afterward?"

If enough people kept asking this question, I would have to come up with a better answer. "I don't know. What will you do?"

"Go to Thelleron, as I planned. But with a heart so heavy it might chain me to the ground."

"Yes," I said. "I am afraid I will feel the same way."

As before, having no responsibilities back at the palace, I dawdled on my way home. I even stopped at a food vendor's to buy a midday meal, since I wouldn't be welcome in the servants' hall and I wasn't sure I could count on Daniel at this time of day. The food was cheap and greasy, of much lower quality than I had grown accustomed to. *Your fancy life has spoiled you,* I jeered silently.

But my fancy life hadn't shielded me from heartache. That came to all of us, whatever our stations in life.

I made sure I was back well before the three o'clock hour. The king would hear evidence and announce a verdict in the throne room—the huge chamber where Marguerite and all the visiting nobles had had their audience with royalty shortly after they arrived. Today, however, the crowds were outside, not inside. When I arrived, there was already a sizable gathering in the hallway: the Banchura triplets and their echoes forming their own formidable delegation; Elyssa with all three of her echoes, though one of them appeared wan and weak; Vivienne, looking as stunned and sad as ever, though I had to think she was wondering if Marguerite's death might reverse her own fortunes. Also present were Darrily and Dezmen and Nigel and Deryk and a few other nobles Marguerite had barely talked to. None of them noticed me lurking nearby, keeping to the shadows as much as I could—or if they did, they didn't recognize me. Why would they? Anytime they had seen me in the past two weeks, I had been one of Marguerite's echoes. They had never encountered me as Marguerite's maid. And even if they had, they would not have bothered to note what I looked like.

They were all talking and arguing as they waited, though I got the sense none of them condemned Marguerite. The triplets certainly didn't. Leonora, always the most outspoken of the three, was expressing her opinion most vehemently—ostensibly addressing Dezmen, but obviously expecting the whole world to hear.

"If they condemn her, I'm leaving Camarria," she said. "They'll have to arrest me and set a guard outside my door if they want me to stay."

"If they condemn her, I think both princes will have a hard time finding brides among the noblewomen with echoes," said Darrily. She had always been one of those who vied for Cormac's attention, but she spoke with a simple weariness that made it obvious she was done with that game.

"I'd still marry either one of them," Elyssa said. "But they'd suffer for it."

"The last thing they'll be thinking about will be finding brides!" Leonora exclaimed. "They'll be spending all their energy trying to prevent secession and war!"

"You might want to lower your voices," Dezmen said. "I believe Harold, Cormac and Jordan are already in the throne room. They might hear you."

"I *want* them to hear me," Leonora said. "I them to know how violently I disagree with this—this tribunal."

"Hush," somebody said, and they all fell silent to listen. We could hear the sound of many footsteps coming down the hallway—eight or ten people, I thought, moving in one big cluster. In a few moments, a tight phalanx swept into view. Three guards led the way and three trailed behind, with Marguerite, Patience, and Purpose at their center. I felt my hands clench as I saw her walk by. She looked pale as death, weary and tense, but oddly calm. She kept her eyes trained on the floor and didn't look at any of us as she passed. I saw Leonora reach out as if to touch her arm, but one of the guards shoved his body between them. Leonora smacked at his shoulder with her open hand, but Letitia pulled her back before she could actually hit him.

Nico came behind them all, glancing around as if to memorize the faces of everyone gathered in the hall. *He* saw me, if no one else did, but he did no more than grimace and nod.

The guards and the prisoners marched into the throne room. "Quick, let's follow!" Leonora exclaimed. But before anyone could react, guards on the inside shut the doors with a thudding finality.

There was a moment of uncertain silence. "Now what?" Nigel asked. "Do we wait?"

"I don't think it will take very long," said a nobleman from Sammerly. "Judgments tend to be swift in cases like this."

"What will happen if they find her guilty?" Vivienne asked.

The nobleman looked at her. "They will condemn her to death and carry out the sentence tomorrow morning."

The others all reacted with dismay.

"So soon?"

"It's shameful and unfair!"

"What about her family?"

"Can't she mount an appeal?"

"I am leaving this city the minute I can pack my bags."

I wished they would all be quiet. I wished I could creep forward, and press my ear against the door, and hear the evidence that Malachi had gathered. I hoped with all my heart that he was describing the location of the lake, the condition of the bodies, and the statement made by the landlady. I hoped he was not offering as evidence of Marguerite's guilt the testimony of her perfidious maid.

It turned out that the man from Sammerly was right. Barely ten minutes later, the doors opened again and a small man hurried out. He was dressed in palace livery but didn't look like a footman or a personal servant; I guessed he was a scribe or a herald. A man whose sole function was to carry news.

"What's the word?" Dezmen demanded.

The small man drew himself up to his full, unimpressive height and tried to look imposing. "Marguerite Andolin of Orenza has been condemned to death for the crime of murder. She will be executed at eight o'clock tomorrow morning in Amanda Plaza."

Nico didn't want me to go. We argued about it half the night, since both of us lay awake for hours.

"Why should her death be the last picture of her that you carry in your head?" he demanded.

"If she can endure it, I can witness it."

"Your witnessing changes nothing for her and everything for you."

"It is the last gift I can give her. It is the least I can offer in return for her last gift to me—which was my life."

We were still at odds when we finally fell asleep, and we silently agreed not to discuss it any more in the morning.

Nico had to leave before I did—to him had fallen the dreadful chore of making sure the six archers arrived at the square before the prisoner even left her room. Malachi had reserved for himself the task of escorting Marguerite from the palace to the plaza. Making sure, I supposed, that Marguerite was not in the hands of someone who might be bribed to set her free.

Nico was ready a few minutes before I was. He kissed me, said "I'm so sorry," and left. I finished dressing, choked down a chunk of bread, and headed out the door—to find Daniel there standing guard.

I glared at him. "I hope Nico didn't tell you to prevent me from leaving."

The boy shook his head. "Said I was to go with you if you want company."

"Thank you, but I don't."

"It'll be crowded in the square," he offered. "You have to go early if you want to see."

"I thought maybe I'd get a place on the bridge."

Daniel shook his head. "Too late by now. Some people will have spent the night there, just waiting."

I shivered, passionately hating all those ghoulish lowlifes who found the spectacle of a public execution to be great sport. But maybe some of them, like me, felt obliged to attend, to bear witness to the unjust ending of a gentle life. "I'll find a place," I said.

I headed toward a side exit that Nico had showed me the night before, not wanting to encounter servants in the back halls or Lourdes in the front foyer, then made my way across the great courtyard half-enclosed by the curving walls of the palace. I found the space crowded with spectators—some of them residents of the palace, some ordinary citizens, all buzzing with excitement. It wasn't hard to guess why. Waiting in front of the grand door was a simple cart drawn by a pair of matched black horses. Marguerite's transport to Amanda Plaza.

As I stood there a moment, trying to decide if I should linger there or hurry on ahead, the doors swung open and the crowd broke into a roar. A knot of people emerged from the palace, moving in one awkward clump. There was Malachi at the forefront, striding over to swing into the driver's seat and take the reins. He was followed by a handful of guards surrounding Marguerite, her echoes, and a brown-haired priestess wearing the black robes of justice. I was unutterably grateful to see that Taeline had been allowed to accompany Marguerite this morning since this was the last act of mercy the goddess would ever be able to grant her.

I fixed my eyes on Marguerite. She and the echoes were all wearing simple white dresses and the rose-encrusted headbands I had just made for them. Her face was so pale and so set that if her headpiece hadn't been more elaborate, I might not have been able to pick her out from the others. She seemed unsteady on her feet, as if she could hardly remember how to walk. Indeed, Purpose and Patience had positioned themselves on either side of her, and they were holding her hands as though to keep her from tripping and falling. She watched her shoes as she proceeded and never once looked up to notice the crowds gathered to savor her humiliation. Taeline helped her into the cart and the four of them crowded together on the single bench. The guards fell into formation around the vehicle, and Malachi slapped the reins to set the horses in motion.

The whole crowd surged after them, and I was carried along in its wake. Like Marguerite, I was unsteady on my feet, stumbling and almost falling as the people around me shoved and shouted. The streets were so crowded it was clear the cart would not be able to manage a very fast pace; I could take a different route and make it to the plaza first. So at the first opportunity, I turned down a side road and hurried through back alleys toward Amanda Plaza. I could still hear, from two and three streets away, the sound of fresh voices raised in excitement as the cart carrying Marguerite passed every new corner.

I arrived at the plaza a good ten minutes before Malachi, but Daniel was right—the place was mobbed, and the stone bridge was so packed with spectators that some of them were hanging from the railing. I would never be able to push my way to the front; I would not be able to see a thing. I would not be able to bear witness after all.

Unless...I glanced around quickly to orient myself, then elbowed my way back out to the edge of the plaza. Just one block over I found myself in front of the decrepit old building that recently had served as a trysting spot for more than one pair of lovers. Now it would be my observation point for the saddest day of my life.

I didn't have the key but, as arranged, Taeline had left the lock open. I slipped inside and barred the door, not wanting any other enterprising onlookers to join me. I hurried up to the fifth story, cast only a cursory glance at the rumpled blankets on the floor, and pressed my face to the window overlooking the square.

From there, I could see everything. Tightly pressed throngs were packed into every inch of the plaza; small boys had even climbed into the branches of the century-old tree and onto the shoulders of the statues of Queen Amanda and her echoes. The only clear space was right before the dais where the prisoners would be arrayed. There, a line of guards kept the unruly crowd about twenty-five feet from the stage.

Just inside the line of guards was a second human chain, this one composed of about twenty priestesses. Half of them wore black robes for justice and half wore white for mercy. Unlike the guards, they faced inward, so they could serve as witnesses to the execution.

A few steps closer to the dais were six archers, all dressed in black, all wearing featureless hoods with small holes for their eyes and mouths. They stood motionless, tilting their heads down and appearing absorbed in staring at the brickwork of the plaza They seemed oblivious to the thousands of people gathered to watch them carry out their task. Off to one side of them stood Nico.

There was a sudden roar from the crowd as the cart pulled into view. The palace guards forced a brutal path through the dense sea of onlookers, and the cart inched closer and closer to the dais. Finally, it couldn't make any more headway. The guards hauled Marguerite and the echoes from the vehicle and fought their way through the crowd on foot until they passed through the line of blockading soldiers.

Then suddenly everyone was silent. Everyone was in place. Marguerite stood between Patience and Purpose, each of them with their backs against the tall stone wall, facing their accusers and executioners. Taeline had dropped back to join her sister priestesses, and I saw her clasp hands with the women on either side of her; then all the priestesses joined hands in one unbroken line. Nico and Malachi stood together just behind the executioners.

The archers raised their bows and took deliberate aim. I didn't see a signal, I didn't hear if someone ordered them to shoot. But suddenly, simultaneously, disastrously, impossibly, six arrows flew across the slim space and buried themselves in their targets. Patience. Purpose.

Marguerite.

They cried out—they staggered and flailed—they fell to the ground and were still.

I couldn't believe it. I stood with my hands and my nose still pressed against the glass, my whole body tingling with shock. They couldn't be dead, they couldn't be. Not until this moment did I realize that I had kept expecting *something* to avert the catastrophe—I had believed Nico would manufacture an escape or the king would grant clemency or the crowd would rise up in protest or the bricks and stones of the plaza would fly apart as the world itself rebelled.

But none of that had happened, and Marguerite was dead.

No one in the crowd had much interest in the aftermath of death; the plaza started clearing out surprisingly quickly. Even the official palace delegation didn't seem disposed to linger. I saw Malachi bend over each body to double-check that the execution was complete, then he turned to wave the archers to disperse. He called Nico over for a brief consultation while the guards broke ranks and huddled together, talking and occasionally laughing, waiting for their next set of orders.

The only ones who cared about the corpses were the priestesses, who knelt between the three bodies and began unrolling simple canvas stretchers. They gently moved the dead women onto the stretchers and assigned one priestess to each corner. Carefully they rose and carefully began carrying their sad burdens through the plaza in the direction of the temple. The few spectators who still lingered in the square either gawked with curiosity at the bodies, or turned away, oddly unnerved. I saw Malachi cast them one indifferent glance before resuming his conversation with Nico. Nico's eyes followed the funeral procession as long as it was in sight.

I ran headlong down the stairs and fled from the building, desperate to join Taeline and the others. I had to wind my way through streams of departing spectators and cross two narrow roads before I was able to meet up with the small parade of priestesses. They all seemed to recognize me; several of them nodded, and one or two came close enough to touch me on the arm or shoulder. No one spoke.

I fell in step with the women carrying one of the echoes and I stared at the corpse's face so hard I was in danger of taking a misstep. It was Purpose, I thought; even in death, she wore an expression of determination. I wondered how quickly her features would lose their particular individual stamp—how quickly she would stop resembling Marguerite. How quickly everyone in the world would forget that Marguerite had once existed.

One of the women carrying the stretcher lifted her free hand to pat my back. I nodded at her and let my pace slow just enough that she and her sister priestesses were able to pull ahead of me by a few steps. Before we made it all the way to the temple, I would speed up again. I would come alongside the canvas sling holding Patience, the one holding Marguerite, and pay my respects to the dead. But I didn't have the heart for it just yet. I tilted my head down and forced myself to keep walking.

Another priestess came up beside me and put a gentle hand on my forearm. I didn't even glance at her, just nodded in acknowledgment. To my surprise, she didn't pull away and stride on. Instead, her grip tightened with such urgency that it was actually painful. My gaze flicked to the fingers so insistent on my wrist.

She was wearing my triskele ring.

CHAPTER THIRTY

I was suffused with astonishment so profound that my whole body flashed with fire; my chest caved in from the lack of air. My eyes instantly went to the priestess's face. She wasn't wearing her brown hair pulled back in the usual severe style that the priestesses affected, but let it fall loose along her shoulders and drift across her cheeks, partially obscuring her features.

But this was no priestess. It was Marguerite.

My lips moved to shape her name, but I couldn't speak. The only reason I kept moving was that she retained her hold on my arm and I dumbly allowed her to pull me forward. The smile she gave me was weary and threaded with pain—and also limned with amazement and wonder. I was too emotional to smile.

"How?" I finally managed to ask. I knew how she'd gotten the robe, and the brown wig was the very one I had purchased a couple of weeks ago when I bought a blond one for my own use. But how could she be alive when there were three dead bodies and only two echoes?

She shook her head. "I can't explain it," she said, her voice so soft no one near us could overhear. "When I woke up this morning, there was a third echo in the room. It is as if the other two *made* her for me."

My head was spinning, but I remembered the tale Nico had told me the very day I met him. How King Edwin had lost most of his echoes in battle, but later regained one when a new echo spontaneously appeared overnight. But I had thought it was a myth, a story Nico might have made up on the spot.

"I didn't know that was possible," I whispered.

She shook her head again. "I didn't, either. Even so, I didn't want to let her take my place. I didn't want *them* to die for *me*. But Purpose insisted. Every time I would reach for my white dress, she would pull it away from me and hand me the black robe instead. I finally gave in."

I remembered how unsteady that third echo had been, how Purpose and Patience had kept her hands in theirs as they guided her to the cart. She had been a newborn, an entity created for a single purpose. Such a short life, such a noble one. "Did you name her?"

Marguerite nodded. "Purity."

"The guards did not suspect?"

"They were a little surprised when they came into the room because, of course, they hadn't been told that a priestess had spent the night with me. I could see the confusion on their faces. But the king's inquisitor entered right behind them, and I suppose none of them wanted to confess that they hadn't kept close track of all my visitors. So they said nothing."

I glanced around, but I couldn't tell who was who among all the priestesses in their white and black robes. "Does Taeline know?"

"Yes. When the cart arrived at the plaza this morning and I joined the line of priestesses, I took Taeline's hand. She almost fell over from the surprise and joy." She nodded at the cluster of women walking ahead of us. "Word spread up and down the line. They all know."

"I can't believe—I don't have words—I thought you were *dead*." My voice trembled. Now, *now*, when there were so many reasons to rejoice, I could feel myself starting to cry.

"I know. I am still nearly dumb with wonder. And gratitude and sadness and emotions I don't even know how to name."

I lifted my free hand to touch my face and body in the ritual benediction. "The goddess is merciful," I whispered through my tears. "She is just."

Marguerite mimicked my gestures. "And she graces our lives with joy."

As we approached the temple, the women carrying the stretchers veered off toward another building, which I assumed held materials for preparing the bodies for burial. The rest of us clattered across one of the bridges and into the sanctuary, entering through the door for justice just in case anyone was watching and might wonder why a funeral delegation considered joy a proper emotion. Not until we had all filed through the hidden door and down the spiral staircase did anyone speak. And then it was pandemonium, a babble of rapid voices and delighted laughter and quiet whoops of excitement. I think everyone there hugged Marguerite, hugged me, hugged each other at least once and maybe a dozen times. I wasn't sure I had ever seen so many happy people together in one place.

"But what happens now?" someone asked, and that caused the group to settle down a little.

"Here—let's all sit and discuss it," someone else replied, and we passed into one of the larger underground rooms where we could all fit around a square wooden table. There were ten or twelve of us, so the space was somewhat cramped, but no one seemed to mind. I found myself across the table from Marguerite, who had pulled off her wig and was leaning her head on Taeline's shoulder. They both wore smiles of almost transcendent peace.

"You can stay here as long as you like, Lady Marguerite," said the abbess whom we had met on one of our earlier visits. "But it is hardly a permanent solution."

Marguerite straightened up, but I was pretty sure she was still clutching Taeline's hand under the table. "I think I have to leave Camarria, which I was planning to do anyway," she said. "But I don't think I need to leave the Seven Jewels after all. If everyone thinks I'm dead, no one will be looking for me."

"You could come to Thelleron with me," Taeline said. "In fact— you have to! I can't bear to be parted from you again."

Everyone murmured agreement at that, although the abbess looked thoughtful. "Are you interested in taking vows? I could write a recommendation to the temple in Thelleron."

"I don't know," Marguerite said. "I've never thought about it. But after today I feel a more powerful connection to the goddess than I ever have, so maybe."

"Not everyone who joins the order feels a great spiritual call," the abbess said. "Some serve the goddess because of the good they can do in her name. If it is lack of deep faith that makes you hesitate, do not let that be the reason that stops you."

"Thank you," Marguerite said. "I will consider it."

One of the younger priestesses spoke up. "But I don't understand. If Lady Marguerite could always take refuge in the temple in Thelleron, why didn't we send her there as soon as we knew she was in danger?"

"Because the situation is very different now," the abbess responded gravely. "Before, if she had disappeared, there would have been inquisitors across the Seven Jewels searching for her. The abbess in Thelleron strongly believes that the temple has a responsibility to shield fugitives, and she would have done what she could to keep Lady Marguerite safe. But there might have been a priestess or two with a jealous heart or a different view of the temple's role. And if one of those women recognized Lady Marguerite—"

"As doubtless they *would* have because she would have been accompanied by two echoes," I interposed.

The older woman nodded. "Then the inquisitors would have descended on the temple. And the abbess would have been discredited and—who knows?—perhaps the temple would have been closed. It was a high risk to us and no guarantee of haven for Lady Marguerite."

"It's wonderful that everyone thinks you're dead now, but it's sad, too, isn't it?" said the younger woman. "What about your family? How terrible for them! Can you let them know?"

Marguerite's smile dimmed as she shook her head. "I have never been close to my parents or my brothers," she said quietly. "I don't worry that they will mourn my death. I worry that they will use my execution as an excuse to arm for war."

The abbess tilted her head. "Ah. That might be a reason to let them know—very quietly indeed!—that you survived."

"Do you think so? My fear is that they would use that fact to taunt the king, and war would come anyway. Perhaps it is best if they believe me a murderer who was justly executed." She paused and glanced around the table. "At any rate, at this moment, I don't believe anyone outside of this room needs to know I am still alive."

One person outside of this room has to be informed, I thought. Marguerite must have read the expression on my face because she gave me a private smile and a small nod. I would have told Nico anyway, but I was relieved that I had her permission.

"When will you leave for Thelleron?" asked a priestess who hadn't spoken till now.

"I was scheduled to go tomorrow or the next day," Taeline answered. "But I can wait a few days if that's better for Marguerite."

Marguerite shook her head. "Nothing is holding me here. I will go whenever you like."

"You'll have plenty of funds for your trip," I told her, "since I pawned all your jewels and left the money with Taeline." I considered. "I wonder if the king's inquisitor would let me gather your clothes and other items from your room. I could say I want to return them to your family. Or drop them in a pauper's box."

Marguerite shook her head. "Don't bother. There's nothing there I want. If I'm going to start a new life, I don't want to take anything from my old life with me."

"And a lady's ball gowns and fancy shoes would be most inappropriate in a temple setting," one of the priestesses said practically.

Taeline looked at me across the table. "What about you, Brianna? Will you come to Thelleron with us?"

"Again, I would be happy to write a letter of recommendation for you, if you were interested in taking vows or looking for some kind of employment," the abbess offered.

Marguerite was watching me, again wearing that knowing smile. "I wish she would join us, but she won't."

I felt a blush rise to my cheeks. These were women who had felt a much different pull than sexual attraction, a different kind of love than that between a man and a woman. Would they understand? "I think—there's someone here—I want to see if I can build a life for myself in Camarria," I stammered.

"Ooooh, a romance," one of the women cooed. They all laughed and nodded. My blush burned hotter.

"Well, without him I wouldn't have been able to escape," Marguerite said. "The morning before Taeline came to visit the first time, I could hear Nico in the hallway telling the guards to expect her. One of them said that prisoners were never allowed visitors, but Nico made it clear that any guard who failed to admit a priestess would find himself without a job the following day. So when Taeline arrived, they showed her right in."

"Then we shall include his name in our prayers of thanks," the abbess said. She glanced at the others. "Is there anything left to decide?"

We talked for a few more minutes, but it was clear most matters had been settled. We all rose to our feet, and the other priestesses headed off to their normal duties, but Taeline and Marguerite and I lingered in the room.

"I still can't believe I am here—and safe—and talking about my future," Marguerite said. "I keep thinking it must be the night before the execution, and I'm just dreaming."

"I never could have imagined a dream this good," I answered.

Marguerite pressed a hand against her chest. "As grateful and joyous as I am, I also feel devastated and lost," she said. "I miss them all—my echoes—there is so much pain in my heart that I don't think it will ever go away. I *felt* the arrows strike them. I felt the pain in their bodies as if it was in mine. I could tell the minute each of their lives ended. Even Purity's, and I only knew her a couple of hours. I think I will mourn them forever."

"As you should," Taeline said. "But you should celebrate them as well. Keep them alive by honoring and remembering them."

"And who knows?" I said, trying to cheer her up. "Maybe you'll wake up some morning and there will be a *new* echo in your room. Or two. Or three!"

She laughed shakily. "Oh, I hope not! How would I explain *that* to the abbess of Thelleron temple?"

"You would say it was a gift from the triple goddess, as of course it would be," Taeline said with a smile. "But I admit it would be simpler if such a thing did not occur."

"You'll have to stay in touch with me," I said. "I suppose you cannot use your own name, but you'll have to send me letters. Let me know how you are. I can come here every day and see if you've written again."

"If I'm not using my own name, I can send the letters to wherever you happen to be living," she pointed out. "Where do you think that might be?"

"I don't know yet. I'm not very popular at the palace right now."

"Why? Oh—because I denounced you?" She frowned. "That might make life difficult for you," she agreed. "What will you do?"

"I don't know yet," I repeated. "But I'm looking forward to finding out."

Marguerite pulled the triskele ring off her finger and handed it to me. "I can't tell you how much it meant to me to receive this and know why you sent it," she said. "But it belongs to you and you must have it back. Now when you look at it, let it remind you that your mother is not the only one who loves you."

That made me cry again, and I hugged her, and I hugged Taeline, and scrubbed my sleeves across my face to try to wipe away the tears. "I don't know why you think I'd need a ring to remind me of that," I said, trying to sound jaunty. "I'll never forget."

I spent the rest of the day at the temple, keeping Marguerite company and taking the chance to store up conversations against the days and months and years we would be apart. I promised to come visit her in Thelleron sometime, though she couldn't make a reciprocal vow. And I promised to come back tomorrow so that I could see her one last time before she left the city.

It was dusk when I finally left, slipping out the door for mercy. I paused before the statue positioned there and placed one of my hands on her outstretched palm. It was warm from the summer heat; I could almost believe that I touched a living hand. *Goddess, hold my life in yours,* I said silently. *Keep me and the ones I love safe for ever and ever. Amen.*

I dropped my hand and turned toward the narrow white bridge. I had just set my foot on the first wooden plank when I realized there was someone standing in the middle, waiting for me. Nico.

"I figured this was where you must have gone," he said.

I walked slowly up the bridge, trailing one hand along the smooth railing. "How long have you been here?" I asked.

"An hour or two."

I guessed it was actually closer to four or five. He looked tired and sad and worried and very dear. "Why didn't you come in and find me?"

He looked even wearier. "I wasn't sure you'd want to see me. Because I was there—because I didn't do anything to—because—" He let a shrug complete the sentence.

I just kept walking until I walked right into him. I put my arms around his waist and rose to my tiptoes and pressed a fervent kiss on his mouth. He responded with alacrity, wrapping his arms around me and drawing me close, but after a moment he broke the kiss and looked down at me, puzzled.

"Why aren't you more upset?" he asked. "You don't even seem like you've been crying."

I kissed him again and then, with my lips still against his, I whispered, "She's alive."

"*What?* But I *saw* her. I was right there. The arrows—"

I nodded and kept my voice to a whisper, though there was no one nearby to hear. "Three bodies. Three echoes. The woman dressed as a priestess was Marguerite."

His expression was dazed. "*Three echoes?* But—the body in the lake—"

"Marguerite's echo. Yes. But last night, while she slept, another one appeared in her room."

His hold slackened as he stared down at me. I saw the disbelief on his face slowly give way to comprehension. "Like King Edwin," he said. "Like Queen Toriana. I didn't know it was really possible."

"I didn't, either. But it is because Marguerite's alive."

He shook his head, then he laughed, then he scooped me up in a ferocious hug before dropping me to my feet again. "Well, *that's* an ending I never could have predicted," he exclaimed. "And she's not even a fugitive, since everyone thinks she's dead." He thought about it. "She probably shouldn't stay in Camarria, though. And I'd advise against returning to Oberton."

"She's already making plans to leave."

Now he looked worried and his hands tightened. "Are you thinking of leaving with her?"

I shook my head and leaned up to kiss him again. "She's taking someone else with her."

"*Another* echo?"

"No—someone who loves her more than I do. I'm not going to tell you who, though, so don't ask me."

"So then what are *you* planning to do next?" he asked. I could tell he was trying to keep the question casual, but he didn't even come close to succeeding. "Will you return to Orenza—or stay in Camarria?"

"There's nothing for me in Orenza except my mother's posting house, which I already left once," I pointed out. "So it looks like I have to stay here."

He leaned his back against the railing of the bridge and drew me close to him. I wrapped my arms loosely around his waist and rested my head on his shoulder. "That's good news," he said. "Though I suppose you'll need to find an occupation."

"I'm not too worried about that," I said. "I can cook and clean and sew, and the abbess said she would write me a letter of recommendation, so I think *someone* will hire me. But I'm not sure where I'll live. Since I won't be welcome at the palace much longer."

"We could rent a place," he suggested, "while we figure it out."

I craned my neck to look up at him. "*You're* still welcome at the palace."

He absentmindedly began running a hand up and down my arm. "Maybe," he said. "But I don't think I want to stay there much longer. After today—" He hesitated and then plunged on. "Watching Marguerite die—or, rather, watching her echoes die. Knowing I couldn't save her. Knowing that, in some other situation, it might be *my* words and *my* investigation that causes somebody's execution. I'm just not sure how much longer I can keep on doing this job."

I was silent a moment. That was a powerful realization, and I imagined it had hurt him to come to the point where he questioned the worth of everything he had worked for so far. "Your uncle will be disappointed if you leave," I said softly.

"I know."

"But *I* will be relieved. I always thought you were too good a man to be an inquisitor."

"Thank you," he said, managing a shaky laugh. "I suppose."

"So then what else will you do with your life?"

He sighed. "Like you, I don't really know. I have some skills and abilities, so I imagine *someone* will hire me. But I would like to think about it awhile before I tender my resignation. I would not like to be wrong twice."

"I imagine most people are wrong more than twice in their lives."

He pulled back enough so that he could gaze down at me, putting one hand under my chin to make sure I was looking up at him. "At the moment there's only one thing I'm sure I'm right about," he said. "That's you. If you'll stay with me—"

"I will."

"And figure it out alongside me—"

"Of course."

"Then I don't think it will be so hard."

"Or even if it's hard, it will still be wonderful."

That made him laugh. He kissed me again, then drew me back against his body, and we stood there, embracing on the bridge, for a very long time. My mind was busy with thoughts of the future. I would return tomorrow to see Marguerite, but after that there were almost limitless possibilities before me. Maybe I would look for work, but maybe I would open a boutique of my own. I had developed a flair for designing floral headdresses for fashionable ladies; maybe I could turn that into a business. I would make arrangements with my favorite flower vendors and buy scrap fabric from the milliners' shops. Maybe I would first set up a stall at the flower market, just to see how well my products sold. After that I could investigate renting a more permanent property.

Maybe Nico and I could find a small shop with a tiny apartment situated above it. We would hardly need much space, not at the beginning. Neither of us had collected many possessions in our lives so far; we were both used to turning our attention and our energy outward. That might change, though, when we had a place of our own to furnish and a relationship of our own to tend. When he wasn't his uncle's assistant and I wasn't Marguerite's shadow.

When we were living our own lives, chasing after our own dreams. Who would we look like then, who would we be? What griefs would color our days, what joys would shape them? We could only find out the answers by living.

"I wonder what you would think of this idea," I began, but suddenly I realized I had lost his attention. He had pushed himself away from the railing and was staring at a young man who was racing in our direction. The boy clambered noisily up the bridge and came to a halt before us, almost doubled over in his effort to catch his breath.

"Nico!" he panted out. "Come now! Malachi needs you!"

"What's wrong? What's happened?" Nico demanded.

"Someone tried to kill Prince Cormac! He's alive, but he's injured."

Nico muttered an oath. "Who did it?"

The boy shook his head. "No one knows. And he escaped out a side door of the palace before anyone could catch him."

Nico turned to stare at me and we shared a look of mutual dread. "Someone from Orenza avenging Marguerite?" he said.

"Someone who merely hates the king?"

"I have to go."

"I'm coming with you."

The young man gestured impatiently and started back across the bridge. "Well, don't argue about it! Malachi wants you *now*!"

Nico grabbed my hand and we followed the boy away from the serenity of the temple, into the clamor of the city. Was Marguerite right? Would her death be the catalyst for war? What could be done to stop it?

I couldn't guess what might come next. Six months ago, I never would have predicted where I would be right now. All I knew was that, whatever happened, I would face it at Nico's side. I tightened my grip on his hand and quickened my pace, and soon we were almost running through the streets, never stopping, never asking questions, holding on to the one thing we were sure that we would keep.

Be sure to read the next Uncommon Echoes book, *Echo in Emerald*.

A Misfit and a Mystery

In the royal city of Camarria, a street urchin named Chessie lives by her wits, always attended by her two faithful friends, Red and Scar. What no one realizes is that the "friends" are really echoes, creatures who look exactly like their originals but who possess no volition of their own.

Echoes normally are only born to high nobles, and Chessie doesn't want anyone to start asking questions about her past. So she's developed the ability to move between bodies so rapidly that she can maintain the illusion that she and Red and Scar are three separate people.

After someone tries to murder the crown prince, Chessie gets entangled in the investigation when she comes to the aid of Lord Dezmen, the high noble who's trying to solve the crime. From the back alleys of Camarria to a society party to a rural province, they track down clues.

Until one of those clues leads right back to Chessie.

ABOUT THE PUBLISHER

This book is published on behalf of the author by the Ethan Ellenberg Literary Agency.
https://ethanellenberg.com
Email: agent@ethanellenberg.com

Made in United States
North Haven, CT
03 May 2024

52052415R00222